GRUDGING

By Michelle Hauck

Birth of Saints Trilogy
GRUDGING

Coming Soon
FAITHFUL
KINDAR'S CURE

GRUDGING

Birth of Saints Book One

MICHELLE HAUCK

HARPER

VOYAGER

IMPULSE

An Imprint of HarperCollins Publishers

Excerpt from *Faithful* copyright © 2016 by Michelle Hauck.

EPub Edition NOVEMBER 2015 ISBN: 9780062447159

Print Edition ISBN: 9780062447166

10 9 8 7 6 5 4 3 2 1

For the dreamers who refuse to give up.
Take chances.

CHAPTER 1

Ramiro guided his horse to the waiting ranks of the *pelotón*, taking his position at the back of the long file of riders along the dusty road. Sweat slicked his palms inside his leather gloves, and his helmet wobbled despite the chinstrap. He maneuvered his mare, Sancha, sidestepping her into position among the other soldiers. In their rightful place, he laid the reins across his knee, signaling that he'd be using his legs to guide Sancha, not the leather straps.

Ramiro wedged his feet in the stirrups as Alvito moved his mount alongside, pinning Ramiro between him and the next man. "Don't look so pale," Alvito said with a grin. "You'll not earn your beard this day." He stroked his own neatly sculpted black whiskers, adding a wink to cut the sting of his words. His beard was artwork, all straight lines and right angles, shaved to the edge of the jaw with a square patch under his lower lip.

His hair tended to curl, a fashion Alvito encouraged with musk-scented oil. The heavy aroma didn't seem to discourage women; Alvito never seemed to be without at least one hanging on his arm.

From Ramiro's other side, Sergeant Gomez gave him a playful push with a fist the size of a ham. The force would have knocked Ramiro off his saddle if he hadn't locked his legs. Gomez's beard was a study in opposites from Alvito's. A nest of brambles to his chest, his hair grew wherever it could sprout. "Rookie. You'll stay the *bisoño* until we tell you otherwise."

A gentle ribbing to let Ramiro know they remembered this would be his first real ride. "Peach face," someone said from the middle rank.

First ride. First time as something other than a trainee squire brought along to clean armor or mind the warhorses. First chance to earn his beard and be considered a man. Bare chin or not, he was a part of it now, and no amount of needling was going to take that away from him.

At the front of the *pelotón*, Captain Salvador raised his sword to indicate they hold position. The captain wore his beard trimmed short and covering chin and jaw—neat but not fanatically styled.

Ramiro touched the flattened metal coin bound close to his throat. His gloved fingers couldn't trace the image of San Martin, but San Martin would send his blessing anyway. A blessing from one soldier to another.

Only then did he register what waited sixty yards

up the road under the spreading mesquite trees. Here, the way narrowed between two steep hills, creating essentially a box canyon. The Northerners had positioned themselves into a square, extending themselves across the road and onto the sand along the edge, wedged defensively like a cork in a wine bottle. They ranged right up to the spindly trees at the edge of the sheer hills, pikes protruding like six-foot spines from a hedgehog and shields tight. Like all the Northerners they'd seen, these had no horses.

Their commander, who couldn't be bothered to lift a weapon, strutted across the front, a proud rooster in his black-and-yellow uniform. Why would he need a weapon when the Northerners outnumbered them by better than ten to one?

Ramiro swallowed, the motion tight against his helmet's strap. This was no line of straw-stuffed practice dummies. They were experienced soldiers. The pale-skinned, unbearded Northerners had appeared one day by the thousands, snapping up each *ciudad-estado* before the sun set on the next. The city-states that included Ramiro's home were unused to working together, and too often they resorted to petty bickering. Vulnerable in their independent isolation, the *ciudades-estado* were easy targets. And now the Northerners blocked the most direct route to their closest neighbor, which meant that in order to find out what happened with Aveston, they had to go through the hedgehog of spears.

Ramiro stroked Sancha's neck. "We'll be fine, girl." He said it as much to assure himself as his horse.

A single desert wren called in the distant trees, signaling a mate with its come-hither song. The men of the north began to shift, their ridged ranks rippling. Ramiro frowned, trying to determine what would cause them to break formation. Their officer gave a shout, his words lost on the summer breeze. His meaning became clear soon enough.

Two men broke free of the hedgehog, pushing a handbarrow ahead of them. They raised the handles and shoved. Bodies toppled out. Ramiro hid an embarrassing flinch from his companions and squinted to gain a better view, lifting himself in the stirrups. Splashes of green-and-gray clothing.

By the saints, it was their missing scouts.

One of the Northerners held a severed head by its dark hair. A gash of red covered the lower jaw. The beard had been hacked off, leaving the face mutilated. No doubt other parts had been equally violated. Ramiro kept a check on his anger and tried not to imagine the scene in detail, glad the distance between them let him avoid seeing the staring, sightless eyes of men from his home city, not to mention the thick cloud of feasting flies.

The Northerners did the same to any civilians they caught, regardless of age or gender. Ramiro had helped bury what was left often enough to know the enemy's depravity.

Growls came from the men around him, and many spat, their eyes hard. As if he were in church, Ramiro brushed his fingertips against his body's centers of emotion to clear his pathways of unwanted passion: mind, heart, liver, spleen. Only cowards disfigured the dead or camped in front of cities, relying on starving women and children instead of engaging men in honest combat.

Captain Salvador turned his mount to face his *pelotón*. He had no need to raise his voice like the rooster peasant of the Northerners. Breastplate and armor gleamed bright silver, while the sleeves of his green-and-gray, close-fitting uniform were neatly crisp and crease-free. The eagle feather of his rank waved proudly on top of his helmet. His beard and mustache were the same thickness, without a scraggly patch, and for some reason, the neatness of his appearance steadied the men. "Ready?" he asked, meeting their eyes with a nod and an unwavering gaze.

"Hi-ya," rippled through the ranks. Men set their shoulders and drew their swords. Here and there, they tapped fists to breastplates for luck. The *caballos de guerra*, warhorses, shook themselves and tossed their heads and tails, sensing the anticipation in the air.

"Hi-ya." The corners of Gomez's eyes creased as he grinned. His white teeth were a sharp contrast against skin the color of black olives. He set his helmet over the dark stubble of his summer-shorn hair. The gleaming dome of silver rode low enough in the back to cover even Gomez's thick neck. Gomez touched each of his weapons in turn with ritual somberness.

"Hi-ya," Alvito agreed, giving a last curl to his mustache.

Captain Salvador pierced Ramiro with his sharp gaze. "Ready, brother?"

"Hi-ya," he managed, though his belly wanted to reject his last meal of cheese and bread. He tapped his steel breastplate, then gripped the horse bow tight and gave a nudge to the quiver at his knee to be sure the arrows were loose and ready at hand. "Brave and bold," he whispered to Sancha. Captain Salvador's trick would work. It had to.

Salvador's sword came down, and the *caballos de guerra* responded without a sound. As one, the *pelotón* broke into a canter, a hundred varieties of dapple-gray horseflesh. They took advantage of the smoothness of the road to risk an all-out gallop.

Ahead, the hedgehog of Northerners drew in on itself, then solidified. Their officer scurried behind the protection of their ranks.

Fifty yards.

Forty.

Ramiro gripped his bow and tried to glory in Sancha's speed and the companionship of the *pelotón*. Wind caught their standard, lifting it out to display San Martin as a simple priest. *I am death. For the saints, I bring retribution.*

Thirty yards.

He eyed Gomez and Alvito to make sure Sancha held perfect position, nudging her forward a little. Now he could identify individual features among the Northerners, their too-pale skin, odd hair colored like sand, and, worst of all, their light eyes. They looked kin to the swamp witches though surely even those legendary murderers would not want to be related to these mutilating barbarians.

Twenty yards.

Death! Retribution! For Colina Hermosa and Santiago! The road thundered with hooves. Ramiro kept the horse bow hidden behind Sancha's mane as Salvador had instructed, seeing Gomez and Alvito do the same.

His heartbeat thudded in his ears, and his vision tightened in on the points of the pikes. The steel heads were sinfully sharp, a good five inches long, ready to pierce flesh whether it be horse or man. To tear and rip while impaling.

Screams of defiance burst from the throats of the thirty men surrounding him. He added his own to the din. "Death! Retribution! Santiago!" The Northerners remained eerily silent. They didn't even understand the tactics of true war. They simply steeled themselves for the impact of this suicidal charge into their wall of spears.

They would find out the truth soon enough.

At less than five yards, close enough to see the Northerners' gritted teeth, Captain Salvador swerved. Instead of throwing themselves onto the pikes, the head-forward charge of the *pelotón* became a gentle arc, following their leader in perfect formation. Their screams changed, becoming full-throated, mocking laughter. Taunts and jeers erupted from Ramiro's companions.

"Motherless goat fuckers!"

"Twice cowards!"

"Saintless barbarians!"

Captain Salvador passed the hedgehog close enough to give one of the pikes a slap with the flat of his sword and added his own jeer. "Dogs! You're not worth our time," he shouted as the *pelotón* thundered after him, reversing direction to curve back the way they had come.

Whether the Northerners understood the language or not, the intent was unmistakable, and their pale skin turned blotchy red. Astonishment turned to outrage as the enemy streamed by just out of reach of their weapons. As Salvador predicted, the first Northerner broke ranks—a short man with a thatch of dirty, straw-colored hair—to stab his pike in their direction. The *pelotón* corrected, adjusting to maintain their distance.

Another man charged forward some steps, taking his neighbor with him. Then another left the hedgehog formation.

Exactly as Salvador had planned.

Just coming into range, Ramiro lifted his short, curved bow, drawing back the string. He aimed not for the men who broke ranks, but for the infantry left vulnerable behind them. He released and sent his arrow into a Northerner's chest. The hum of Gomez and Alvito's arrows echoed around him.

He scrambled for a second shaft, and released in a blur, unsure whether he'd struck true. Then Sancha completed her arc, and he was away, following the rest of his troop back to their starting point.

The *pelotón* kept up the insults, but now the laughter sounded unforced. Ramiro checked over his shoulder and saw the Northern officer burst forth from the hedgehog. Gone was his strut; now he screamed in a hoarse language at his men. A gleam of steel appeared in his hand, then the short Northerner with the strange thatch of hair crumpled. Unable to catch his mounted opponents, the officer had turned on his men, who'd broken ranks.

Alvito muttered a curse at having to break away and not satisfy his bloodlust against the Northerners. Ramiro pushed down his own surge of disappointment. He wanted to turn and give fight—only in close, hand-to-hand combat could he earn his beard—but they had their orders. Search and report only. There would be other days.

Many of them.

Captain Salvador slowed their withdrawal to a trot, letting the horses breathe and heading them toward Colina Hermosa, leaving a handful fewer of the Northerners to trouble them and something for the barbarians to think about.

Ramiro's helmet swung from its strap on his saddle, allowing the cooling breeze to reach his neck as they followed the road back to Colina Hermosa and home. His breastplate straps weighed heavy on his shoulders. Sancha swished lazily at flies with her tail, the skin over her flank quivering as the hum of cicadas filled the afternoon air. Olive trees grew in the stony soil on one side of the road, while the other side contained grapevines woven across metal wires. A windmill spun in a slow circuit, pumping water from deep wells to irrigate the fields. Smoke rose in the distance, the column too thick to be a campfire. The Northerners had done little damage to crops, only burning small sections of land, mostly grainfields. They were too assured of their eventual victory to ravage the rest. But humans and their habitations were another story: Neither were left standing.

Other members of the *pelotón* remained vigilant, looking for ambushes or enemy patrols, but such was not Ramiro's duty on this day. He could allow his mind to wander . . . or would if his companions ever closed their mouths.

"Still got that razor, I hope," Alvito teased, touching his artwork of a beard. "I think you're going to need it for a while longer, kiddo."

"*Bisoño*," Sergeant Gomez said fondly from his towering height, his bushy beard thick and ratted as a magpie's nest. "We shall keep you in our pockets as a mascot."

"Perfect idea," Alvito said. "A mascot. Why, we'll keep you safe as a newborn lamb."

Ramiro rolled his eyes. "I took down two."

"Two, he says." Alvito laughed and touched his bow. "Didn't you see my three? Two is the work of a child."

"Or a mascot," Gomez added. "I believe I may have

hit four. But the bow is a coward's weapon. One should not brag about such kills." He glanced toward the olive trees as coyly as a modest maiden seeking to avoid praise, a laughable sight from the mountain-sized man. "Skill with a bow is necessary, but one shouldn't pretend it gives honor or can make you a man."

"Now," Alvito said, "drinking is a true bragging skill. I'll bet a copper our little mascot will be under the table before he finishes one glass. What say you, mascot? You'll come out with us tonight to celebrate your first ride. I know a plump serving *chica*, and I believe Mencia has a shrew of a sister who might like a *bisoño*."

"Mencia?" Gomez asked. "What happened to Estefania?"

"Old news, my friend," Alvito said with a wink. "Old news. Now, how about it, kiddo?"

"You can keep your shrew," Ramiro said. "But I'll join you and show you how a real man—" A shadow fell over him.

Captain Salvador still wore his helmet. Unlike Alvito, with his almost-Northerner paleness, or Gomez, with his roasted, dark skin, Salvador was a honeyed brown, the same tone as Ramiro's own skin. "I'd have a few words with my brother if you please."

Alvito gave a bow and a wink. "By all means, *Capitán*. Tonight after our report, *bisoño*, I'll see you under the table." He and Gomez put heels to their mounts and forged ahead in the slow-moving line to put a horse length of space around them.

"Did all fare well with you?" Salvador asked. "You are unhurt?"

Ramiro sighed. "Our father bid you keep an eye on me."

"And if he did?"

"Then he did me a disservice. I'm no child. Did I earn my place in your *pelotón* fairly?"

Salvador twitched at the hit. "You know you did."

"Then leave off the coddling."

Salvador gave him a nod of equals though five years the elder. "So be it. No more coddling—I mean it when I say you did well. Too, we learned much."

A weight left Ramiro's shoulders at the rare compliment. His brother was the youngest man ever to captain a *pelotón*. Some attributed it to Salvador's skill at fighting, others to his almost eerie ability to anticipate trouble. Regardless, there was no man Ramiro would rather follow—brother or not. Still, he pondered over what Salvador meant by "learned much."

"The west road is closed," Ramiro said, reflectively. "Hardly a surprise. We guessed that when the scouts didn't return."

"But what does it mean?" Salvador prompted.

Ramiro considered. "That Aveston is besieged now, exactly as we are. Why else would the Northerners bother to close the roads?" Aveston was their closest neighbor and their most-likely ally.

"And?" Salvador asked.

Ramiro watched Sancha's withers rise and fall. "One or more of the smaller *ciudades-estado* have fallen, or they wouldn't have enough troops to set a siege at Aveston."

"And so we add to the knowledge of our situation for our *Alcalde* and the council, with few casualties." Salvador smiled sadly. "And maybe while leaving a sting of humiliation on our enemies."

"Next time we should bring more bows with us," Ramiro suggested. "We could have inflicted greater damage." They'd put the four bows in the hands of the best archers and among the last of the ranks to keep the surprise. Ramiro hadn't expected to be one of those chosen.

"Next time the fight will be real. Our mission wasn't to engage the enemy but to scout and gain information. And there's no point to trying that trick again, little brother. The Northerners are not fools. They will not give us the opportunity." Salvador shook his head. "Don't count on your enemy to be stupid."

"Then we should have attacked today and not played peekaboo," Ramiro said hotly. It stung that his first ride had given him no opportunity for the close combat needed to earn his beard.

"What is the top precept?" Salvador asked without raising his voice.

"Follow orders," Ramiro snapped out.

"Ours were to search and report," his brother said. "Not waste lives on opening the road to Aveston that the Northerners would only reclose the next day and with twice the number of men. Not when we have so few to lose. A good soldier doesn't question." Without another word, Salvador booted his stallion and returned to the front of the column.

Ramiro shrugged, trying not to feel the sting of Salvador's rebuke. He had thought only of his own desires and not what was best for his city. With a sigh, he bundled the regret for his beard into a small corner of his heart and tried to forget about it.

After the olive fields turned to bare desert and among high hills topped with rocky outcrops, they'd find the secret path to the hidden tunnel. The tunnel, one of several, would take them safely past the blockage of Northerners and straight into the citadel.

Ramiro kept a loose grip on the reins and gave Sancha a pat with his free hand. As he rode, a question that had been gnawing at him rose once more to the surface: Why had the Northerners invaded the territory of the city-states in the first place? If the *Alcalde* had captured Northerners and forced them to talk, none of the answers had drifted down the bureaucracy chain and into his ears.

Was it purely a thirst for conquest? Unlikely. They'd never invaded before. Nor was there much to be had in this dry land. Had something else driven them south? Perhaps a famine or a drought had struck. Or maybe their leadership had changed. Or worse yet, a greater threat might ride behind them, driving these pale men from their homes, only to come after them. It bothered him to have to battle so many unknowns.

The first sight of Colina Hermosa, appearing in the valley spread before them, pulled Ramiro from his thoughts. He could make out the citadel at the center of his city, rising above walls and other buildings. The white stucco of the building shimmered with heat waves, almost as if it were burning, and despite the hot sun, Ramiro shivered at the illusion of his city consumed.

Whatever the reason, Aveston had joined the ranks of the besieged. There would be no help from the west.

CHAPTER 2

The aroma of bread baking drew Ramiro like flowers
bring bees. He entered the small kitchen at the back
of the citadel, almost drooling in his eagerness. A fire
roared on the ox-sized hearth, though at this late hour,
all but one cook had gone home.

Lupaa set down the bowl of goat meat marinating
in olive oil and turned in his direction. "Come to fit
those long legs under my table again? I've not seen you
in a dog's age." The head cook had a plump, motherly
face and muscled arms that could challenge Sergeant
Gomez in a wrestling contest. A large white apron
covered her voluptuous skirts and the bright yellow of
her blouse. Her long hair was knotted atop her head
and out of the way of accidental touches from floured
hands.

Ramiro shrugged, guilt running in a flush up his
neck. Since turning seventeen and being accepted in

the *pelotón*, he'd had no time for his former childish haunts. Tonight, though, his feet had drawn him to the quiet here to avoid the barracks full of noise and rough men. The ache in his head and the grittiness of his eyes suggested neither would be good for his hangover.

Alvito had lived up to his promise. Almost. Ramiro managed to stay above the table, but somehow it didn't seem right to celebrate. Despite his first ride, he hadn't earned his beard, and his horse had done most of the work this day. He'd escaped the drinking as soon as he could. An hour spent grooming Sancha cleared away the cobwebs but did nothing to make him ready for sleep or settle his stomach.

"Still providing fresh bread for hungry *chicos*?"

Lupaa grinned. "You're rather more than a *chico* now." With a long-handled, wooden bread peel, she drew down a loaf from the warming nook beside the fireplace. Quick work with a knife produced a hearty brown slice, which she slathered with honey. His mouth watered as she placed it on the plate, bordered with large red roses, she'd reserved for him since he could toddle. "I suppose you earned your beard today."

Ramiro winced and dropped his eyes. Until he was a man, he could not speak in assemblies or be taken seriously anywhere. He could not even officially court a girl. Unlike shop keeping or crafting, where you only had to pass your apprenticeship to be considered a man, the army had tougher standards. Lupaa might have downplayed it, but he still felt like a *chico* with his bare face. "Not yet. Soon though."

Lupaa caught his mood and changed the subject. "Out doing the work of the saints or *del diablo*?"

"A little of both," he said, as alcohol sloshed in his stomach. Only pride had gotten down that last glass. He bit through the thick crust into delicious sweetness. Rumor said Lupaa got her honey straight from Santiago's heavenly garden.

Lupaa waved her hand in front of her face. "That's not the smell of you I remember. You abandoned the *Alcalde's pelotón* to work in a distillery?"

"Alvito."

"Ah. That handsome scoundrel." She walked to a shelf and fetched a mug, then filled it with milk. "If you can hold this down, you'll survive." She waited for him to swallow half the mug. "How goes the news from the outside world?"

He swallowed a mouthful. "Ill."

Her eyebrow quirked. For the first time, he noticed the gray spreading through her hair and the pucker of worry above her brow, how her hands, normally so sure, plucked at the apron around her middle.

"The Northerners have settled into camps surrounding Aveston, or so we surmise." The spies would verify whether their ally Aveston faced a siege of its own.

"Thank the saints the *Alcalde* had the forethought to bring plenty of supplies through the gates." She glanced at the icon of Santiago hanging over the door, but the worry lines deepened.

"And plenty of farmers, laborers, and peasants with bellies to feed."

"It's what Santiago would expect from his people." She tapped forehead, heart, liver, and spleen in quick order.

"Aye." He touched the medallion at his throat. "It is." He couldn't speak to her of the old men of the council arguing for hours about what war strategy might keep the people from starving, being killed, or enslaved. Salvador was surely still there with the other *capitanes del pelotón*. The discussions of evacuating the people through the tunnels, knowing there was nowhere for them to go; the arguments for and against direct assault with their tiny army. His stomach rolled, threatening to heave up, and the bread tasted like road dust in his mouth. He owed this kind woman better than giving her more to fret about.

"San Martin shared his cloak with a beggar, so if we pray hard, he will divide our foodstuffs to last as long as necessary," Ramiro said. "Santiago taught us stubbornness. These Northerners will get tired of our hot lands and go home." She looked doubtful, so he added, "*Alcalde* Alvarado has told me so."

Immediately, her face cleared at words coming direct from the mayor. "You give this old woman relief. I shall light a candle to San Andrés on my way home."

The deep toll of dozens of church bells penetrated the kitchen with a suddenness that momentarily stupefied Ramiro. He fought off the fuzzy effects of the alcohol and jumped to his feet, dropping his second piece of bread. Lupaa's head came up, eyes wide.

Warning bells.

"The gates!" he shouted. He shook his head to clear it and dashed from kitchen to hallway, catching the doorframe to straighten his course. Several turns later, he burst from the citadel doors and paused to orient himself. Built upon the crest of a hill, the castle-like structure of cream-colored stone rose as the crown at the top of the city, complete with arrow slits and heavy doors. The fortress was several stories with a flat roof and housed government offices as well as the *Alcalde* and his family. Unlike a castle, though, no walls surrounded the structure to fence it from the rest of the city.

Citadel guards stood at the ready beside the doors, their gazes directed down the avenue at the wall. Distant shouts and clashes of metal reached all the way from the edge of the *ciudad-estado*, sounding over the deep ringing of the bells and the hum of frightened people.

Ramiro leaped down the steps two at a time to join the crowd of grooms and other men headed for the fortifications around the city. All military men had been assigned spots at the walls for the first sally. The *Alcalde's pelotón* belonged at the gates. Ramiro dodged servants staring openmouthed at the night sky, their hands clasped or clutching skirts. His head pounded in time to his boots' thumping against the cobblestones. Damn Alvito and his drinking challenge. Damn himself for not being strong enough to resist it like a real man.

Despite his nervousness, he kept his breathing

even as he dashed past storefronts and homes along the wide avenue, all the time weaving around clots of civilians holding lanterns or torches. The road led steadily downward, dim and hazy in the darkness, like the gullet of a monstrous beast. The dry air sucked the sweat from his skin, not letting it collect.

The crowds increased, then diminished as Ramiro shoved his way through the courtyard before the city's protective stone skin. Twenty feet high and more, the limestone wall encircled the entire city, wide enough to house guard barracks and storage rooms inside its length. Only one gate broke its surface, and that toward the west, where their most-and-least-trusted allies lay—Aveston and the legendary witches. Even at the time of the wall's construction, they knew the witches never left the swamp, so they used the witches' presence to become Colina Hermosa's secondary ring of protection.

The great gate at the center of the courtyard was crafted by the best metalsmiths and was twice the height of a tall man, and more, its width allowed for a *pelotón* to ride forth in full formation. Forged of the strongest steel, bars of metal—heavier than six armored men—barricaded it closed. The metal had aged to a black patina, dark as the tomb of the blessed Santiago. But not as silent. Now the ringing blows of a battering ram came from its other side. The sound drove the last alcohol fumes from his brain.

In the early history of Colina Hermosa, the city had mobilized to take part in the wall's construction. All citizens had given a year of their time toward its completion or drafted someone to take their place. Stone by stone, it had grown, built in pride and raised with surety that it would see them through any crisis. And so it had.

Now it was being asked to do so once more.

The gate guard of Colina Hermosa stood along the parapet above, arms and backs bending in a steady rhythm of arrow fire. With the thud of the first scaling ladder against the wall, the noise of battle pounded at Ramiro. His heart galloped in his chest, corresponding to the fearful tingling in his fingers and toes. He fought against panic not to shame himself.

Ramiro put a hand to his hip and came away empty—he'd left his sword and dagger in the barracks during Alvito's celebration! All he had was the small knife he always kept in his boot. He didn't even have a bow, and there were no unused ones in evidence. He couldn't go back to get his weapons, yet he also couldn't just stand here while his city was invaded. Innocents would die and his city fall without the soldiers—without him—to protect them.

He scrambled to a hulking, uniformed sergeant—built from the same mold as Sergeant Gomez of his own unit—giving orders at the center of the courtyard. His beard was a veritable tangle. "Where can I help?" Ramiro panted.

The sergeant turned and lifted one overgrown eyebrow to sweep Ramiro from head to heels with a contemptuous glance. "Go back up the hill where you belong. Boys and civilians need to stay out of the way."

Ramiro cursed his lack of uniform. He'd donned a crisp white shirt over leather pants to impress Alvito's ladies, and he'd never changed back. He spotted his brother atop the battlements, thrusting at a ladder with Gomez. The ladder resisted, then ground backward and fell amid screams from its climbers. Even as it was vanquished, his brother swung around to meet a new ladder rising at his back, almost as if he felt it arrive without needing to see it. Salvador hadn't been caught out of uniform though his brother could never be mistaken for anything but a soldier.

"*My pelotón* is assigned here," Ramiro said.

"Then where's your sword . . . and your beard?" The sergeant huffed, his attention clearly elsewhere as he gestured more troops to the stairs to the left of the gate. He turned away, shouting for someone to fetch more polearms.

Ramiro reeled when a flight of arrows overshot the height of the wall and arched down into the courtyard. One caught a groom in the arm and another hit the sergeant in the throat. The man lurched, blood flooding around his fingers and into his beard as he sought to keep the life fluid in. His eyes formed pools of fright.

Ramiro gagged and sidestepped a trail of blood on the cobblestone as healers swarmed the injured men, taking them under cover. Noise and confusion pounded at his senses. His hand fastened on the medallion at his throat. "San Martin, save us," he prayed, wishing for his weapons. Every self-preservation instinct urged him to flee. He released the medallion and straightened.

Never. Never would he shame himself or his family.

Perhaps he could scrounge a weapon atop the wall, already berating himself for not grabbing the sergeant's before the healers spirited the injured man away. He touched his heart for luck and staggered to a pile of arrow bundles, shouldered two, and made his way to the stairs with a young boy who was also carrying a load. A soldier rushed past them with an armful of polearms, almost sweeping them off the stairs with the trailing ends.

The first archer atop the wall hollered at Ramiro to take his burden farther down the sheltered passageway, away from the gate, directing the boy in the opposite direction. Ramiro crouched smaller to take up less room in the tight quarters and to keep below the wall, out of arrow shot, as he worked his way along the line of busy men. Missiles flew all around him, while more ladders plunked against the wall behind him above the gate. He soon reached men eager to reload their bows with his supplies.

His shoulders freed from the bundles of arrows, he cautiously raised his head above the wall to look below. A mass of Northerners seethed in the barren desert soil, stretching in both directions. It seemed they'd emptied their entire camp for this push. Those without ladders brandished swords and evil-looking, hook-tipped polearms as they waited their turn to climb. Set farther back, ranks of archers provided cover for the Northerners attacking the walls. There were enough ladders to blanket the entire length of the wall, and enough men to match the grains of wheat in a harvest.

The stone wall of Colina Hermosa would be their mill.

To his left, more Northerners rammed tremendous tree trunks affixed to leather straps into the gate—the gates held. The trees splintered and failed against the immense metal of the blocked entranceway. The gate guard had concentrated their own archers there, and arrows streamed into the men wielding the rams despite the wooden covering meant to protect them. They fell away in droves, only to be replaced the instant they were struck down.

A ladder clunked into place beside Ramiro. His heart leaped.

"Hold! Hold!" someone shouted from nearby.

"For Colina Hermosa and Santiago!" called another.

Joining with an archer, Ramiro struggled to push the ladder free as Northerners scaled its length. A polearm carried by the topmost Northerner caught Ramiro's helper, punching through his shoulder. The archer screamed as a guard seized a stone from a nearby pile and sent it crashing down to sweep men from the ladder right and left. The topmost Northerner toppled, pulling the polearm and the archer in whom it was embedded with him.

A flight of arrows whizzed past, making Ramiro duck and close his eyes.

Below, more men must be climbing the ladder. Determination burned in Ramiro. His eyes flew open. No Northerner would stand atop this section of wall. Not if he lived to stop them.

Ramiro stood, revealing himself to the enemy bowmen, and gave a mighty heave. The ladder hung upright a foot off the wall and slowly fell backward as the Northerners on the ground lost control. Ramiro scrambled for the lost archer's bow, but before he could locate it, another ladder replaced the last. Someone put a six-foot polearm into his hands.

He quickly formed a pattern with the soldiers around him, thrusting at the ladders while others cast down stones and reduced the weight by knocking loose the Northerners. Oftentimes, a well-placed stone could break apart the rickety, overlong ladders. Push and duck. Duck and push. No time to think. Never let them breach the wall. Ramiro dodged spears and avoided swords. Men died or bled around him and were pulled away. At other spots along the wall, especially closer to the gates, Northerners breached the defenses and climbed over the wall to engage in hand-to-hand combat. Here, none made it off the ladders. He fought and sweated until his mind was numb, and his body ached.

It was both lifelong dream and nightmare.

The winding sound of horns split the air.

Ramiro knuckled the small of his back. *What now? There couldn't be more of them?*

"Look!" someone shouted.

He spun, and his body grew chill despite the heat. In the distance, hulking wooden structures rose. Scores of oxen teams towed other contraptions with a single long arm ending in a cupped basket. Trebuchets and siege towers.

Ramiro's heart sank. They'd hoped the Northerners wouldn't bring such weaponry. The desert certainly couldn't supply any trees to suit the purpose. They must have brought these up from the siege of another *ciudad-estado*. How could his city resist the siege engines when they barely held their own now?

But the gate guards around him lifted their arms in triumph. The enemy arrows had ceased. Ramiro leaned over the edge and watched as the Northerners pulled back in neat ranks, dragging their dead with them. As they retreated, the remaining ladders were quickly dispatched.

"They're quitting?" Ramiro asked, his breath coming in ragged wheezes.

"Nay, *chico*." A gray-haired soldier clapped him on the back. "They'll come another day when they've readied their siege machines. This was just a test of our readiness." The man must have seen his expression because he laughed. "Celebrate each day. Likely we won't have many more."

CHAPTER 3

Shortly after the combat, Ramiro made his excuses to the men at the wall and left, returning to the citadel and taking the stairs to the roof. Some *alcalde's* wife from the past had turned this spot into an outdoor garden and dining room, making it a favorite retreat for many. A peaceful place when he felt anything but.

Other people's blood spotted his white shirt. Had things gone differently, it could easily have been his own. He needed a bath and a rest, but his mind hummed from the conflict, leaving him unable to stop pacing. Cold chills claimed his limbs. His stomach was sourer than when alcohol had filled it. With no clear single-combat victory, he hadn't earned his beard. The night reeked of disappointment.

How long? How long could they keep the Northerners out?

Stars spotted the night sky here, where the citadel

met the top of the world. Or so it had always seemed to him as a child. Life was no longer so certain now that he was older.

He drew in the cool scent of creeping jasmine, carefully tended and watered by hand in pots across the rooftop. Colina Hermosa spread before him, a humbling sight. The city stretched away from the citadel on all sides, a jewel shining with lights. It spread down the hill, becoming wider and grander as it sprawled, with imposing avenues and white-clad stucco buildings whose thick walls and small windows kept out the noonday heat. There was squalor and dirt as well, fits of temper, rudeness, and often impatience. But the darkness hid all that, washing the city of its faults and giving it a fresh life until it tumbled like the sea against the immovable stone walls that now held out the Northerners.

His heart swelled with love. Something worth defending. Home.

Outside the high, white walls, well beyond arrow shot, was a sight not so welcoming. There, jammed between the city and a deep, old quarry used to build the city walls, campfires burned. A red swarm of rage and death, brimstone and smoke, offering a grim contrast with the peaceful firmament. Not by the hundreds did they burn, but by the thousands, mirroring the stars in the sky. How many peasants' houses did they demolish to feed so much hungry fire? They must be down to burning cacti. How they kept it up night after night, he couldn't begin to comprehend. Salvador had talked on about supply trains and quartermasters, but Ramiro had let his imagination dwell on his first ride instead. An indulgence he regretted now.

If only each fire meant a single enemy, but that was wishful thinking. Each fire contained tens of men. Tens and thousands. And behind them, the siege machines waited their turn. A lethal combination for Colina Hermosa.

He touched the spot above his spleen, and whispered, "Santiago, don't let me give in to despair."

A shadow moved briefly and settled against the wall. Ramiro blinked and, as vision settled, he distinguished one of the *Alcalde's* personal guards. A second later, two new shadows strolled around a grouping of flowering prickly pear and palms, heads bent in conversation. He quickly made to leave but was stopped by a wave from one of the figures.

"Here you are," Salvador called. His brother looked as clean and fresh as if he had come from a dance instead of a bloody battle. "I knew you were near. Stay. Father has been looking for you."

Light flared as a servant with a lantern hurried to set it on the edge of the wall before bowing himself away. *Alcalde* Julian Alvarado was an unassuming man, a head shorter than his eldest son. Gray had conquered his bristling mustache and close-cropped beard and made inroads on his dark hair. Even in the lantern-light, deep bags were prominent beneath his eyes. And yet something about him commanded respect, and Ramiro stood a bit straighter in his presence.

"Two this morning. Your firsts, my son. And you helped defend the wall."

Ramiro glanced at Salvador but saw only neutrality. His brother must have made inquiries to learn such detailed information. "I think two with the bow, Father." Instead of pride, disappointment surged for failing to achieve his dream twice in one day.

Julian took him by the upper arm and squeezed. "And you are well? Your mother's convinced I need to speak to you. She would steal her baby back from the army, I suspect." His father smiled, giving new life to his eyes. "Speak up, my son. Are you ready to return to her skirts?"

Ramiro had known his path in life since before he could toddle: wherever his brother led. "It is my duty and honor to protect Colina Hermosa from all enemies. No matter the task."

"Just so. Just so," Julian said. "She faced the same when this tall one went his own way. I warned her that you would follow in his footsteps. She believed that because I was never in the army, her sons would escape it likewise. She still sees the boys," he said with a small smile, "but I see before me men." Ramiro tried to stand even straighter.

"But that is not why I was looking for you, Ramiro. We've had several new reports from *pelotónes* sent east." The *Alcalde* glanced toward the seating area. "Come—let us sit and discuss this in a more relaxed way."

Curiosity sparked as to why his father would share

such news with him. His father chose the bench against the outer wall, and Salvador took the chair closest to him. Ramiro pushed aside pots of orchids to set the lantern on the table, then dragged his mother's footstool over for a seat. "What did the intelligence say?"

"Zapata has crumbled to the Northerners," his father said. "Their council refused the terms of surrender, and three days later, the city was put to the flame. The people slaughtered. The siege towers came from there."

"Saints." Ramiro drew in a tight breath. *Zapata destroyed*. He'd never been to the small city by the sea, but he'd heard of its beauty and legendary gardens, possible because of their more plentiful rainfall. There, Santiago had performed his first miracle. The saint had lain down to sleep on the ground, hungry and unsheltered like a beggar. As he slumbered, a great olive tree rose at his back, providing fruit to satisfy and broad limbs to shade. The people of Zapata honored Santiago through horticulture. Through growth and life.

The Northerners could work no greater sacrilege on Zapata than to destroy its gardens.

"So some of the Northerners do speak our language," Ramiro said. "I guess we know their intentions."

Salvador nodded. "When they are challenged, they push back. They sent an ambassador to our gates today while we were out patrolling. To offer terms."

"What happened?"

"Father turned him away . . . unseen."

"What?" Ramiro asked. "Why?"

"For good reason," Julian said. "I told them I must consult with the council before any meeting can occur. I have not heard their terms, nor accepted or rejected them. They did not give us their ultimatum or their time period until our extermination."

"So they cannot say you have defied them," Ramiro said.

"A technicality." Salvador rolled his eyes. "You cannot expect our people to be saved by such tactics."

"Stalled. I can expect them to be stalled," Julian said. "A few days to arrange a meeting, more days to give our answer to their terms. It is the way of politicians, a universal language even barbarians comprehend, much like mathematics."

"They have no honor," Salvador said with a shake of the head. "They will not wait because you refused to hear them. Likely the attack today was because of it."

"Such attacks we can handle. And there are many types of honor, my sons. Never forget that. If it soothes their conscience to give their victims a sevenday to decide whether to live or die, they will stick to it. Let us hope they do not try to breach the walls until they have delivered their terms."

"But they could not get inside," Ramiro said quickly. "We would repulse them." The words were foolish pride; he knew it the minute they left his mouth.

And yet his father didn't rebuke him. Rather, Julian looked out over the wall at the flickering campfires, "Aye. That we would. We will be no easy meat. But it's not just walls we must worry about."

That was what Ramiro had come to realize. Yes, they could stop the Northerners for a time from breaching the walls. But fire was a different foe. When the enemy used the siege machines or even arrows to fling fire at them long enough, they couldn't extinguish every one. Their wells were deep, but there wasn't enough water if the whole city was burning.

If only they understood the Northerners' motives, Ramiro thought, they could find some ransom to spare Colina Hermosa.

As if reading his thoughts—and coming to the conclusion there was nothing these Northerners wanted, Julian said, "No—we cannot wait for the Northerners to decide our fate. And while the council bickers, it is up to us. We must take action without their approval. There is an alliance we have not tried.

"In the swamps."

Ramiro stood, his surprise flooding out in words. "You would seek out the witches? The witches are friends to no one."

"See, Father," Salvador said. "I told you he would disagree. Now will you give it up as impossible?"

Julian raised a hand. "Spoken from your spleen and not your mind, just as the Northerners see our small numbers and underestimate us. Yes, our ally Aveston cannot help us, and with the siege engines, our enemies do not need to breach the gate. But you both mistake the purpose of this conversation—I am not looking for advice this night from either of my sons. The witches may or may not aid us, that is true. Sometimes risks have to be taken. Sometimes the impossible attempted. And for that, there is no one I trust more to give this task to. The two of you and three others will go."

Shock kept Ramiro silent. Go to the witches! Why would his father pick him? He was one of the least experienced men in the *pelotón*. There were so many more likely choices. Not that it mattered, though, he thought bitterly. Stay here and fight uselessly to save the city or venture out practically alone on a suicide mission. His brother was shaking his head, obviously coming to the same conclusion.

"The witches will never agree to help us," Salvador said. "They'd dance to see us eliminated."

"They may hate us"—Julian held up a finger—"but would they rather *we* lived here or the Northerners? Will the Northerners stay out of the witches' swamp? The witches know we will ignore them. Can they say the same of a new enemy? That will be your negotiation point."

"Why me?" Ramiro said in a whisper, then louder, "Why me? Why not someone better suited." Pride, worry, and confusion took equal shares in his head.

"As I said, I need ones I can trust to keep this mission secret. If the people learn of our desperation, they will panic. And why not you, my son. Are you not fit and ready? Do you not love our home and follow duty as much as anyone?"

For that Ramiro had only one answer. And yet, it didn't seem his father was being entirely truthful about his reasoning . . . or this mission.

CHAPTER 4

Claire wiggled her toes in the grass, studying the shape of her feet. Maybe a little too thin, like the rest of her, but not bad. Her dress of undyed linen showed too much leg, but it couldn't be let down any more. No hem remained. She hoped there was time to sew a new dress before winter arrived, but so many other things had to be done first. Firewood. Garden. Harvesting herbs for medicine. It was hard to manage all of it between just her and her mother.

A clear day wasn't such an uncommon event in late summer but still to be enjoyed. And she didn't really need shoes on dry land and so close to home. It wasn't as if she got to walk across the swamp to the village to trade beaver and mink skins for supplies. Sometimes, it seemed like she'd *never* be given the chance to do that. Especially with all the chores her mother piled onto her.

Beside her, the pot containing lye, lard, and water boiled merrily. Molds lay beside her, waiting to receive the hot liquid when it reached the right consistency, which wouldn't be for a while yet. Claire stayed upwind to avoid a noseful of stink. Making soap was no picnic, but she got a day alone.

She dropped the stir paddle and flopped onto a hillock of grass, letting the sun soak into her bones. With no lessons to be learned and nothing to do, she sighed and wrapped her long braid of wheat-blond hair around her wrist until the end nearly reached her elbow. The goats' bells tinkled in the distance. "I can be as lazy as I want!" She shouted because Mother wouldn't allow it and to see if there'd be any echoes. There weren't.

There never were.

She let go of her hair and lay back in the grass to watch the clouds. Before the first batch of white puffiness drifted past, movement caught her eye. A small brown rabbit ventured from under the dangling, ball-like flowers of a buttonbush. She sat up on an elbow.

"Should I?" Mother wasn't here to interfere. What good was magic if you never had permission to use it? She was a Woman of the Song—or a Girl of the Song at least. How was she to decide whether the magic was useful or something to be learned but kept hidden as her mother insisted? She looked around furtively—no one there.

The opportunity was too tempting.

Claire sat up taller and drew air from her diaphragm as she'd been taught, making sure the sound could carry far enough and the rabbit hear her. Her mother said the magic took the sound farther than a normal person's voice, but Claire had no idea of the distances involved as her mother wouldn't go into detail.

She sang, putting the intention of the words firmly into her heart and mind, letting the words match her voice and become her will.

> *"Come along to me.*
> *Come along to me.*
> *All is safe.*
> *All is sure.*
> *Come to me."*

She made the words simple so the rabbit could understand, but caressed them with music as Mother had shown her. For over two thousand years, Women of the Song had used such magic to defend themselves—used it sparingly and with sound judgment, but they used it. A rabbit might not be a mighty foe, but a girl had to start somewhere. And it was better than singing to the trees or a fence post. It had a mind to be persuaded. The rabbit loped in her direction, leaving the safety of the bush behind.

> *"Skies are clear of hawks.*
> *Good food to munch.*
> *Come along to me.*
> *Come along to me."*

Claire hardly dared to move as the small creature inched closer. "Friends to be found—"

White hindquarters flashed as the rabbit disappeared back under the bush faster than Claire could blink. *By the Song!* She scowled at her miscalculation as the sun vanished behind a thick patch of clouds.

Silly creature. She should have known. Rabbits didn't understand the term "friends." The concept was completely foreign to them. That was the one basic rule her mother had explained thoroughly, when she left so much else to Claire's too-active imagination: The Song didn't work effectively unless you matched it to the intended target.

But that's why I need to practice.

She picked up the paddle and gave the soap mixture a hard stir. Animals didn't care about friends. Neither did her mother. And neither should she if she was going to get this soap finished. A hard, little knot formed in Claire's chest. She couldn't help thinking about it.

What would it be like to have someone her age to share secrets with? Someone who would act silly and giggle with her?

She loved her mother—no girl could have a better— but the ache in her heart longed to be filled with something or someone else—something new.

Friends were not allowed. Practicing the Song on anything that could hear her was not allowed. Venturing out of the swamp was not allowed. Meeting anyone was not allowed. *Fun* was not allowed. She gave the soap another halfhearted stir. It might be babyish to mope, but she wanted those things.

The sun poked out from behind the clouds, and Claire squinted, smiling. Her mother trusted her with the soap. That was progress. Maybe soon she'd get to be the one trading at the village. She put her attention back on the kettle, determined to make this the best batch ever. Let Mother see how grown-up she could be, then maybe every "no" would turn to "yes."

CHAPTER 5

First Wife Beatriz thrust a slim volume under Ramiro's nose. He leaned back wearily. "What about these?" she asked.

"Mother, those are children's tales meant to frighten the gullible. You can't take those seriously." Plump and set in her ways, his mother devoted her life to sewing, pampering small dogs, and worrying. Working herself to an anxious frenzy was her favorite hobby, especially where her children were concerned. Ramiro had grown used to redirecting her rants though not always successfully.

She turned to seize another old tome from an elbow table. "And these? This is a book of serious history." She flipped pages to stop at a painting of a thin woman with wolflike fangs and a matted torrent of hair colored like sunflowers. "Your father has lost his mind."

Ramiro started to believe he'd lost his own mind

for visiting her. Salvador had made it sound so sensible that one of them had to take leave of their mother. Certainly, Salvador wanted to spend his free time with his sweetheart, Fronilde, instead. Ramiro couldn't blame his brother; he had better plans also. Yet he knew it was honorable to devote an hour to their mother before going on a dangerous mission.

If only he hadn't drawn the low card, and if only Mother hadn't been in her sitting room.

Fabric swathed almost every inch of the claustrophobic, windowless room, even the tables and walls. And what wasn't drowned in lace was satiny and bright yellow, blue, or red. The high ceiling and thick walls might make it pleasantly cool, but the room suffocated Ramiro anyway.

"I won't argue that history records the witches, but they might be only history. I've never seen hair that color, Mother, not even on the Northerners. Too, all we have to go by are old books, rumors, and ghoulish embellishment." He pushed aside two embroidered pillows that filled the overstuffed armchair and put a third on the carpet at his feet, disturbing his mother's latest lapdog, who promptly yipped at him. Better to play down the danger and pacify her before she worked herself up. He couldn't let her sense his own nervousness.

It was perhaps too much to hope for.

Because, undeterred, she lifted an arm with a sleeve covered in dangling white lace and turned more pages. The next painting showed a woman with the same bizarre hair, only clutching a bloody dagger. The woman's eyes stared, round and dilated.

Beatriz sniffed. "And when rumors all agree, we call that fact." She slammed the book shut. "They use magic. Not that there's anything wrong with magic—my own grandmother had the Sight—but the witches are murdering lunatics." She glanced at the icon of San Gerald, patron of motherhood. "How can a mother protect her children if they persist in going among murderous cannibals?"

"Cannibals?" Ramiro asked, blinking in astonishment. "Now that's one I haven't heard before. You cannot believe what is in such stories." His mother grabbed at the book in her lap as if to show him more evidence, but he stayed her hands. "I don't deny that all the stories say witches use magic. But then again, they wouldn't be useful to us without it."

"They murder good, honest people."

"They murder people who enter their *territory*," Ramiro said.

"Or outside it," she insisted, picking up her small dog to place it atop the book in her lap.

"Possibly. Murderers or not, we could use their skills to beat the Northerners. But it's all beside the point, Mother. Think of it in a different way," he said, squinting, trying to come up with something convincing. Finally, he settled on, "Salvador has a duty to go where Father sends him. You must allow that. He has no choice in the matter. His *pelotón* belongs to the *Alcalde*." No sense in sharing Salvador's own doubts with his mother or anyone else. She raised some of his own misgivings, but the choice had been made for him. He followed his superiors' orders, and in turn, Ramiro would follow his.

Beatriz's mouth pressed into a thin line, and her eyes narrowed. "So you're saying this is your father's fault."

"No," he said with a sigh. "I'm saying that Salvador is going, and you need me to keep an eye on him. Protect him. You know how my brother gets tunnel vision." In this stuffy, overdecorated drawing room, he might as well have been in a tunnel himself—he felt just as trapped. But he could see some light that just might get him out of here. "It will be much safer with both of us together. It will only take a few days, then we'll be back. You can't grudge us a sevenday. I've been gone for much longer during training, and I will be away from the Northerners. Orders are orders. It's only for a short time." He threw ideas at her rapid-fire, hoping that something might stick. The sooner he got out of here, the sooner they could begin the mission.

And the sooner they returned, the sooner he could prove to everyone he was a man.

His mother switched to a new worry as if she were resistant to his arguments. "But what does one pack to venture into a *swamp* and meet with a *witch*?" The dog yipped each time she raised her voice as if it agreed. "You must promise to change your socks after every meal. It's very wet in a swamp."

"I promise," Ramiro said, too knocked off-kilter by

her capriciousness to think of a better response. Only with effort did he hold his face in an appropriately solemn pose. It wasn't like his mother to surrender so quickly. Something didn't add up.

"And be back by San Cristin Day. I won't have either of you missing my dinner party."

"That's two months away. How can you be con—?"

She held up a hand to stop him. "Someone must be concerned about morale. Keeping up spirits is every bit as important as soldiering. Your father agrees with me."

"Yes, Mother. You're right, of course."

She nodded in satisfaction. "And you'll come to Santiago's shrine and light candles right now."

"I have to go add more socks to my bags."

She reached across to grip his chin between two fingers. "Don't sass your mother. You haven't got a beard yet. You're still my *niño*." Ramiro cringed, but she laughed and handed him the lapdog. "Come along. It won't interrupt your little trip to make friends with a witch."

He stood and put the dog under his arm. "The witches don't make friends. We're bringing them back so—"

"Blah, blah, blah, magic. I've already heard it from your father. All very secret. Not to be talked about around untrustworthy ears. Come along." She headed for a door concealed by more fabric, this one with peacocks sewn into it. Her skirts rustled, so stiff and full they were capable of standing up by themselves when she wasn't wearing them, like miniature versions of First Wife Beatriz. Her clothing was another tool in his mother's arsenal of intimidation.

The little lapdog got Ramiro's best shirt in its mouth and began worrying at it, leaving a wet patch until Ramiro shifted it under his other arm as he followed his mother out the door. Servants bowed and stood back as she led the way, a tall, old-fashioned mantilla of lace dangling from the top of her piled hair adding almost a foot to her height.

"Since when do soldiers dawdle? Hurry up there. And don't drop Pietro."

Several corridors, six staircases, and many minutes later, Ramiro decided his mother was luring him to a dungeon to lock him inside with the lapdog until after the *pelotón* had left. "Where exactly is this shrine?" He tugged at his tight collar. Somehow she'd done more exploring of the citadel than the gang of ruffian boys he spent his childhood with.

"Here," she called over her shoulder. She rounded a curved wall that concealed one of the spiral staircases and stopped in front of a dead end. Up ahead was a little grotto, complete with kneeler, metal shelving, and enough unlit candle stubs to illuminate a cathedral. From the amount of soot staining the walls, this place had been active for centuries. "This is one of the holiest of places," she whispered, pointing to a glass jar in the exact center of the grotto, placed upon a velvet cushion. "That is the sacred finger bone of Santiago himself."

"If you say so, Mother." The amber-colored liquid in the jar was too thick to show if there was a bone inside or not. He'd be more likely to believe it if he hadn't seen enough of these for sale in the market to make ten of Santiago since the Northerners had arrived. Yet some of his apprehension did lift, whether it was the finger bone or his mother's belief.

"Shhh," she hissed. She lit a stub of a candle from a tall pillar set there by the priests for that purpose and put it next to the glass jar. "Your turn."

Ramiro lit candle after candle until Beatriz showed signs of being pacified, then he knelt between her and her lapdog while the ache in his knees slowly grew. She kept her head bent in prayer, and the dog fell asleep, snoring loudly. He wondered about witches and what exactly their so-called magic could accomplish for them. Or even if the witches could be brought to cooperate. Historically, the women of the swamp liked their privacy and reacted with hostility to anyone entering their territory. It had been so for centuries. Every once in a while, an *alcalde* decided to try to exterminate them, but such efforts always failed. Badly. So badly that none were recorded as ever returning. But that had all happened long ago. What Ramiro needed to know was what changes had taken place since?

Beatriz suddenly rose, dragging Ramiro upright with her. She placed a hand on his stomach. "Santiago, keep worry and darkness from building in my son's spleen." She shifted her hand to suit her words. "Keep anger from controlling his destiny and filling his liver.

Make his heart valiant. Let his mind take the lead in all he does." She seized him in a rough hug and squeezed tight. "Bring him home."

He patted her back and tried not to wiggle like a five-year-old. "I'll be back, Mother. It won't take long."

"You'll take this." She released him and picked up two candles from next to the finger-bone jar and blew them out. "These candles are blessed by Santiago now. Use the wax to block your ears when you meet the witches. It will protect you. It's their voices that hold the magic." She pressed the candles into his hands. "How many are going? Will two candles be enough to protect all of you?"

"Only five of us, Mother. Two will be plenty." This time, when she hugged him tight, he squeezed back.

CHAPTER 6

Julian Alvarado stood at the map covering much of the front wall of his study. Dark, masculine wood paneled the walls, except for where overfilled bookcases took up space. The massive desk, used by hundreds of *alcaldes* who preceded him, was planted at the center of the room before the empty fireplace. It was practically the only furniture in the room besides two plain chairs for visitors, and the one he had sat behind for over ten years. A painting of a saguaro cactus, tall with many long arms, reminded all who entered of the reward of stubbornness and persistence. Each arm represented seventy years of the plant's continued life in one of the most inhospitable climates in the world. His own determination could be no less.

He studied the gold stars painted on the large map to signify each *ciudad-estado*, the size of the star indicating the extent of the city. Names had been embossed by each *ciudad-estado*, also in gold. No star was bigger than the one marking Colina Hermosa though you had to squint to detect a difference from Aveston's. Much of that accomplishment was his doing, a thought that filled him with pride.

With a finger, Julian traced a nearly straight line west across the map from Zapata and its smaller, satellite towns along the seacoast to Colina Hermosa, then on slightly north to Aveston. All three *ciudades-estado* were the most northern, the first the enemy found. Its first victims. Seven other cities and a few smaller towns were located south from them, waiting to be next.

Worry boiled in Julian's gut. No amount of tea or plain broth was enough to soothe it. Did he make the right choice? Did he go too far, accept too much risk? But what other move could he make? Never had his leadership been such a heavy burden.

He had sought help from all the *ciudades-estado*, both those now under siege like themselves and those still free. A few of the cities had rejected him outright— Zapata, Aveston—the rest never responded, playing for time. Like the hare with a hawk overhead, they hunkered into the grass and hoped to go undetected, not realizing the hawk circled back for them. Their *alcaldes* were unwilling to take the risk of banding together to escape the talons. Even now, they feared treachery and deceit from their neighbors more than the swords of the Northerners. Julian could not blame them. Hiding, fear, repeating tactics of the past, avoiding liability— such was human nature.

Their spies had reported that Zapata had been as accommodating to the Northerners as humanly possible without actually opening their gates or accepting their terms. Zapata had taken the line of appeasement, hoping to buy survival. The smoking ruins of their *ciudad-estado* proved passive resistance hadn't worked. Julian suspected Aveston would try battle, would wait until the last moment, then throw everything it had at the hordes of Northerners. So vastly outnumbered, this approach was certain doom as well. Every military captain agreed to that fact. Aveston would fall unless something changed.

Just as Colina Hermosa would fall if it relied on a military solution.

The *ciudades-estado* acted as they always had, following time-honored trials of history. Doing as their forefathers had always done in times of desperation. Adhering to the past would get no one out of this new threat.

Man must follow his nature. But Julian couldn't hide like some old hare behind walls, waiting for the talons to fall. The talons already clutched Colina Hermosa's throat. He could not force himself to wait for them to slash.

Julian turned from the map to pace; the route was ten steps from map to fireplace when he felt relaxed and at peace. Today, his longer stride cut the path to six steps as if events drove him to hurry.

Acting was all well and good, but did he do the right thing? Was it best to run from the hawk? Sending his sons to the swamp in search of the witches. His other plans for the children of the city. Would he lead his people to life or devastation? Salvador and Ramiro might be safer here. Would his risk be to their harm? Could he live with the results?

And keeping his plans secret from the councilmen and his closest advisors . . . he still wasn't sure if he should regret that or not. And yet, he'd told no one but those necessary to carry out his orders—and his wife, Beatriz. He had done so because then only he would be to blame if they failed. To be fair, he also didn't believe the *concejales* would approve his choices. Despite many years of friendship, they would censor him, perhaps strike him from his seat as *alcalde*.

It was not too late to change his mind. To keep his sons here with him. To put none of his other plans in motion. To go the safe route and leave the life of his city in the hands of the saints. He could spend his days and nights on his knees to Santiago, praying for deliverance.

He rubbed a hand across his beard as doubts tore at him. Would he be the savior or the villain? Did he have the right to risk, not only his own family, but the entire city with his secret plans? He had never been a religious man, but if only the saints would help him decide.

"Give me a sign," he demanded, looking up at the ceiling. "If you're real, let me know what to do!" He listened with all his might.

Common sense said that they wouldn't answer and,

indeed, nothing changed, except for a wave of sheepish embarrassment flooding Julian. The burden belonged to him alone.

The *alcaldes* of the other *ciudades-estado* came from political families, from long lines of those used to making decisions for their cities. Like all politicians, they had learned to avoid risk as unprofitable, dangerous even. They would not stick out their necks and deviate from historical choices.

Only he had another background. His father had been a merchant with two stores. When Julian inherited, he had built that small beginning from two to twelve, had branched out into trade between other *ciudades-estado*. When he could go no further there, he had made the move to politics, dreaming of expanding his city just as far.

His empire had not been carved by sitting still and waiting. Taking risks was in his nature. He could not hide in the grass no matter how much he might prefer such safe measures. Not if he wanted to save Colina Hermosa.

He straightened and went to sit at his desk, fingering a report before him. The spies who got inside Zapata said the Northerners had offered terms of surrender and given a sevenday to decide on them. They had not been able to learn the details of the terms, only that they were harsh. If precedent held, the Northerners would do the same with Colina Hermosa.

The Northerners' pattern seemed to be holding from the envoy who had approached them this morning—the one Julian had delayed and turned away. Tomorrow, he would see their representative, hear their demands. Would it be for riches? For land and domination? For something else? He believed the Northerners would not destroy the city until Julian gave them an answer to their terms. The Northerners wanted something, and he might learn what tomorrow.

The *alcalde* from Zapata had taken this momentary calm in the storm of a sevenday for a chance to placate its way out of the Northern talons. Aveston, no doubt, built up its armaments.

He planned to do both and go further. He would use this momentary calm and take advantage of it. Seek out new allies. Find ways to fool and delay the Northerners. Unlike the other *ciudades-estado*, they had the blessing of their secret tunnels, giving them access to the outside world.

This moment would make or break, not just himself but all of Colina Hermosa. They trusted him to get it right.

Julian closed his eyes and drew a deep breath. He held it, seeking calm, seeking answers. He had felt foolish asking the saints because that wasn't his way. Always when troubled, he sought deep within himself for the solution. He did so again, and his gut told him to stay true to his nature. That hazarding it all was the only way to win this time.

So be it. He would take the consequences as his alone. He opened his eyes, his hands stilled against the papers. His stomach settled. His eye lit on the saguaro painting, the cactus tall and majestic. If he and Colina Hermosa were to go down, let it be with flare and dignity. Let it be with a fight that might succeed or at least save some of their people.

He stood. It was time to see his sons off.

A young groom tugged at a blindfolded packhorse, who danced in panic. Most horses didn't care to be underground; it took them awhile to settle once in the tunnels, but *caballos de guerra* weren't ordinary horses. Moving past the panicked gelding, Sancha butted the back of Ramiro's uniform as if to say move faster as he guided her down the temporary ramp that led into the citadel's cellar. He reached down to steady his sword, which had been set swaying by his horse's antics. His armor was all stacked and tied among his belongings on Sancha's back.

Ramiro smiled at the sight of the troubled horses and nodded at the boy. He'd handled many a frightened horse. Being the son of the *Alcalde* had earned him no favors. He'd started out as a groom when he was ten years old, following in his brother's footsteps instead of preparing for the university as his mother wished. Tradition dictated every candidate for the *pelotón* start in the same way. Days spent with horses and evenings spent training with any soldier who would put up with him long enough to teach him how to use any weapon he could get his hands on. At fourteen, he'd become a squire to his brother's newly won squadron, and three years later he was one of them, with his own mount.

Besides their unusual gray coat, *caballos de guerra* all had the same qualities—loyalty and intelligence. A single farm outside Colina Hermosa had produced the stock over many generations. Stock that was now safely cramped into lodgings within the walls of the city.

Ramiro stroked Sancha's long nose to comfort her though he needed the calming just as much. The same excitement and anticipation, mixed with nervousness, radiated from her as coursed through his veins. He'd picked Sancha out as a colt when he'd first begun his apprenticeship with the *pelotón*. Or perhaps Sancha had picked him. Whichever the case, only death would part them now. They had come of age together.

It was hard to resist crouching under the low ceiling of the cellar although the rafters were a hand's length above Sancha's ears. Unlike most cellars, this one had been cleared of all the food and drink stores and the accumulating junk that usually collected below stairs to make way for another use. The smell of dry earth and cobwebs didn't help the feeling of being buried alive. The cellar might have been heavily guarded since the Northerners arrived, but no one had felt a need to clean it.

He struggled against a lump caught in his throat. He could almost hear the big clock outside his father's study beating down the days and hours left of Colina Hermosa's life. *Hurry, hurry,* it seemed to say with each tick in his head.

Guards stood straight, made extravigilant by the presence of the *Alcalde*. The packhorse finally surrendered, allowing its attendant to take it into the west tunnel. Packhorses would be ready for them on the other side.

Over a hundred years ago, mad *Alcalde* Domingo had ordered the tunnels dug. Some paranoid whim drove him to put hundreds, perhaps thousands, of laborers to the task. It must have seemed insane then, with no invaders terrorizing the land. Seven tunnels had been completed, leading into the distant hills, before the people deposed him and elected a new *alcalde*. The tunnels were an amazing feat. What would those people think now that their bane might be their descendants' salvation? Ramiro sent them a swift prayer of gratitude.

Salvador, Alvito, and a ball-shaped groom waited with *Alcalde* Julian at the center of the space, their horses around them. Salvador wore a surcoat over full armor. Like Ramiro, Alvito settled for his uniform only though a plumed hat like a chevalier of old was pulled rakishly over one eye. Farther off, his brother's second-in-command, Muño, waited against one wall. The competent lieutenant would take over with Salvador gone.

A horse shifted, and Ramiro fumbled Sancha's reins. Coming closer, he realized that the fat figure he took to be a groom was a woman. Her hair had been shorn off short, perhaps due to some illness, and she wore—he stared again to make certain—trousers of a dull shade of brown held up by a rope like the triple belt of a priest. Over that undignified attire was a homespun poncho covering a plain peasant smock. A large straw hat hung by its thong from her hand. Her complexion was rough from wind and sun. Only polished boots of rich leather peeking under the trousers gave her away as something other than a farmer. Her eyes sparkled with laughter as he approached and joined them.

His father bowed to the strange woman. "Ramiro, this is—"

"Teresa," she interrupted. The word tickled her, for again her brown eyes danced, causing them to nearly disappear in her plump cheeks. "Well met, cousin. I thank you for the escort home to Aveston. I'm sure we shall slip right through the Northerners."

Ramiro frowned. His large family was a web of interconnected chaos, but he didn't remember this woman. He opened his mouth to profess his ignorance of their family relationship when Salvador prodded, "Lucky for our cousin to have such good connections. It's not every scholar that claims a military escort."

A quick glance at the listening ears of all the men and boys standing provided the answer for the sudden relationship though there was the possibility they could actually be connected by *sangre* kin lines. Fiction or no, escorting kin was a perfect excuse to leave the city and keep their true mission secret. But why was she *really* here? Salvador and his father had agreed on a party of five to hunt for the witch. Didn't the nature of their task require all their members to have fighting ability? How would this unnatural woman help them?

He understood her presence no more than his own. Again, he couldn't help but wonder why his father included him? There were older, more experienced, more skilled men to take his spot. For all his bluster and boast, Alvito had more talent with knives than men twice his age, and he was a practiced healer. Gomez had great strength to offer, not to mention skill with a variety of weapons and time as a scout. Salvador was a born leader. But Ramiro added nothing unique to the mix.

An awkward silence descended as they waited for him to reply. Lies didn't come as easily to him as they did to Salvador. Ramiro covered it by giving a stiff bow. "Honored . . . welcome . . . cousin."

Alvito jumped into the breach. "Then we are all cousins together, for I'm connected to these rogues on their mother's side." He primped his mustache and winked. "You know the old saying, go back seven times seven generations, and we're all related. Luckily, the priests don't know, or no one would be allowed to marry."

Teresa snorted a guffaw and clapped Alvito on the back like a comrade. "Spoken like the philosopher Destomones, himself."

A large shadow darkened the cellar entrance as Gomez and his horse appeared, then came forward to join them. Gomez bobbed his head in greeting, running through his usual obsessive premission weapons check by touching each of his armaments to be assured he'd packed them on his person. Sword. Dagger. Bow. Quiver. Lastly, he checked a thick coil of rope tied to his saddle.

Alcalde Julian cleared his throat. "Since we're all here, the sooner the departure, the sooner the return. Good fortune on your journey. May the saints guide you to a quick and *prosperous* resolution." His calm confidence suggested there could be no other outcome. He turned to the stranger with another formal bow. "Farewell, Cousin Teresa."

Gomez and Alvito got a kiss on either cheek from the *Alcalde* as old acquaintances. "For you two, behave yourselves. Keep Alvito away from the drink, Gomez."

"No promises," Gomez said in his gravelly voice.

As the trio moved toward the tunnel, Julian turned to his sons. "Stay safe and stay well. Defend each other. All honor." He directed a nod at Salvador. "You know what to do."

"All honor," Salvador said gravely.

"All honor," Ramiro echoed a second behind, wondering what Salvador knew that he didn't. Then he was enfolded in a crushing hug that encompassed him and his brother.

Julian pulled back with a sharp nod to them. "Do what must be done for Colina Hermosa."

"Hi-ya." Salvador strode for the tunnel with only a single nod toward Lieutenant Muño, drawing his stallion Valentía along by the reins. The narrow width of the tunnels forced them to enter one at a time, and his brother was soon swallowed up with the other three. Ramiro followed more slowly. At the first support timber in the passageway west, he turned to find his father wiping away a tear, his shoulders slumped as if the weight of the city-state rested upon them. Ramiro touched his sword hilt. With this mission, that weight now rested on him as well.

Whatever it takes.

CHAPTER 7

Only after the stars lost their sharpness and became indistinct blurs in the awakening sky did Salvador lift his ban on talking. His older brother made sure they'd slipped through the Northerners' lines before risking any noise beyond the horses' hoofbeats on rocks. He'd also insisted they put on their breastplates. A precaution Ramiro understood but which made him sweat all the sooner.

Alvito, in his plumed hat, rode beside Salvador at the front of the group, keeping up a running conversation, which Salvador occasionally answered. Ramiro yawned and stretched his back. The armor weighed heavy on his shoulders. His brother had more patience with Alvito's wild tales than he did. Or perhaps Salvador wanted to avoid Ramiro's questions about what their father hadn't said—he had been rebuffed when he had asked the first moment Salvador had given them leave to speak.

With the sun solidly up, Gomez led the two pack-horses behind them, a good twenty yards back, proving he had the least patience with constant boasting this early in the morning. The scenery alternated between glimpses back at the city-state and the wild desert in front of them, depending on which side of the hills they trod. The west road was strewn with rocks and dusty enough to raise tiny puffs with each step of the horses, who had to pick their steps carefully. After much climbing and winding, they descended toward flatlands again.

The tall saguaro cacti, with their many and varied-placed arms, stood like silent sentinels, scattered randomly across the landscape. Clusters of buds crowned their tops like strange hair. As a child, Ramiro had used them in his make-believe, often pretending them to be the foe to his soldier hero. He hoped other children got a chance for such innocent play—if they survived.

As if to mock the dark mood settling on him, birdsongs rang from thornbushes, greeting the new day. At Ramiro's side in the center of the group, the strange woman balanced atop her chestnut gelding— "balanced" being the only word to describe her cautious seat in the saddle. She looked like an overweight cat ready to leap clear before the dog could appear. Did she fear the Northerners would attack or that her horse would throw her?

Probably both.

"That horse may not be a *caballo de guerra*, but it should be well trained. You're safe with it as long as you don't spook it, and we can outrun them, you know," he offered his silent companion.

Teresa looked up from her focus on the gelding's neck. "Eh?"

"The Northerners. They have no horses. If they should ambush us, we can outrun them. Not that they could find us while in the hills. They don't know the pathways."

"But we're leaving the hills, and don't they use bows?" she asked, and her mouth lifted in a grin. "But you know the truth of that. You've heard the reports of the destruction of Zapata."

"Well, the infantry doesn't use them. The pikemen we met yesterday had none. And it's not so easy to hit a moving target anyway." They lapsed into silence, and once again Ramiro studied the woman. A maturity in her homely face suggested she must be a decade older than Salvador. What was she doing here? This was no place for a woman. She carried no weapons he could see. She was obviously unused to horses, and the way she stared at the *caballos de guerra* said she hadn't encountered the breed up close before.

She looked up from the gelding again, wobbling in the saddle. Her eyes danced with mirth as they had back in the cellar. "Your face is an open book. Ask. Ask before you burst, cousin."

"We're not cousins, *cousin*, unless we share a *sangre* kin relationship of which I'm unaware." He didn't believe they fit any of the blood kin laws. He'd certainly never seen her before, let alone saved her life. Nor had they gone through a traumatic battle together, or had relatives who'd drawn death blood in some vendetta— though the ludicrous idea of this tame woman in a blood feud made him smile.

"No *sangre* kinship." She grinned wider as if to out-shine his amusement. "But I'll not be responsible for *your* death. Get your questions out."

"Are you really a scholar?"

"Indeed I am," she said. "A specialist in cultural anthropology at the university. Shall I explain that to you?"

He snorted and leaned away from the hooked nee-dles of a barrel cactus. The yellow fruit atop it had been hollowed out by pack rats. Did she think him an idiot just because he wore a sword? "You study other people. Their ways. A rather limited field. Until recently," he corrected himself.

"As was a specialist in military exercises . . . until recently."

He warmed to her. "Aye. We've been busier of late. So you studied the Northerners and the witches? Father sent you as a source of information for us?"

"And a diplomat," Salvador called back. "She's to handle the negotiation side of the mission."

Teresa nodded at him. "Correct. As this trip in-volves relations between two modern cultures—ones that don't get along—the *Alcalde* decided it would be best to have an ambassador with experience in mat-ters other than the military." She turned her attention back to her horse, giving it a pat as if it were a dog.

"I have studied the witches and what is known of the Northerners. Mostly, though, I researched the other *ciudades-estado*. That's where my true expertise lies, cousin. Truthfully, I'm almost as much in the dark on how the witches will react to our offer."

"So how are you a help to us?"

"Because I understand people, cousin," she said, not offended at all by his impertinent question. "Just as I understand that you question my place here because you question *your* own place."

And now it had been voiced aloud. If any of the others heard her say it, they said nothing. Embarrassed, Ramiro changed topics. "I'd heard little of the Northerners before they entered the territory of the *ciudades-estado*," Ramiro said. "You can tell us more?"

"Aye," she said. "The university has information on them. The Northerners rebuffed our offers of trade centuries ago, preferring to keep to themselves in their own land. They operate as a unit, identifying not by home city but by shared physical traits. In other words, they formed an interwoven community of cities operating together instead of separately, as we do. They worship statues of a golden god—kept in their churches—who dwells in some invisible land beyond the stars. Their women are merchants, while the husbands tend the home and do the fighting. Their god hands down proclamations through their priests. Proclamations such as 'horses belong to god and not man. Man must rely on his own feet so that the toil of his travel makes a stronger vessel before their god.'"

"That's idiotic," Ramiro said.

"Don't be so quick to judge them. I'm sure our use of horses is equally idiotic to them." Once more, Teresa silenced him. "But those are just customs. What is key to know about them is that their god tells them not to welcome strangers. They most certainly follow that declaration even though they're on our land now."

Alvito touched his liver and heart. "Santiago preserve us."

"And why would they come here?" Ramiro asked the question that had bothered him since the Northerners arrived.

Teresa shrugged. "I'd love to talk to one and find out, cousin. Will you capture one for me?"

Salvador looked thoughtful though Alvito laughed. "A good way for the *bisoño* to earn his beard, no? What say you, kiddo? Shall you capture a Northerner for your cousin?"

Ramiro scowled. "Would that be so impossible?"

"Leave off," Salvador interrupted, with a glare at Alvito. "We didn't come here to argue among ourselves, or to tease."

"'A man without his beard is a source of potential possibility,'" Teresa quoted from an old proverb. "It is no shame, but a limitless prospect. One that makes a man think deeply and act bravely, cousin."

"Except that without a beard, a man is no man, cousin," Ramiro answered, annoyed. Now she sounded like his mother. "But a boy, no matter his age."

"Let's get back to our mission," Gomez said like

the peacemaker he was. He had picked up his pace to ride closer. "The swamp witches. Is it true women are immune to their magic? That they beguile and drive men insane and foster an irrational hatred of anything male?"

"We have no idea if the magic works only on males," Teresa said. "That, like most else, is only a rumor. There is no corroborating evidence of any women meeting a witch. There are few reports of men meeting them." She wobbled on her gelding again, the smile vanishing. "Perhaps we'll find out firsthand."

Ramiro stared at her. She might be here for her knowledge, but it could also just be because she was a woman and protected from the witches. It sounded like a decision his father would make: anything to increase their chances of success.

What about the witches then? They preferred to dwell alone, away from the presence of men, even though it meant choosing the swamp over more desirable dry territory. Had their magic developed because a woman alone was so vulnerable? Did they really hate men?

"So there's little information on the witches," Alvito said with a twist of the head. "And isn't that because no one survives an encounter with a witch? We're all dead men who just haven't realized it yet."

"Two days until we reach the vast swamps of the western lands," Salvador said. "And then, as Teresa said, we'll find out firsthand. There's no sense in letting our imagination have control." He gestured ahead toward a massive pile of boulders that covered the cross trail running north and south. The wider, more used road north went toward Aveston. A powerful flood must have deposited the enormous rocks there years ago, where they caught in the depression between hills. "We'll make camp after that crossroad. Catch a bit of sleep."

Ramiro's heart lightened at the hint of a goal. Scattered brush and thick groupings of saguaro grew among the rocks, further screening the crossroad from view, but he hoped for a clear space close by. His seat was beginning to grow stiff. He couldn't imagine the discomfort Teresa must be feeling, unaccustomed as she was to the saddle. Even Gomez the Inexhaustible urged his horse faster.

The birdsongs had ceased, and their horses made little sound since the dust muffled their steps. As the company entered the crossroads, Ramiro cocked his head as the slight clink of metal beating against metal came from his right. His muscles tensed.

"Wait," Salvador said, frowning. "Something's not right."

A squad of Northerners burst from the road to their left, legs moving in a full trot. They marched in neat lines, wearing chain mail and burnished helmets. The neat lines dissolved as the five riders entered their midst, creating confusion. The astonishment on Northern faces said they were just as surprised.

Everyone reacted swiftly. The Northerners drew weapons. Ramiro's heart sped as he dropped his reins and pulled his sword. There's wasn't time to don his helmet. Salvador struck right and left, fluid as quicksilver, avoiding blows and showing how he'd earned his *pelotón* so young. His sword bit into necks, then slashed and parried. Leaving the packhorses, Gomez gave a full-throated shout and simply spurred his *caballo de guerra*, his mount riding down a Northerner, trampling him into the road. As his horse slowed, Gomez pulled his leg from the stirrup and used his big steel-booted foot to kick another enemy in the face.

A sound between bellow and maniacal laughter emerged from Alvito's throat. He'd distanced himself from the fray so his daggers could bloom from Northerner flesh.

Teresa pulled and twisted on her reins. Her chestnut gelding reared with a scream. She slid off its rump and toppled into the dust, disappearing beneath churning hooves. The gelding raced up the road.

A big bear of a Northerner with unbelievable red hair and brown spots on his pale skin lunged. Ramiro screamed a battle cry. He caught the sword thrust on the hilt of his own sword, only his greater height on horseback allowing him to match strengths with the giant. They strained, trying to overpower the other. The giant Northerner pressed close, pinning Ramiro's right leg against Sancha's side. The man grabbed at Ramiro's uniform, trying to yank him from the saddle.

Ramiro fumbled for his concealed knife. Left-handed, he plucked it out and slammed it into the Northerner's chest. The blade penetrated an inch, then caught in a steel ring in the Northerner's chain mail. Caught in a stalemate, the man roared and fought harder to unhorse him.

Sancha sidled seconds before a sting scraped along Ramiro's left ribs. A thin Northerner had come up on his blind side and penetrated under his backplate, but the enemy had been deflected from piercing deeply by Sancha's actions. Besieged, Ramiro couldn't release his grip on the right to defend his left. Sancha arched her neck to seize the thin Northerner's arm in her teeth, her normally gentle eyes now narrowed and furious. The man screamed as she shook him and spun him around.

Sancha's movement unbalanced the giant, crowding him tight against Ramiro. With the pressure on his left gone, Ramiro stood in his stirrups, using the greater height to slam down on the knife. The steel ring split, allowing the dagger to penetrate deep. The giant stumbled, only to take Salvador's blade through the neck before Ramiro could bring his sword around. A throwing knife from Alvito finished off the opponent in Sancha's teeth.

Ramiro gasped, trying to slow his racing heart. None of the Northerners remained on their feet. As he watched, Gomez moved among them, making sure they'd be no more threat. It'd happened so fast, they hadn't even considered taking a captive for Teresa.

Teresa!

Still wearing his plumed hat, Alvito secured his knives and began rounding up the loose packhorses before they could run off like the chestnut gelding. Gomez hefted a body and headed toward the rocks, intent on removing all the evidence of their skirmish. The wound in his side stung, but Ramiro swung down from Sancha to go to Teresa. Salvador beat him there.

"Cousin?" Ramiro called, touching her short hair.

"Are you hurt?" Salvador asked.

The plump woman uncurled from the defensive ball she'd assumed. She held tight to her shoulder. Her eyes showed fright atop pain, which she struggled manfully to conceal. "Here," she hissed, nodding down at her chest, unable to move her other arm. "Something stepped on me." Did Ramiro imagine her cringing away from the blood on his hands?

"Collarbone," Salvador said gruffly. "Likely broken. It'll have to be bound in a sling."

Ramiro settled back on his heels to await instructions as Alvito rummaged in packs for cloth. Alvito came over bearing one of Gomez's extra shirts. Instead of offering the shirt to Salvador, he froze. "You're hurt, Capitán."

A spreading stain of red darkened Salvador's surcoat below his breastplate, and Ramiro felt like he'd been stabbed himself.

CHAPTER 8

Salvador's wound proved neither dangerous nor deep. A sword thrust had slipped below his armor, cutting skin and muscle near the top of his thigh. The gash stopped bleeding almost before Alvito finished sewing it back together. The cut along Ramiro's ribs bled less but required one more stitch than his brother's, leading Alvito to declare Ramiro the bigger idiot.

Teresa sat on a dried saguaro skeleton and watched the scene, her left arm in a sling to immobilize her collarbone. It didn't seem to be a clean break, but it might be deeply bruised or the muscles damaged. Nearby, Salvador nursed a teakettle and lifted roasted sausages off the same small fire of dead cacti that had been used to boil the needle and other supplies.

"Fine lot we are, by the saints," Alvito grumbled. "Caught unaware. Three injuries in the first hours. One lost horse. A sad, sorry lot." He tied off the fine catgut of Ramiro's last suture and broke off the thread with his teeth, then gave Ramiro a push. "The only redeeming light—our mascot has earned his beard! That is, if he can manage to grow one instead of peach fuzz."

Gomez held up a razor with one hand and stroked the fierce beard that ran from his face to his chest with the other. "You won't be needing this anymore. A real man lets everything grow as it will."

"Well," Alvito hedged, "I don't recommend losing it altogether." He kicked over the pot of cooling water onto the fire and slipped the needle back into his pack, careful not to disturb his plumed hat, set there to be out of the dirt. "A nicely trimmed sculpt lets you look sweet to the ladies, unlike a hairy bear. I'd rather be a man than a beast." He touched the crisp lines of his straight-angled beard.

Gomez growled and waved his hands like claws. "Jackass, you mean. A bear has many virtues over a jackass."

"Jackass? Nay, I think you mean cat. A cat I will allow." Alvito directed a smile toward Teresa. "We must appeal to the woman among us. Would your sex prefer a hairy bear or a sleek cat?"

"Oh," Teresa said, her grin bursting forth despite her injury. "How can one possibly choose? I say yes to variety. One isn't enough, eh?"

Ramiro smiled at their banter and glanced up as Salvador's hand settled on his shoulder. "Nicely earned, brother." Before he could answer, Salvador moved off, and Ramiro wondered again what his brother concealed that kept him so quiet.

Ramiro stirred on the rock he'd chosen for a seat, spreading his hands before him. Clean now, they'd been covered with blood only a few minutes ago. His left hand trembled, the motion barely apparent, and he quickly formed it into a fist. If not for Sancha, it would have been *his* body dragged off the road and into the rocks. Salvador would be mourning him instead of praising.

The giant Northerner had not gone into their meeting expecting to die. In fact, his eyes had expressed utter confidence, right up until the moment they'd filled with horror and shock. The saints had turned the giant's fortune in an instant. They could turn Ramiro's just as fast. Or Salvador's. Or anyone's.

They don't talk about this in the tales.

Alvito walked around the fire to whisper to Salvador, but Ramiro overheard. "He's awful quiet, no? Shouldn't this be a celebration?"

Salvador gave Ramiro a glance. "Leave him be. The first time in close combat isn't easy."

Ramiro pulled his shirt on over his head so he need hear no more. He strode to the edge of their camp and began grooming Sancha, determined to give her the thorough going-over she'd earned. Despite the twinges from his raw wound, he rubbed and curried her with brushes until the work smoothed away all other thoughts, even lifting each hoof to scrape caked sand free with a pick. Sancha nudged him in appreciation, leaning her weight on him until he staggered and almost collapsed.

A hummingbird, all green and red, zoomed closer to inspect them, and discovering they offered no nectar, it zipped away.

Ramiro stroked Sancha's chest, then he reached upward to encircle her muzzle in his arms. "Salvador thinks I'm feeling guilty for killing," he whispered to her. Salvador was the perfect soldier. He couldn't bear for Salvador to think less of him. "Perhaps that's what I should feel, but I'm relieved. Glad it's the Northerner and not us."

Sancha blinked her large eyes in perfect comprehension. To her he could say anything. It was no sin for a soldier to be scared, but he had reacted in panic and not with a clear head. He'd acted out of desperate self-preservation. There hadn't been time to recall Salvador's endless lectures of, "use your brain and not just your muscles." He'd barely had time to react, let alone form a plan. He just wanted to survive and protect his friends and his city even if it meant taking another's life. "It's war," he said. "We have to do what we must."

If there was a next time, he wanted things to go differently. He would keep himself under control and use his brain. He'd do better than merely reacting. The wound across his back had settled into an ache that throbbed along with his heartbeat. He fingered the bandage. *Yes, I will not lose my head next time.*

And I'll wear all my armor.

Sancha nickered softly as if to say he'd dodged his

friends long enough. Ramiro took the hint and headed back to the fire to grab a sausage before Gomez ate them all.

Julian stepped from the carriage and turned to wait for Beatriz as she fussed busily with the drape of her shawl, the frills and flounces of her dress, and finally with her little hairball dog. Instead of sighing, he smiled. More than twenty-seven years of marriage had taught him patience. It had also trained him to be prepared for cold hands. Winter or high summer, the woman never got overheated though she'd often dragged him back from that state.

Somehow, the familiar touch of those chilly hands brought sense and sanity to him. Almost as if by their sheer stubborn refusal to change no matter the weather, he could hold on to his convictions. That, and they certainly helped to soothe a headache when the air was too thick to breathe, and the sun baked all else. Plus, she worried enough for three men. With Beatriz by his side, his cares were often light as a feather.

She arranged dog and attire to her taste and let him help her from the coach. Once she was out, grooms led it away to make room in the busy courtyard. Julian waved, and his bodyguards departed with it. Against the far wall, a blacksmith worked under a sheen of sweat, his hammer throwing sparks as he beat out an arrowhead. Smoke drifted from the forge and from cook fires inside the nearby barracks. Soldiers hurried on numerous errands: carrying dispatches, going to their duties, topping off lanterns with oil.

We do not give in so easily, he thought with pride.

Julian escorted Beatriz across the cobblestones to a flight of stairs. The stair would take them to the top of Colina Hermosa's wall.

Beatriz's cool hand twined around his arm. "Did you have to send both my sons on this impossible mission?" She raised her voice to be heard above the din, moving slowly on the stair, clinging and pulling.

He hugged close to the wall to allow a sergeant carrying a stack of arrows to pass. Here, Julian was the unimportant one; their work was more urgent. They reached the top of the wall, where all was orderly and quiet. Guards stood at attention in their spaces along the stone fortification. Julian gestured outward over the parapet at the Northern army. "Would you have them here, *mi amor*? Knowing that is coming for us soon. We agreed they are safer away."

"But sending them to the witches . . ." She held the dog close to her nose and buried her face in its fur. The stifling breeze caught the lace mantilla atop her head, lifting it in a gentle wave.

"The witches are only a plausible excuse to send them in that direction," he said. "It had to be a reasonable fabrication, or they would see right through it. Now Salvador can scout the way for the evacuees who will follow, and only he has to know about them. Besides, no one has seen the witches in decades."

Beatriz stuck out her lower lip as if she were still a

girl, and he couldn't help but smile. To Julian, she would always be the beauty he'd wed before becoming rich or being elected *alcalde*. He wrapped an arm around her. "They are doing what is important. Making sure the way to the swamps is safe." He squeezed her shoulders. "Now and forever."

"Now and forever," she echoed with a sigh. "But did they truly have to go?"

"Who knows?" he said. "Perhaps this side mission will succeed. Perhaps the witches still exist, and our sons will persuade them to use their magic in our favor."

She huffed and rolled her eyes. "By the saints, Julian. Of course the witches live. Evil doesn't die that easily. But the witches help no one. Isn't that so, Pietro?" The little dog under her arm panted happily. She looked back at Julian. "When do you go on this foolish quest to meet the barbarians and settle these terms so they can destroy us?"

Julian cast a swift glance at the enemy camps spread across the plain. One group of them marched in a square formation, while elsewhere soldiers moved more freely. The siege machines waited in silent isolation near the rear. He detected no change among the enemy though the scouts assured him the numbers had grown. "In the morning. But as we've already discussed, I go nowhere. So you can stop worrying. They are coming here, where I'll be well protected."

Her lips thinned. She'd already given ground on that issue as she had on their sons' departure. "You'll be guarded by bodyguards, not kin. You could have kept our sons here with you or sent them with the children."

"When the first group of children goes through the tunnels tonight, they will have *pelotón* members to protect them. We decided our sons would be safer elsewhere. It may be selfish, but I want them out of the city. Let's not rehash that argument. They've been gone over a day; there is no getting them back. Besides, the children are the priority now. They will go to the swamp as long as the hill tunnels remain undiscovered—with the *pelotónes*. Hopefully, the Northerners won't find them there."

The little dog squirmed as she hugged it tight. Beatriz's lip trembled. "I hate to see it come to this. Bad enough you meet with these . . . people. But the children, will they be safe? They are like our own."

"As safe as anyone. And Salvador has his orders. Our sons will take their trek through the swamp and join the evacuees. Then the children will have more protection." He put his hands on her arms, and looked into her eyes. "I promise, *mi amor*."

"*Alcalde* Alvarado," a captain who had been waiting out of earshot called. "They are ready for you."

Julian took his wife's hand to lead her down from the wall. Below, a wagon had arrived, and with it came the first of the evacuees. Of course, a wagon couldn't fit through the tunnels, so the older children would have to walk while the smallest rode on mules. But it would be quicker to get them to the tunnels with the wagon.

Already, parents and grandparents helped small ones into the wagon. Larger children climbed in under their own power. All carried some sort of cloth sack containing provisions and extra clothing. All wore their best: skirts of brilliant red, white blouses, black pants for the boys, all without a tear or a mend. Red skin around ears or knees showed where a hasty scrubbing had been performed before arriving. Damp hair gave further proof. The scene left a nostalgic ache in Julian for his own children's time as this age.

A circle of adoring tots formed around Beatriz with eager hands reaching out to touch the fluffy hairball. "Pietro, no kissing," Beatriz said, laughing as the tiny dog slurped faces, adding his own brand of grooming.

"Thank you, *Alcalde*," one white-haired grandfather said, seizing Julian's hand. "Thank you for harboring the children in the citadel, where they will be better protected." A tiny girl with reddish streaks in her brown hair clung to the old man's leg. She squeezed a rag doll tight with her other arm, thumb in her mouth.

"It is nothing," Julian said, shifting his feet. Telling the people their children went to the swamp of the witches for their own safety would go over like a dead fire on a winter morning. But it was safer for the children out of the city and hidden in the swamp—it had to be. Thus, this deception was for everyone's benefit. It was much more easily and quietly done when the parents didn't know the truth.

"But my sister's children," one bright-eyed matron appealed to Beatriz. "What will happen to them?"

Beatriz gave him the look, and Julian cleared his throat. He forced a reassuring smile. "The citadel has plenty of room. All the children will be safely sheltered until this Northern threat is eliminated. More children will be brought every hour until we have them all. Santiago had a heart without limit; so, too, is our citadel without limits when it comes to the children of Colina Hermosa."

Even as the lies left his lips, he said a silent prayer: Santa Bridig, patron of fugitives, defend them all. For surely the swamps would be kinder than the death they would find here.

CHAPTER 9

Ramiro rode beside Teresa as the sun reached midday. Only their third day on the hunt, and already the land had turned wet. The thorny cacti and saguaro had vanished, leaving flat, open meadows of thick, tall grasses. Gone was the road dust. Now the horses' hooves squished against the ground, leaving behind tiny pools in their prints and casting splatters. Though the sun shone every bit as fierce and no rain had fallen, the ground did not drink up the water but let it remain close to the surface.

Even the air felt wet as it entered Ramiro's lungs. It clung, damp and unpleasant on his skin. How did people live in a constant state of moistness?

Teresa's brown skin had gone gray, but she managed a smile. "I promise I will not overreact again and lose another horse. You can stop being my shepherd, cousin."

"It is not the loss of a horse that worries me. You look like you need a rest."

She shrugged, then winced when the motion disturbed her sling. "To keep suffering the rocking of this beast or to have to climb off it and eventually back up again—which is the worse punishment? It's a philosopher's question. Is the misery you know better than the misery you anticipate? I'll stay where I am rather than have three of you boost me around like the useless lump I am."

Misery was no understatement. Ramiro couldn't but admire the round woman for her determination. His own wound still ached and throbbed dully, but the ride must be a constant torture to her. She'd refused to slow their pace, though, claiming she, too, could do her part to save Colina Hermosa.

They'd off-loaded the supplies from one of the packhorses, distributing them equally to all the steeds. Now Salvador rode the packhorse and had coaxed his stallion to accept Teresa. Valentía had the smoothest gait of all the *caballos de guerra*, but it made little difference. Teresa grew more drawn by the hour.

"Spare some of your worry for your brother." Teresa nodded ahead, where Salvador led.

His brother sweated freely in his armor, a flush over his skin. Unlike Ramiro's wound, his was not healing cleanly. Alvito fussed over it with alcohol and said little, calling it an infection that the alcohol, the fever, and Salvador's own constitution would soon banish. Regardless, Salvador, like Teresa, would not turn back.

"Salvador wouldn't accept my concern," Ramiro said with a forced smile. It did no good to show the worry he felt for his brother. Salvador would get better. "He has much more pride than you, cousin."

Teresa chortled. "Perhaps my pride is just as deep, but it is overcome at having a handsome young man at my beck and call. So what is your decision? What type of beard shall you grow, cousin?"

Ramiro touched the rough stubble forming on his chin. "You'll have to wait and find out."

"Oh ho. A tease. But I believe you will be just as hairy as the rest of these ruffians soon; and then how will I tell you apart? You should stay clean-shaven and defy convention. A beard doesn't make a man, the man makes the beard. Why not dare all and go without?"

Ramiro grinned. "Next you will want to put me in a skirt though you don't favor them yourself."

"Ah," Alvito called. "A hit. I do believe our mascot has scored a hit."

Sancha twitched an ear and did a bouncy sidestep, as if she agreed. Teresa patted her leg, encased in very manly trousers. "You see I have no trouble defying convention. Is my cousin less brave with the face he shows the world?"

"Tell us what look the witches would prefer?" Gomez called from the rear of their group. "Beard or no beard? It is them we need to impress. That is the direction our mascot should take, though a beard on a mascot will make us a laughingstock."

"Then perhaps we will hold you down and shave

you," Salvador said with a suppressed smile. "Gomez can be our new mascot."

"Sounds fair to me," Ramiro said quickly.

"Listen to them," Alvito said. "The brothers gang up on our poor bear. But what's a bear without hair? A goat? Nay, a pig. Pigs are hairless, are they not?"

"I've met many a man that was a pig." Teresa snorted. "But none among present company unless it be disguised as a cat."

Alvito gave a mock frown. "And a hit for the lady against my own self."

Ramiro clapped Teresa on the back as he would any comrade, then froze in consternation. But she winked at him as if he'd caused no pain to her shoulder.

Alvito tossed Teresa a waterskin. "But back to the topic at hand—I'd venture a guess the witches prefer their men with glazed eyes and maggots eating their insides," he said.

Teresa drank deeply and wiped her face with her sleeve, grimacing before handing the skin back. "Very likely, cat. Very likely."

"Quiet," Salvador called. "Look there."

Ramiro guided Sancha to the edge of the grassy roadway to see around his brother. He squinted against the stark sunlight to make out dark smudges ahead. Across a cleared space, a village was built right alongside the road in a little hollow. What sort of people would live hard against the only track? People who didn't care for their own defense or people who felt very sure of it?

In no time, the structures resolved into low, rounded huts comprised of mud slathered over sticks. A cleared field of mud surrounded it on all sides, holding back the woods. The grass in the village had been worn away by many feet, packing the ground into sludge. Woven marsh grasses made up the roofs, a dubious shelter from the rain. The road ran straight through the center, splitting the group of houses in half, without a solid wall or a rickety fence for the barest protection. There was no sign of any shops or even a church to give the Lord's comfort to the poor souls who lived here.

The village appeared deserted, except for a small child in a torn smock and bare legs. The child raised a grimy finger. "*Ciudad* men."

Salvador halted in the center of the cluster of huts as a dog started to bark. "What say you, Teresa? Do the witches live here?"

She shrugged, then winced again. "Santiago. I've got to stop doing that." She glanced around, adjusting her sling. "It seems unlikely. We're not in the swamp yet, and they'd be too easy to find here. Too, that young one is male—from all we know, no men live among the witches."

As if they were called, figures emerged from the huts—men with the sullen eyes and unsmiling faces of those who had lately been at their *siesta*. Their dark hair hung long and tangled. They leaned on tall cudgels of hard oak, their dark-haired women and children keeping well behind them.

A short, bent man stood at the front of the growing crowd. He eyed their armor and weapons, then the dappled, gray coats of the *caballos de guerra*. "Soldiers of the *pelotón—ciudad* men." He spat. "Come to take from us yet again? What do you want, city men?"

"We're looking for witches," Salvador said.

"Witches. You mean the *sirenas*?" The man grunted. "What do you know of *sirenas*? On your way, city men. Take your hunt elsewhere while you can."

Ramiro tensed, touching the San Martin medallion at his throat. The men were small and battered with hard living, but there were over twenty of them, and all with strong clubs. He was glad they'd donned their full armor after the skirmish with the Northerners. Better the heat than bleeding flesh.

Salvador dismounted from his packhorse as calmly as if they were home in the citadel. No stranger could have detected he was sick. "We bring trade goods in exchange for information and assistance." He strode to the loaded packhorse and threw open a bundle to reveal a stash of hand mirrors jumbled among cheap beads. A woman with strings of hair hanging in her face gasped. Salvador opened another bag with small iron knives strapped inside.

The man stepped closer. "For information about the *sirenas*? The *sirenas* are no allies of ours. We leave them alone, and they do the same for us." He nodded and spat in his hand before holding it out. "Done. The two bags for your information."

"Then the witches are not legend," Ramiro said.

"Oh, they're very real, city man. One was here yesterday to trade. But if you go looking for them, you'll
pray that they weren't."

Salvador hesitated to take his hand. "Ominous
words. We'll need a guide."

The village man nodded. "My son. You won't get
better than that." He gestured to a wiry boy of about
ten years. The boy wore leggings and no shirt, his
brown hair a thick mop against brown skin.

This time Salvador took his hand. The man shook,
then disengaged his grip and stepped for the packhorse, open greed on his face. Salvador intervened,
putting himself between them. "Where can we find
the witches?"

"Not in this village or any village. The *sirenas* live
alone, except for their brats. They keep to the swamp.
My son can take you to the nearest. The swamp is just
as dangerous as the *sirenas*. Maybe more. It can kill you
quicker. My son knows the ways of the swamp. Can
you say the same, city man?"

The rock Claire used as a milking stool every morning was cold under her bottom. Her thin summer dress
couldn't keep the chill away. The cool early breeze in
front of the cottage would turn steamy soon enough.
Instead of focusing on the task of sending the goat milk
zinging into the pail at her feet, she yawned and let her
mind wander, leaning her cheek against Dolly's warm
flank.

Why was the magic so finicky, so hard to control? She'd practiced with the Song for as long as she could remember, but it never got any easier. Not like it did for her mother. If only she could use it on something real instead of theoretical practice.

Dolly used her distraction to bring forward a hoof. Claire jumped to grab at the bucket—too late. The goat kicked over the pail and spilled the milk into the grass, then turned to give her an impish grin as only a goat could.

Several feet away on a wooden stool, her mother shook her head and kept right on sending streams of liquid into her pail. She was slender and straight, tall as any man. Her hands were rough from work, an odd contrast to the delicate curves of her face. "If you paid attention, that wouldn't happen." Tessa—the goat her mother milked—winked one amber eye in Claire's direction.

"Spiteful things," Claire huffed. She righted the pail and shook milk from her bare foot. "If I sang to them, they'd stand still for me."

"No." Her mother kept right on with her chore.

"But why not? Wasn't the Song given to us to use— for a reason?"

Her mother paused long enough to nod toward the swamp pool at the edge of their homestead. "The frogs have long legs for jumping, but you don't see them jumping for fun. The Song is not for frivolous exercises."

Claire pursed her lips. She hated when her mother

used this argument. She could never think of a way to counter it.

"Everything in nature is given for a purpose," her mother said. "The wolf doesn't kill for sport. The blackbird doesn't fly for show. We don't use magic except to defend."

"The mosquito doesn't sting to cause itchiness," Claire said. "Wouldn't forcing the goats to stand still for their milking be useful? Humans are smarter than animals. It's what makes us better."

Her mother scowled. "Humans."

"We're humans, too, Mother."

"We of the Song will never settle among humans again. We might be human, but that doesn't make us one of them. Men manipulate. Men control. One and all, they deserve death. Men." Her mother almost spat the word, then she clicked her tongue in disgust. "I cannot even talk about them without losing composure. It's why I've only lived once among humans and never will again."

Alternating between pats and pulls, Claire coaxed Dolly back in place to finish her job. Her mother had lived in a village for two years in order to fulfill her duty and produce a daughter. The Women of the Song lived apart, even from each other, having little in common, except for the Song and the obligation to carry on their kind.

Her mother would never speak of those two years—the lost years, she called them. Claire could learn nothing of her forgotten father. Not even the features she saw in the mirror gave her any clue to his identity. She looked exactly like a miniature version of her mother, from her blue eyes to the curve of her chin, right down to the wide spacing between her toes.

"But I can never improve the Song if I don't practice more."

Her mother sent Tessa off and waited for Jorga to take her place for milking. Her mother's eyes turned inward. "Perhaps improving is not a good thing. The Song is evil. The Song manipulates just as a man. It robs a living thing of its free will and hands it to another. My mother did not think so, and that is why I have such skill. But it was bought at a painful price. A price I will not have my daughter pay."

Claire growled low in her throat, so her mother wouldn't hear. Yet another thing her mother wouldn't speak about. Whatever her grandmother had included in her mother's training had not been pleasant.

Her grandmother had believed in using the Song at every opportunity and had trained her daughter at it hard. Once grown, her mother had left home and never looked back. Grandmother had visited once, so long ago that Claire could not even remember her, back when she couldn't yet walk. They had argued, and the matriarch of their family had never revisited from her home at the southern end of the swamp. Claire didn't want to be trained so obsessively, but a happy medium would be nicer than practically no training.

"When you are grown, then you will make your own choices," her mother said. "Until then, you follow my word. The Song is not for games. I speak thus because I love you."

Anger evaporated like fog under the sun. Claire milked in silence. She could no more disobey her mother than she could cut off her own arm. Too much love existed between them to cause her mother any additional hurt. Mother had lost her own mother—she'd never survive losing her daughter.

"Tell me about your trip to the village yesterday."

"What's to tell?" her mother said. "It was just like every other trip. I've described it to you a thousand times. It's muddy and smelly. I traded for what I could, but they don't have much. They tolerate us but give no welcome. Always the same."

"Then tell me something that happened yesterday. Something that was new."

Milk zinged into the pail as her mother seemed to consider. Finally, she smiled. "The village children are getting braver. I caught one peeking at me from behind a barrel. They stalked me down the street, hiding behind corners and rotting stumps." Her mother laughed. "Not very effectively. I heard them giggling and whispering the whole time."

"What do they look like?"

"Small and brown—exactly like they looked the last time you asked."

"Are there any my age?"

"Their women don't come near me. Only the village leader, but I did see a girl through a shutter. She hid about as well as the smaller children, only quieter."

"Did she look like me?"

Her mother paused in her milking. "You know they don't." Then she relented. "She wore her hair up as they do in the cities."

"Hair up," Claire said. She grabbed her long braid and piled it on the top of her head.

Her mother laughed. "More toward the back. Not on the top."

Claire stretched her neck and lifted her chin, holding the braid against her skull. "How do I look?"

"Silly."

Dolly tried to take a bite out of Claire's dress. She sighed and released her hair to push the goat away. "If I wore it that way, would they like me?"

The smile slid from her mother's face. "The villagers would hide from you. The city men would try to kill you. Women of the Song aren't welcome in the cities. You'll never go near another human because I love you too much to risk it."

"But you lived there."

"I kept my hair covered and my eyes down. It was necessary." Her mother's smile returned. "I was better at hiding than those children yesterday."

"Don't the cities have thousands of streets?" Claire asked. "Easier to hide. I wish I could see one. Or at least the village. Maybe that girl would talk to me." She stared into her half-empty bucket. Her mother had never been in a city, but she had seen them from afar. And her grandmother had ventured inside one. Maybe someday she'd be like her grandmother.

To see other people. To see a city. To make a friend. Her throat burned. "It's necessary," she whispered, so her mother couldn't hear.

Her mother drew the last milk from Jorga and stood. "You've been quiet a great deal lately. Get the berry baskets and change into walking clothes. The blueberries should be ripe. We're taking a holiday."

Alcalde Julian sat at the head of the council table. Without a ruler or king, they had no throne room to welcome an ambassador or a herald from a conquering nation. But the council room had tall brass candelabra in each corner to shed light over any gloom. A crystal chandelier, large enough to hold twenty candles, hung in the center of the ceiling directly over the glossy mahogany table. Table legs carved in fantastic shapes by expert craftsmen matched the carving on the padded chairs. A plush carpet and murals of the saints on the wainscot walls completed the picture.

He'd had the citadel scoured for silver or gold statuary to set about the room. A mantel clock ticked above the tile fireplace. An empty chair waited at the far end of the table. If the room failed to impress the Northerners, then they had nothing better. Displaying wealth was risky before such greedy invaders, but it might also convince them that the city had power and strength as well. It was a delicate balance.

Julian's bodyguard waited behind him, standing silently against the wall. To his left and right sat the oldest and most venerated members of the council. Tall and straight, *Concejal* Adulfo had sparse white hairs on his bald head and a wild bramble of thick beard. *Concejal* Diego, on the other hand, had thick gray hair and a meager beard. He seemed to fade into his chair, his belly being the most obvious part of him as it strained against his waistcoat. A vote among the seven members had picked these two to provide support through the meeting. He was glad to have the support of their presence today.

Julian stared at the dark wood of the closed doors and fingered his beard. They had no idea what to expect from their soon-to-arrive visitor, in either his appearance or his message. If they were young men, they would have let words express their nervousness and trepidation. Being old men, they sat in silence and kept their thoughts to themselves. No need to express doubts and worries that could cease to exist in moments. Time had taught them that dwelling on speculation solved nothing. One merely had to wait, and answers would come. Young men lived in the future, but old men lived in the present.

A knock boomed from the doors, and they swung inward. Two soldiers of the council *pelotón* escorted a single person, hidden between them. A person who, no doubt, had her own share of confidence to beard the lion in its den—and alone at that.

"Santabe, priestess of the Children of Dal," one of the soldiers announced. The soldiers stepped aside with a click of their boots, dropping back and standing by the chamber door.

Julian sat taller in his chair, sensing Adulfo and Diego stir at his sides. Indeed, they couldn't have predicted this outcome. Matters just got more interesting—and potentially more to their favor.

The Northern ambassador was a woman.

The woman was tall, easily over six feet, the height of a soldier. Judging by her face, she was not quite young enough to be one of Julian's children, but not much older, either. The pale blemishes—freckles—adorned her cheeks and nose, and her yellow-tinted barbarian hair dangled in a braid instead of being properly coiled about her head. Gold chains circled tight to her long neck, while a large gold earring in the shape of a sun hung from her left ear, drawing down the lobe with its weight. She wore a simple robe of white that could have been a long flour sack with sleeves sewn at the shoulder. It hung straight until tapering at the bottom, except where it lay over her breasts. Her only adornment was a small knife at her hip. He found her both exotic and intimidating.

Julian stood, as was proper. One did not offer a woman a seat at the council table, not because he personally found a woman any less intelligent or capable but because it was the law. He found this law old-fashioned and outdated, but today it worked in his favor. He must take command of this situation and use everything the Northerners gave him if the city was to have any hope.

"I am *Alcalde* Julian Alvarado, elected official of Colina Hermosa. These gentlemen are representatives of our council." Adulfo and Diego dipped their heads. As honored elders, they need not rise. "You bring the terms of your people?"

"I do," she said in a ringing voice though with an odd accent.

"Then let us see them."

Her head lifted, strange green eyes meeting his. "They are memorized, to be given orally."

Julian shook his head. Had he heard her correctly, the accent made it difficult. "Spoken word can be misspoken, especially when given in an unfamiliar language. Do you rule over the Northerners that your word can be taken for their will?"

"I am a high priestess of Dal. I speak the word of Dal, but I am not one of your kings."

"The word of Dal, however great His might, is not accepted here. We want the word of the one who rules you, or a written presentation of your terms." He gave her the look he bestowed on his sons when they were young and had broken something valuable. "Moreover, according to our law, a woman cannot act in matters of politics."

Anger flared in her face. Julian blessed the Northerners' fair skin, so ill equipped to hide their emotions. This one was not used to being questioned or invalidated.

"You insult us," she said, voice ringing.

"Not at all," he said quickly. His gut said he'd pushed enough. Time now to withdraw and placate without conceding. "You misunderstand my purpose. I wish only what is best for the survival of Colina Hermosa. We are most anxious to settle these conditions, but this city is governed, not by divine will but by a council. All must be carried forward in the law. To overset that law, the council must first confer and find agreement.

"We would willingly discuss and accept a woman as ambassador from your people, but that will take time. You may, of course, speak the terms now, but we'd need them in writing also. Bringing us your terms in writing makes it easier to share with all the council members so we might best consider those provisions. It only speeds matters to do so."

She lifted her chin. "Bring all your council here now, and they may all hear Dal's terms."

"They are elderly and would be slow to comply. Scribes would have to be gathered to take down the conditions. It would be faster to go and return with written terms that may be shared before our people. Written terms are a better guarantee to us that they will not change upon a whim."

"*Alcalde* Alvarado speaks wisely," Diego added. "As elder of the council, I back his words."

"And I," Adulfo said.

"The will of Dal is that all bend before us." She put her hand on the small gold knife she wore at her hip. "Or be broken."

Julian nodded. This priestess saw in terms of black-and-white; with her there was no gray. "Colina Hermosa is the largest of the *ciudades-estado*. We are not so easily broken. You'll find us no easy meat. To do so will cost your Dal more time and many lives. Does your Dal wish us to hear the terms? Does he prefer we are gathered to *his* cause? Then we must act within our laws to have our decisions accepted by our people."

He saw by her reaction that he had guessed correctly. Their god was after living converts. Probably in order to gather more wealth at the least cost.

He moved around the table to stand before her. "We are the ones asked to bend; we ask only that we be allowed to consider with dignity—by our laws. Bring us your terms in writing, give us a day to change law and accept a woman as ambassador, or send your king to confer with us directly." He gave her a bow, keeping his eyes cold. "Or, of course, you can always attack instead. But, I promise, such actions will cost Dal many followers. You can speak your terms now, but it will get you nothing if the law is not followed."

"You are full of tricks, old fox, but they will not avail you." She glared. "I shall enjoy watching your city burn." She turned crisply on her heel and marched out.

Julian's strength ebbed as she withdrew. He sat in the empty chair. She had great force of will, but sometimes a gamble paid off best.

"Was that wise?" Adulfo asked. "You've antagonized them more."

"We're at war—I don't think we *can* antagonize them more. We never intended to concede to their terms," Diego countered. "Does it really matter how we answered them?"

Julian touched mind, heart, liver, and spleen. "What matters is we've gained another day."

CHAPTER 10

Barefoot and shirtless, the village boy hopped from one hillock of grass to another before dodging between bushes with thin, pointed leaves of a type Ramiro had never seen before. The plants he was used to all had thorns.

The boy moved nimbly as a goat down the narrow but well-defined path. They'd left the village and the road behind hours ago. The scenery alternated quickly and often between soggy grasslands and scrubby woodlands with stagnant water. Ramiro shook his head. Knowing such standing water existed and actually seeing it were two different things.

The shirtless boy stopped and waited for Salvador astride his packhorse to reach him. He pointed across a short rise to a lone tree of dead branches in the distance. "Follow the trail to there, and I'll meet you."

Salvador gave the boy a stare of equal parts distrust

and warning, then he proceeded silently up the trail. He appeared flushed and sweaty, his eyes red, but he rode upright and under control. Single file in his wake, Alvito and Teresa followed, with Gomez close behind. Ramiro clicked to his packhorse and set Sancha in motion.

The boy fell in beside him, walking among the grasses. He grinned to show missing teeth on top and bottom. Ramiro refrained from rolling his eyes. They entrusted their mission to a child who didn't even have all his adult teeth.

"Your leader is sick, eh?" the boy said.

Ramiro tried to mix fierceness and suspicion in his gaze, as Salvador had done, but he felt sure he failed miserably because the boy continued to grin. "Alvito traded for willow powder and honey at your village. Salvador will be well soon."

"Alvito?" The boy laid a finger vertically under his lower lip to mimic Alvito's beard. "The one all the women looked at?"

"Apparently," Ramiro said, and this time he did roll his eyes.

The boy laughed. "Some of them looked at you, too. My older sister said you have pretty eyes, and you're still young enough to be changed to fit in at our village."

"Marvelous," he scoffed but pulled himself taller in his saddle. "The hairy one is Gomez, and I'm Ramiro. The woman is Teresa."

The boy nodded. "Call me Bromisto."

"Trickster?" Ramiro laughed. "That's not a real name, and I wouldn't advise sharing that hoax with my brother." He pointed ahead. "Salvador, I mean. He won't like it. What's your real name?"

"Ermegildo." The boy's chin sunk to his bare chest. "My sister says it reminds her of a flower. Do you have sisters?"

"I have a fussy mother. Does that count? Let's stick with Bromisto."

"Thanks." Bromisto snapped off a round, ball-like blossom from a shrub before flinging it over his shoulder. "I'm ten. How old are you?"

Ramiro blinked at the swift change of subject. Besides being nimble like a goat, his new friend was as capricious as one. "Seventeen."

"Then you are the perfect age for my sister, Elo. She's studying to be a healer. Do you have a wife already? Are you looking for one? You could pick her and take her *far away* to your city."

"I'm afraid my mother might have other ideas. I'm sure she plans to be the one who picks my wife."

Bromisto shrugged. "Maybe one of the others will take her. Are all city men so stupid?"

"Stupid?" Ramiro silently cursed at speaking his surprise aloud. He'd encouraged the boy enough.

"Wearing all that metal into the swamp." He pointed at Ramiro's breastplate, while standing on a hillock of grass to make himself taller. "You do know about quicksand? You plan to sink faster? It will certainly rust fast enough with all the water around.

We've already had to take the longer route because of your horses."

Ramiro leaned forward, and Sancha stopped at his unintentional signal. "Longer route? How much longer?"

"How should I know? A day or more. I don't go to the *sirena's* house to visit. Too dangerous."

"Then why were you chosen as our guide," Ramiro asked, angrily.

"Because I know how to get through the swamp at all—you'd be dead without me. And I have been there once—on a dare." The young boy grinned, then glanced ahead. "Your sick friend has reached the syca-more. He'd better wait unless you want trouble."

"Quicksand?" Ramiro asked.

"Not here." Bromisto kicked at a tuft of long grass. "It's too dry here. But there are panthers and snakes and poisonous plants. Not to mention the *sirenas*. Enough to trouble city men. Besides, the path ends there. He'll go the wrong way. I'd better stop him."

"Wait," Ramiro said. "Tell me about the *sirenas*. Are you sure you can find them? Why do you call them that? Are they more dangerous than the quicksand?"

"Ugh, I don't want to talk about them." He gave a mock shiver. "Not even in the daytime. Hurry up. You have a horse, and you're still slower than my *abuela*." The boy scrambled off at a trot toward Salvador.

When they stopped for a meal several hours later, Ramiro helped Gomez settle the horses with feedbags full of oats and other grain, while Alvito tended to his brother's wound. Salvador's gash looked less angry and

red, and the swelling had gone down. Even more encouraging, the tightness had gone from Alvito's face
as he wrapped Salvador's torso with a clean bandage
smeared with the fresh honey, then went to check on
Teresa's collarbone. The boy trotted eagerly at Alvito's
heels, poking his nose into everything.

As Bromisto had promised, the trail had ended at
the dead tree, forcing them to wind in a meandering
fashion around pools of stagnant water and clumps
of thick brush. The smell of rot had done nothing
for their appetite, while the footing had grown ever
more treacherous and damp. Mud became thick muck,
creeping up to the horses' knees, though the boy's light
frame managed to stay clean of it. Ramiro found it the
stuff of nightmares and was sure, at the very least, the
overpowering smell would find its way to his dreams.

As the horses munched, Ramiro joined his brother,
grateful for some quiet after a morning of Bromisto's
constant chatter. Their garrulous guide seemed to
have picked him out for a companion, sharing every
detail of village life and gossip. He'd learned more
names in one ride than a census taker. His boots sank
an inch or more with each step on his way over to the
high patch of ground Salvador had chosen.

"The boy told me a squad of Northerners came
up the road toward the village," Salvador said, looking worried. "Apparently, they didn't actually explore
far enough to reach it yet. But if the Northerners have
been here once, they'll return. We'd be wise to keep
weapons close and armor on."

Troubled, Ramiro stretched out his legs, layering one muddy boot atop the other. "The Northerners would cut through the villagers like ripe cheese. They need to get out of there, go to a city."

"Aye." Salvador wiped his forehead and took a bite of cold sausage. "Though they'd take the advice better from the boy. I doubt they'll listen to a city man. We'll let Bromisto carry the message. He seems to have taken to you. He say anything useful?"

"Not much, but he did mention we're taking a longer route because of the horses." He waited for Salvador's nod. The calm way his brother took the news showed clearly he'd either expected it or already heard the same from Bromisto. "He also said that there are a lot of dangerous things here besides the witches."

"Undesirables are often pushed to live in the most uninhabitable spots."

"You learn that from Cousin Teresa?" Ramiro joked.

"From observation." Salvador handed him a slice of bread spread with the same honey they used for wounds. "Did he tell you anything about the witches?"

"He won't talk about them, but he has told me exactly how many goats he shepherds and the best spot to find spring mushrooms. I can name every type of tree in this waterlogged place. And I believe he wouldn't be shy about selling his sister to the highest bidder—or the lowest. I'm keeping a count on my coin pouch, and you should, too."

Salvador laughed. "Just be careful, little brother. And I don't mean of our guide. Remember your training. Mother would kill me if I failed to bring you home."

"Saints forbid Mother be disappointed." Ramiro touched the sword he always kept close. "But I'll remember—no fear of that. Speaking of Mother, though, I can't help think she gave in awfully easy. Is there something more going on? Father acted strange, too, and you seem to be keeping se—"

Bromisto came bounding across the small clearing to their spot. "Can I see your sword?"

Little nuisance. Ramiro sighed for his lost peace and crammed the slice of bread in his mouth, holding up his spread fingers covered with honey and mumbling excuses. Salvador shook his head and drew his own weapon.

"You can see mine as my brother is too busy . . . and sticky."

The boy gasped and bent close to inspect it, reaching out a tentative finger. "I thought it would be longer."

Salvador turned the double-edged blade to allow the boy to touch it. "You're thinking of a broadsword. Those are for infantry. You'll find them worn by the men who guard Colina Hermosa's walls. On horseback, we wear shorter blades. They're more maneuverable, more useful than those oversized giants of the foot soldiers."

Bromisto nodded. "I saw broadswords on the guards who came with the tax collectors."

Salvador looked up. "Then your village is part of

Colina Hermosa. You are our people. We are responsible for you."

"Tax collectors come from Aveston, too. We don't pay any of them. No coin." The boy skipped away to investigate Gomez's meal, calling over his shoulder. "We belong to ourselves, city man."

"Well, I guess he told you," Ramiro said, wiping his fingers on some grass. "They belong to themselves."

"He can claim what he wishes, but if our tax collectors visit, then they are our responsibility." Salvador gave him a nudge. "And be more patient, little brother."

Ramiro glanced up sharply. Was Salvador referring to the boy or whatever other instructions their father had given? His brother's silence made him anxious.

"You'll be teaching the likes of him for the *pelotón* soon enough. If I wasn't tolerant with you and your hero worship, you'd still be cleaning stables."

"You try listening to him all day," Ramiro said.

"You have a beard now. Act the part."

"Ramiro," Teresa called from atop a grouping of rocks she'd claimed with the others. "Your promotion is safe. We found a replacement mascot."

"I believe he's an improvement," Alvito said. "He eats less and smells better than you."

Gomez handed the boy a chunk of sausage. "And he's tame, too."

"Very funny," Ramiro called, letting the annoyance slip into his voice.

"Calm," Salvador whispered. "A good soldier must have calm."

Ramiro reined back the frustration. "I beg pardon for acting ungrateful. This delay and this place . . . Plus, worry for home and how Father is faring with the Northerners has me on edge."

"We are all on edge. Father instructed me to clear the path and make sure there were no Northerners between home and the swamp. Lucky for you, there were no groups we couldn't handle, or you'd have been sent back with the warning."

"That's the secret? Why?" Ramiro asked. "Unless . . ."

"Evacuation," his brother confirmed. "Father is sending out the children. If we find no witches, we are to remain with them instead."

"By the saints . . ." That was what Salvador was hiding from him. His father would push things so far. To desert the city. He had trouble finishing the thought in his mind but eventually found his words.

"Why keep that secret from me? From us?" Ramiro corrected, indicating their group. "Why didn't Father just tell all of us? Wouldn't that be easier? I think we need to know. And why not take it to the *concejales*? There are laws. Father will be in serious trouble when this is found out."

Salvador frowned. "Perhaps he feared to disappoint you. Perhaps he wanted to worry as few people as possible. Certainly he didn't believe the *concejales* would support him.

"Perhaps we should give him our trust."

"To take the risk, though. He could be arrested. Thrown from office."

Yes," Salvador said calmly.

"But that must mean that Father finds the situation—"

Salvador grunted. "Dire, indeed. I very much wish we had news."

Alcalde Julian stood in the road that circled the outside of Colina Hermosa's walls, letting dust settle onto his pristine boots. He stood because no horses had been allowed. He'd gotten the delay of one more day added to the negotiations, but in turn he had to forfeit setting the conditions of their second meeting.

The Northerners had demanded an appointment outside the city to the south, on foot, and with no more than five delegates. It made little sense to drag five old and infirm men outside the walls to wilt in the heat. Julian smiled. One would have to suffice.

Instead of wisdom, Julian had brought might; four heavily armed soldiers of his *pelotón* were arranged in a semicircle at his back. Here, they were out of bowshot of the city guard and miles away from the rescue of Colina Hermosa's gate. With the bulk of the Northern army camped a mere three hundred yards away, they could never cross the distance to the gate before being captured or killed.

Surprisingly, curiosity about the terms almost outweighed the jabbering fear that was turning his guts to water. If self-pride abandoned him, though, he had a stronger incentive to stay firm. The saints preserve him, he could not panic and give in to the rising terror without proving that Beatriz's worries were right and his bravado wrong. Never would he give the love of his heart the ability to say "I told you so." Not even to his corpse.

A cloudless, blue sky stretched overhead, allowing the fierce sun full reign. The hum of the army and the crowd on the walls behind him drowned out the swell of insects, but the scent of foliage bleached and baked by the sun was everywhere. Julian lifted his chin as a small party, also on foot, broke from the main mass of Northern soldiers. At their head was a woman in white robes. The priestess, Santabe.

He steeled himself. *Now it comes.*

The small party crossed the distance without haste, taking another petty revenge by making him wait. Soon Julian determined their five consisted of the priestess, one beardless servant in plain linen clothing, and three extremely short figures covered from head to toe in brown robes, like pilgrims. Their hooded heads were turned down to stare at their feet. One of the *pelotón* guards behind Julian grunted, no doubt struck by the lack of weaponry—unless weapons were concealed under the robes. Even the small gold dagger at Santabe's hip was gone though she carried a slender white rod as long as a forearm in its place. Other than the missing knife, the priestess looked the same in every detail, right down to the large, sun-shaped earring pulling down her lobe. Dread filled Julian at her expression.

"By Dal, you have come," Santabe said in her halting accent. The Northern party stopped at the edge of the road. She gave a quick glance as of victory to the servant figure waiting behind. "From such a wily fox, one would expect more . . . how does one say . . . subterfuge."

"Subterfuge can take place equally well in full sight," Julian said.

Her large earring swaying, she chuckled—an unpleasant sound, like a sharp echo in a hollow room. "Here are your terms. Written fair—so they cannot be changed by a misspoken word." She gestured with the rod, and the servant stepped forward, producing a rolled scroll from his sleeve but keeping it out of reach. "Do your people accept this *woman* as an ambassador?" she asked. "Or have you another excuse to delay?"

"We have voted to accept the unusual situation, but we would prefer to negotiate with the ruler of your people."

"Then Dal grants your wish." She stepped back and bowed her head, and the servant stepped forward. "Make of it what you can. Here is Lord Ordoño."

"You . . ." Julian stuttered. "You are the hand of this army?"

The beardless man inclined his head, but no humility marked his face—and that was the least of the surprises about his looks. His coloring and features were not Northern. Rather, his appearance would fit well on the streets of Colina Hermosa. Ordinary in every respect, the man was neither tall nor short, neither handsome nor plain. In the clothes of a servant or dressed as a prince, he would go unnoticed in any drawing room. Until one saw his eyes.

Eyes of hard brown stone, layered in determination and fitted with intelligence, but cold like the ice they say formed in the north. The eyes of a man who had killed much and didn't let it trouble his soul.

The short, robed figures shifted, and the clink of metal sounded. Chains. Black-iron chains bound the three together.

"You are not Northern," Julian said. "The name Ordoño is from the *ciudades-estado*."

"Brilliantly deduced," the man scoffed without the slightest accent. "It took much trouble and might to get the Children of Dal to accept me. Many of their more inflexible priests had to disappear. And it took more effort to turn the might of their army against my former homeland."

"No one would be exiled from the *ciudades-estado*, except criminals."

Lord Ordoño flung his arms wide like a bad actor in a troupe. "Who is to say I was exiled? Perhaps I chose to leave an unfair system that discriminates against those they call peasants. But you have it on the first call. I will not argue over semantics. See how my new land loved me, providing me learning. I'm fit to bandy words with the *Alcalde* of one of the biggest cities. And you call yourselves civilized and us the barbarians." He wagged a finger. "Do not deny it. I know you do."

Julian held his ground. "Revenge. That is the cause of your war, then."

"Revenge. Gain. Loot. Conquest. It is many things, but I will not argue with you there either." He held out the rolled scroll until Julian took it. "Here are the dictated terms. Open your gates by the seventh day and give us one in ten of your men, one in ten of your women, and one in thirty of your children." He let that sink in before smiling—an expression that didn't touch those troublesome eyes. "See, we do not discriminate as some would. A woman can be just as deadly as a man. Is that not so, Santabe?"

The priestess didn't react.

"And what will you do with them?" Julian asked.

"Sacrifice them on the altar of civil obedience," Lord Ordoño said with no trace of emotion. "But it will be quick, unlike if you defy us." He pointed to the scroll. "Read the terms. It is all there. You have a seven-day. That gives your city plenty of time to decide their fate. Fail to open your gate, and we kill all.

"Now, to other business." Lord Ordoño walked unhurried until he stood behind the robed figures. "*Alcalde* Julian, we treated you truthfully and honestly, and you gave us deceit, like the fox you are." He yanked back a hood to reveal the face of a boy, perhaps ten summers old. "What, I ask, is this I found traveling on a mule toward the swamp? Trying to send people to safety. You're cheating." He pulled back the other hoods to reveal young girls, barely more than toddlers. One of them was the girl who held her grandfather and the rag doll, both now lost. Tears leaked from their eyes as they looked to him in silent appeal.

Julian's grip on the scroll constricted until the tight roll gave and warped. He recognized the other girl by an intricate braiding of her dark hair. She'd boasted to him that her grandmother had done it. She'd also been in the first group of evacuees. Did that mean other groups had successfully made their escape? The *pelotón* guard behind him fanned out around him, hands on their sword hilts. Julian tensed as well—if miracles were real, now would be the time.

"How many of these children have you dispatched from your city?" Ordoño asked.

Julian kept his mouth shut. He would not surrender the number and give this animal a target to hunt.

As if expecting his reticence, Santabe moved in a graceful blur of white skirts—one second she was paces away, the next pressed against the nearest guard. The other three drew their swords, but the man she held only managed to extract his halfway before she brought up the white rod to touch his throat.

He shuddered, arms and legs flailing in spasms like a seizure. Eyes staring in blind panic. Bearded chin pointed at the sky. Then he went rigid and collapsed in her arms, limp as a fish. Her feet already in motion, she let the body drop to the ground, moving not toward Julian but to the children. A satisfied smirk split her beautiful face as she stood behind the boy, holding the rod to his neck.

Julian hissed in outrage.

"Such is the power of Dal," she said. "Do you doubt now?"

Yells came from the wall. Julian didn't have to look to know arrows had been notched all along the stone edifice despite being out of range. He shared their rage and helplessness.

"How many groups of brats, *Alcalde*?" Lord Ordoño asked again. The children sobbed, their eyes darting in frantic glances from the body to the safety of their city, just out of reach.

Disaster. Julian held up a hand to stop his remaining guards from rushing forward or any arrows from being loosed. How had she done that? What kind of magic existed in that strange weapon? The woman pressed the rod closer to almost touch the boy's tanned skin.

"Two groups. One per day," he lied, desperate to conceal the true number. Two sounded more believable than trying to convince there had only been one. Five had escaped thus far. Or so he'd hoped.

"I will find those as well." Ordoño nodded. "Do not do so again. Any more attempts to cheat will cancel the grace period granted and bring destruction and fire upon your city. Santabe."

The priestess began dragging the children back toward the army of Northerners. The rag-doll girl fell limp, but Santabe yanked her upright by her hair and shook her.

Hands clenched into impotent fists, Julian stepped forward hurriedly. "Give me those three as a sign of good faith. No doubt you have other hostages."

"No deal, old fox. These we will keep for your good

conduct, along with the others who survived," Ordoño said. The way he said the last word, it seemed clear to Julian that very few still lived. "Do not test me again. And we will find your tunnels."

Julian flinched.

"Did you think children wouldn't give up your secrets? Such lack of foresight. Children break so easily that we didn't even have to torture your surviving soldiers." He grinned once more, a feral look. "That we did for the gratification and the glory of Dal. We *will* find your tunnels. And any small advantage you believe yourself lucky enough to have will be gone. Surrender while you can."

CHAPTER 11

"**H**ere we are," Bromisto sang out. The boy stood with his feet ankle deep in a stagnant lake, which stretched as far as the eye could see. A green scum, consisting of tiny, floating plants and some kind of slime, covered the surface.

"The witch's house?" Ramiro asked doubtfully with a glance at his brother. The horses stood in a row on the shore. He waved uselessly at the cloud of gnats that had swarmed above his head for the last hour or so. Willows and sycamores rose out of the deep water, along with the tops of scraggly bushes. A thick mat of reeds lined the shore. It was the strangest vista imaginable. So much ground covered in water. Somehow it made him feel unclean.

"City men." Bromisto put a world of scorn into the short phrase. "Do you see any houses? This is where we get wet."

Alvito and Teresa laughed. Not a single member of their group was dry below the waist, and even Bromisto had been dunked all the way to his neck when a platform of grass proved to be unable to bear his weight. Only the height of their horses kept them from being soaked through and through. Ramiro couldn't count how often branches had dripped moisture on his head and neck from the moss that clung to everything.

"Isn't there a way around it?" Salvador asked. "There's always been a way around."

"Not this time," Bromisto said. "I kept you out as long as I could, but the only way to the *sirenas* is across the lake." He pointed left. "That way is full of quicksand, and the double-bite spider likes the other end of this bog. This is the shallowest and safest place to cross. You are very lucky I know about it."

"Oh yes, very lucky," Alvito said. "Thank the saints for our new mascot, who can lead us to such wonderful new places."

"Double-bite spider?" Ramiro asked. He wasn't sure he wanted to hear the answer.

"It bites you twice to make sure the venom kills you." Bromisto grinned. "That way it only hurts for an instant, then you swell like a stuffed toad and never wake up. Very fun."

Gomez sighed. "And they only live over there?"

Bromisto shook his head. "No. There are just more of them that way. They're everywhere. Black and red, and you'll be dead," he chanted. "But they usually don't bite unless you crowd them."

Salvador dismounted the packhorse and began undoing the strap that held his breastplate in place. "Armor on the horses. We'll have to walk. Teresa, wait where you are, and one of us will lead Valentía."

"I won't argue." Teresa gripped her sling with her good arm and shuddered at the green water.

Ramiro dismounted from Sancha. They'd walked in a few places already. There were plenty of spots where it wouldn't be safe for the horses to carry extra weight because the ground was so unreliable. No one wanted their mount to step in a hole and break a leg.

He looked at his new boots—a gift from his mother upon entering the *pelotón*—and sighed. They'd managed to repel the water so far, but no amount of water-proofing could survive this lake.

"It's not so bad." Bromisto stood knee deep in the water. "I told you, you were lucky. I've seen it much deeper, especially in the early spring." He bounced in place. "Hardly any ooze. I'm barely sinking at all."

Ramiro pulled off a boot. Barefoot it was, then. He quickly arrayed his armor and footwear in a neat pile atop Sancha, tied the pieces down with leather straps, and stepped close to the disgusting water. Sancha rolled her eyes, pulling back on the reins. Ramiro couldn't agree more. Could this day get any worse?

"Stay out of the shade," Bromisto advised. "That's where the leeches hide."

"Wonderful," Alvito said. "Dive right in, I always say." His face set, he strode forward, dragging his reluctant *caballo de guerra* and a packhorse behind. Gomez followed more slowly with Valentía and Teresa besides his own horse. Gomez whispered encouragement to the animals to get them to move.

Ramiro gave a last look at Salvador, and the two of them stepped in. Mud slithered up between his toes and tugged at his heels, resisting his efforts to pull free just enough to be noticeable. He gritted his teeth and took a few steps. What was he afraid of? A little nasty water? Nothing more harmful than a sharp stick could lurk beneath, right? His brother didn't look bothered. Why was Ramiro letting his imagination get to him? He was a man of the *pelotón*, not a frightened child to be jumping at shadows.

A green-and-brown-mottled snake longer than Sancha emerged from the reeds where the ripples of their passing had disturbed it. Ramiro shrieked like a girl as its flat head turned in his direction, skimming the top of the water with sinuous movements. He splashed at it, but the snake kept coming. The mud pulled, making it difficult to retreat, especially with Sancha surging forward. She whickered at the serpent, showing her teeth. Ramiro cringed and shouted.

Salvador's sword blade descended and guided the snake around their position, pushing it until it disappeared into another clump of reeds. All the air went out of Ramiro in a gust.

"You should see your face," Bromisto crowed, slapping his sides in helpless laughter. "It's not the big ones you have to worry about. Those are harmless."

"*Caramba.*" Ramiro scrubbed at his eyes with a forearm. Why hadn't he thought to use his sword? Again, he had lost his head and forgotten to think. He might have earned his beard, but he had a long way to go to match his brother.

The half-full berry basket pulled at Claire's arm. They would have enough berries to make gallons of jam, but her mother seemed content to remain to gather more. A good thing as it had taken two afternoons of berry picking for Claire to work up the nerve to bring up this subject. "Were you scared?"

Her mother looked up from the nearby blueberry bush. "Of what?" she asked. The gentle breeze wasn't strong enough to lift sweaty hair away from equally sweaty foreheads.

"When you left home and went to that village to create a daughter . . . me, were you scared? You went all alone. It must have been scary."

A faraway look entered her mother's eyes. She remained quiet long enough for Claire to add another handful of fruit to her basket. The only sound in the swamp came from the harsh cry of a jay and the drone of insects. Claire held her breath, afraid to say anything that would cause her mother to close off.

"Of leaving home, yes," her mother finally said. "Of the village, no." She pulled loose a berry. "I was only a little older than you are now." A few more berries went into the basket before she sighed. "I suppose you should know—I'd been to villages many times by then."

Claire's hand froze in the middle of reaching toward a high branch. "*Many* times?" Her brown scrunched. "You were allowed to go many times?"

"My mother . . . my mother wanted me to become the Thorn Among Roses. It's considered an honor—to some at least. When Women of the Song reach their sixteen year, they are sent for training—"

Claire interrupted, anger blooming. "But I'm past that age. Why have I never heard of this?"

"Obviously because I didn't tell you," her mother said. Instead of seeming upset, she set her full basket on a rock to keep it off the damp ground. "It's a tradition I choose to ignore. Girls of sixteen are sent to a secret location at the heart of the swamp to hone their skills with the Song. It's one of the few times our people ever come together. Girls train, and news is spread, women catch up with one another. The best among the girls each year is named the Thorn Among Roses. Your grandmother wanted that title for me as she had won it herself in her time.

"She didn't believe in waiting on training, though. She made the villages my training ground well before I was old enough to know better."

Again her mother became lost in the past, her eyes seeing something beyond. "Your grandmother sent me to the villages to learn to sense or sniff out men's fears, to find their weakness, the better to manipulate them with the Song. It wasn't enough to use the traditional Songs handed down through generations. Your grandmother wanted me to learn how to create Songs to fit the moment, to innovate and design my own. I learned to instill terror and drive minds mad. At her urging, I used the Song on men, women, and even children. She never had me kill . . . but I believe she would have worked up to that if I hadn't left."

Pain rippled across her mother's face. Claire took her hand.

"By the time I'd gone for my training," her mother continued, "a sickness grew inside of me. I began to enjoy controlling others. Not only could I fool the villagers who didn't suspect, but also the girls of my own kind who should have been harder to trick."

"But how?" Claire asked. "How did the villagers not see you and know you for a Woman of the Song?" Claire held out her wheat-colored braid. "We sort of stand out."

"The Song can do many things for those who explore its depths. It makes people see what isn't there. It can even disguise my features.

"By the time of the competition among the girls my age, I'd had enough." For the first time, her mother met Claire's eyes. "I took my belongings and I left your grandmother's house. I told your grandmother I was done with her and the Song, and I didn't look back. Just as I want for you, I had to learn to sing my own tune and not dance to my mother's."

Claire struggled to think, to even decide how she felt about this revelation. She knew her mother's rejection of the Song didn't match what her people considered normal. She knew her mother's training had been rough. But for her mother to turn her back on everything about the Women of the Song? Claire sighed. Not everything. Her mother had had a daughter to carry on the line when she could have remained alone.

"I'm sorry, Mother." She caught her mother in a hug, crushing her basket between them. "That must have been horrible. You did the right thing by leaving. I'm sorry you weren't given a choice. But . . ." Claire gathered herself and took the plunge. "I haven't really been given a choice either: a chance to try the things you taught me. I feel like you don't trust me to make the right decision." And that revelation stung, knowing her mother had kept opportunities from her. That her mother didn't believe in her. Why else keep her here unless it was because Claire wasn't good enough with the Song?

Claire didn't want to deceive people, she just wanted to experience for herself, to make up her own mind. Was the Song evil or only a tool or was the truth somewhere in between?

"It hurts that you don't have faith in me."

Her mother stroked Claire's hair. "So I've been thinking for the last few days. You are a woman grown. The Thorn Among Roses competition takes place at the end of fall as work settles down for winter. We will be there."

Claire stepped back. "We will?" Her feet did a happy, little dance. "We're going?"

Her mother did not smile. "It's time to trust you. We're going." She turned back to the bushes and dropped more berries in a basket already weighty, closing the conversation.

Feeling like she was lost in a dream, Claire forged ahead among the bushes. She needed time alone to absorb the change of her fortunes. There could be no doubt of her wishes. Claire swung her basket as excitement sang in her veins.

She'd get to meet other Women of the Song, maybe even find friends among them. She'd get to make up her own mind about the magic, and even learn more about the Song that she so desired to sing.

A nagging tugged at her heart. Her mother's lesson ran too deep. She mustn't let the freedom go to her head. There were dangers to using the Song. Risks to relying on magic, especially for someone without much practice. Peril to being among other people. Mother had shared many stories about men and their deceitful ways. Even Women of the Song might not have Claire's best interests, as they would have their own agendas.

That drew her up short. Danger waited around every corner in the swamp. One must always guard against quicksand and other threats. It was the same for the whole of life.

But then Claire glanced back and felt relieved. With her mother at her side, she could get through anything.

CHAPTER 12

Ramiro slogged forward, anxious to reach the other side. The water approached midchest in this part of the swamp, forcing him to hold his arms high to keep them dry. Besides being disgusting, it was also cold enough to numb his toes. Ahead, Bromisto was all but swimming to keep his head above water. The others followed closer to the boy, while Ramiro and Salvador lagged behind.

"Good thing the Northerners aren't here now," Salvador said. "We'd be easy pickings." His brother also had his arms raised high, hands empty as he'd put his sword on the back of his mount. "Or they'd die laughing at us."

"Can you hear Mother?" Ramiro asked. "'You promised to keep your feet dry,'" he minced in imitation. "'You'll catch your death of cold.'" They shared a grin.

"'No son of mine will go to his wedding stinking of swamp water,'" Salvador imitated. "'Fronilde will turn up her nose at you, and I'll never be able to show my face in public again.'"

"Wedding?" Ramiro's feet stopped moving. He shook himself. "Fronilde? Then you've asked her finally. Congratulations!"

"Aye," Salvador said, not stopping. "Before we left. We had the first set of banns read. Fronilde is starting the arrangements."

Ramiro labored forward to catch his brother, creating a surge of ripples. "Mother doesn't know, does she?"

"Would *you* tell her? Fronilde suggested we wait until I get back."

"Fronilde suggested? Yes, *I'll bet* it was all Fronilde's idea. You've picked one of the smartest and most competent women I know, not to mention the softest-hearted. There's no way she went with that plan willingly." Ramiro raised his eyebrows. "Keeping that kind of secret from Mother. She'll kill you."

"Well . . . it's not like Fronilde exactly wanted to manage Mother alone, either."

Ramiro threw back his head and laughed. "I'm glad you have to explain this to her and not me." His foot slipped in the ooze, and he sobered quickly to keep from slipping under. "But Mother would be right about one thing: You shouldn't be in this water with your wound. The infection could return."

"List the priorities," Salvador said, his face setting back into its "mentor" lines.

"Always see first to Colina Hermosa and its civilians," Ramiro recited obediently. "Then fellow *pelotón* members, other military brothers, and lastly self."

Salvador nodded. "The mission comes first. Remember that, little brother, and you can't go wrong. I'll survive."

Ramiro rolled his eyes but refrained from objecting. Salvador had beaten the precepts and priorities into him since he was Bromisto's age. He couldn't go against them if he wanted to.

"I see dry land," Gomez said, his neck craned for a better vantage.

A surge of relief went through Ramiro, and he rose to his toes but couldn't see anything except the backs of horses. Teresa lifted herself uncertainly in Valentía's stirrups. "I see it, too."

Everyone rushed ahead, to much floundering and splashing. Ramiro fought against the water's resistance to go faster, eager to be out of this plague. Considering the only place he'd ever had a chance to swim before was in the old quarry during a particularly rainy season, he was glad now to have learned how.

Ahead, Alvito and Gomez split to go around a half-submerged tree trunk, Gomez getting the near side closer to the unseen shore. Bromisto scrambled up the bleached-white sycamore trunk, avoided the lethal-pointed, dead branches, to stand head and shoulders above the horses.

"Not that way!" he called shrilly. "Hairy one! Not that way! Quicksand!"

Salvador seized Ramiro's shoulder, bringing him to a halt while the others also froze. Teresa shrank down against Valentía to grip the horse's neck.

"Where?" Salvador demanded.

Bromisto pointed ahead of Gomez. "A small patch, right against the land. We'll need to go to the right to get around. Come back this way, city man. Stay to the other side of this tree."

As Gomez retreated and worked to persuade the horses to step away from the promise of land, Ramiro joined the boy atop the log. At first, his eyes stared greedily at the reed-lined, firm, dry ground, but then he scanned the area where Bromisto had pointed. The same greenish water. The same offensive smell. "It all looks identical. How can you tell?"

"Look at the ripples," Bromisto advised. "See the sediment in the water."

Ramiro followed the ripples leaving Gomez and the tree trunk until they entered the dangerous area and compared them to the undulations coming off everyone else's movements. The curved swells in the quarantined section moved slower, and the water darkened in its wake, becoming brownish. Ramiro suddenly felt very thankful Salvador had insisted on a guide.

"There's only a thin layer of water over quicksand," Bromisto said. "Underneath." He clutched his throat and made bubbling noise like a drowning man. "It sucks you down. Hard to judge unless you know what to look for."

Unbothered, the boy hopped off the log and maneuvered back in the lead, but Ramiro hung back until the ripples over the quicksand died. It looked deceptively peaceful now under the veneer of the lake. No different than any other section of the swamp. Sancha, whickering her impatience as her fellow horses left her behind, broke him out of his reverie. Ramiro shivered and slid back into the muck, more eager than ever to reach dry—or relatively dry—ground.

Already, Bromisto and Alvito fought through the reeds to emerge from the water. Head-high bushes grew all around the spot, creating a sort of clearing. Alvito drew his horses after him, getting farther from the water to leave room for the others. He shook like a dog, sending water spraying. Bromisto stayed among the reeds and used the edge of his hand to seemingly strip the water from his bare chest and arms.

"Saints," Teresa breathed as Gomez led Valentía from the water. "I'm glad that's over. Ugh, quicksand. What a horrible way to go."

Gomez clapped a huge hand on Bromisto's shoulder, staggering the boy. "A thousand thanks to our new mascot. We'll have to start calling you Eagle Eye."

"Aye, mascot," Teresa said, still clutching Valentía. "Thanks from me also. You saved us. I'm glad I was only a passenger because, even above the water, I'm chilled all over."

Alvito pulled a flask from his belt. "This will warm you up."

"Hold," Salvador said sternly. "How close are we to the witches?"

"From what I remember, an hour's walk or less," Bromisto said.

"No alcohol." Salvador gestured. "Not now. Standard scout formation. Something doesn't feel right."

Emerging from the water last, Ramiro kicked his legs to send water drops falling from his pants. He eyed the burning sun, grateful for once because it meant he'd dry quicker. By San Martin, he wished they didn't have to go back that way on their return.

When Alvito and Gomez moved upwind of Salvador, fanning out, he spread in the opposite direction. If Salvador said something wasn't right, then it was time for extra caution. Sancha nosed at the bushes, lipping the small berries. Ramiro glanced closer. *Blueberries.*

He scanned deeper into the nearest bush, searching, on high alert. And although he was being vigilant, he started at a pair of eyes, as blue as the berries and filled with astonishment, focused on Sancha from the opposite side of the bushes.

A thin girl held a basket over one arm. It was half-full of berries. She wore a skimpy dress of unbleached homespun that was inches too short over trousers of the same material. Her long, braided hair was the color of a sunbeam breaking through the clouds, just like in his mother's book.

At his noise, her eyes darted from Sancha to him, and her mouth popped open.

Sancha's reins fell from Ramiro's hand when he realized exactly what he was looking at.

A witch!

He launched himself through the bush, twigs tearing at his wet clothing. The force of his leap sent him plowing into her. Basket and berries flew upward, hitting the ground seconds after he bore her to the earth. His weight came down atop her, driving the air from both their lungs as he plastered his hand over her mouth.

She squirmed under him, thrashing like a cat, but he overbore her easily even one-handed, pinning her to the ground. Fallen berries made a carpet around them among crushed leaves. Her mouth worked under his palm, but no magic was able to emerge. Water dripped from him to dampen her clothing. Everything went deadly quiet for the length it took to get air back in his lungs, then birdsong resumed.

Shadows fell over them as the others arrived.

"By Santiago, cousin." Teresa chuckled astride Valentía. "We're supposed to negotiate with the witches, not embrace them."

Ramiro felt his cheeks heat. He'd reacted without thinking again. "I feared she'd use magic against us."

"Is it a witch?" Salvador pressed.

Bromisto backed toward the swamp, his face grayish. "It's the nit of a *sirena*."

Salvador exchanged glances with Alvito. "And she has the magic?" his brother asked.

"Not as strongly as a full-grown *sirena*, but yes."

They all stared at the skinny girl, and Ramiro instinctively increased the pressure holding her secure. Her eyes had gone from astonishment and shock to pure fury. She bucked and fought uselessly against him. She might have been pretty if not for the rage marring her features.

The boy retreated farther until his feet were under the water. His eyes darted in all directions. "A *sirena* is never far from her nit. This is not for me. I take you to the house, not help you against the *sirena* herself."

"We wouldn't ask you to," Salvador said calmly though the tension in his body spoke his readiness. Already, he buckled his sword about his waist, Alvito and Gomez quickly imitating him. Salvador's voice lowered, his eyes already seeking. "No time for getting into our armor or tying her up. Well done, Ramiro. Keep her here and keep her quiet until we find the other, but don't hurt her."

"Hi-ya." He straddled the girl's chest, using his legs to pin her shoulders and pressed both his hands across her mouth. "She's not going anywhere."

Gomez touched his sword hilt, then the dagger at his waist.

"Wait a minute," Teresa protested quietly, gripping her sling with her good arm. "This is why you brought me. Give diplomacy a chance. It's persuasion that will make the witches help Colina Hermosa. The Northerners are a danger to everyone, not just our city."

Salvador nodded. "The show belongs to you, cousin. We'll back you up. And if diplomacy fails, then force will take over. Our backup plan is you convincing her *as* we take her to Colina Hermosa. Ready?" He secured the packhorse he'd been riding to the remains of the bush while Gomez did the same with the other one. The *caballos de guerra* could be trusted to stay with their owners.

"Hi-ya," Gomez and Alvito said.

A woman called out from a short distance away. The tension in their group increased tenfold.

"Salvador," Ramiro whispered. "The wax from Santiago's candle. Use it. It's in my saddlebags."

Salvador hesitated, then fished in the bags until he withdrew a handkerchief wrapped around earplug-sized bits of tallow. Swiftly, everyone took a share, adjusting them to fit. Alvito bent over Ramiro and pushed wax into his ears.

"Hold her safe," Alvito said in his ear, the sound a mere trickle through the wax.

The others edged away from him, leaving Bromisto at the water's edge. The men spaced themselves, with Teresa astride Valentía at the center. Blood rushed in Ramiro's ears, helping to drown any other sound. He craned his neck to keep them in view as they maneuvered through the bushes.

Then she appeared. The woman was identical to the girl he held against the ground, only older, more mature. Tall and cool, she was an icy spire atop a mountain as she watched the men surround her, Gomez at her back and Salvador in front. Her blueberry-colored eyes focused on Teresa, seated up high.

Ramiro ducked through a different gap in the bushes to see Teresa's mouth move, but the sound was too muffled from this distance. He shifted again to determine the witch's response. She spoke fast, her face hard. An angry response or a demand. No doubt asking for her nit. Ramiro ducked lower, even knowing the witch couldn't see him behind the bush or that he restrained the girl.

Sensations under his hand told him the girl he restrained was growling and attempting to sink her teeth into him. The flat of his hand gave her nothing to bite.

When Ramiro glanced up again, Salvador and the others had their swords in hand. Teresa's face held a measure of fear and desperation. Bromisto was nowhere in sight. The chill from the swamp water had dissipated, allowing sweat to slick Ramiro's arms and back. A trickle ran down his face to drip from his nose and drop onto the girl.

Santiago, please, he begged. *Let it work. Please let the witch listen. Let Colina Hermosa be saved.*

The witch threw her head back. Cords in her neck stood out as her voice soared, pushing right through the wax protection. Her song roared forth, a melody of the dark and twisted.

"*Bite.*
Pain.
Everywhere.
Sting.
Agony.
Bite."

Stabbing pain like the sting of a horsefly penetrated Ramiro's shoulder, his chest. The girl twitched and struggled, eyes watering, feeling it, too. Everyone was slapping and spinning in an effort to find the invader, but Ramiro kept his weight on the girl. Though he screamed his throat raw, he kept his hands over her mouth, holding with grim determination.

"Bite.
Sting."

The horses went mad. All around him they kicked, skin flinching from horsefly attacks. An instant later, they broke and ran. The packhorses pulled free, and Sancha vanished along with them. Valentía screamed and reared. He dashed for the swamp, taking Teresa with him.

The witch's eye gleamed as a gloating smile crossed her features. The tempo of her song changed, growing more vicious, filling with hate.

"Foes.
Deceit.
Surrounded.
Protect.
Defend.
Foes."

Ramiro's scream turned defiant. The Northerners were here. They'd been tricked. All around, the foes hid in plain sight. Waiting to kill. Waiting to snatch victory. Northerners everywhere. Their weapons ready. He must defend. He must defeat. Protect himself.

A glance down showed he sat on a slim, sandy-haired boy, no older than himself, but he wore the Northern uniform and held a knife. *Bastards!* They were right in front of him, slipping in unnoticed like snakes! Ramiro snatched at the shoulders and neck under his hands. Heedless of the dagger, he beat the Northern boy against the soggy ground over and over. Desperate to kill in order to protect himself.

His foe went limp, but Ramiro couldn't relax. Vaguely, he was aware of swords swinging, the clash of arms. Where was his sword?

"Foes.
Defend."

Salvador, Gomez, and Alvito struggled against each other.

Ramiro blinked. No, against the hated Northerners. Swords stabbing. Flesh parting. Blood flowing. The giant Northerner from his nightmares took a blow from a smaller dancing enemy that slashed open his guts, spilling intestines. But the giant fought on, bellowing, his sword penetrating. Their captain took two stabs to the chest even as his own sword took the dancing Northerner.

Ramiro frowned. Something wasn't right. How could the giant be back? He'd killed that opponent yesterday. The Northerners fought each other. No, they fought his friends. They'd slay his brother, himself.

He climbed unsteadily to his feet. His enemy remained still, an unconscious pile on the ground.

Brow twisted, Ramiro's hands lifted to cover his ears. To block out the sound.

*"Foes.
Defend."*

No. It wasn't right. There were no foes. No Northerners. They couldn't have gotten so close unnoticed. The body at his feet lay in a puddle of gold hair. A girl, not a soldier.

"Salvador!"

His brother swayed on his feet, one arm dangling uselessly. Bleeding profusely, his brother blinked. Gomez and Alvito were down. Realization bloomed in Salvador's eye. He understood the trick played on them.

Salvador spun and advanced on the witch, closing the space she'd kept between them. Confidence slid from her expression. She turned to flee. His sword flashed once. The witch's song cut off. Her body hit the ground, a savage slice down her spine.

Salvador dropped. Bleeding his life into the morass.

"Salvador!" Ramiro staggered toward his brother, pulling the worthless lumps of wax from his ears.

"Cousin," came a pleading cry. "Cousin! Help!"

Ramiro whirled. Valentía thrashed in the pool of quicksand, already buried deep. Teresa clung to his back, fighting to calm the horse.

And Ramiro had no idea whom to try to save.

CHAPTER 13

"**S**an Martin, help me." Ramiro clutched the medallion at his neck. His breath rushed through a throat grown too tight. *Quicksand*. And his brother—his friends—bleeding out into the ground. *Hurry*. Bandages. Tourniquets.

He looked around, but nothing moved. The horses had gone, taking all the supplies.

Even with the needed material, saving them would consign Teresa to the quicksand. Buried alive. His legs refused to move in either direction. *His brother. Teresa. Saints . . .* what to do first? He was only one person.

"Bromisto!" he called wildly.

Not a sound answered. The boy probably wouldn't stop running until he reached his village. Ramiro couldn't blame him. He wanted to run also. Pretend that none of this horror had occurred. How could they have let this happen?

"Cousin," Teresa begged.

No movement came from the area where his friends had murdered each other in ignorance. The lifeless body of the witch showed she'd gotten what she deserved.

Saints. Ramiro kicked savagely at a broken branch, sending it flying.

Then he took a step.

Then another.

Away from his brother.

Tears stung behind his eyes, and he thought his heart would burst. *It's what Salvador would want.*

His feet reached the reed-lined water's edge. Valentía was trapped only three feet from the shore, just out of reach. The horse's eyes rolled with terror, not understanding what was happening to him. The ground sucked at the stallion like a hungry mouth, taking Teresa with it. Foul water of treacherous thickness reached past her waist, lapping at her ribs.

"The reins, cousin," he called. "Throw me the reins." The light leather floated on the surface before trailing into the quicksand.

Teresa looked at him with eyes wide and no comprehension.

"The reins," he ordered again, putting force into his voice. "Hurry." This time she moved. With effort, she got her arm free of the clinging muck and drew the trailing end of the leather strap to herself. She cast it in his direction, but it coiled in a pile a foot short of him and began to sink.

Ramiro stepped into the lake and immediately the ground gave way, trying to take him down. He retreated, his glance going to his brother and the other two. Was it his imagination, or had Alvito changed position? Painful hope flared.

He stepped to a straggly blueberry bush growing by the water's edge and heaved. Two more yanks, and the entire plant lifted from the wet soil, spilling mud from the roots. With the top half, he raked at the reins, slowly drawing them across the treacherous ground to him.

The reins in hand, he pulled. Perhaps sensing help, the stallion struggled. Valentía thrashed, his head and neck stretching. Muscles cording in his arms, Ramiro exerted a steady force backward on the reins, trying to give Valentía the leverage with which to fight.

The *caballo de guerra* sunk another inch and went still. Brackish water settled higher, eager as a lover, only this lover dealt death. The reins went slack, sending Ramiro stumbling off-balance. He wasn't strong enough. He yanked again, but Valentía didn't respond. The horse knew it wouldn't work. Ramiro collapsed to his ass on the boggy ground. A mosquito whined in his ear as if laughing at his failure.

"Cousin," Teresa called. Tears ran down her round cheeks. "It's all right. You did what you could. Do not blame yourself."

"A rope. If I had some rope, I could anchor back to a tree and have more leverage."

"There is no rope," Teresa said reasonably. "Nor any

trees close. See to your brother. The others. Just . . . just keep talking to me. I don't want to die alone."

"No." Ramiro clambered to his feet and seized the reins anew. "I'm not giving up. You can't either." He pulled, and once more Valentía thrashed, lifting a little in the water, gaining ground toward shore. Ramiro heaved like a madman, the reins cutting bloody streaks into his hands. He screamed for added strength as the soggy ground gave him no support, sending him sliding toward the quicksand. Before he could lose all ground, he managed to anchor his feet against a skull-sized rock to stop his slide. A burn settled into his muscles, slowly growing, but Valentía made no more progress. The thick liquid neared Teresa's shoulders. Valentía had his neck stretched to keep nose above water.

Ramiro pushed down on the gibbering panic that threatened to unnerve him only to have the fear grow stronger. *Too long.* It was taking too long. He risked a glance toward Salvador but could see nothing but the covering foliage of the bushes.

It wasn't going to work. He hadn't the strength to pull a horse free. Teresa had given him permission to quit. She kept her face turned from his, making it easier for him. Then he could help Salvador. *No. Think! Find a way.*

"Teresa, get the bridle off Valentía. Tie it around yourself." He might lose the horse, but he *could* at least pull her free.

She flailed at the horse's head, one-handed, the

quicksand reluctant to let any part of her escape. He saw instantly it was a losing battle as she couldn't brace herself higher and reach the leather.

"Both hands! Take off your sling!"

She fumbled at the knot around her neck. So slowly. Too slowly. Ramiro loosened his grip on the taut reins long enough to set two fingers in his mouth and blow a sharp whistle.

"Hurry," he urged to Teresa, but the woman hadn't undone the sling yet. By the time she worked the knot loose, something pushed Ramiro in the back and a wide nose was thrust under his arm, a broad forehead butting against his shoulder.

"Sancha." Ramiro's knees almost gave way. She'd heard his whistle. He spun, coaxing her closer and getting the reins over her saddle horn, looping them three times. In no time, he had a rope from his saddle to Valentía and tied off. "Hi-ya," he shouted. She took the strain, pulling as if she understood the dire nature of their struggle.

The already-stretched lifeline of reins and rope grew still tighter. But Salvador's leatherwork would be solid throughout; he would never allow a weak spot in his equipment. It was not the reins that would fail.

"Saints," Ramiro said through gritted teeth. Sancha struggled forward two paces.

Valentía sensed the new strength and added his efforts to theirs, lashing out with rear legs, drawing ever so much closer to shore. The quicksand shrank back to Teresa's waist. Her thighs. Its lover's touch was weakening . . .

And then Valentía's hooves found purchase. With a great sucking belch, he came free. Teresa slithered off his neck to collapse on the firm ground, sobbing her relief.

Weak-limbed, Ramiro clung to Sancha with bleeding hands and gasped like a stranded fish. His heart thumped as if he'd run twenty miles. The world spun. He squeezed Sancha and buried his face in her coarse hair until things slowed, then he lurched on drunken feet toward his brother.

Salvador lay where Ramiro had last seen him, next to the witch's twisted and broken body. His hand still clenched his sword. Curled on his side, two spots of gore stained his chest. One rested over the heart where a breastplate would have given protection. Salvador hadn't stirred, but Alvito had crawled to Gomez and pressed cloth to the ghastly wound at the other's mid-section.

"No." Ramiro dropped to his knees next to his brother and fumbled for a pulse. Nothing. He tried again and again, touching neck then wrist.

"He's gone." Blood ran unheeded from the corner of Alvito's mouth into his immaculate beard.

Ramiro stiffened. Alvito faced a wound to the lungs at the very least. "He's not . . . the saints . . . they wouldn't . . . he's not . . . dead . . ."

Hands touched him as Teresa knelt beside him. Muck dripped from her clothing and skin. She turned Salvador, revealing his wounds to the sunshine. His brother's eyes were glazed and sightless. The expression she sent him showed pity, remorse, as she pressed Salvador's eyes closed. "I'm sorry."

"No," he continued to say, but Teresa stood and hurried to Alvito. Her drawn face grew still paler, and one look under the cloth covering Gomez, and she began to retch, gagging into the weeds. His eyes closed tight, Gomez remained mercifully unaware.

"Find my Constanza," Alvito said, coughing blood. "The medical supplies are on her."

Ramiro couldn't get his legs to respond because none of this was real; he dreamed. He must be stuck in some horrible, unending nightmare. Teresa wandered uncertainly, peering behind bushes as if the *caballo de guerra* could be playing a child's hiding game with them.

A huff of air hit the back of Ramiro's neck, and Valentía lowered his head to nudge his master. The stallion lipped at Salvador's clothing and stamped a hoof demanding his brother pay attention. Valentía brushed at his brother's hand again before turning limpid eyes in Ramiro's direction as if demanding reassurance.

A crushing weight descended on Ramiro's chest. He couldn't breathe. Salvador would never ignore his horse. Never. And that drove the truth of it home: By the saints, Salvador was dead. Humming rose in his ears, and the world grew dark.

"No. No. *No!*" The word grew into a scream that left the swamp ringing with its echoes. Sobs tore at him. He doubled over, searching for something to strike out at, but found nothing but bare ground. He seized at it, and chunks of mud flew. Valentía shied back from his rage.

If only he'd been faster. Done more. Gone to Salvador first.

"Ramiro! Cousin! I need you!"

He turned his back from Teresa, so she wouldn't see, fighting for control. His hands shook. A man didn't disgrace himself before others. He clutched at his medallion, desperate to pull it together.

Duty. Duty dragged at him.

Ramiro fought off the darkness and raised his head, swiping at the shaming wetness on his cheeks, pushing all the emotion deep inside. He wanted to scream again, to rage, but he packed it all away, trying to fill the empty ache in his chest that only grew by the moment.

By some miracle, Teresa had found Alvito's mare, but Constanza wouldn't let her approach. Pawing and rearing, she backed from the woman's outstretched hands.

The strength to stand and leave his brother took an eternity. It bruised worse than the thump of a thousand practice swords pounding his body. Cut deeper into his soul than his most heartfelt prayer.

His feet stumbled over ground blurred by eyes that wouldn't obey his order to return to normal. "Something in my eye," he said, gruffly, dabbing at them.

"Oh, cousin." Sorrow split her face.

He avoided Teresa's offered hug and moved her aside to catch the reins to Alvito's mare, leading the *caballo de guerra* to her master. Ramiro knew he wouldn't be able to ride him, but every stable boy of the *peloton* had to know how to handle another's warhorse. Only standing beside Alvito did Constanza settle, for the same reason Valentía continued to stand beside Salvador.

"Loyal until death and beyond," Ramiro whispered. "Eh, cousin?"

Teresa hesitated to touch the mare and unload the supplies they needed, so Ramiro did it for her. Alvito had lapsed into unconsciousness, but his chest rose and fell in ragged, bubbling breaths. "The *caballos de guerra* will accept no touch but their bonded master," Ramiro said.

"But I rode—"

"Because Salvador *told* Valentía to allow you."

Teresa stopped short holding a bandage. "The horse understood him?" She shook herself and knelt by Alvito. "Hold this here. Hi-ya," she panted in frustration. "If only I had some knowledge of what I'm doing. I'm not a healer."

While Teresa peeled away obstructive clothing to inspect another wound in the chest, Ramiro stooped to press a cloth against the oozing gash in Alvito's side, concentrating on his words and actions to block out any other thoughts. "Stop the bleeding. Keep the wounds clean."

"That's the limit of my information, too," Teresa confessed. "Maybe I could set a bone. But I don't know how to handle this!"

Ramiro took a deeper examination of his friends.

The giant form of Gomez had a shrunken look like a child's bladder balloon that lost air. Alvito had packed the intestines back in the wound, but it needed stitching, and only Alvito had the skill for the task. The saints knew the depth of the internal injuries or how they should be treated. How to clean it? Whether to give substance and water or withhold them? What medicine would help?

Alvito's already-pale skin had gone ghostly from blood loss though little enough leaked to the outside of his body. The liquid gurgle to his breathing told the story of where it had gone, and Ramiro knew not how to get it out or stop further bleeding.

Teresa used a bandage soaked in alcohol to sponge off Alvito's chest, dribbling the liquid inside the lung wound. With a screech of pain, Alvito jerked from their hands, only to settle again as if he was too weak to evade them. She held out a water bottle, but Alvito batted it away and instead clamped onto Ramiro's arm.

"The witch," Alvito demanded in a wheeze. Fresh blood ran into his groomed beard.

"Dead."

"The girl. The nit?" Alvito asked.

"I don't know. Alive, I think."

"You must get her home. Get her to our people."

Ramiro shook his head. "I must take care of you—of Gomez—first."

Ramiro had to lean close to hear the fading reply. Alvito's eyes met his with force and utter conviction. "Too late. For us. Get nit. Colina Hermosa. Order."

It was starting to dawn on Ramiro just how terrible a thing duty could be.

Father Telo waited on the plush bench of the confessional booth instead of using the kneeler provided. Why rush discomfort when he could ponder great matters of sin and redemption just as well sitting? Light came through the mesh grill at the top of the box, and a smaller wooden lattice on the left wall gave access to petitioners come to speak with him. Otherwise, he might as well have been in a vertical coffin, closed in and dark. Much practice had taught him to accept the close walls, but he still swung the end of his triple-rope belt worn over his robe, the emblems of his profession, unable to keep entirely still. Other might learn patience, but waiting never got any less tedious for him.

Strange that the siege would send him from visiting small mud churches to this grand cathedral in the center of Colina Hermosa, yet he'd spend most of his hours inside this little box. Whatever he could do to help—and sitting here freed up another Father to venture outside among the people and lead by example. They who knew the city could best bestow calm and comfort. He was happy to assist where he could—anything to serve Santiago and the people.

Telo muttered a swift prayer for the city's deliverance.

In the past, it had been saints, holy men, who led

in times of crisis. Now they relied on politicians. The ways of God were not for him to judge, but if the Holy Father were by chance taking a nap or distracted by some heady matter of the universe, perhaps a few extra prayers could direct his attention back in their direction. Surely the blessed priests of this sacred cathedral were entitled to produce a miracle or two, especially if others asked for it.

He said another prayer just for good measure, then crossed a sandaled foot over his knee and thought about what Father Vellito might be making for dinner. Not exactly a saintly occupation, but his ample stomach wouldn't be denied. Santiago would forgive his lapse. The saint had forgiven much worse, and Telo was only a humble monk; he left great matters to his betters.

The door to the adjoining booth creaked open, and a weight jolted both confessionals as someone entered. Telo crossed mind, heart, spleen, and liver. "May the saints and our Lord be in your heart to make a good confessional today," he said automatically. Let him give the right hope and comfort this time. Since the Northerners' arrival, tedious waiting for new petitioners was short, especially since the terrible events of that morning outside the walls. Telo smiled weakly. *Look to me for strength, sayeth the Lord.* And since the Lord was busy, the people accepted their priests as the closest substitute.

"Bless me, Father, for I have sinned," said a familiar woman's voice. "It's been one day since my last confession."

"Yes, my child," Telo said automatically when First Wife Beatriz hesitated. He didn't even twitch at having the *Alcalde's* wife back so soon. She was one of those who spent much of their time at the church lately, and he suspected she exaggerated and prolonged her confession just to linger.

"These are my sins. I knew of my husband's plans to evacuate the children, and now they are captured." She sniffled.

Telo waited, but no more seemed to be forthcoming. "Hmm," he said for time to think. "Supporting your husband is not a sin. If only we had more such sinners as that, we'd have more happy marriages."

"But the children are captured by the enemy. Who knows what is happening to them! And it is all my fault. Santiago, saintliest of God, have mercy on my sins. I should have spoken against it or told someone. Now my husband must go before the *concejales* for judgment. They question his motives!" She went on in a breathless rush. "The poor children. It breaks my heart."

"You must pray for them."

"Prayer doesn't seem enough." First Wife Beatriz gasped. "I'm sorry, Father. That was wrong of me."

Telo shook his head though she couldn't see it in the dim light of the booth. "*We* must all pray for them." He looked at the dark skin over his prominent knuckles. Going from village to village, he had to make use of his own hands—and sometimes his fists if bandits appeared—as there were no servants for monks. Strong his hands might be, but they felt ineffective now, which he shared with Beatriz. "I have felt the same at times. It is easy to think prayer is not enough. Yet it is the greatest power we have in this life. That doesn't mean our faith in it doesn't waver. That's very natural, my child, and expected. In the case of the children, it doesn't seem enough—they are innocents swallowed up by evil. But it is in times like these that we must hold on to faith even harder. Can you do that?"

"I shall, Father. I shall pray every minute."

Telo smiled at the simplicity of her words. "That's all our Lord can ask."

"Yet . . ." Her voice choked off.

"Yet what, my child?" he finally had to prod when it seemed she wouldn't say it otherwise.

"Oh, Father . . . If the *concejales* remove my husband from office, how can he help fix this? They might not believe that he acted rightly. That he took an unacceptable risk . . . and kept it secret. That his common sense lapsed."

"That is not for me to judge. But what man opened the doors of this *ciudad-estado* to all the poor villagers nearby to give them shelter? What man made sure the farmers were paid fairly for their crops and out of his own pocket, too? I don't believe anyone would question *Alcalde* Julian's motives."

"And put together the group paying for the villagers' housing if they have no relatives to take them in," she added proudly.

"As you say," Telo agreed, "no man can question his motives."

"But they do questions his choices. And Julian feels terrible guilt. He does more than hold himself responsible, he punishes himself. I'm so afraid he will do something foolish to make amends."

Telo uncrossed his legs, sitting up straight. It was easy to imagine the *Alcalde's* pain. He would feel much the same were their positions reversed. "Your support, along with the Lord's, can help him through that, my child."

"I try, but . . . I was hoping you would speak with him also."

The triple-rope belt fell out of his hands. "Me? You want the Bishop, I think."

"Oh no," Beatriz said quickly. "My husband and the Bishop hardly speak. They do not see eye to eye on things. Julian does not like . . . well . . . the holy Bishop . . . he has much learning and . . ."

"He's full of himself," Telo supplied. "One is not blinded from pomposity for belonging to the church. Another priest perhaps?"

"That's exactly what I thought." She leaned closer to the latticework. "*You*, Father Telo. You are the only kind of priest my husband will hear out. Julian is not as fond of religion as I. But it's my duty to see my husband gets the counsel of the church—even if I have to be sneaky about it. You can catch him before his meeting with the *concejales* if you hurry to the citadel. You're the only one who can comfort him. Just like you've comforted me these last weeks." Before he could say anything in response, she launched into a prayer.

"Santiago, I've examined my conscience, I've confessed my sins." Beatriz rattled off. "I am sorry for my sins, and I'm determined to do my best to see that I live in You, and You in me. I ask your forgiveness and your grace. Amen.

Telo sat stumped. He'd just been bamboozled. "You could have just asked, my child."

"Hurry, Father, unless you have a penance for me."

He heaved a sigh. A penance might ease his heart, but it wasn't called for. What had he let himself get drawn into? Well, he'd wanted to help, and what bigger assistance than speaking to the *Alcalde* himself. "I absolve you of your sins, in the name of the Lord, and of Santiago and of the saints. Amen." He moved to get up, but paused. "I cannot guarantee it will do any good."

"But you'll go?"

"I'll go." Telo opened the door of the booth and stepped into the light. He blinked, letting his eyes adjust, and tightened his rope belt. "May the saints and our Lord be in my heart today."

Telo had a feeling he was going to need them.

CHAPTER 14

"**Hi**-ya." Ramiro's hands curled into fists as he backed from the unconscious Alvito and Gomez, gesturing to Teresa to stay and attend them. Alvito was his kin, best friend of his brother. Ramiro had tagged after the two of them since his legs were long enough to keep up. Alvito had shown him how to use knives and how to chase women. Gomez had taught him to use a sword, how to fight with his hands. The sergeant had dandled Ramiro on his knee and given him his first seat on a horse.

Throat tight, Ramiro turned, looking for the nit, and his gaze fell upon his brother's body, sending a fresh punch of pain to his gut.

By the saints, the magic couldn't be anything other than evil. They had journeyed here to save lives, and yet all they found was death.

He wrenched himself away, dodging through bushes toward where he'd left the witch's apprentice. A branch scratched at his face, and he tore it loose savagely, breaking it into a thousand pieces and casting it away. She lay with her limbs sprawled in all directions, and her neck turned at an unnatural angle. A dark bruise stood out on her throat.

His work.

No—not mine.

More evil done by the magic. He'd never have hurt her otherwise. He saw now she was older than he thought, closer to his own age. What he took for skinniness was in fact a matter of small bones, giving her the slenderness of a child.

For the space of a sigh, he stood still, wishing she were dead. If that were so, he could forget Alvito's orders and stay with his friends. Stay with Salvador. But he couldn't pretend her chest wasn't moving in even breaths. She lived.

And she had the same skill as the cursed witch, meaning she might be Colina Hermosa's only hope.

Yet he had no intention of letting her work any magic on them. Never again. They'd given the witch nothing more harmful than words, and she had gone for blood. This girl had to be tamed or controlled although Ramiro doubted the witches could ever be brought to hear reason. Not after what he had witnessed.

Not after seeing his friends and brother murdered. He forced himself to relax, thinking of the precepts.

Thinking of reasons why he *shouldn't* kill this witch.

Claire woke to dampness seeping through her clothing, but that small annoyance was quickly replaced with a throbbing pain in her head and neck so violent, she wanted to spew her stomach contents. Where was her mother? Her jaw ached, and a dry taste filled her mouth. Something gummed and matted her eyes, making them difficult to open. She tried to reach to clear them only to be brought up short. A restraint bound her arms and legs, giving her little movement.

She forced her eyes open to focus on leather straps cutting into her skin at wrists, elbows, ankles, and knees. She worked her mouth, but couldn't close it. The dry taste came from a rag stuffed between her teeth. More straps secured around her head held it in place. Trying to get her feet under her resulted in such a sharp pain to her head that it set her ears humming and her sight darkening with encroaching unconsciousness, making it a necessity to sit absolutely still.

Her breaths came fast and sharp, but panic worsened the pain, so she fought it back. Forced herself to figure out her situation: What happened? Who did this to her? It was hard to concentrate on anything, so she tried to focus as her mother had taught her.

She'd been deposited in a small clearing among the blueberry bushes, in a puddle of swamp water judging by the wetness. The sun beat down on her, reddening her skin. Directly across from her, only a short distance away, two bearded men lay in the shade of a clump of the bushes. In a raised dry spot, they'd been covered in blankets despite the heat, and supply bags sat around them. Two unsaddled horses of mottled gray waited nearby. Swords lay within the men's easy reach. She tilted her head for a better view. Their chests rose and fell slowly. *An odd time to nap in the middle of the afternoon.*

Movement at the edge of her vision caught her attention. She ignored the blast of fresh pain as she hopped on her bottom, allowing her to swivel. A man—no, a youth with dark stubble on his face—rolled a dead body in blankets with the help of a shorter, fat man with an arm in a sling. The youth wore the uniform of one of the city-states, a sword at his hip. He looked the part of the nobles her mother had described, and for the first time she could understand the contempt toward those from the cities. He looked like a strutting fool, wearing the costume of someone he wasn't. The fat man, on the other hand, was dressed in a peasant poncho under the mud that covered him. His pants were held up by a rope belt.

But they were free to move about, and she was stuck here, nearly overcome with pain.

They were the ones who had tied her up, then. She'd been picking blueberries. She vaguely remembered the youth pinning her to the ground. Minutes later, she'd heard her mother's magic, and the youth had gone berserk, throttling her.

And that's when she'd lost time.

As if sensing her scrutiny, the one-armed peasant turned, and Claire saw it was a woman. An ugly woman in pants, with hair cropped short. Tears burned in Claire's dry eyes. Why would a woman do this to her?

The youth and the woman hefted the covered body to the back of another unsaddled horse, and Claire's world fell apart. Behind them, her mother . . . rested on her side in the grass and . . . a giant wound . . . a bloody wound . . .

Sobs tore at Claire's throat. Tears streamed as she toppled over into the mud. *Her mother. It couldn't be.* She screamed her shock, but the gag muffled the sound inside, trapping her jaws. Her stomach heaved, sending up bile that couldn't escape. She choked on the rag in her mouth. Her nose clogged. And suddenly she couldn't breathe. She thrashed across the wet ground, trying to free the straps about her mouth, but only succeeded in making it worse.

Hands dragged her upright. The gag came off, and someone thumped her back as she spewed into the wet grass and weeds. She choked and retched, blinded by tears, until gradually she cleared her airway enough to breathe easier. As soon as her rapid panting ceased, hands roughly thrust the gag back into her mouth and secured it by the straps again.

"No magic," the youth said. His eyes blazed with anger.

Anger at what, Claire couldn't imagine. She was the one being mistreated, while he was free. Murderers. They had killed her mother. She matched his gaze with a white-hot glare.

The peasant woman helped Claire to a more comfortable sitting position. "No time for that, cousin," she told the youth. "It will be dark soon, and we haven't an extra horse. If we're doing this, I want to cross the lake before nightfall."

The youth retreated to add more bindings around the body aboard the tallest horse while the woman went to fuss around the blanketed men. As they left her alone, Claire's fury faded though the hatred remained like a tiny flame in her chest.

She glanced around, anticipating her freedom. The murderers had obviously gotten what they came for—her mother's death. Since they hadn't killed her already, they'd release her and be on their way. Wouldn't they?

Her body didn't accept that wishful thinking. Her limbs trembled uncontrollably like they were gripped by the first killing frost of the season instead of under the warm sun.

Think. Had they said anything about her? Her brow wrinkled. What had the peasant woman meant? There were plenty of horses if someone rode double. Why would they need another? And why didn't the two men under the blankets get up and help? From the way the peasant woman held a flask to their lips, they were either sick or injured.

Not enough horses?

The youth headed in her direction with a rope, and Claire's heart skipped. They didn't have enough horses unless they were bringing another . . .

The murderers weren't leaving her. They were taking her!

The pounding ache in her head shot up in intensity. Face set in cold hatred, the murderer reached for her, and Claire shrank away. He's the one who'd hurt her. She couldn't stand for him to touch her again. He grabbed her roughly, yanking her to her trembling feet. Despite her efforts to evade him, he wound the rope around her already-bound arms, and then fastened it around his torso in a knot. A quick flick of a knife split the leather straps around her legs, setting them free.

To Claire's surprise, he went to the reclining men, forcing her to follow. Sweat covered their bearded faces. She could only stare from the bloodstained blankets covering them to their drawn faces. They were awfully hairy. The youth dropped to one knee and bowed his head.

"By Santiago, I vow to do my duty and reach Colina Hermosa with this witch." He reached out to touch one of the men's knees. "I won't fail you." Claire had never seen a face so wiped clean of emotion.

He turned to the peasant woman with a tight jaw. "Ready, cousin?"

They left the two men and went to the only saddled horse. The rope pulled Claire along even as she fought to hang back. The youth was too strong. And once more she was reminded how her mother had always warned: Men used their physical strength to dominate.

Her pain, her despair—they mean nothing to this callous boy.

Yet again the youth surprised her. Instead of taking the mount for himself, he helped the peasant woman climb awkwardly to the animal's back. She'd been taught city men were selfish, especially ones with any power. What she saw shook that, but just as quickly she dismissed her doubt. Obviously, he only did so because of the peasant woman's sling.

Without a single glance in her direction, the youth took the reins of that horse and the one with the body, then turned toward the stagnant waters of the swamp. Claire set her feet. What was happening? Why were they taking her and abandoning their obviously ill comrades? Why not take the extra horses if the sick men couldn't use them? Why bring the body of their dead friend?

Body. . .

Her mother! They were forcing her to leave her mother to rot in the mud like some animal they'd slaughtered without a second thought. Leaving her for beasts to devour and bugs to crawl over.

Strength blazed through her, overcoming her pain. Claire pulled back on the rope connecting her to the murderer and threw herself at her mother. She sank down to her knees and refused to budge when the youth tugged. The city people turned; it was their turn to be surprised.

"On your feet!" the youth yelled. "Walk!"

Claire matched his glare, wishing her mouth free. How she'd like to scream her loathing right back at the horrible murderer. She shook her head, working her legs deeper into the loose ground next her mother's body. The youth hauled on the rope, and she found herself being dragged by inches. Again she shook her head and toppled backward in an attempt to make it harder for him.

"By the saints," the woman called. "Stop, cousin. This won't work. You're not going to outhate the little witch." Awkwardly, the peasant woman clambered down from her horse and came to kneel beside Claire.

"My name is Teresa," the peasant said calmly. "That angry hellhound is Ramiro, and we need you to walk." She glanced toward Claire's mother and back to Claire. "I realize this must look bad to you, but we have no intentions of being your enemy. In fact, we wanted to be your friend. We wanted to be *her* friend."

Claire stared. This Teresa was insane. How could they come claiming friendship after their actions? She sat up and rocked her legs to sink deeper into the mud. Trying to show the woman she wouldn't cooperate. Not for anything. She'd never leave her mother's side.

Ramiro spit out an angry oath. "For heaven's sake, I'll carry her."

Teresa turned, looking irritated though her voice held none of it. "Cousin, you cannot lead two horses and manage her. Not through the swamp. Let me reason with her."

"She is not to talk!" Ramiro said. "Don't let her free to work her magic."

"Settle, cousin. I'll do the talking." Teresa arranged her hands on her knees as though to show her patience. "I'm sorry we must keep you tied. After what happened with the other . . . you must understand."

Claire shook her head, trying to make the woman understand. Trying to understand herself.

"It was a terrible misunderstanding that turned

into a disaster," Teresa continued. "We came to speak with a . . . witch. To seek help. And, well, she reacted badly. Salvador—our leader—is dead. The others are hurt. And she"—Teresa pointed to Claire's mother—"is dead, which, I assure you, is the last thing we wanted. So now we must take you. It's the magic, you see."

Claire shook her head again. She didn't see. Did they want a Woman of the Song or magic from one?

"The Northerners are laying siege to our home. They've already defeated a number—"

"She doesn't need to know that." Ramiro paced between the two horses. His face set, the cording of the tendons in his neck demonstrating his irritation. "Can you get her to walk or no?"

Teresa rolled her eyes, gesturing to the covered body and lowering her voice. "Young men have little control. Salvador was his brother." She cleared her throat. "We want something, and so do you. Can we make an exchange?"

Claire worked her jaw, producing growls as fury built. Help the murderers? *Never.*

"I don't want to see you hurt again," Teresa said. "But time is of the essence, and he'll knock you out and carry you. I've seen how much duty means to them. You'll come with us no matter what. Better to get something out of it and come on your own two feet."

The peasant woman reached out to wipe mud from Claire's face, and Claire ducked away. "Murderers," she shouted, but the gag reduced it to inarticulate noise.

Teresa climbed to her feet. Her face filled with sadness. "I'm sorry, Ramiro, but we'll have to leave your brother. It's the only answer. She won't cooperate, and who can blame her."

The youth reddened, clutching at his sheathed sword, but his voice sank to a violent whisper. "I cannot. We've no shovel to give Salvador a proper resting place. And even if we had, the ground is too soft for burying. Bad enough I must leave Alvito and Gomez; I won't leave my brother."

Against her will, Claire's eyes went to her mother. They'd leave her to rot; her soul trapped inside her body. One way or another, they'd take her and let her mother lie here like trash. All they cared about was their own dead and their own desires. Tears rolled into her gag. Her mother's soul would never find peace. Never return to the ancestors of the Women. It would be forced to wander lost forever.

And she'd be dragged away from her, losing her forever . . .

Claire reached out with her bound arms to touch the peasant woman. When she had Teresa's attention, she pointed toward her mother, then climbed to her feet.

"You'll walk?"

Claire nodded and pointed to her mother.

"If we bury your mentor?"

Claire shook her head and kicked at the ground, making a stamping, negative motion.

"No burial." Teresa examined their surroundings. "They obviously have other funeral traditions. A cairn of stones? No, there are not enough stones. Or quicksand? Do you sink your dead in quicksand?" she prompted.

The gag cut across her face, abrading the corners of her mouth. Claire shook her head with a growl for the barbarian notion. How could she make the woman understand?

Ramiro strode to them, and Claire stepped back, though some of the anger had left his face, leaving him almost a different person. "Too wet to bury," he said. "They must do something else." He studied the ground, and then his head came up. "Fire. They must burn their dead."

Claire nodded.

He stalked closer, all grace like a deadly panther, putting his face close to hers in confrontation. "You promise to walk if we burn the witch?" His eyes drilled into her, catching her agreement.

"Deal."

CHAPTER 15

Julian exited the council chamber and pulled the door shut. He slumped onto a bench set against the wall for petitioners, sinking into the velvet cushion. The waiting area was empty as a tomb, the guards having shuffled everyone out of the building but the officials. *Concejal* Adulfo suggested Julian return to his rooms while they debated, but it seemed like the coward's way. Better he stayed and took his medicine as soon as it was spooned to him.

The council had every reason to expel him as *alcalde*. He had gone behind their backs with a momentous decision. And it had gone terribly wrong—children captured by the enemy. Julian stared without interest at the tapestry opposite him, one of Santiago planting his staff in the soil that would become Colina Hermosa. A crowd of people were woven in lifelike detail at the saint's back—people who would become his countrymen.

Those men and women would hurl stones at him if they were here now.

Of course it had been a risk all along—a risk that had landed squarely on the most innocent. He was more than willing to take all the blame if that would bring one child safely home. By the saints, he wanted to turn back time.

Well, he accepted the responsibility; they could find a replacement who would not make such horrible mistakes. Julian scrubbed at his face and slowly sat upright, only to jerk in surprise at a priest in a coarse brown robe and triple-rope belt standing right in front of him, blocking out the tapestry of Santiago.

Unlike the saint in the wall hanging, this priest had skin so dark it practically shone. His hair was cropped short and, like all priests, he wore no beard. "May I join you in your rest?" he asked.

Julian pushed aside a surge of superstitious nonsense and slid farther along the bench to make room for the burly man. The bench creaked loudly as the man took his spot, dispelling Julian's vision of ghostly apparitions sent from Heaven.

"You are spiritual advisor to one of the *concejales,* Father?" Julian asked.

"I am an advisor to any who need me," the man answered vaguely. He settled square-knuckled hands in his lap atop the simple trirope belt that signified his station. Instead of boots, he wore dusty and worn sandals, a hole actually worn through in one spot.

"You've taken a vow of poverty?" Julian asked.

The priest patted an emerging paunch. "Of the material, but not, I fear, of the flesh. I'm too fond of my meat and drink." He smiled, revealing not the perfect white teeth Julian expected but ones crooked and slightly yellowed.

"Indeed," Julian said as prelude to the silence he hoped would follow. He left the priests to his wife. Beatriz had enough interest for both of them.

"In times of tumult, look to Me sayeth the Lord."

"One can look," Julian said drily.

The priest nodded. "Have faith in Me, and the Lord will have faith in you."

"The Lord has many platitudes."

Instead of taking offense, the priest chuckled. "Glory to the Lord. Turn the other cheek in a quarrel, and I shall shelter you from harm."

Julian cleared his throat to keep hot words from escaping. "I don't see the Lord protecting us from the Northerners, Father." Priests and their ambition. Though no new saints had been created in—what—three hundred or so years, they never gave up hope they might be the next if faith and benevolence and fuzzy words could make it so. Better they kept their opinions to themselves until asked for. Even the most good-hearted couldn't ignore the ultimate prize. They wouldn't know a true miracle if it stepped on their toes.

"An eye for an eye suits you better?" the priest asked. "Do you believe that fate controls our destiny?"

"If I did, I'd spend my days hiding under my bed."

"And faith? Can faith turn the tide?"

"That and a copper will buy you a cup of *sopa de cordero*." Not that one could get mutton soup for a copper since the Northerners. Julian gave himself a mental shake. "I mean no disrespect, Father. Faith is a power I don't have much dealing with, but a power nonetheless. My wife—"

"Faith is for women and the weak-minded, you mean to say."

Julian shrugged, secure in his convictions. "No offense meant, Father."

The big priest held up a callused hand. "No offense taken, my son. I've felt the same myself many a time." The man grinned and winked. "On my bad days, you understand."

"Don't mistake me, Father. There is a place for faith."

The man's belly shook as he chuckled. "Spoken like a politician. Now who has the platitudes?"

Julian offered his hand. "A wise man stays out of religious argument."

"Amen, brother." The priest gripped Julian with a huge, callused hand. "Father Telo."

"An honor."

Father Telo settled his hands back on his stomach. "Better if you had kept the children here. Sending them away to keep them safe? Idiotic idealism. Better we hid under our beds, as you put it, and do nothing so the children could be culled like cattle as the Northerners pick their one in thirty after our surrender. Or suffer a violent death when our walls come down. Or burn in their homes before that. Certainly the parents won't thank you for giving their most precious possessions a chance at life and freedom. Such selfishness. After all, we should sit on our hands and wait for the Lord our God to save us all."

Julian stared in shock as the man continued with a perfectly disinterested face.

"It's not like He gave us free will for a reason. Or that some of our choices are often less than perfect. We are as omnipotent as Our Lord, are we not?"

Julian scowled, but the priest continued before he could get out a word.

"And when the council deposes you, can they not find someone with experience of a lengthy siege and invasion to replace you? You, who are doing such a poor job."

Julian made a *hmmph* deep in his throat. "How many times a day do you get called an ass?"

"Isn't that what the city pays me for?"

"Remind me to cut the church's tithe from the budget," Julian said. A sudden suspicion struck, and he sat up straighter on the bench. "Did my wife send you, Father?"

Father Telo flashed his teeth in a crooked smile. "Is that not her prerogative, having her own share of free will from Our Lord?"

Julian shook his head. "Tell her she made a wise choice. I've been thoroughly dis—"

The door behind them cracked open, spilling forth the seven councilors. Such had been their haste to call this meeting that *Concejal* Antonio still wore the blood-stained apron of his profession as butcher, and *Concejal* Pedro had flour from the mill on his collar and hair. Julian rose to face it on his feet.

Tangled beard bristling, Adulfo settled a hand on Julian's shoulder. "The council has voted to stand behind you, my friend. While better to have shared your plans with this board, we cannot see another option you could have taken to better secure our children. They were in every bit as much danger here."

The other *concejales* mumbled their agreement.

A mist gathered before Julian's eyes. *Sentimental idiot.* He dismissed it with a sniff. The stress was getting to him. The true test came when he faced the people and let them know what he had done. A test he would face now. The people deserved to be acquainted with his disgrace. He doubted they would be nearly as forgiving.

"Father," the *concejales* said in greeting to the priest. *Concejal* Lugo even knelt for a blessing. But then again, the small man was known for putting a thumb on the scale in his business dealings, so no doubt he needed the extra favor.

Julian inclined his head to the priest. "If you'll excuse me, Father. Time to come out from under the bed."

The *concejales* looked at him in astonishment, but the priest nodded gravely. "May His blessing go with you."

All seven councilmen followed Julian to the door,

where two uniformed soldiers and Julian's bodyguards kept the portal closed against concerned citizens. Usually, the great bronze doors stood open to all and sundry, even during the glaring heat of the midday sun. Today, it needed no imagination or glass set into the bronze to tell Julian what waited outside. Already, the sounds came through metal and wooden obstructions alike.

The soldiers pushed open the doors onto a mob. People strained against one another below the steps of the council house, their faces contorted in anger or worry. Women with mourning shawls covering their heads wept. A general hum of voices filled the large square, while the crowd reached to the shops opposite and spilled into the roads. The council *pelotón* held the entranceway against them with spears raised and crossed to bar the way.

At his appearance, someone threw a fistful of vegetables to splatter against the bronze and plop in a glancing blow against a soldier. The hum grew into a roar as bodies surged forward like a furious tide. "Where are our children? What have you done to our children? Children!" The word echoed across the square, thrown from a thousand throats.

In ten years as *alcalde*, Julian had never dreamed such a dark day could exist.

A cold hand touched his arm, and Beatriz stepped to his side from the protection of the soldiers where she'd been hiding. Her face was pale and strained, but determined. Julian sensed the *concejales* flinch at his back but stand firm. Astonishingly, the sight of so much righteous wrath washed the rest of his reservations away. He had done what had to be done. His choice had been right—no matter the consequences. Now he had to rectify what had gone wrong.

Pulling free of his wife, Julian held his arms wide for silence. In only a few breaths, he had it, the mob dwindling to mutters somewhere in the depths.

"Where is my child?" a thick male voice shouted.

"You shall all be reunited with your children or told where they are as quickly as possible," Julian shouted so all could hear. "Most are in the citadel. Some have been sent to the swamps for their safety and some, as you saw, were captured."

"Safety!" The roar returned, hotter. Most of the heated words drowned in the tumult.

Julian spread his arms again and waited as the shouts and mutters died for the second time. "Yes, my people, safety. Do we fool ourselves that our lives here are any more secure? Our situation is ominous, and no amount of pretending can make it otherwise. But remember: The enemy is outside the gates, not within. To tear each other apart will not help the situation."

He continued over the talk this raised. "The Northerners expect us to close the tunnels—to hunker down and pray for salvation. They push us to give up our city, our freedoms, our souls." He darted a glance at Father Telo, who had joined them on the portico, and inspiration struck. A plan, clear as crystal, formed in his head. "But such is not the path of Colina Hermosa.

The people of Colina Hermosa make their own fate. We do not surrender to infidel invaders. Give up our homes and lives without a fight? Never."

The mutters held a note of approval. They waited to hear what he could offer, for people desired someone to take charge—as long as that someone brought a likelihood of success. But the crowd would be just as quick to return to outrage.

Saints, allow it not to come to that.

"It's my responsibility to see this sorted out and families reunited," he continued. "Then the evacuations will continue. We may not be able to hold our city, but I will ensure you escape from it. I will make good on my mistakes, and we will get our children back. This I swear by Santiago himself!"

This time the angry roar held purpose behind it. Speech done, Julian now had one more task.

It was time to create a miracle.

Ramiro sliced through foul, stinking water of the swamp lake. He glanced back at the column of black smoke falling behind them along with the dry land. It had taken more time than it should to collect enough wood. Too much of it was either green or wet, and it sent a thick plume into the air for that very reason. The fire wouldn't be hot enough to consume the body of the saint-cursed witch, though apparently the nit didn't understand that. She walked, albeit it at the very end of her tether to be as far from him as possible.

Ramiro shivered. *Saints preserve me.* Burning the dead. The witches were barbarians. How could a person go to the afterlife with no body?

She walked, but her eyes focused on him and not her steps. Her white-hot scorn focused along the several yards of rope connecting them and into his soul. If looks could kill, her glare would have a knife in his back. But if looks could kill, he'd have her head under the water. No doubt Teresa had chosen to go with them for that very reason. Someone had to keep him from killing the result of their botched mission. Despite that, he wished the scholarly woman would have remained behind to tend to the others.

Ignoring the witch, Ramiro returned his attention to the treacherous waters ahead—already they lapped to his waist—and kept the western, sinking sun at his back. Everything in him screamed at him to go back, to ignore duty and orders and be with his dying friends. But . . . he'd given his word. Coward that he was, he ached at abandoning them, but hadn't the guts to turn around. By Santiago and San Martin, he swore he'd return for them, no matter the cost. Once the burden of Colina Hermosa's survival didn't weigh on his shoulders.

Now that weight was all too heavy. What would Salvador think of that? Alvito would have rolled his eyes. Gomez would shake his head to see a *bisoño* at the helm. His brother would tell him to do what must be done. Ramiro gritted his teeth. He was not fit to be the leader.

But there was no one else.

"Do you remember the way, cousin?" Teresa asked. Atop Sancha, she would have the best chance of spotting any threats. Hopefully, she kept her eyes open.

He pushed against the muck sucking at his heels and got a tighter grip on the pair of reins, checking to see that Valentía followed. "Hi-ya." In truth, he'd paid little attention to the trail Bromisto had taken through the swamp. He spared a fleeting thought that the boy had made it home safely. Better Teresa didn't know his clueless lack of direction. Beyond the landmark of the fallen tree, he remembered none of it, too sure someone else would be there to be the guide.

How could he have been so stupid?

As far as he knew, they'd cut straight across. He'd keep a watch on the ripples, pray the saints kept the snakes away, forge east, and hope for the best. *Welcome to wise leadership.*

The Northerners were still out there. He had to keep the witch under control. He would have to tell his mother about . . . *Oh God.* If only he could have a second alone, a second without this burden. Already, he preferred the lesser task of quicksand and snakes.

A great heron, walking on stick-thin legs in the shallows, followed them with one beady eye. It looked like God had put it together with leftover parts, its looping neck seemingly meant to swallow snakes.

A tug on the rope around his torso demanded his attention. The nit had slipped and fallen to one knee. Instinctively, he increased the tension on the rope so she could pull against it and avoid slipping beneath the stagnant water. As soon as he caught her, he wished it undone, but she was already climbing to her feet.

He stroked his hatred. "A reflex and nothing more, witch."

The witch gazed ahead, refusing to look at him.

Teresa rolled her eyes. "The girl did not kill your brother. Ramiro did not kill the witch. It was all a tragic accident. How many times do I have to say it?"

Ramiro turned away. "Forever. She would see us dead." The older witch hadn't hesitated, and the younger would be no different. That Teresa couldn't deny.

Apparently she could. "She has as much to fear from the Northerners as us."

"I doubt she'd see it that way," he snapped, sending ripples rolling ahead as he moved forward, pulling his three tethers with him.

"Then she'll hear the story from the beginning and make up her own mind." Teresa turned and directed her words at the witch. "The Northerners appeared for the first time over a month ago. They strode into our city in several small groups, immediately standing out with their jade-colored eyes and dust-light hair, and gave no indication of being our enemies."

Ramiro shook his head. Only the whir of the cicadas and the sluice of the water as they walked impeded the witch's hearing, but that didn't mean she'd listen. Teresa might as well address her words to Sancha or the stump up ahead that Ramiro would have to detour around. She carried on anyway.

"Like any other travelers, they inspected our markets, attracting no small attention with their foreign appearance. They watched our blacksmiths at work and sat in our inns, trying to pay with bits of jewels. They entered our churches and loitered near the great gates. All the time, they were sizing up our strengths and weaknesses—a pair even hiked a circuit around the outside of our walls."

"I did not hear that," Ramiro admitted. He splashed ahead of him to chase away a particularly dense patch of green scum to avoid walking through it. Teresa had more information from his father than he did, since no doubt an expert on other cultures would be a valuable resource to consult. Still, it bothered him that he'd been—once again—left in the dark.

"We thought nothing of their appearance," Teresa continued. "A free and easy people, we welcome all within our city—even witches," she said, smiling. The girl ignored her, and Teresa shrugged, once again wincing at the gesture, before carrying on. "Then a week after they left, panicked travelers brought word of an army appearing. The Northerners surrounded Zapata, and the villages of Suseph and Crueses, killing all they found outside the safety of the city walls. Our *Alcalde* took heed and brought people and foodstuff inside."

"Salvador said they had settled there," Ramiro mused reflectively. "He believed they'd be busy in the east, until the day they split their army, and Northern troops set up their siege outside our walls. Their force was powerful enough to pin down two cities at once."

"Just before we left, we heard more news," Teresa said, taking back the story. "The Northerners blocked the gates of Zapata and used their siege machines to shoot fire inside the walls. So much fire.

"Zapata tried a direct offensive to force an opening in the Northerners to get the civilians out. Thousands of arrows cut them apart. That and the ferocious battalion the Northerners had installed before the gates. So the people of Zapata burned. All of them. The city collapsed around them. Women, children, little babies, the old . . . the innocent and the sinful. Our scouts brought word that thousands perished."

Frogs croaked, and insects hummed in the silence that descended. The air reeked with rot. Ramiro's jaw tightened. His mother, father, the remaining members of his *pelotón*, innocents like Lupaa and her sweet honey bread waited for the Northerners to send fire over the walls of Colina Hermosa. Waiting for them to take it down as easily as they had the ancient walls of Zapata. And the only foreseeable hope rested on the shoulders of a just-bearded soldier and a slip of a girl with only hate in her heart.

"Look, cousin," Teresa whispered. "She sympathizes with our plight."

Ramiro turned. The girl still kept her head turned away from them, staring resolutely at the stump they'd bypassed, but tears made tracks down her cheeks and vanished into the gag.

Ramiro let the sullen lines on his face harden. "She feels for herself, cousin, not for us."

The witch cried in front of her enemies. Did she feel no shame? Ramiro shook his head. Not if it killed him would he give in to the ache in his chest and show tears to anyone. Furthermore, a slight wind could knock the spindly thing off her feet. The girl walked head-on through the swamp instead of turning her body sideways to offer the least resistance, sending splashes of water fountaining up before her like an ungainly bear. She wallowed as badly as one, too. The horses made less noise. She didn't even bother to wash away the mud covering her. Grief should never consume a person. Duty came first.

This weak thing was to save his city from the hordes of Northerners? What chance had magic against such numbers?

The shadows had grown long and spindly. Time got away from him. He didn't want to be caught in the water when night arrived.

"She slows us down," he told Teresa. "Hurry up back there!"

"It's been a day of shock for her," Teresa protested.

"And not for me? For you?" Ramiro growled back. He sought the shrouded bundle securely tied on Valentía's back. Why did the witch deserve more right to mourn than he did? "I don't let myself fall apart."

"No," Teresa agreed. "You fill with anger instead."

He scowled at her, then traced a path back along the trailing rope until he reached the nit, leaving hardly a ripple with his smooth passing. "Walk faster or ride." She didn't increase her pace, so he reached for her shoulder. She thrashed and flailed to avoid his hand, and he settled for seizing the rope just before it wrapped around her wrists.

He half guided and half dragged her sloshing over to Sancha. "Get on. You can ride behind Teresa."

The witch stared at him in horror, the whites of her eyes showing all the way around like Sancha when the *caballo de guerra* saw the snake.

"She's a horse, not a wolf. You won't be hurt."

More tears leaked, but the witch turned to face Sancha though she made no move to mount. Ramiro heaved a sigh. *Cursed civilians.* Sancha turned her head, and he thought he read the same disgust in his horse's eyes. He put a hand under the witch's bottom and gave a push and a yank, practically throwing her over Sancha's rump, where she clung, dripping foul water all over Teresa and Sancha. He removed the rope attaching him to the witch and anchored her instead to Teresa.

Ramiro *hmmphed* with relief at having that settled. Teresa didn't know what she was talking about. He was not filled with anger. Frustration, maybe, but that's because he had a mission, and it was as if the saints were conspiring to prevent him from accomplishing it. No, he was perfectly rational. The only rational one in the group, beyond the horses.

I'm not angry, he told himself.

I'm . . . not.

Scowling again, he said, "Let's get out of this mess before we lose the light."

CHAPTER 16

The ever-pervasive stench of the swamp as vegetable and animal matter slowly rotted filled Ramiro's nose. Covering his face or holding his breath did no good when surrounded by the foul water. There was no escape from it any more than he could avoid the burn of the sun. If there was one positive, the smell nullified the rank stink of his body odor.

Thank the saints for small favors.

As the hours wore away, so did his irritation, replaced with a dull numbness that sank through skin to muscle and bone. The numbness of exhaustion settled deep and ran from his toes to his hair, encompassing his brain in a foggy haze until nothing existed but the reek and the urge to find dry land. Even Teresa no longer attempted to engage him in conversation, riding slumped against Sancha's neck. The witch lay upon Teresa's back—in either a *siesta* or a swoon, Ramiro cared not which.

As the reed-lined bank of the eastern shore drew nearer and nearer and the water shallower, Ramiro fought within himself to stay on his feet and not crawl onto the waterless land like a *bebé*. His legs wanted to collapse, and his spirit, sunk so low, agreed with the idea. Only pride kept him upright as he led the horses out of the water and into a clearing of matted grasses, scraggly bushes, and a scattering of white-clad birch trees. Frogs greeted their safe return to land by springing for the water with muffled plops.

"We can camp here," he said, not even bothering to shake off the fetid liquid clinging to him.

Teresa slid down from Sancha with a groan of relief. At the same time, the little witch came to life, springing off the far side of Sancha's flank. She dashed for the safety of the trees with a flash of long braid. For a split second, Ramiro's mind staggered, unable to comprehend. Then came the dull thought that he could let her go and be done with her. Stand still, and he could wave good riddance to one trouble.

What was one more failure?

"Hell and damnation!"

He threw down the reins and dodged around his horse to hustle after her. He couldn't blame her for the escape attempt—who wouldn't do the same?—but they didn't have time for it.

The rope still hugged Teresa's middle. The witch must have worked her end loose over the long, miserable ride. What surprised him more than that, though, was her speed. The girl could run.

But so could he.

He caught her just before she broke past the edge of trees not far from the water's edge, grabbing a fistful of her hair and dragging them both to a halt. Her arms remained lashed together, her skin red and swollen from the leather straps. Somehow, the sight brought up his anger.

"That was stupid," he shouted, swinging her around. "Never try it again unless you want me to thrash you."

Her odd blue eyes shot defiance and anger, while her garbled shouts from under the gag were better left unheard. He almost slapped her as if she were a spoiled child—and the thought disgusted him. Hitting a woman, witch or no . . . that wasn't the man Ramiro wanted to be, no matter what threat he might make. Mustering his control, he marched her back to their camp, where Teresa handed him the rope that had recently bound her to the witch.

He couldn't resist a taunt as he made sure her gag was secure. "You should have worked this free and used your magic on us instead of running. I guess you're too stupid to realize that." Without looking at the witch's face, he lashed her securely to a slender birch, then turned his back on both his guilt and her and went to Valentía.

Where he hesitated. Finally, he reached out, but even then, his fingers fumbled on the bonds that would release Salvador's body. He wanted to hide his head against Valentía's flank, hide from the truth, but someone had to set up a camp.

"I'm sorry, cousin," Teresa said, coming to stand next to him. "I should have kept a better watch on her." She turned around, showing him her back. "Untie my sling. I want to help, and two hands would be more useful."

"But your injury," he protested. "You shouldn't be doing this."

"Let me decide. It's not broken, and you need help." She gestured at the horses waiting to be cared for. "Besides, it is a danger to me to be one-handed here. The knot, cousin."

Water and tension had worked their power on the material of the knot, forming it into a tight mass, so Ramiro pulled out the knife from his boot and sliced through the fabric in a smooth tug.

Teresa hesitantly swung her arm, bending and flexing while her brow contorted with evident pain. A forced smile crossed her face. "Not nearly as bad as I expected. Hardly a twinge," she lied. She jerked her head at the witch. "You'll have to deal with her sometime. You can't deny her existence forever."

"I'm not denying her existence," he said. "I'm *loathing* it." Yet even as he said it, a pang cut at Ramiro as he remembered the welts on the witch's arms, the bruising on her throat. This rough, brutish behavior wasn't him, but maybe it was a new version of him. After all, Teresa had lost the laughing and jesting countenance she'd showed the world ever since he met her. None of them was untouched by change during this cursed journey. But the thought frightened him.

Trying to shake that thought, Ramiro worked at the straps covering his brother. Blankets could conceal Salvador and shut out the sight of his brother's mangled body, but it couldn't change the truth. Just as denying the facts would only lead to further pain and fail to solve anything.

"*Think, brother,*" Salvador would urge.

He had to face the situation sometime. Painful as it was to admit, the witch had used a magic that made them attack one another. Best of friends since childhood, and still they'd been unable to see through the cloud in their minds and resist her. Common sense shouted that sort of magic turned on the Northerners could swing the tide in their favor.

Common sense shouted they needed the little witch.

If, he thought, the slender twig of a girl actually had the same magic. Because for all this effort and their assumptions of her power, so far she'd shown none. Ramiro might infinitely prefer she never did, but Colina Hermosa needed it otherwise. He looked at Teresa.

"Dealing with her is last on my list," he said curtly, and went back to his somber task.

Together they freed Salvador's body from its confinement and laid it in the driest spot they could find. Then, while Teresa collected dry wood and prepared what food remained, he tended the *caballos de guerra*, finding a thin stream that trickled relatively clear into the swamp lake for them to drink. Ramiro's own tongue was gummed to the inside of his mouth with thirst. By the way Teresa attacked her canteen, she felt the same. They'd have to boil more water for tomorrow.

He lifted his canteen to his lips and caught the witch staring at him fixedly with her red-rimmed eyes. A hint of pleading entered them. Ramiro cursed himself for a fool. The witch would have to drink and eat sometime. Dread ran through him. That meant lifting her gag.

Apparently last on his list had come sooner than he'd like.

The horses grazed free on marsh grass, and a fire crackled happily at the center of the murderer's tidy camp. It held the gathering dusk at bay, except where Claire slumped against the tree at the edge of the light. There was nothing happy or content in her position, though at least the rough feel of the tree's bark was less intrusive than the straps around her body. At first her arms had throbbed and burned, but now they'd gone dead, a lifeless weight. With her arms numb, thirst was the prime pain that tortured her. Her throat already sore from the throttling, it now ached with a double torment, while the gag acted like a sponge to absorb the little moisture her mouth could produce and stole it away.

Thirst and fear.

She held back a shiver. The two murderers knelt

opposite, favoring her with their unwanted attention. The peasant woman sat with hands neatly folded in her lap as if the damp ground didn't deter her. She sat so close their knees almost touched. The youth, on the other hand, kept a distance between them. He held a canteen, the sight of which made her throat work, while a knife rested on his bent thigh.

"Tell us what we want to know and you get this." He held the canteen before her eyes, taunting her with its proximity.

The murderer had handled her as easily as if she were a newborn goat. He'd moved with a fluid grace, compared to her floundering run. Stopping her flight had given him no trouble, and the idea terrified her. Even if she escaped, he'd find her again. Primal determination shone from his eyes whenever he condescended to look at her.

His meaning was no great mystery. He wanted to know about the Song. Her mind raced, trying to decide what to tell him. Did she admit everything? Say she had no magic in the hopes they let her go? Say nothing? She searched her brain for the advice Mother would give, but came up with nothing.

He seemed to sense her intention to lie. Holding up the canteen, he said, "Give me any trouble, and you can go without until we get back to Colina Hermosa."

"Really, Ramiro," the peasant woman Teresa said. "We're not barbarians."

"We are what the world makes us."

"But, through the saints' grace, we can strive to be more than that."

He scowled and picked up the knife. "Hold still," he directed Claire.

She shrank against the tree, but he seized her bound arms in one hand and brought up the knife with the other. She closed her eyes, only to feel tugs as her arms pulled at her shoulders. Opening one eye revealed him using the tip of the knife to wiggle lose the knot on her bindings. The leather thongs came away, and, for a moment, Claire felt nothing. Then blood rushed back, proving her arms weren't dead—far from it. She writhed against the tree as pain bloomed in her wrists like sharp, tingling daggers.

How had this happened? She wanted to go home. The goats. Who would tend them now? Her mother. The deep ache in her chest stirred to life, leaving her feeling so alone. Why had she ever wished to leave home? To test the Song? This day proved there was no one to save her. No one to care.

She sobbed.

Oh so gradually, the agony lifted. The world stopped whirling, and she heard a rough, keening moan coming from her gagged mouth. Hot mortification flooded her skin, but she forced her head upright.

Did she imagine the hint of satisfaction in the murderer's eyes? There and gone in an instant, it allowed her to reclaim her hate. She reached for him to scratch out those eyes, but the rope binding her to the tree wouldn't allow her to reach.

He held aloft the canteen again. "Tell me what I want to know."

She let her arms drop. Fighting solved nothing. Not with thirst twisting her thoughts. Without water, she'd soon be good for nothing. Without water, her escape chances went from slim to zero. There would be other chances to show her resistance.

"Ramiro." Teresa frowned. "Don't torture her like that."

The murderer shrugged. "Listen well, witch. I'll give you water when you tell us if you have the voice magic. I'll even feed you. When I lift your gag, you'll make no attempt to cloud our minds. You'll say nothing unless asked, not unless you want to go without. Is my point clear?"

Claire nodded, having no doubt he was capable of anything.

He leaned close, and she smelled swamp and sweat and something musky but not unpleasant, like a mix of cedar shavings and leather. His hands fumbled in her hair, and the pressure around her head vanished. She lifted trembling hands to her face and touched welts at the corners of her mouth.

The murderer held her gag as if posed to replace it. "Do you have the magic?"

Her attempt to speak came out as a dry croak. Did they really fear she'd sing when she could barely get her swollen tongue to move?

"Cousin," the peasant woman remonstrated. "We'll get nothing this way."

The murderer put the canteen in Claire's hands. She grasped it with difficulty, surprised to see her hand shake. The water was flat and warm. Pure heaven.

Before she could manage a second swallow, he plucked it away. Claire held what was left in her mouth, letting it soothe her parched tongue.

"You want more?" the murderer said. "Tell us. Do you have magic?"

The peasant Teresa shifted in the flattened grass. "We need magic to stop the Northerners. To turn the minds of their army so we can act to save our people. Just as the other witch acted to save you."

The youth frowned but sat quiet.

Claire's gaze turned to the canteen on his knee. To get more water . . . "Some," she admitted, raw throat robbing her words of music. "I have. Some magic."

"Some?" the murderer asked. His eyes hardened. "What kind of answer is that?"

"Please—" Saying such a word to them shamed her, but her mouth was a desert, killing her by inches. "Please water. I'll. Answer."

The peasant Teresa brought out a second canteen from behind her back and handed it over without even receiving a nod of permission. Didn't city men dominate the women? This one argued and acted on her own often enough. It went against everything Claire knew about city people. Was their relationship typical or extraordinary?

But the answers to those questions were nothing compared to the need for water, and Claire drank like a glutton, trying to get as much down as possible before they took it away again.

"Well?" he said.

By his tone Claire knew he expected her to go back on her promise. Maybe hoped she would so he could make good on his threat to withhold future drink. She reluctantly let Teresa take back the water. They would not believe she had no magic. Yet claiming to have the full ability could be a potentially lethal lie. What if they forced her to use it? She could not defeat an army even if she wanted to do so.

"The magic grows as a woman matures. I do not have my full power."

"Because you're young," Teresa prompted.

Claire nodded. "I could not work it against hundreds of people. Not successfully, anyway."

"The Northerner army is tens of thousands," the murdered said. "Not hundreds."

Claire gaped. *Thousands.* Could there be so many people? She tried, but could not picture it. Why hadn't her mother warned her of their numbers? Her strength, revived somewhat by the water, wilted. So many of these horrible city dwellers. How could she hope to win free against so many? She must make them see her as useless.

"There's no way thousands could hear me. Your plan is impossible." She knew from her mother's tantalizing hints that there were ways to stretch the magic and make it reach farther—running water being one of them, even a thick fog—but she'd never say as much to these city people. Yet, she doubted even an ocean could help her reach thousands. She hadn't that kind of strength.

Her captors exchanged glances.

"Is it a learned magic?" Teresa asked. "How does it work?"

It cost her nothing to answer such a question. Let the barbarians understand they couldn't acquire it or use her for their own ends. Maybe then they'd let her go and look for a new method to destroy this army. "It's inherited from mother to daughter."

"So witches don't have sons?"

"Rarely," Claire said.

"And men are born without the magic?"

Claire nodded. "I cannot stop an army. I'm useless to you." The murderers didn't need to know she'd never used the Song against another human. Barely used it at all and knew little of how it worked. Let them retain some fear of her. Perhaps it'd inspire them to let her go sooner.

The murderer leaned close again and returned her gag. Though she tried to wiggle free of his grasp, he pinioned her head and shoulders and tightened the leather around her head. Forcing it into her mouth and restraining her tongue.

"I don't believe her," he said. "She'll say anything to get free."

"Perhaps." Teresa tapped the nearly empty canteen against her leg. "But one thing is true. A single voice cannot reach thousands of men. They simply could not hear it, and it's clearly the only way her power can be released. How does that bode for your father's plan?"

"Ill." The murderer stood. "Like we came all this

way for nothing. But my duty is to fetch her. We take her back to the city anyway. My father can work out some use for her. And maybe she can lead him to others. Others like the one Salvador killed."

Frustration hit Claire in a wave, her hands curling into fists. She wanted to strike out at them, claw the indifferent expressions off their faces. But the murderer anticipated her once more. He seized her hands and rewrapped the straps around them, though this time not so tightly.

"Mother to daughter," Teresa mumbled as she labored to her feet. "Cousin . . . the dead witch must have been her mother."

Claire squirmed inside, unable to escape the cold pity in their brown eyes. She didn't want their attention, and she most certainly didn't want their pity.

"So?" he asked, harshly.

"Your brother. Her mother," Teresa said. "Ramiro, you *know* what this means. The two of you are *sangre* kin. Related by blood. Bound together with the same ties as family. Under obligation to each other."

What? Claire struggled to understand. She was kin to the murderer under some impossible rite of their city kind? She felt vaguely sick.

The murderer seemed to feel the same. His skin had gone a shade paler than his normal honey brown. "No," he said through clenched lips. "We're not." He turned and stalked toward the swamp lake.

CHAPTER 17

Claire leaned against the tree, letting it steady her, and stared at the peasant woman. The gag kept back her disagreement. She was not kin to this man who treated her . . . like the way *he* deserved to be treated.

The murderer turned and stalked back to them. "The witch killed Salvador."

Teresa laid a hand on his chest. "And your brother got his revenge and killed her. One of the very definitions of blood kin. When two people owe a blood debt, their kin become kin."

"The witch attacked first," he said, shaking his head. "It was her fault."

Teresa sighed and went to sit by the fire. "Which makes no matter in the case of *sangre* kinship. It only matters that they fought, and in this case died. Preventing this kind of unreasonable hatred in the living relatives is the very purpose behind blood kin."

"That doesn't make it acceptable. Does it?"

Impossibly, the murderer turned to her for confirmation, and Claire nodded. For once he made sense. Just because the murderer's brother killed her mother did not make them kin. Did not mean she owed them anything. She hadn't even promised to walk once they crossed the swamp lake, and she didn't plan to cooperate when they broke camp in the morning.

A chorus of frog calls filled the silence. Teresa stirred something hanging over the fire, something that smelled suspiciously like beef stew. The scent sent Claire's stomach rumbling with hunger. Her mother had traded their animal furs for dried beef a few times. She remembered the taste and forgot about the notion of being kin with this monster for a moment.

Did they intend to feed her or let her starve?

It was such a base thought, she felt ashamed for a moment, as if she were already forgetting the burning body on the other side of the swamp. She closed her eyes and formed an image of her mother. Tall. Strong. Independent. Exactly what Claire would need to be in the coming days. The only thing she could do for her mother now was concentrate on escaping.

She flexed her arms. The leather had more give this time. The murderer might actually have human feelings after all. He was much too thorough to have accidentally made her bindings less tight, which meant he'd done so on purpose.

Most likely because he found her too weak to be a threat. She could work with that.

The woman Teresa got up and came toward Claire carrying two bowls of the stew. Her mother had always said city women were dominated and controlled by the men. Yet Teresa clearly made her own choices. Was her mother mistaken or was the only man here too young to be so controlling? It was a puzzle, and puzzles gave her something to think about other than her sorry situation.

While the murderer sat at the fire staring at the wrapped body of his brother, Teresa sat by Claire's side, careful not to spill the full bowls. Claire's mouth watered, and she looked away before she betrayed more weakness.

Teresa ate a spoonful from one of the bowls as if to show the food was safe. "Will you promise not to use the magic if I feed you?"

Weak. She was weak for caving in. Claire nodded anyway.

Even if she used the Song against them, what would it accomplish? She couldn't manipulate them to cut her loose when it wasn't in their subconscious. Even she knew subjects had to be willing or open to suggestion for the magic to push them. Or it had to be something they already feared. Getting them to cut her bonds was beyond Claire's ability, not when they were on the watch for it. But if she could catch them off guard . . .

Teresa lowered Claire's gag and set the first spoonful against her lips, feeding her like a baby. The stew was salty from the dried meat, and it burned her tongue with hot spices. A taste like nothing Claire had tried before but still savory.

It was the best thing she'd ever eaten, and even though she knew that was because of her hunger, she hated the fact that she appreciated any part of their treatment of her.

The woman alternated turns between feeding herself and offering more. Claire took two mouthfuls and found herself staring at her captor's shorn hair. Longer than a man's, it was still too short to tuck behind an ear. Teresa caught her glance and lifted a hand to touch her ear, then held up another spoonful.

Claire hesitated, then slurped down the cooling food. "*He* said you could feed me?"

A small grin touched Teresa's lips. "*He* is not in charge of my decisions. It was my idea."

Claire waited for Teresa to finish her bite, emboldened at not being rebuffed. Escape meant lowering their guard. Observing the murderers and learning their patterns would help, too. Plus, she could admit she was curious, and of the two, she'd much rather interact with the woman. "You are the exception among your people?"

Teresa laughed. "You mean because I make up my own mind? An oddity, but I'm hardly alone in that. I'm afraid my hair and my decision to forgo dresses stand out much more than my ideas."

"But your men . . . they control . . ."

Teresa let the spoon hang frozen in the air. "Men control the women? That's what the witches think, isn't it?" Teresa offered the full spoon, then rested it on her knee, heedless of the wet spot it left on the coarse material. "We're not slaves if that's what you've heard."

She touched her shorn hair. "It's true my parents wanted a boy. Boys support the family in their old age. Girls care for their husband's family. But my parents understood my wish to go to the university. A girl isn't forced to marry. She can choose. I did."

Teresa took another bite of her dinner. "And it is better than it used to be. Women have more freedom. There are more of us at the university. More merchants, more artisans are women. Women may not sit on the council, but that doesn't mean we don't rule our families. Not a perfect system, but workable. And hardly slavery." Teresa offered another spoonful.

"More stew?"

Claire chewed slowly, trying to decide whether she believed the woman or not. Teresa seemed so tolerant, almost eager to talk. Such earnestness was hard to discount. Cautiously, she said, "It's not what I've been taught of city people."

Teresa nodded. "We all have our biases. I'd love to hear about your life. About your beliefs, your customs. It's why I went to the university."

"That's the second time you used that word. University?"

"School. A place of learning. A university is a higher-level school for those who want to learn more."

Claire met the woman's strange, mud-colored eyes. "I had this wish. To learn more. My mother . . . she . . . was not so sure."

"Then we have something in common," Teresa said.

"That cannot be. We are enemies."

"Are we?" Teresa scraped out the bottom of her bowl. "We're not killers. We don't wish you harm."

Claire stiffened with a glance at the solitary figure eating by the fire. "*He* does."

"Ramiro and his friends took me in as one of their own on this mission. They joked with me. They accepted me. They didn't care that I was a woman or even that I was an ugly woman. And here we are sitting and talking like reasonable people. People with things in common." Teresa gathered the bowls and spoons into a neat pile. "You and *he* are both mistaken in each other."

Claire said nothing. She could accept that Teresa believed she was acting in the right, but she could not believe that of the murderer. Her capture, her bruises were his doing. He'd tried to strangle her. Whether it was due to her mother's magic or not, it had to have been in his heart for him to act on it.

"Can I have your name?" Teresa asked, startling Claire out of her thoughts. "I mean knowing your name—"

The murderer by the fire looked her way, a hint of contempt and condemnation in his face. Claire drew defiance around herself.

"Makes it more acceptable? Less like you're making a slave of me?" The words came out with more vehemence than she intended. That was not the way to lull their suspicions. But she could not share her name with these people.

"If that's how you feel . . ." Teresa pulled the gag back into place with an apologetic shrug. "Sorry for this. When you're ready, I'd be honored to hear your name. And when we trust each other more, we'll be happy to do without this."

Claire sat perfectly still. Escape meant doing more than refusing to cooperate with her captors. Refusing to walk would not get her free. She must come up with something more.

Luckily, she had nothing to do but think.

Julian feared his ass would become molded to fit the chair if he did not move soon. The chairs in the council chamber were comfortable, but all comforts had their limits, and an entire night of discussion had stretched him to his.

"Let me see you closer," he said as an excuse to move. He stood gingerly with due care to avoid falling on his numb posterior and circled the three men at the center of the room.

Father Telo looked the same from his worn sandals to his seen-better-days robe—the only change being cleaner feet and hands—the very picture of a priest, if a rather brawny one. The two men on either side appeared to match his profession from their clean-shaven jaws to their triple-rope belts. But these two men were scouts from the army. The best of their scouts. Julian had worked with Vimaro before, but the other man was unknown to him.

"I cannot tell the real from the fake," Julian said. "Are you satisfied?" No doubt Vimaro and the other fake priest had enough concealed weapons under their brown robes to prove the true difference between soldiers and men of God. But that was their business.

Concejal Lugo tilted his head, like he was inspecting cloth at one of his stores he suspected was shoddy. "Their appearance is well enough. But can they act the part? The Northern leader Ordoño was one of us. He'll be able to spot a fake."

"Which is why Father Telo volunteered to do the talking."

"He is merciful and will send me the right words," Father Telo said.

"Hands," *Concejal* Pedro said, showing his large splayed ones from working his mill. "Their hands will give them away. Too rough, like mine. They have the calluses of swordsmen."

Father Telo held out his own hands, revealing his own set of calluses. "Toil in the cause, sayeth the Lord. Not all priests sit behind desks, occupied with books."

"I do not like the whole—" Lugo began.

"It is my privilege to offer myself," Julian interrupted. "The council has no say. It is personal." He'd enough of the arguing. It only robbed them of sleep. The council discussion had been heated. First about whether to accept the Northerner's insane terms of surrender—which they ultimately rejected—then on the finer points of his plan of insurgence. And the two *concejales* remaining with him were far from the worst on that score. They'd been among the first to be convinced, but politicians had debate in their blood.

Julian slapped his palm against the shining mahogany tabletop, making crumb-covered porcelain rattle and wineglasses vibrate. "If the Northerners will take me hostage in exchange for our children, then it is my wish to go."

Concejal Lugo wore a scowl that made him look like a prune. "It is your choice," he conceded, "but we need you here."

"The plan is in motion. All that needs doing is administrating it." The saints knew the *concejales* excelled at directing. As they wasted time here, *Concejal* Osmundo met with the *capitanes del pelotónes* to fill in the military on their part. Diego used his skills to organize the clerks and scribes of the priests informing the people of the location of their children. Other *concejales* worked at other aspects of the plan near the tunnels and the city wall.

The plan was happening, and these delays had to end.

"Let us talk as we go to the gates," Julian said. "I shall go insane if I spend another minute in this room."

The quickly hid grin from Pedro proved he sympathized; the man was used to spending time outdoors at his mill. The group was soon welcoming the earliest rays of the new day. The sweet touch of coolness lingered in the air. A few vendors pushed carts along the roads, but otherwise the city slept as though dead. Just streets away in the main square, parents would be anxiously waiting for information on their children.

Julian's urged his cramped body to take long strides in the empty streets as he maneuvered himself by the priest and left the scouts to the *concejales*.

"Do not worry about trying to map their camp in your head, Father," Julian said. "That's for the professionals to accomplish. They will pinpoint the strategic locations as well as try for more information about their magical weapon." Julian still dwelt on that. It seemed unfair the Northerners had numbers *and* magic to help them. He could only hope this new plan would help turn the advantage to Colin Hermosa. Hope was for the future, though, and he had to stay in the present. "You have only to play the spokesman and make my offer," he continued. "You're certain you want to do this?"

"He is my shepherd and walks as my companion. I shall fear no wolf."

"Platitudes," Julian huffed. The priest's dark skin gave no clue as to his level of courage, but his eye held no worry or indecision. Perhaps the tired words were not empty in his case.

"The Northerners sent their priests to walk among us, my son. We can only assume they will accept the same ambassadors from us."

Julian remembered the fierce priestess Santabe and her white rod murdering his guard without leaving a mark and somehow doubted the comparison's validity. Those cold killers were no servants of the Lord.

"Get in and get out, Father. Make my offer and locate the children."

"Understood." The priest pinned Julian with an appraising glance. "And you? Your soul is prepared if they say yes to the exchange?"

Julian grimaced, unable to hide his worries like the priest did. Fear made a tight knot in his gut. "If they say yes, you can give me the final rites before I go. Just don't tell my wife. I would not have my last moments cause her worry and recriminations."

"The Lord gives strength when strength is needed."

"Amen, Father," Julian said, willing this platitude, at least, to be true.

They walked the rest of the way in silence until Julian waved to the gate guard. "Three men to go forth." The guard eyed them curiously but hurried to the heavy metal doors and opened the small portal set within them.

The wicket creaked, protesting its change of position. Julian clasped hands with the priest, nodding to the scouts. "Farewell."

Father Telo touched mind, heart, liver, and spleen in a silent benediction. Vimaro and his companion copied the gesture with the fluidity of regular practitioners, looking every bit the genuine men of God. Then the gate clanged behind them, shutting them out of Colina Hermosa.

"I must return to my businesses," *Concejal* Lugo said abruptly. He turned away without further parting.

Off to fleece more customers. Julian caught the uncharitable thought with a wince. Lugo had supported his plan, and it'd been long years since Julian had sold his stores when it became clear his sons had no interest in them. It was hard to remember sometimes that he and Lugo were no longer rivals.

"Shall we watch from the wall?" Pedro asked. Unlike the departed *concejal*, the miller had nothing to keep him. His mill was outside the safety of the city—if it still stood. He could only spend so much time dawdling at the more fortunately located mills of his many sons and sons-in-law.

"My thought exactly." Julian followed the broad shoulders of the miller to the top of the wall, then moved down it until they stood above the gate. A press of soldiers made room for them.

The enemy army sprawled across the desert, skirting the edge of one of the old quarries where the stone for Colina Hermosa had been pried from bedrock. Julian eyed the mass of the camp. They suspected the leadership lived and worked at either the center of the enormous throng or the rear near the siege machines. But given the Northerners' oddness, Julian doubted it would be so simple.

"They'll get through, sirs," one soldier said with a confident nod.

Julian felt less certain. Nervousness danced like electricity down his limbs as he squeezed into a space against the stone. He might have just sent all three to their deaths. Crossing the road and moving through the dry and flattened grass toward the Northerner army, Father Telo and the scouts looked surprisingly small from above. A wisdom to remember as it applied equally well to all men, including himself.

But that reminded him that Salvador and Ramiro were still out there, too. Had they met with a witch yet? Made contact with some of the evacuated children? Julian sent a quick prayer to Santiago to keep a watch over them as well as their newly created spies.

All too soon a troupe of Northerners hurried out to surround the three and enclose them. Julian held his breath as weapons were drawn and figures took tense attitudes. The group paused as if talking, then weapons were put away as they resumed an unhurried pace toward the army. He caught a glimpse of brown robes here and there among the soldier's black-and-yellow uniforms before tents and supplies wagons swallowed them from view.

"They've been accepted," Pedro said. The soldiers murmured in acknowledgment and began to drift back to their posts, curiosity replaced with duty.

And so the end of Colina Hermosa begins, Julian thought. Let it be a grand one. If the Northerners accepted his offer of a trade for the children, Julian wouldn't live to see it.

CHAPTER 18

Ramiro stood in Colina Hermosa, in the square outside the citadel. A drifting white fog clung and concealed. Everything seemed taller, and he realized he was the timid ten-year-old who followed his brother like a puppy. The white world mocked him, keeping him from those he sought. He batted it away, looking for Beatriz or Julian, even a priest, but saw no one. No one to put a comforting arm around him to scare away the demons. No one came to take the burden he fought to hide. He spun in place, yet not a soul moved in the square.

"Mama?" His voice emerged as the voice of a boy with a stubbed toe who needed his mother to kiss it and make it better. "Help!"

The fog parted. Salvador stood across the square. His brother wore all white as he never had in life. Joy filled Ramiro's heart, and the weight he'd been carrying slipped away. He was his true age again, his full size. It had been a dream. Not real. He threw back his head and laughed in anticipation of seizing his brother's hand.

Salvador looked at him and smiled. Everything was well. He lifted an arm, and Ramiro felt the danger. Swords appeared, aimed through the fog at Salvador's heart.

Ramiro screamed a warning, but a gag kept him silent. He tried to run, but quicksand held his legs fast. He couldn't get there. Couldn't stop it. The swords descended, stabbing and slashing into Salvador's unprotected flesh. The hand holding them was his own . . .

He woke with a start, covered in sweat, unable to move as memory overwhelmed him. The blame belonged to him. The promise he made to Beatriz to bring Salvador home lay broken. Now he transported a corpse. He wept silently, a blanket pressed against his face, until a troubled sleep claimed him again.

Years of discipline woke Ramiro at first light despite his nightmares. He turned his eyes as he'd done countless times throughout the night to the witch. Seeing her still securely bound to her tree, and not about to murder them in their sleep—though to be fair, he pictured her as more likely to sneak away—he sat up and spat to rid the taste of rot from his mouth. His eyes felt thick and gritty.

The frogs had shut off their nightly chorus to be

replaced by the early stirrings of insects. The air felt thicker than ever, as if he could swim through it today. He quickly tended the horses—Sancha's tail swished in surprise at his not lingering with his usual affection— then set about dismantling their camp. Despite his pains to keep quiet, Teresa woke and soon joined him, taking over the breakfast duties as Ramiro rolled up the bedding. While she fed the witch, keeping up a running stream of one-way conversation with the sullen-faced girl, he busied himself strapping on parts of his armor, not so easy by oneself.

Salvador had considered it wise to wear the armor in case they met Northerners, so Ramiro would follow his brother's example. He'd considered fitting a few pieces of Salvador's suit onto Teresa, but their body types were too dissimilar. Still, he couldn't bring himself to abandon the now-useless metal, any more than he could leave his brother's body.

He'd expected thoughts about Salvador to keep him awake last night, or maybe worries about finding their way out of the swamp, the welfare of Alvito and Gomez, or even the fate of his city. Those had been in his head, but they were nothing compared to a new, smaller nagging trouble, the fresh torment enough to make him toss and turn. He scowled at the witch for causing his added guilt, then focused on a stubborn strap of his breastplate. Let them pack the rest of the camp, and he'd deal with the new guilt once and for all.

With most of their gear put away, Teresa awkwardly

helped him settle Salvador across Valentía, then she picked up Ramiro's helmet. "Mind if I borrow this?"

"Why?" Ramiro asked, catching her arm.

"Getting some water to wash out the fire."

"What!" Ramiro plucked his helm from Teresa's hand and traded it for the iron cooking pot. Sancha nickered as if amused. His equipment was already starting to rust—as Bromisto had predicted—it didn't need help. "Not my helmet. Try this."

For the first time in a day the dimple showed in Teresa's cheek. She gave him a wink. "Got ya. I knew my cousin was under all that gruff silence." She hefted the pot. "Knew that would wake you up. Who could imagine you'd get so much stuff in those saddlebags. Cooking equipment, food, fire starter. I thought it all lost with the packhorses."

"Survival gear. We all carry it." Ramiro surreptitiously rearranged some packing Teresa had done. He still felt stiff, words coming with difficulty. She might be ready to admit life moved on, but one moment he couldn't accept what happened, and the next anger filled his soul though he tried to contain it. Maybe he should try to be himself again for Teresa's sake. "Stow everything just so, and it fits. But the food's all gone."

"Then we'd best find that village today, eh cousin," Teresa said, coming back with the water.

"Easier said than done." The swamp all looked the same, and Ramiro had no idea if continuing to head east toward the sunrise would run them to the village or the middle of nowhere.

Teresa splashed water over the fire pit, producing a faint hiss from the dead coals.

"You're not a saint, cousin. I don't expect miracles from you. That's not a burden you have to bear. And don't think I don't see you trying. I'm not military. I'm not the lieutenant to your general."

Ramiro managed a grin that was only partly faked. "Officer? Given yourself a promotion, have you? You're a *bisoño* and no mistake. Remember that, will you? Keep your place."

She threw the pot at him, and he snagged it neatly out of the air before it could hit the ground at his feet. "Weak, *bisoño*. We'll have to build up that arm."

"Listen to the man. Putting down a woman with an injury." She rolled her shoulder. "We'll see when I'm healed. I'll wager I'll throw better than your beard manages to come in. Patchy, scruffy thing."

"Is it that bad?" he asked, his hand going to his jaw before he could stop himself. Without time to consult a mirror, he had wondered if he would be shamed instead of proud. All he could tell was that it itched.

Teresa laughed. "Not a thin patch anywhere, cousin." She cocked her head. "It suits you. Especially with the armor."

His face felt hot, and he quickly ran an eye over their campsite, searching for signs of their passage. No need to give the Northerners any help locating them. If they were looking. "Bury that, would you please?" he asked, pointing to the wet, glistening cinders. "I'll get our guest ready."

Worrying about his beard. This wasn't time for such vanity. He was as bad as Alvito had been. *Had been? Was it so?* The thought wiped away the last of his smile.

Forcing himself to joke with Teresa could only lighten his heart so far. Too much remained to drag it back down into the "gruff silence" she disliked. One such stared him in the face right now with disturbingly sky-colored eyes.

"Get ready to walk, witch," he said.

The sky-colored eyes narrowed in a look that should have included spitting, hissing, and biting—with probably a bit of cursing for good measure.

The witch couldn't have spent a comfortable night either, forced upright. He'd seen her awake as often as sleeping, her head slumped sideways in an awkward kink. He suspected she'd spent as much of the night crying as he had. He shivered with embarrassment, hoping he hid it better. Remorse might not trouble him for her lack of sleep, but one thing did.

Ramiro put himself between the girl and Teresa so Teresa couldn't possibly overhear. Best to get it off his conscience . . . it wouldn't get easier for waiting.

"I'm sorry you lost your mother."

To be clear, he wasn't sorry the witch was dead. That was a whole different feeling. But he was unhappy he'd offered no sympathy for someone suffering such a loss. He knew loss too well.

For a moment, surprise registered on her face and in the bizarre eyes, then contempt came back. He applied himself to undoing the rope holding her to the tree. "I don't care if that makes you feel better. I said it for my own benefit."

She grunted, then growled something he knew by the tone was meant to tell him off.

He finished unlooping the rope off the tree and gathered it in a loose coil, the other end wrapped around the little witch's arms. Mosquito bites marred her face, neck, and arms. His own bites itched in sympathy. "Stand up, and Teresa can take you into the bushes."

A shake of the head was her only response.

Ramiro clutched tight to his patience. "Don't make me drag you. You don't want that. I'm trying to give you a little privacy."

She stubbornly kept her place against the tree.

He rolled his eyes, then bent to jerk her upright. The last thing he wanted was to use more force. As Teresa constantly reminded him, they needed to win the girl over. But if someone had to be the mean one, better it was—

What—

He froze. "You've got a spider." He pointed to the spot of red and black on the little witch's trouser and had the satisfaction of her eyes rounding. *Black and red, and you'll be dead.*

Teresa brushed by him. "Is it that the double-bite Bromisto told us about?"

"Judging by her reaction, I'd say that's a safe bet," he said. "There's another." The second spot of red and black was about the size of a coin, all hairy legs and bulbous body. It clung to the tree, close to her head. Ramiro dropped to one knee and flicked the first spider from the little witch's leg.

"Swell up like a dead toad," he said as if to himself. "I wonder what that looks like. If you don't plan to walk, we can leave you tied here and find out." He smirked. "This tree is probably crawling with them."

Claire widened her eyes and put fear into her face, playing along as if the murderer's attempt to frighten her was succeeding. Double-bites were lazy and seldom bit unless you squished them. She'd encountered enough to know. They liked to hide under cabbage leaves in the garden. Maybe she could use this.

She tried to see the one by her head and pretended to flinch. Then she rushed forward like panic had seized her, moving on hands and knees, bumping against the murderer as she fled. Quick pats at her clothing looked like checking for more spiders, but allowed her to slip the small knife she'd filched from his boot into her waistband.

She'd have to move fast. The murderer would notice it missing soon.

"Very wise and you're welcome," he said. The murderer had strapped sheets of curved metal across his chest, back, and shoulders over his uniform. Looser pieces of shining silver hung from his waist, covering the top of his thighs. Though his sword hung on his horse, another dagger was attached to his waist. The whole ensemble made him look bigger, somehow more impressive. Harder. That combined with his red-rimmed eyes aged him. She wasn't the only one crying last night.

She wasn't crying now. Claire hid a smile, already moving. She was welcome to his weapon. Thank you very much. And the murderer had given her the perfect place to use it on her bonds. Dried reeds crackled under her feet and deflected off her shoulders. She sought a thick spot and hunkered down in the middle of them. As expected, Teresa stayed thoughtfully out of sight, though still close.

"Do you need help?" the woman called. "Since your hands are tied, I mean."

Claire used the knife to slit the straps around her wrists, then pulled at the gag around her head. She drew in great lungful of damp air, unsoiled by stale leather under her nose. The only help she needed was what to sing.

She dropped the gag. Trying to blind their eyes and have them fail to notice her slipping away wouldn't work. It would go against all their conceived notions—they were on too high an alert. She needed something that worked *with* their worries and fears—or to remove them altogether.

The idea of using the weapon on Teresa put a small knot in Claire's stomach. The woman had been kind to her, however misguided her reasons. And trying anything with the murderer would result in her knife's being taken away and her being returned to prisoner status . . . if not worse. She had no doubt, *he* had the training, the skill, and the desire to overwhelm any attempt she made to stab him. She hadn't the courage to attempt it. No—escape was her best choice.

Quick. There was no time.

The city people had been very particular to conceal their campsite from their supposed enemies. Very careful to remove all signs. Claire began to hum without words, almost under her breath. Gradually, she added words and increased her volume, so her Song would reach Teresa. Claire hoped the thickness of the air, loaded with moisture, would act like fog and carry the magic even farther. Perhaps reaching the murderer. She filled her words with emotion and pushed them into her soul so they'd become thick with magic.

> *"Unfinished chore.*
> *Thing left undone.*
> *Carelessness.*
> *Forgotten task."*

She let that seep on the wind for a breath and set a foot forward, trying to keep the reeds silent. Ever heedful, she crept through the concealment, her Song gaining in volume. Would it work? Could she fool them? Would they even hear her?

> *"Smoke from a not-dampened fire.*
> *Blanket left unpacked.*
> *Unfinished.*
> *Careless."*

"Cousin," Teresa called. "I think I didn't get the fire out. Can you check? Cousin?" The city woman moved away, trailing the rope and heading a few feet closer to their campsite.

Claire kept the Song alive, letting the same magic fill it. She edged out of the reeds and into a clump of bushes. Mother warned the more complex an idea she put into the Song, the harder it was to maintain. Harder to fool. She needed to recross the shallow swamp lake. Home—safety—lay on the other side.

Moving silently, she reached the shore of the lake and looked out. It was completely open, dotted by a few dead trees and ragged stumps. Out there, she'd be in plain sight. *He'd* catch her.

Running and taking a parallel path to the water would achieve the same outcome.

Again, he'd catch her. It would be the second place he looked.

Her Song faltered.

"Forgetfulness," she tuned, catching herself. "Second-guessing."

If she couldn't run, she could hide. Her time tied to the tree had let her learn the area. She'd spotted a fallen pine tree, its numerous boughs still green. It had topped against a sycamore, creating a little cavity between them, screened by broken foliage.

Claire turned away from the swamp lake and headed toward Teresa. The woman was still shouting at the murderer. Picking each step with care and holding a steady Song, Claire skirted around Teresa and crept back toward the overnight camp. The moist ground and damp tinder helped make her passage noiseless, and when she could she stepped in puddles or on dead timber to hide her tracks. In no time, she was hunkered between the evergreen and the peeling bark of the sycamore trunk with a fringe of branches to conceal her.

Her low position gave her a partial view of the camp. The murderer walked the area, bent over hands on his knees to better examine the ground. She choked back a shocked giggle. Her first use of the magic on another human had not only worked, it had carried all the way to the camp. He was looking for traces of their passage to conceal. She nestled deeper into hiding, dropping the Song in order to catch her breath. She'd never held the magic for so long.

The murderer stood up straight and gave a little shake. She pictured him frowning for his strange behavior. She held her breath. *Now comes the test*. Would they guess at her decision to hide?

He passed out of her range of sight, and Claire counted to three until he reappeared near his horse. He leaned against the creature, putting his arms around its neck as if taking comfort. Claire snorted, then glanced around uneasily. Like the murderer needed consolation. The man had a stick up his butt and no mistake.

She racked her brain for what Song to use now. Something to screen her hiding place or something else? She didn't want to insert anything to do with concealment in their minds. Maybe . . . She hummed a tune of panic, then added words, letting the wet air carry it. Let them think less clearly. That could only help her.

A loud shriek came from the direction of the reeds, then shouting and rustling. Claire hunkered down as the murderer jumped to his feet. Teresa came crashing back into camp. The gag was clutched in her hand, and she held out the loose end of the rope.

"Tricked! She's gone!"

For the first time in the last few days, Claire felt a rush of joy.

CHAPTER 19

The bronze door had closed behind Father Telo and his companions with a clang of finality, shutting them out of Colina Hermosa. Neither of the scouts posing as priests had flinched. Hardened men, they had known how to control any signs of trepidation. Telo had searched for fear in his own soul and had found too much.

More sturdy than the great wall at his back was his trust in the Almighty. Telo had had faith in the Lord for four decades to lead him along the hallowed path. This day had been no different. If only he had remembered that.

Telo had touched head, heart, liver, and spleen. That was not to say he took the Lord's intervention for granted. One was not stupid merely because one believed. One still needed to act with common sense and not put the Lord in a position of keeping one out of trouble.

The taller scout, a man with the rough and weathered skin and face of a farmer, all hard planes and sharp angles, had gestured to the dusty road lined with scrub bushes and cacti. "After you, Father."

Telo had inclined his head and taken the lead. Telo had offered to be their spokesman. *The Lord forgive him.* Let that offer have come from an honest desire to act as a shield for these men and not vanity for his quick wit and ready mouth. Further, let that ready mouth keep levity off his tongue for one day. He had managed to keep his mouth shut as they progressed and studied the army ahead.

Being outside with the enemy and on the same level had made the concentrated mass seem smaller. A most welcome illusion. The Northerners were sprawled on the generous plain, gathered well beyond the reach of the largest trebuchet. Not that Colina Hermosa had such a machine, the Lord forgive them for shortsightedness.

A group of nearly a dozen black-and-yellow-uniformed men with the strange light-colored hair had caught sight of their approach and advanced to meet them, keeping carefully out of arrow shot and on the bare dirt of the road. The Northerners had learned the danger of cacti thorns both from the plants and from a bow, Telo had noted with amusement.

One of the Northerners with peculiar green eyes had gestured to him and spoke in a guttural language, all hard consonants and all equally unintelligible. The squad of soldiers had surrounded them, hands resting on sword hilts. The same man had spoken in another flood of words, this time pointing to their sandals and robes.

The shorter scout, the one Telo called Taps for his resemblance to the cubby-faced, frequently smiling cellarer at the monastery where he'd first taken orders, had given Telo a prod.

"Hello, my son," Telo had boomed in his heartiest voice. The Northerners had jumped, and half pulled their weapons. "May the Lord shine upon you and your ability to speak in tongues."

Farmer-faced scout had rolled his eyes. "What if they understand you?"

Telo had put on a big smile and held out his arms as if in friendship. "Just look at them. They don't." Indeed, the Northerners had shown all stages of confusion with frowns and puckered brows.

Their green-eyed spokesman had tried again, showing a God-given persistence. Telo had waved him off and walked toward the army, only to be grabbed by the spokesman. Now weapons had left scabbards, and Northerner faces had borne dark scowls.

As the scouts had sunk into defensive crouches, Telo had freed his arm to point at the army camp. "Lord Ordoño." Logically, as envoys they had been granted protection. Even the Northerners had honored that right—or they had thus far.

The soldiers had broken into nervous chattering as Telo had pointed back to the wall of Colina Hermosa. "*Alcalde.*" He had pointed to himself. "Envoy. Talk."

"Tagh." the spokesman had mimed with a shrug. "*Alcalde*," he said clearly, proving the term was familiar. He had nodded and spat out a short stream of words, after which weapons had returned to holders. "Ordoño." He had waved toward the army before walking in that direction.

"See, my friends," Telo had told Farmer-face and Taps. "The Lord provides."

As they approached the army, though, Telo's steps faltered. The stony ground had been hacked and scraped of plant life. Everything from the tiniest pincushion cacti to the seven-foot-tall ocotillo with its many pole-like branches had been removed to make way for the camp. Even the giant saguaros had been chopped at their base. Like the gravest sin, life that had taken centuries to mature was gone in moments. Telo struggled to remember he'd been sent with a higher purpose than saving plants.

The green-eyed spokesman gestured at their feet and ankles showing under the robes and said something that drew a chorus of laughter from the other soldiers.

"They have no respect," Farmer-face muttered.

"Mind your spleen," Telo said mildly as he hurried to catch up. "The Lord commands we forgive the ignorant and the simpleton. Besides, sticks and stones . . . It is other things for which they'll answer to Our Lord."

The scouts had much time to examine the camp as their guides led them deep into the heart of it, taking several different pathways across the scarred ground.

To Telo, one square foot of it looked much like another. Squads of men. Very few women. Wagons and tents and crates of supplies. No doubt it made better sense to the two scouts, but his mind ran ahead to dwell on the coming meeting.

Would they accept the *Alcalde's* offer or reject it? And how was Colina Hermosa to survive if they accepted? But it was not his job to judge the *Alcalde's* decision. No, his objections had already been given.

Instead of taking them toward the rear or center of the army, their guides led them to the left, close enough to see the rim of the old quarry. Telo looked around for a large tent to indicate the housing of the leadership of this beast, but their escort halted before a red-and-gold-wool carpet with no discernible pattern, easily the size of an alehouse—alehouses being the perfect places to bring hearts and minds to the Lord while quenching one's thirst, hence Telo's familiarity with their dimensions. The rich carpet stood open to the sky. At the center were a single throne-like chair and a rather battered table.

The wooden chair was carved and embossed with a flaring gold sunburst. Gold objects covered the table, from elaborate miniature statues of deer to expensive tea services. The largest of the statues, at the center of the table, was a depiction of the sun. Pushed to a far corner of the wooden surface were gold-framed icons of Santiago and other saints. Their faces had been scratched out of the paintings, torn free as if only the gold mattered. Telo touched his forehead and heart as he realized they must have been looted from Zapata by the heathen devils. Had they no reverence for art?

At the far side of the carpet was a large screen that concealed whatever hid behind it. A good ten yards separated the carpet from the nearest supply wagons, which formed a sort of fence around it for privacy. More wagons made another barrier along the hundred-foot drop of the quarry rim.

Telo met Taps and Farmer-face's curious stares with a shrug. The Northerners must have some purpose for the outdoor display, but without a common language or culture, there was no way to discover the reasoning.

Suddenly, soldiers surrounded him, subjecting him to a quick but thorough search. They seemed disappointed when no weapons turned up. Telo was surprised when similar checks on the two scouts turned up nothing either. Maybe he'd misjudged his companions' preparedness.

The green-eyed spokesman dropped to his knees facing the carpet and put his forehead against the sand, leaving it there while he spoke. A tall woman came out from behind the screen, and Telo tensed as he recognized the description he'd been given of the aggressive priestess, Santabe. In her hand she carried the white rod that killed so easily.

Telo felt a flare of fear. He hoped the Lord knew what He was doing.

Santabe carried a gold tray full of food, including roast mutton and mashed turnip, which she deposited on the table, drawing the throne chair closer before crossing the carpet to them. She stood on the edge as a nearly naked servant ran from one of the wagons with a folding canvas stool. He arranged the stool on the carpet without once letting his body touch an inch of its fibers, then scurried back whence he came.

Telo glanced from the empty throne chair with the heaping table to the plain stool. Was the elaborate display for Ordoño? And if so, where was the man?

Hands grabbed him from behind and forced him to his knees, pressing his head against the sandy and rocky soil. At the same time his two companions met a similar fate. Telo did not resist, but when the hands lifted, he raised his head.

"The body can be manipulated; it's not so easy to bend the heart," he said.

"You are priests?" Santabe asked in a cool voice of unconcern. "We have studied your priests." She sat on the stool without a single twitch to her long white skirt, her feet and hands perfectly still, and settled the white rod across her knees. "You priests are full of weakness. Putting yourselves and people before the needs of your god. Caring for the sick and elderly. Worrying about right and wrong. Giving away food and drink. It is weakness."

"There are many types of weakness," Telo said. "Kindness is not one of them."

Santabe sniffed. "This life is where the weak are winnowed from the strong. Only the best go to the afterlife to fight and become favorites of Dal. Dal is everything. We are nothing. You priests pervert the holy and interfere with the natural order. Blood and sacrifice are the true calling of a priest—or priestess."

"So some believe," he said carefully. "But our views are fundamentally different. We must agree to disagree, then, for the sake of harmony."

"I do not seek harmony," Santabe said harshly. "Neither does Dal. Why are you here? Do you bring the answer to our demands?"

"Not yet. We bring a different offer to Ordoño from our *Alcalde*."

"If you don't come to answer our demands, you have nothing of interest to say." She stood and pointed with the rod. She spoke in her harsh tongue. "I told the guards to take off your hands and let you bleed out as punishment for presumption. Don't let your foreign blood tarnish the sacred altar."

What? Telo had time to share one glance with Farmer-face before hands gripped him roughly, seizing his arms and pulling them forward while others held his shoulders. Stones bit into Telo's knees. Shock held his tongue still. The green-eyed spokesman stood over him with a drawn sword. Even as Telo made no sound, shouts came from around him. To his astonishment, Farmer-face had kicked out, miraculously managing to connect with a stooping soldier's chin and clamber to his feet with the same movement. He joined Taps, who was already a spinning whirlwind of punching and blocking. Taps seemed to lean out of the way of a sword swing and delivered a quick thrust with his bare hands under the ribs of his opponent, stealing the man's breath and making him fold. Farmer-face took down another with a foot to the groin and tossed a second man over his back. He tried to reach Telo, but fresh soldiers hurried to join the fray from all sides, called by the shouts.

Telo twisted unsuccessfully to get free as Green-Eyes pushed a flat rock under his outstretched wrists, then raised his sword high. Telo's dark skin stood out starkly against the pale-colored, yellowish stone.

Strangely, Green-Eyes hesitated, looking not downward at his victim, but skyward where a small cloud obscured part of the sun. Another breath and the shining orb reappeared, too bright for eyes to hold. Sunlight glinted on the razor-sharp blade. Heart thudding, Telo closed his eyes and ceased resisting. He'd failed at his mission. Failed to help his city. At least he could cease to be a burden to his companions and maybe they could win free alone.

"Father and Santiago, into your hands I offer my sins!"

"Stop," a new voice called. "That one is really a priest."

All sound ceased, except for the roaring in Telo's ears that must be fear. He opened his eyes and squinted, trying to detect the newcomer. A single man leaned against one of the supply wagons, his feet crossed idly at the ankles. The man pushed off from the wagon and walked toward them. Telo waited for the man to assume the throne-like chair, but he, too, avoided the rich carpet.

"Why have you come, priest?"

"I . . . I have an offer from *Alcalde* Alvarado." Telo was amazed his voice barely shook.

"An offer." One dark eyebrow rose. "You intrigue me, priest. What could it be? Even if I reject it, it might be entertaining. Walk with me."

The soldiers surrounding Telo stepped back, and Telo struggled to his feet. He spent too little time on his knees lately and now, daresay, he'd be even less inclined to adopt the pose after such a close call. His companions had been driven to the ground, overcome by numbers. "And my fellow priests?"

The man who must be Ordoño smiled slyly. "Santabe, have the goodness to keep your knives off these *priests* for the time being."

Ordoño led the way to a supply wagon, which was covered by an undyed canvas tarp. Not a single guard or solider trailed at his heels. Nor did any stand outside the wagon. Telo gave nothing away on his face, but what kind of leader had no protection? Even the *Alcalde* had a token pair. Did he fear harm so little?

Ordoño held a wooden door aside to reveal a tiny sitting room, complete with tidy desk and comfortable-looking chairs with pillows. Short shelves up against the side of the wagon held a selection of books. A square of carpet stood at the entrance. Ordoño climbed the few steps and wiped his boots on the rug. "Clean your feet, priest. I can't abide sand. Nasty stuff."

Feeling he'd entered a dream, Telo complied and took the chair the supreme leader of the Northerners offered him. He plumped the pillow behind his back and leaned against it as if he were at home in a drawing room. The man facing him had the brown skin and eyes of the *ciudades-estado* and the hawk-like nose, looking nothing like a Northerner. "These are your living quarters?"

"My study," Ordoño confirmed. He waved toward the front of the wagon. "My bedchamber is there, in a separate wagon. Dressing room beyond in another. The Children of Dal are not complete savages. Nearly, but not completely. Wagons are much more convenient than tents, wouldn't you agree?" The man took a chair and settled. "Father . . . ?"

"Father Telo."

"Well, Father Telo. What is this offer of yours?"

"*Alcalde* Alvarado offers an exchange—himself for the children."

"Hmm. Unexpected for the old fox. And yet I can see no gain from this idea on your end."

Telo asked the question that had been burning at him since before he left Colina Hermosa, "Are the children alive?"

"Look for yourself." Ordoño turned to the side and loosed a rope that bound a canvas window closed. He pushed aside the flap to reveal a line of figures in the sand, separated by ten feet or so between them. Chains went from each small child to a stake in the ground. Clinks attested to movement, and bowls of food and water sat within reach of each. A canvas had been erected over the entire line to provide shade. As Telo began to count, Ordoño let the flap close.

"I see no reason to accept," Ordoño said. "Let your fox of an *alcalde* stew in his guilt."

"'Truly the mighty favor charity, sayeth the Lord. Those that least need, giveth most abundantly and prove their holiness.'"

Ordoño snorted. "Priests. Do you truly believe what you peddle? The Children of Dal make much less pretense."

"The quicker to lop off a hand?" If such was to be his fate, let it be earned by speaking the truth to this man who used to be one of them.

"Simpler, certainly." Ordoño tapped his knee. "Their bloodthirstiness does become wearing. Useful, but wearing. When you solve everything in such a way, there is little need for debate. Or reason."

"And have you any? Or does your soul trouble you even now. They are children. The innocent of God. The soul of a—"

"Stop." The man held up a hand, but his eyes held no heat. A gentle smile crinkled the corners of them in abundant laugh lines. "Ah, priests and their ability to instill guilt. Better than one's mother, wouldn't you say? You make me nostalgic."

"So we are taught in seminary though some do seem to learn it at their mother's breast." Telo leaned forward. This man was not what he'd been expecting. "Which city were you born in?"

"Does it matter? Is your mission to ferret out my heart or the children?" The man's voice grew sharp, his amusement fading.

"Does not God call upon us to save all sinners?" Telo put away the touchy personal subject for firmer ground. "You have us cornered. You have all the leverage. The children are no real use to you. You and I both know it. You need to save face this badly?"

"I have no need to save anything. I have already won." Ordoño sat easy in his chair, crossing one leg over the other at the knee and leaning back. "From the moment I crushed the spirit of a people and controlled their destiny. What does God think of that? Why hasn't he come to save you or sent a saint?"

"Are you so sure he hasn't?"

Ordoño chuckled, slapping his leg. "Ah, priests," he repeated. "Master manipulators. I will make you a deal, priest. I will let the youngest children go, if . . . if you stay and annoy Santabe. I grant you full immunity from her bloodthirstiness. Minister to the savages. It is your calling, is it not?"

"And the *Alcalde*?"

The leader of the Northerners waved as though at a fly. "Keep him. What would I do with such a fox? Santabe would insist on cutting him into tiny pieces for her Dal. More mess. I'd rather be amused."

"One does not take half the chicken when one can get the whole."

"Half is what you get, priest. Take it before I change my mind."

"Priests are also known for their bartering. All the children under twelve and my two fellow priests go free, alive and well, and safely escorted back and inside the walls of Colina Hermosa." Telo chose his words carefully to leave no loopholes. This man seemed like one to exploit any mistakes you offered him. "And I stay until I feel the call to leave."

"Let free some dozen hostages when I'll soon have a city of them, in return for endless lectures and manipulation." Ordoño spat into his hand and held it out. "How can a man of sense refuse? Blame it on nostalgia. But I hold you until I tire of you. Deal, Father Telo?" The man's eyes gleam like he'd captured a great prize.

A sinking feeling struck Telo's heart as he took the offered hand. His common sense had just landed him in a cartload of trouble, but if it saved even one child, he had no choice. "Deal, Lord Ordoño. Let us talk about the older children now."

"My dear Father, there's nothing to barter. I gave those to Santabe for Dal."

CHAPTER 20

"Saints!" Ramiro jerked his head away from Sancha's mottled-gray hide as crashing sounds came from the bushes. The witch girl was gone. Instantly, he turned to get orders from Salvador and was met with the sight of the swathed bundle on Valentía's back. Fresh pain lashed him like a whip. *Dear God*. He was in charge. He'd let his city's slim hope escape. "*Mierda!*"

The rope looked cut. *How?* How had the girl—

He felt at his waist, but his dagger was intact. A quick scan of his boot, though, revealed the little knife gone. Curse him for a fool. The witch had tricked him.

"What'll we do?" Teresa begged, practically dancing in a circle and wringing her hands. "What'll we do?"

Everyone in his city would die, and it was his fault. Strangely, though, that thought was nearly buried under the heartbreak that he'd let his father down. That he'd dishonored his brother's last mission. His heart thudded like he'd run ten miles, muscles weak, breath coming too fast. He reached for his sword strapped to Sancha and cursed himself. *Stupid*. He didn't need that to subdue the girl. Instead, he grabbed the rope from Teresa.

"Watch the horses. I'll catch her."

"Yes. Watch the horses." She nodded vigorously, legs still working although she went nowhere. "I can do that. Watch the horses. You find her."

Thoughts skittered in and out of his head faster and harder to catch than mosquitoes. He couldn't concentrate, even while running from the camp. His body tried to take him in a dozen directions at once, causing him to zigzag all over the place. Vines and trailing moss caught at him, and he batted them away. How long could she have been gone? Three minutes? Ten?

He swallowed hard and tried to force away the overwhelming panic. A strange buzzing packed his ears.

"Think. Think." But his brain felt clogged, like it was filled with Lupaa's honey. He grabbed his short hair and yanked. The small pain helped clear his mind. The swamp lake. Her mother's body lay on the other side. Bromisto had been taking them in that direction. The girl's home must be that way, too.

His feet took him to the shore of the lake, pressing right into the water until his boots splashed. No girl. He scanned the lake. It was open, no place to hide. Without a thought for snakes or quicksand, he ran for yards in either direction to get different angles, searching up and down the shoreline for a glimpse of her. Nothing.

Like Teresa, he couldn't stand still. He tromped in circles through reeds and high grass. It was impossible. She had to be here. Where else could she go? *Think*, estúpido. *What's wrong with you?*

Something was wrong. Very wrong. But there wasn't time to figure it out now. He had to find the girl. He hurried through the brush, seeking her fleeing ahead of him, going one way than another. He found the spot where Teresa had taken her for privacy and tracked across every inch, spreading out in all directions.

Nothing.

Nothing.

Nothing.

And yet he continued searching, getting farther and farther from camp. She had to be found for Colina Hermosa. He lost track of everything but moving and searching, always searching. He tripped over fallen logs, soaking his legs and feet in muddy water, and battled with stickers and thick brush. All the while he muttered prayers to Santiago and every saint who might intercede, knowing that he'd let her escape. Why would any saint help such a fool? They'd be more likely to help the witch.

Estúpido. He'd found her less and less of a threat the longer they'd spent together. Seeing her bound and powerless against the tree and her feeble attempt to run from him had all contributed to underestimating the girl. By God, he'd even begun to feel sorry for her. And here she proved she had cunning and could plan. Much better than himself.

His foot sank up to the knee in muck, and he sprang back, dragging against the suction that captured his leg. The quicksand released his flesh with a slurp that sounded like regret and a promise to win next time. Ramiro panted. *Close. Too close.*

Sweat covered his body, dampening his hair and pasting his shirt to metal and flesh. The normally comfortable armor dragged at him, so much deadweight. His stomach growled. Vaguely, he heard Teresa calling his name in the distance. Still blaming himself, he stood stock-still and rested against a giant tree trunk, then glanced up.

The sun was high in the sky, dazzling him with afternoon light. How could that be? It was minutes ago the girl escaped. Wasn't it?

The weary set to his muscles and drag to his steps told a different story. The sting of welts covered his arms and back where branches had whipped against him in his headlong search. His hands were marked with scratches from brambles.

For calm, he ran a hand over his face, rough whiskers scratching his palm, then touched mind, heart, spleen, and liver in resignation. Tricked. He'd been running aimlessly for hours, like a hound without a scent. Slowly, he made sense of it. The girl must have used her magic to lead him astray—to make him

forget reason and caution. But for it to last for hours . . .
no. She wouldn't have wasted her time. Would have
gotten far away instead. At some point she'd stopped
using the magic, and the panic had been all his. Had
continued long after the magic stopped causing it. All
the time the witch girl used *his* mindless distraction to
get farther away. Shame filled him.

Just the latest example of his failure to use his head
and think before he acted. Even if the girl used magic
against him, he still *let* it continue to happen. There
wasn't a word strong enough for his stupidity.

A newt scurried down the trunk to rest near his
hand as if flaunting its ability to escape unscathed.
Just like the girl. Ramiro lashed out to grab it, but it
evaded his reflexes and shot into the leaves. *Mierda*. He
couldn't manage anything. He'd ruined the mission,
ruined everything.

Head bowed, he trudged in the direction of Teresa's voice. She greeted his return with silence, merely
watching him drop the empty rope to the ground. As
he took a seat on a rock near their cold fire pit, she
handed him a waterskin. He drank, then poured the
rest over his head. It brought no refreshment to wipe
away his miserable failure.

"It was smart," Teresa said, sitting across from him.
"The girl, I mean. What she did to us was smart. She
knew she couldn't best you physically, cousin."

Ramiro sat up and rubbed his damp neck. "Exactly
the kind of smart Colina Hermosa needed, and I lost
her."

"*We* lost her. It was me she got away from in the first place."

"With *my* boot knife. The mission was my responsibility."

Bad arm and all, Teresa had unloaded the horses, laying Salvador's body neatly on the ground and piling his armor and other belongings in a stack. Sancha and Valentía had water and foodstuff. He hadn't even the heart to compliment her on what must have been hard work.

Sancha wandered over and butted at his shoulder as if she sensed his pain. A flash of pink flesh showed as she widened her nostrils and blew a puff of air at his face, enough to ruffle his hair. A heartfelt gesture wasted on a useless man, who couldn't even capture a lizard.

Teresa sat opening and closing one fist as the quiet grew. "We should head back. We're out of food. You have to take Salvador home to your family. It's hopeless." She chuckled sadly. "The university is my only home, cousin. I mean, my parents were always there for me, but they've passed on, and the university has been my life for fifteen years. Home, family, god, sanctuary, and world." She clenched her fist, then forced it open with her other hand, twining them together. "They'll burn it, won't they? Your father won't surrender the city to them."

His throat felt squeezed by a noose. "Yes. They'll try."

"Try?"

"Try." He caught her eyes and held them. Her misery lashed his soul. What was he doing giving into despair and blaming himself? That didn't solve anything. Would Salvador quit? Would his father lie down and wallow in self-pity? His mother had more stubbornness than he. He needed to show the strength of his family. With more conviction, he said "Yes, try. Which is what we need to do. Our city won't give up easily. Neither can we. The girl will go home. She has nothing else. No food. No supplies. I checked the lake again. No sign of her though I tromped everything so thoroughly there's no way to find her tracks, but she'll be headed in that direction. Physically, I can overpower her."

"She knows the swamp, while we don't," Teresa said. "She might have taken a longer path around the lake to avoid us. But we don't know where we're going. We don't know where she lives. Maybe we could pick up her trail across the lake, but she's too smart for that. And it would take too much time. She'll be long gone by the time we've caught up. And we've nothing to eat. Can you hunt while we chase her?"

He stood and handed her back the waterskin. His sword hilt gleamed atop the pile of his possessions. "Not without slowing us down."

Everything Teresa said to him was sensible. But he didn't want to be sensible right now. It was time to make up for his failure. Cunning would be met with cunning. He belted on his sword. "We have the location of a person who does know the swamp. Let's check the lake one more time, head across, and double-check where we burned her mother's body to make sure she isn't there. It will add a few hours, but then if we can't pick up her trail, we can circle back to the village and get food. Bromisto knows where she lives. We'll find her one way or another."

Claire smiled as she watched the murderer and Teresa repack the camp in preparation for leaving. She'd dropped her Song of panic hours ago, afraid that using it longer would only tip them off that she remained hiding in the area, waiting for them to be gone so she could head across the lake. Besides, she couldn't hum any more—her mouth was so dry it hurt. She'd never maintained magic for that long in her life.

It had astonished her to see the murderer continue to blunder around as if she still used the Song. Why had that happened? Years of trying to draw hints from her mother, and she still had nothing but guesses. Either the magic lingered in his system—unlikely—or she'd hit on an emotion so near to the surface that it was how the murderer would have reacted without her interference. At this point, it didn't matter. She just wanted them to leave and be done.

Jammed in a crack between the fallen pine tree and the sycamore, her legs pressed against her chest giving her no space to move. Sap stuck to her hands and clothing. Pine branches poked her from all directions, and she could barely take a deep breath, let alone find a more comfortable position.

Despite the aches in her body, she couldn't help the feeling of pride that warmed her. And why not, she'd beaten them. She'd managed the situation as well as any Woman of the Song could have done, even her mother would admit that. The murderer was giving up. She was safe!

She could survive another hour of torture in this tiny hiding place—it was still better than being tied up by the murderer—and then she could go home. *Home.* Her heart sang in her chest, despite the pain of loss that attacked her again. Her mother might be gone, but at least she could go *home.*

The murderer gave one last look around the campsite and took his horse, while Teresa held the other huge beast by the end of its reins. Claire slapped a hand across her mouth before a gasp could echo in the stillness. The murderer didn't go in the direction of the village. Her pulse began to hammer as he headed for the lake.

It can't be. Not after everything she'd suffered.

They were going after her—toward her home. Blocking Claire from the only direction she wished to go. She caught a last glimpse of her kidnappers before the brush and trees swallowed them up, taking them out of range.

Her position suddenly strangled her. Her legs screamed for space. The branches pressed too close. She couldn't breathe. She couldn't stand being penned in another moment. What did it matter anyway? She couldn't go home. The murderer had outsmarted her.

Or had he? She needed to make sure.

Careful not to make a sound, she inched free of her cramped hiding place, keeping close to the ground. For long seconds, she lay flat out, letting life return to aching limbs, then she tiptoed toward the lake. The murderer and the woman were already yards into the dirty water, moving toward the far shore and her home. Claire dropped to her bottom, feeling the tears come.

So it was true. The murderer had outsmarted her. He headed for her home, keeping her from it. She swallowed against a parched throat.

A drink. If only she could find some clean water and moisten her mouth and throat. Then she could sing again, have a little bit of protection. She couldn't go home, and she had no fire to boil water, but the village would have some. She feared to go there alone. Yet, what choice did she have? She couldn't go on like this much longer. But then he couldn't lay siege to her home forever, either. Eventually, the murderer would give up. Somehow, she'd get water and food at the village; and then she'd wait him out.

She took a last look at the murderer's retreating form, then she took off in the opposite direction.

CHAPTER 21

"I don't suppose you studied anything about snakes, cousin?" Ramiro eyed the evil-looking serpent looped around the branch alongside the animal trail they'd been following. The snake was easily as thick as his wrist, and the setting sun illuminated a red-and-black pattern along its back. It could be harmless—or not.

"Sadly, no," Teresa said from her seat atop Sancha. Ramiro decided one of them at least should get to ride. "Not my area of expertise. I *can* tell you that the people of Aveston associate snakes with San Pedro, who they say drove away the snakes from their city before it was built and prevented any from coming back. Or at least so they claim. It seems to be a superstitious way of claiming they drove out the heathen tribes that lived there."

"Hmm," Ramiro said, hardly listening. Someone lived in the desert before them? He forced his way into the brush alongside the trail, taking them around the threat at the expense of fresh scratches on his skin. When they'd first reached the swamp, he'd been amazed at the scenery, unable to pull his eyes away from all the new types of plants, with their flat leaves and smooth stems. His friends had been with him then and it had all seemed a lark. Now he hated this wet, dripping place, every leaf and every thornless tree. Even the air held moisture. One could hardly see a foot in front of one's own face. He longed for the open space and the dry heat of home.

If the girl left any tracks, they'd been impossible to find. Certainly, they'd discovered nothing new across the swamp lake even after a quick but thorough search. All it would gain Ramiro was another bleeding gash on his soul for leaving Alvito and Gomez again. He hadn't gone near them, afraid the sight would strip away all his resolve. They'd turned right around and recrossed the lake, heading to the village. And with darkness coming, they'd soon have to camp or risk falling into quicksand, though they'd made remarkable time. He only hoped Bromisto could help them find the witch's home, and they weren't too late.

If they managed to find the village, that is, and didn't stumble around this swamp for an eternity.

". . . and also many *ciudades-estado*," Teresa was saying, "including our own, believe Santa Margarita was swallowed by a dragon, but dragons are often associated with snakes. They do say her medallions can ward away—"

"Have you got one?" Ramiro interrupted.

"One what?"

"A medallion of Santa Margarita?"

"Well . . . no." Teresa simultaneously pushed a short strand of hair from one round cheek and pulled a small metal disk from a pocket. "Santa Catalina of scholars. She always appealed to me."

"San Martin for me," he said, touching the medallion at his throat. He pushed aside a branch and met open space and a beaten track full of muddy ruts.

"That's hardly a surprise . . ." Teresa sputtered to a stop. "Is this the road? The one we came in on?"

Ramiro looked up and down it, recognizing a tall split tree, one side burned black by lightning. A small smile pulled at his lips as he led them out onto it. Now they wouldn't have to stop because of darkness. "I do believe it is. Follow it that way, and we'll reach the village, the other direction . . . would take us home."

Teresa sniffed. "I hope you're not planning to send me home. I would see this through. And besides, then you'd be alone, cousin."

Valentía nipped at Sancha, and the mare moved over to give the stallion a wide space. Ramiro had never known the stallion to be snappish, but without Salvador . . . His throat tightened. It had to be done.

"I said you're not sending me home are you, cousin? Ramiro?"

He blinked. "What? No." He dropped the reins and approached Valentía.

"Well, that's a relief," Teresa said. "Which way did

you say to the village again?" But he was focused on the *caballo de guerra*.

Valentía backed away, shaking his head in warning, and Ramiro held out a soothing hand. "It's time," he told the horse.

The stallion nodded as if it understood and it stood still so Ramiro could approach. He touched the swathed bundle that was his brother. Heat and time had done their work; even holding his breath there was a sickly-sweet odor. Had it only been two days?

"I wanted to take you home myself, Salvador," he whispered. "Wanted us to be together as your mission was complete. But things didn't go so well." His face twisted as he fought off tears. "I've let you down, brother." He gripped his medallion until the edges cut into his palm. "Now we must go a different way, and you must return home alone. I swear by San Martin that I'll fix it. I'll be a brother to make you proud." He could say no more without shaming himself, so he simply touched mind, heart, liver, and spleen and backed away.

"Take him home," he told Valentía.

The horse pawed the ground as if eager to be gone while Ramiro removed the reins from Valentía's bridle. He stroked the stallion's dapple-gray forehead.

"The Northerners will be between you and home. You must be careful." Valentía blew out a breath, and Ramiro smiled weakly. "Yes, I know. You'll do better by Salvador than I did. If you could talk, I'm sure you'd apologize to Mother for me." He turned and gave a slap to the *caballo de guerra's* hindquarters. Valentía took off in a splash of mud and was soon hidden by a curve in the road.

"It had to be done," Ramiro whispered. They were going in the other direction. Who knew when they would return home? Salvador must be buried among his ancestors and soon. And if they didn't get through, his brother's body would be with his most-loved horse, while his soul was surely already with San Martin as part of the saint's *pelotón*.

His reasoning was sound.

Then why did he feel like the world had ended?

Teresa held out a hand, and he gripped it tight, setting his jaw to avoid shaming himself. For a long moment, they stood, saying nothing, then Ramiro bent to retrieve Sancha's reins and headed toward the setting sun and the village. There was a job to be done.

They slogged along the muddy road as full dark descended. The moonless night hardly allowed them to see anything, but it was impossible to mistake the cleared ground of the road. Not that Teresa helped. She drooped against Sancha's back, gentle snores adding their rumble to the chirp of insects and chorus of frogs. Ramiro swiped at a mosquito buzzing his ear. The uncanny sense of eyes on his back grew stronger. He'd noticed it since they'd moved onto the roadway.

The sky lightened ahead, but only in one concentrated area. Ramiro frowned. It was much too soon for dawn, the color too red for moonrise.

Fire!

"Teresa," he hissed. The woman jumped and clutched the saddle to keep from falling.

"What?" she said much too loudly.

"Shhhh. Look." He led Sancha to the side of the road and took her up among the bushes for concealment.

"The village?" Teresa asked.

"Must be." What else in this swamp was dry enough to burn?

The red glow got bigger, and now Ramiro could see smoke where the light lit the sky. That smoke rose above the treetops and vanished into the darkness. He took a tighter grip on Sancha's reins and used the undergrowth to get as close to the village as he could. The night had gone so still he could almost hear Teresa holding her breath, as he did himself.

Let him be wrong about the cause of the fire. Let it be an accident with a cook fire. But the sense of eyes against his back grew stronger.

His first glimpse through the branches at the muddy field and the village in its center told him his fear was not misplaced.

One of the squat mud huts burned like a bonfire. Looking more like bees in their yellow-and-black uniforms than ever, Northerners threw torches at other homes, laughing when they bounced off or failed to catch fire as if it were a game. A man in a white robe seemed to be directing the efforts by waving a white, forearm-length stick at the soldiers. Ramiro's blood went cold. Bodies lay sprawled on their faces or their backs, flickering eerily in the glow of the firelight—a lot of bodies. More Northerners corralled a group of men, women, and children just outside the village in the cleared, muddy field. Dozens of mules stood in a line between the row of houses that lined the road, nervously shifting and pawing in reaction to the fire.

"Saints," Teresa hissed, as Northerners began stabbing and slashing at the mules. "Appalling. I wonder if this is their usual behavior or an uncommon occurrence based on the war. That person in white seems to be in charge. Is he religious or governmental?"

"I don't think it makes a difference to the people down there," he whispered.

"Every scrap of information can help us find ways to beat them. How they think. What cultural activities they engage in. It's all important to us." Teresa flinched and looked away from the gruesome sight.

More laughter rang, and Ramiro felt sick inside as the animals stood while they were slaughtered. Swords rose and fell among the dumb beasts, yet not one animal moved. Ramiro forced his eyes away. How long until they started on the people?

"Children," Teresa said. "Look. There are too many children for this village."

Ramiro stared at the trapped villagers, fearing Bromisto was among their number and fearing even more that he was not. Small figures huddled against taller ones in the semidarkness, most sobbed. "You're right." In this poor village, he expected children to outnumber adults, but not to this degree. There were dozens, way too many for this tiny place to support. He looked closer, letting his eyes get better used to the growing darkness.

Some of the bodies wore green-and-gray uniforms.

His father's plan. The one Salvador had told him about: evacuation.

"Dear God! Some of them are from Colina Hermosa."

Ramiro reached for the curved bow strapped to Sancha and his quiver filled with his and Salvador's arrows. Thank San Martin he'd kept his armor on. Even with the extra missiles taken from Salvador, he wouldn't have enough arrows, but they were a start. Pushing the quiver over a shoulder, he took his sword from the straps alongside Sancha's saddle and checked his dagger.

"No more time for study. I'll give you ten minutes head start," he told Teresa, "more if I can. Give Sancha her nose and let her choose her speed. Hang on and don't fall." He turned to his horse. "Sancha, take her home."

Sancha tossed her head. She heard him and understood.

"Wait a minute," Teresa sputtered. "Don't I have a say in this? There are far too many of them. Don't throw your life away."

"Always see first to Colina Hermosa and its civilians," Ramiro recited. "Then fellow *pelotón* members, other military brothers, and last self. They'll head straight for the source of the arrows. I'll have to move and move quickly. Do you understand? I don't stand much chance, but I can't be slowed down, or I'll have none."

It looked like some civilians and twenty *pelotón* soldiers were dead. There were more than twice their number of lifeless Northerners. The men of Colina Hermosa had fought well. Maybe a dozen Northerners remained. He could get two before they came at him. Maybe another two after; and then it would be all sword work. Someone else would have to complete the mission.

He gripped Teresa's leg. "Do you understand? Tell my father I'm sorry. Sancha, the tunnels. Not the front gate. Take her to the tunnels."

Tears ran down Teresa's face as she touched mind, heart, spleen, and liver, then reached a hand to stroke his cheek. "It isn't the beard that makes the man." She gave a twisted smile. "Though your beard looks well. Very well. The saints protect you." She wiped at her face with one hand. "Don't worry about me. I'll hang on. If there's any horse I trust to have sense, it's this one."

He stroked Sancha, unable to say the word good-bye. The *caballo de guerra* would never allow another hand to tame her. It was their way: one master for life. "Live wild and free, my friend. I have Northerners to kill."

"Would you like some help with that?" a high-pitched voice asked.

A rough hand on Julian's shoulder shook him awake. "Something's coming toward the gate, sir," a voice said.

Julian jerked, nearly losing his perch atop a barrel. He glanced around blearily as stiff joints protested his sleeping arrangement. He'd slept in worse places than on barrels, but not for years. Age had a way of catching up to you.

A few oil lanterns were anchored in niches, giving enough light to navigate the gate courtyard but not enough to strip away the night vision of the guards on the wall. His fellow sleepers—the parents and families of the missing children—began to stir also, emerging from stacks of supplies and cubbyholes. Word had spread that envoys had gone out to the Northerners, and nothing could keep the people away. He couldn't blame them though he would have spared the people this if he could.

A black-lace shawl was draped around Julian's shoulders, and a small fluffy dog lay sleeping on his lap, leaving a wet dab of slobber on his knee. Julian groaned and became instantly awake. Where was she? By the time he set the dog on the ground, Beatriz was headed down the stairs from the upper wall.

"What were you doing up there at this time of night?" he demanded in a last-ditch attempt to head her off. "How did you know I was here?"

She merely sniffed and lifted Pietro to her arms. "Twenty-seven years of marriage, and you think I don't know when you're up to something. What have you done?"

Men ran past them, headed for the gate. Julian tried to sneak a glance in that direction. "Twenty-seven years of marriage, and I'm sure you know, *mi amor.*"

She held Pietro in his face. "Daddy is being funny. Our sons are running around out there—in danger. What about your responsibility to our family? What about your responsibility to this city? Now and forever?" She cradled the dog under her arm. "Sometimes you need to let things go. The children weren't your fault."

"It was my fault." He sighed. "I took the risk. I had to make it right. Now what is happening?"

"Prepare to open the gate," a voice shouted.

Her mouth pursed as she straightened his jacket. "It wasn't your responsibility. Whatever *this plan* of yours is, you shouldn't have done it." She cleared her throat with a huff. "There's a large group headed toward us from the enemy camp. The nice young men atop the wall tell me they believe it is the captured children. Or the Northerners have some very short warriors."

"Give me this," she said, drawing the shawl off his shoulders. "Looking silly in front of everyone," she mumbled under her breath. "Going behind his wife's back and thinking she's not smart enough to know. Men. Babies are what they are. Underhanded, is what it is. Overinflated sense of honor."

The gate commander strolled up, giving Beatriz a wide berth. "A group of children, sir. From the Northerner army. The best eyes report there are two priests with them. We'll be opening the gate, with your permission, sir."

"Excellent," Julian said. Beatriz raised an eyebrow as if to mock their asking his authorization. No doubt the commander had thrown that in to try to assist his situation. The soldier didn't understand that Beatriz was just relieving her feelings and was all bark and no bite.

Murmurs and joyful smiles broke out from the crowd of waiting family members at this official news.

Beatriz slid one cool hand around his arm. "Shall we greet them, husband," she said in her stage voice. "We'll talk about this later," came in a whisper for his ears alone.

An icy flutter of fear ran through Julian's gut, and he clutched her arm tight. "I love you, *mi amor.*" He very much doubted they would talk again. Not if the children were returning. He straightened his back to meet his fate head-on. It was done, and he was glad for it. He'd lived his life; let the children and their families have theirs.

The bronze gate opened, and he drank in the sight of the children limping through it. Family members pushed forward with cries and tears. The small girl who lost her rag doll clutched her grandfather as if she'd never let go. A boy showed welts on his wrist to his sobbing mother. More people pushed into the crowded courtyard, and more and more children were claimed. It was well they were saved, but many parents remained calling for news, looking in vain. The sight tore at Julian, dragging him between joy and heartbreak.

"*Alcalde* Alvarado. *Alcalde* Alvarado," people burst in a ragged cheer that soon grew stronger as more voices united. "*Alcalde* Alvarado!"

Beatriz nodded as if taking the credit for him. She understood it only embarrassed him.

The two scouts came last through the gate. Vimaro, his grizzled face a strange contrast to his humble priest garb, handed the child he carried to a clutching father and turned to Julian. "Halfway successful, *Alcalde*. It was too late to rescue the older children." A slight tightening of the taciturn scout's brow was the only sign he cared one way or the other.

"Too late." Julian touched mind and heart. The poor mothers and fathers. The crushing guilt returned.

"The saints watch over them and secure them a place with our Lord," Beatriz prayed.

Julian had to know if the other purpose of this mission had succeeded before the Northerners took him. "Did you learn what we needed?" he asked the scout. "Where is Father Telo? I don't see him here."

Beatriz released his arm. "Father Telo? My priest? You sent my priest to the Northerners?"

"He volunteered, Beatriz."

"They didn't want you, sir," Vimaro said. "They traded the children for the priest. He told me so himself. He stayed behind. Bravest thing—"

"You offered to trade yourself?" Beatriz's voice rose to a shout, drawing the eyes of everyone in the courtyard. The little hairball began to yip. "That was your—"

Julian dragged her close, suddenly in need of her support. His knees seemed to have gone weak, though whether it was relief at his safety or regret at the loss of the priest, he couldn't say. The way Beatriz settled her shawl with a snap said this discussion wasn't over. "The layout of the camp," he pressed, praying for a positive answer. "Did you find what we need?"

"Aye, sir. That we did. We know just where their leadership is camped."

At last, some luck among the tragedy. "Then get to the strategy room. We have a raid to plan."

CHAPTER 22

Ramiro spun at the voice. "Bromisto?"

The boy crouched under a tree. The bare skin of his chest and arms glowed pale. Ramiro slapped him on the back. "You're alive!"

A young woman waited next to him, her hand on his arm. Slender and not much taller than the boy, her hair, skin, and eyes were all various shades of brown. She carried a bag slung over one shoulder and wore a light-colored homespun dress.

"Bromisto?" she said with a laugh. "Is that what they call you?"

"You escaped the village!" Teresa was laughing and crying at once as she slid down from Sancha and seized the boy in a fierce hug. Ramiro barely restrained himself from joining them, but hurry pulled at him.

"And you escaped the *sirenas*," Bromisto said, his face squeezed against Teresa's shoulder. She released him and stepped back.

"Two of us did," Ramiro said gravely.

"Then the others?" Bromisto's face crumpled. "Your brother and the great soldiers? I tried to warn you. The *sirenas*. They are bad. Nothing but bad."

Ramiro thought of the witch girl. How her big eyes focused on him as she sat bound to a tree. The meek way she'd let Teresa feed her. How she'd snuck away without harming either of them.

Then he remembered the Northerners butchering the mules and how they'd mutilated the dead bodies of those scouts, which seemed like so long ago.

He knew exactly which one he could live with and which one he'd prefer to squish under his shoe like a scorpion that crawled from under a rock. But this wasn't the time to argue enemy virtues with the boy. Perhaps later there would be a chance to persuade Bromisto they needed help to find the witch girl—if any of them still lived by morning.

"Go with Teresa," Ramiro said. "She and my horse will see you to Colina Hermosa, where you'll be safe. This is no place for children."

"Children." The young woman at Bromisto's side straightened and pushed at loose hair that had escaped her coiled braid. "I'm older than you are. You haven't even got a proper beard. We're not going anywhere. Our people—"

"This is man talk, Elo," Bromisto interrupted. "You stick to healing."

Elo crossed her arms over her chest but held her tongue.

Bromisto turned to Ramiro. "You sure you don't want to marry her? Father will give two goats for her dowry. Think it over. She's not ugly when her hair is combed."

Elo huffed, and her scowl deepened. "My brother's name is Ermegildo, not trickster. It's pretty and dainty, just like a flower."

"Elo! Then should I remind them how you said Ramiro has pretty eyes?"

"Enough," Ramiro said. "There are more important things, like getting you to safety."

The boy gestured into the trees. "I said we could help kill these beardless men, and we can. Come this way." Bromisto turned and disappeared into the bushes with a rustle of leaves.

Ramiro stared at the frowning girl, who shrugged. "Come on." Elo too vanished.

"We should hear them out," Teresa said. "What could it hurt?"

"It's wasting time." A glance over his shoulder showed three huts were alight, and all the Northerners not guarding the prisoners were looting the remaining huts. He couldn't find the figure in white.

The boy didn't even have so much as a knife for a weapon. Ramiro sighed. Yet if Bromisto could offer help, Ramiro was going to accept it. He was not so eager to die. And dying alone would do nothing to help the prisoners. "Let's go."

Bromisto took them through the underbrush, keeping the glow from the burning village over their left shoulders. Struggling to get Sancha through the thick growth, Ramiro fretted about the loss of time until he was sure his spleen would explode. At last, they entered a clearing where several sullen-faced men rose from scratching something on the ground to meet them. Ramiro counted six village men, all with stout cudgels, and behind them, a flock of dark-haired women and children, looking none the better for being roused from their houses in the middle of the night. This was their help?

"You found a *ciudad* man and his ugly woman, Ermegildo," the short bent figure of Bromisto's father said. "Why did you bring them here?"

"A fighter, *Papá*. He's a fighter. And he has real weapons."

"And why would a *ciudad* man help the likes of us?"

Bromisto lifted his chin. "Because he's nice. He was going to take on the beardless men alone."

The leader of the villagers lifted his arm as if to cuff the boy. Ramiro stepped between them. He didn't think a litany of the creed from his *pelotón* would make an impression on this hard man. What would Salvador do?

He put a hand to the hilt of his sword. "Because they are my enemy, and they hurt *children*."

At the warning in his voice, Bromisto's father took a step back. The other village men came forward to make a solid front, cudgels raised.

Ramiro held his ground. "I want the Northerners dead. You want the Northerners dead. Every minute we glare at each other is a minute wasted."

Bromisto's father scratched at his beard, then he slowly offered his hand. "I am Suero. We could use the help of your weapons."

"Ramiro. I have a spare bow. Does anyone know how to use it? With bows and your cudgels, we could set an ambush."

A surprising smile bloomed on Suero's face, making him look younger. "I like the way you think, *ciudad* man. One of us can use this bow. Our aim will be as good as yours."

Murmurs of agreement came from the other men.

Whether their aim was true or not, it would be helpful to keep the Northerners off-balance and draw them deeper into the ambush. Ramiro pointed at the village women, standing on the far side of the clearing, then at Teresa. "First, we get them to safety." Sending so many to Colina Hermosa was not practical or wise. Not with the Northerner army between there and the swamp. "The other side of the swamp lake: Would that make a good meeting place? Somewhere the Northerners can't find, but where the civilians could go."

"So I had already decided," Suero said, grandly. "Ermegildo, take the women there."

Ramiro expected the boy to complain, but Bromisto merely ducked his shoulders and nodded. "Yes, *Papá.*"

"We could use the boy here," Ramiro said. "Someone needs to collect the prisoners when we draw off the Northerners. Guide them to safety."

Elo straightened. "I can take the others to the lake,

Papá. I know the way as well as Ermegildo." The young woman's eyes flashed with pride. "Leave it to me."

Suero grunted. "Try not to get them lost."

Teresa stepped close. "I'm staying here to help, cousin," she whispered. "I don't trust these people."

Ramiro shook his head. He didn't trust the adults either, but he thought Bromisto was another story. He hoped the boy wouldn't willfully deceive them. "Go with them. Alvito and Gomez are there. Perhaps . . ." It was hard to even consider. "You can find them enough dry land to give them a burial. And I'm counting on you to organize the refugees and hold them together. Be their leader."

Her full-armed hug caught him by surprise. "You'll meet me on the other side of the lake?" Teresa asked. "We'll hunt for the witch girl together."

"On my honor, sister."

She tucked her head under his chin, and he squeezed her wide frame. "We are double *sangre* kin," he said soberly. "I've saved your life, and we've gone through more hardship together than with any of my *pelotón* comrades. You are the one and only sister of my heart."

"Brother," she said, eyes shining. "It has a solid ring to it." She gave him a playful punch over heart, spleen, and liver, then tapped his forehead with a finger. "At the lakeside, brother."

He retrieved the rest of his armor from Sancha, then drew free Salvador's sword. He held it carefully. This and the bow were the only things of his brother he'd kept back.

"Sancha, go with Teresa."

Teresa gave him a surprised look, and he forced a reassuring smile. "It's too tight here. Sancha won't be able to maneuver or help in a fight. She'll only be in danger."

"Much like myself." Teresa took Sancha's reins. The horse rolled her eyes and lifted her upper lip to show her teeth. "I'll keep her safe at the lake. Whether she wants me to or not."

"Go," Ramiro instructed with a slap to the mare's shoulder. "Behave. Do what Teresa says." He had little hope the stubborn animal would listen for long, but Sancha quieted and let Teresa hold the reins.

Teresa stepped away and quickly vanished into the darkness after the women and children. A hollow opened in the pit of Ramiro's stomach as he began strapping on armor. In the clearing with six strangers, Ramiro had never felt so alone.

In the light of the raging fires, Ramiro stood three arrows upright in the muddy ground and prayed to Santiago that he got all three off before the Northerners reached him. The more he culled the Northern numbers before the close fighting, the better his chances.

Suero had chosen the ambush spot wisely. The brush was thick here. Only a narrow path ran through it. Ramiro couldn't see any of the already-hidden village men. The ground rose upward at a steep incline where the clearing in front of the village met the forest, meaning the Northerners would have to climb the muddy slope. It should slow them. The incline would also add to his bow's range.

It all depended on whether the Northerners could be goaded. He counted on their losing their heads and forgetting discipline, letting him draw them after the ambush started. After all, it had proved not so difficult on the last reconnaissance mission with his *pelotón*.

Seconds passed too slowly as they waited for Bromisto to skirt around to the opposite end of the clearing and get into position. The man Suero had picked to be the second archer was off to the side, waiting to take the Northerners as they tackled the slope.

However, the Northerners hadn't been waiting. By the time they'd set the ambush, the Northerners had finished with the village and turned their attentions to the prisoners. An old, gray-bearded man had been pulled from the huddle of captives. As Ramiro watched helplessly, the one in white directed two men to hold the old man, while a third hacked off his hands and then decapitated him in one sweep. Ramiro felt sick, but rushing in to save the old man would only doom their plan and the rest of the panicked prisoners.

Whatever the outcome, this time he had put thought into it and did not run ahead without a plan. Salvador would be pleased.

"Ready, *ciudad* man?" Suero spat into the mud. "You're sure they have no bows?"

"Reasonably sure." He hadn't seen any on any other infantry they'd met. They seemed to reserve bows for the troops camped around Colina Hermosa. Ramiro donned his helmet. "More of the children from my city will have been sent to your swamp. If something happens to me, I ask that you gather them and guide them to safety where the Northerners won't find them."

"And what would be in it for me?"

"I'm about to try to save your village."

Suero nodded to the prisoners. "More of them are your people than mine."

Ramiro knew it would come to this, just as Suero must have. He had no delusions of the village leader's goodness of heart or loyalty. Suero had traded with the witches for years, then sold them out for a few bags of trinkets. He would hit his own child. Not a man Ramiro wanted for an ally. But perhaps he could be bought and have enough honesty to stay bought.

He took Salvador's sword from its sheath on his back. Bile filled his mouth, but he said the words anyway. "Payment enough."

Suero's eyes gleamed brighter than the steel as he took the sword into his hands. "Payment accepted. For this, I'll see every brat from your city to the swamp lake and out of the pale men's hands. For this, I'll make them part of my own family."

"If you go back on your word, and I live, I'll kill you myself."

"You can try. But Suero never goes back on a bond once given. Start it, city man. Start it and let us be finished with one another." Suero faded away into the cover, taking his place among the ambushers.

Ramiro touched his breastplate for luck and set an arrow from the quiver to his curved bow. The man in white directed a woman to be dragged out and stretched along the mud in preparation for taking off her hands. A sword rose high. Anger burned and Ramiro used the emotion as fuel as he drew back the string. His intended target, the man in white, was blocked by soldiers. He didn't have a clear shot. He changed aim and released. With a hiss, the arrow embedded in the sword handler's shoulder, punching him back. The sword fell into the muck.

Shouts and screams rose from captives and Northerners alike, but Ramiro was already pulling a second arrow from the mud at his feet. It resulted in a square hit to the chest of a Northerner standing exposed like a sheep for the slaughter. Now they began moving. And it was all luck whether the entire group rushed him or they kept a guard on their prisoners.

His third arrow found a neck when he'd aimed for a back. Most of the captives had gotten to their feet. The man in white pointed at Ramiro with his stick. A group of Northerners left the prisoners and rushed in his direction, boots slipping in the mud. From the opposite side of the village, a piercing whistle sounded above all the noise: Bromisto's signal. The whistle came again, and Ramiro saw the captive children turn in that direction. Only a few men remained to constrain the prisoners. Too few.

As Ramiro plucked the last arrow from the mud, the prisoners broke, children shouting and running in the direction of the whistle they'd used all their lives in their hide-and-seek games. The adults were only seconds behind, dodging confused Northerners. One of the soldiers reached for a child and Ramiro let fly with his last arrow, not waiting to see where it struck the soldier.

The four Northerners with drawn weapons toiled up the slope, directly at him. Two more followed close behind. Letting the bow drop, he pulled his sword and took a step back. An arrow skittered across the mud among the Northerners' legs but hit nothing. Ramiro stumbled backward, drawing them closer to the woods. His fellow archer improved with a second shot that took one of the rear guards in a thigh, but more Northerners zeroed in on him standing at the top of the slope. He made a fitting target in his shining armor as the first rays of the morning sun lit the sky.

He straightened his helmet and gripped his sword in both hands, then turned his back and ran into the forest. The Northerners shouted in glee and pursued. As planned, Suero let the first two run past.

Ramiro sought some distance from the ambush spot, then turned to face his pursuers, putting his back against a tree. His armor made him slower and clumsier than the enemy. Three came at him, not the two they'd planned. A mistake or a calculated move on Suero's part? He could see that the villagers had now burst from their cover, heavy oak staves finding skulls and the softer flesh of the trailing group of enemies. With Salvador's sword, Suero skewered a Northerner through the back.

Ramiro turned to his own problems as the three rushed upon him. All of them were shorter, wiry men, wearing only mismatched mail. Ramiro parried a sword strike aimed for his neck. Another blow struck harmlessly against his armor, but thrust him back against the tree. The Northerners spread out around him. His short cavalry sword seemed to put him at a disadvantage.

In reality, it allowed him to be faster.

He waded forward, leaving the safety of cover at his back. His sword struck out like a snake, sinking deep into the stomach of the man in front of him. At the same time, Ramiro snapped his left elbow up and out. Metal connected with the jaw of the opponent, just as Gomez had taught him. The Northerner's eyes rolled up into his head. He folded.

Not that Ramiro had time to watch—he caught it all out of the corner of his eye even as he brought up a knee to push the body off his sword. He tried not to look at the blood on his gauntlets or feel the resistance as flesh parted and his weapon came free. A strike came at Ramiro's face, the vulnerable part of his defense. He ducked, and it clanged on his helmet, making his head ring. For a moment, he saw two of everything.

The village men had ceased bashing skulls, finishing off any who continued to move with their wide hunting knives. They faded back into the bushes as more Northerners scrambled up the slope. Ramiro panted. Where had Suero gone? Were they in the bushes to reset the ambush, or had they abandoned him?

He would have to worry about it later. His last opponent grappled with him, trying to pin him in place until more companions arrived, making it impossible for either of them to use swords. The Northerner brought up a knife to penetrate the chinks of his armor. Ramiro caught his wrist. The oncoming enemy jumped the dead bodies of their fellow soldiers and rushed through the ambush spot.

"Son of a bitch," Ramiro cursed. *Betrayed.* Well, Suero had gotten what he wanted: his people free and a sword to boot.

Curiously, what struck him most about the moment was that the Northerner smelled of onions. It was as if his nose knew death was at hand, and wanted to make the most of these last few seconds. The knife inched closer to Ramiro's neck. He couldn't get enough space to use his sword. Couldn't reach his knife.

But then he remembered his armor.

Dropping his sword, he raised his arm high, smashing his metal-encased elbow on the Northerner's helm. Once, twice, a third time, and he was free.

He scurried to his feet, picking up his sword as he ran away from the Northerners. Ramiro crashed into the brush with four more in pursuit. His breath came in gusts. All the Northerners had to do was overwhelm him, put him on the ground, and they'd be free to hack him apart at their leisure. He couldn't allow them to close if he wanted to survive.

He dodged around a tree and heard them cutting the distance. There was no way to outrun them.

"Salvador." He'd be with his brother again soon.

CHAPTER 23

Claire had sat back on her heels, tucked into a button-bush on the edge of the clearing. The village burned. The place she'd wanted to visit for as long as she could remember consumed in fire at the orders of a man in a white robe. A mosquito had buzzed her ear, and she had flinched, waving distractedly at the insect.

Men without beards had the peasants of the village to sit in the field in a group, under guard. The invaders were all dressed in the same black-and-yellow clothing. Soldiers, but not from the cities. And certainly not from the village. The men who had flung torches and laughed could only be the enemy Teresa and the murderer were so set against.

"They told the truth," she had whispered

She'd wondered if it hadn't been some invented story to get her cooperation though for what she couldn't imagine unless it was something dishonest.

There were so many children down below, crying, holding on to adults. Children shouldn't be treated like this. Her hand had drifted to the hilt of the knife stolen from the murderer, but there had been nothing for her to do. Even if she had gotten close enough, she hadn't the skill of her mother.

She wasn't good enough.

Below her, swords had come out, and the soldiers had killed mules. The poor animals' braying had cut straight to her heart. Claire had spun around and crawled deeper into the buttonbush. Mules. Blood. Bodies all over the village. Her mother. So much killing. She had vomited up the cattail root scavenged on the way here, gagging and sobbing, until she had straightened and wiped her mouth.

Why was there so much killing? Her mother would say it was because men were evil. Maybe her mother was right. Maybe that was the reason.

She should never have come here. But where else was she to go? The murderer was between her and home. She had no idea how to find the grandmother she'd seen once in her life. Her desire to leave home and test her magic seemed childish and naïve now.

Tears blinded her. She huddled into a ball, thrusting her fingers in her ears to keep out the sounds from the village, and rocked. Maybe seeking adventure and wanting to meet people wasn't such a good idea. She just wanted to go home—for none of this to have ever happened. To go back to being protected by her mother.

For long moments, she sat like that as gradually a buttonbush flower came into focus. She stared at the white globular ball, counting each individual stamen. By the time the count got to thirty, her eyes were dry, and her stomach had settled.

A bad tasted filled her dry mouth. The moisture in the roots she'd dug out of the mud had helped, as had the few berries she'd found, but she needed clean water. Time to make a decision. She couldn't stay here.

She brushed off her hands and straightened her clothing. The only place she wanted to go was home. Nobody better try to stop her. She'd keep a sharp lookout for the murderer and simply avoid him until he gave up and left. It should have been her decision in the first place.

Screams came from the direction of the village.

Her heart jumped into her chest, and she froze. Did she want to see what new horror was happening? Maybe it was best to give it a quick glance to be sure no one saw her, then get out of here.

This decided, she backed from the bush. The scene had changed. Soldiers and villagers were running around like a kicked anthill. An arrow zinged from nowhere and caught a black-and-yellow-clad man straight in the chest as he reached for a fleeing child. The figure in white waved uselessly with a white stick, but the crowd stampeded right past him. He touched an older boy with his stick, and the boy dropped into the mud and didn't move again.

Claire blinked. *By the Song?*

Soldiers ran by her hiding place, headed up a muddy slope. At the top stood a figure all in metal. She gaped. The murderer?

How did he get here? She thought he was across the lake, blockading her home. What in the world was he doing?

The answer came in an instant. However he got here, he was doing what she'd been afraid to try.

A soldier near the village shouted, pointing in her direction.

A second soldier stood within touching distance, having crept up on her. Her heart gave a great leap, and her legs moved of their own accord. She fled into the trees with her breathing suddenly too loud in her ears.

The noise of fighting, metal upon metal, came from her left, where the murderer had vanished. Were they coming? Were they close? She veered the other way and kept going, too afraid to glance around and see if anyone was behind her.

She tripped and sprawled against a tree, falling hard enough to feel the sting of a cut on her chin, then she hugged the tree, waiting for a hand to grab her or a sword to slash her into oblivion. Instead, water dripped on her shoulder from the moss hanging above her head. She turned ever so slowly to discover she was alone.

Had that soldier really been pointing at her?

The more she thought about it, the more likely it became he'd been pointing at the murderer. What would he want with her anyway? From what she'd heard of this army, he wouldn't know she was a Woman of the Song.

The murderer had taken on all those soldiers by himself, when all she'd done was hide in a bush—and now against a tree. Why had he done it? She dabbed at blood oozing from her chin. Didn't he know he would be killed?

"How strange." Puzzled, she tugged at her braid. For some reason the idea of the murderer being killed made her sad. He'd kidnapped her. If he hadn't killed her mother, then he'd helped with it. A little burn in her chest suggested she didn't believe that. Suggested Teresa had been truthful when she said her mother's death was an accident.

The little burn of guilt grew as she realized she should have done more to help the villagers. At least the murderer had shot a few arrows, risking himself to help others. Couldn't she have caused just as effective a distraction? Of course, she wasn't encased in armor and hadn't a shiny, sharp sword either. But she had proved herself smarter than the murderer by escaping him. She could have done something.

Her mother would say to mind her own business. That it wasn't her responsibility. But she'd heard so much about the village: girls her age who wore their hair up, children who hid and giggled behind barrels. She had the Song, and they didn't.

And yet the way home was clear. With the murderer here and too busy to hunt her, she could go home. She hesitated, the indecision gnawing at her.

Even in the growing daylight, the glow of the burning village still showed through the foliage. She hadn't gotten very far in her headlong flight. Sounds of vegetation crashing and breaking came from her left. Her throat felt tight, but she produced a quiet hum that would help conceal her as she pushed off from the tree and moved left, still undecided on what to do. The murderer had gone that way, but home was that direction, too.

"Look away.
Nothing to see.
Nothing important.
Nothing worth investigating.
More important things to do.
Look away."

The crashing noise got closer as she moved to get ahead of it. She'd searched for enough wandering goats to have practice judging distance by sound.

Except wandering goats don't carry sharp swords. Wandering goats don't try to kill you.

Light-headedness began to make her vision spin. The mossy dead tree she tried to step over spun in circles, and so did her raised foot. She was breathing too fast. Her heart raced like she'd run three miles. Her mother's instructions on control surfaced, and she made a conscious effort to breathe as normal. She pictured herself stalking Dolly. Safe in her own woods, moving to cut off her favorite goat. Pushing aside a harmless raspberry vine. Going around a bit of swampy ground. Dolly would never stab or trample her.

She imagined the goat on two legs, waving a sword and wearing armor, and she giggled, but the dizziness receded as she calmed. *Breathe in and out. Slow and easy.* She skirted along a thick oak and into the concealing branches of a big willow. Dolly didn't have spirited brown eyes or a smudge of a beard along a square jaw.

She froze and forgot to sing.

Where had that thought come from?

One of the crashing noises changed direction and came right at her. As she looked up, something emerged from the hanging branches of the willow tree and smashed into her. She clung to it to avoid falling.

Spirited brown eyes stared down at her in amazement. "What are you doing here?" Before she could answer, he said, "Get behind me," and hands pitched her around, causing her to stumble.

By the time she regained her balance, what seemed like a million soldiers emerged from the willow. The murderer stood between her and them. He blocked the sword thrust of the first man while stepping into it. The knife in his other hand slid smoothly under the soldier's armpit and up into his chest.

Claire shrieked and covered her mouth with her hands.

Three more followed right in the footsteps of the first soldier. She was going to die. They both would die. She seized on the first defensive song she'd ever been taught.

> "Sting
> Hornets
> Wasps
> Bees
> Pain
> Swarming
> Sting"

Weapons fell unheeded to the ground. The men began beating at the empty air, dancing and hopping in place to escape the nonexistent attack. She should run for all she was worth. Run home and never look back. Leave the murderer to distract them while she got away. Except the murderer had saved the villagers. Had put himself between her and danger. Now he jumped and waved his arms just like the others.

She must be out of her mind, but she couldn't leave like this.

Holding the song, she dodged his swinging arms to get close enough to grab his shoulder and shake him. When he didn't respond, she stood on tiptoes to make her face as level with his as she could and tugged at him with both hands.

His face scrunched in confusion, and then sense flooded into it. "What?" He took in the squirming soldiers and put his hands over his ears. "Will they stay like this until we get away?"

Claire shook her head and kept singing. The magic reached farther than she'd expected when she'd used it against Teresa and the murderer, but it would fade with distance. The soldiers would recover and give chase. Either they risked it or took the soldiers out permanently. She didn't know about the murderer, but she didn't want them after her again.

She drew her stolen dagger and held it tightly, then pointed at the murderer's weapons on the ground, then at the soldiers. By continuing the Song and manipulating their minds, she would be as guilty of killing them as if she held the sword.

But the murderer didn't pick up his weapons. He moved to the closest man and launched his fist into the back of the man's head. Metal crunched against flesh. The man hit the ground and didn't even twitch. He repeated the procedure twice more, and she quit singing to stand in a hollow silence. The murderer was even stronger than she'd thought.

"Are they dead?" she asked, wringing her hands. Belatedly, she considered the small knife, then put it away. It wouldn't be much use against him.

Haunted eyes came up to find hers. "Hopefully not. Does it matter?"

"Yes," she hissed, affronted.

"I believe you." He looked around and gathered his weapons. "We should go before more come."

Fear tightened her dry throat. She stepped toward the willow. "Are you making me or asking me?" The hornet song wouldn't work on him again. Probably no Song would while he was expecting it.

He froze in the middle of straightening as if considering. "Asking."

"Then . . . then no gags?"

"No magic?" he asked. "Truce?"

"Truce."

CHAPTER 24

"You didn't need to come along," Julian said. He'd decided to walk for exactly that reason: an attempt to dissuade his wife. The early-morning air was cool and refreshing, but his knees suggested a carriage would have been wiser. It was a long downhill route from the citadel to the wall. Another scheme that didn't go as planned. His bodyguards kept well back like distant shadows, giving them the illusion of being alone in the city.

"As if I would leave you," Beatriz answered, matching his strolling pace. A hush of gloom and depression hung over the city. She'd substituted her small dog for an equally useless tiny parasol, which she supported over their heads to block the low morning sun. "Trading yourself to the Northerners. There will be no more of that."

"Alcalde." The grizzled, white-haired man pushing

the handbarrow of turnips across the cobblestones smiled and tried to bow, only to have his cart wobble dangerously. Ever since the group of children returned, Julian's popularity with the people of the city had risen exponentially. Beatriz and her loud voice had guaranteed enough people overheard to spread the tale of his attempt at sacrifice all over the city. Though he, like Beatriz and the tradesman, wore black in deference to the children they had lost.

Julian returned the bow, giving his politician's smile. "I'm only going to check on a project," he said to her as the tradesman passed. "It's too early for you."

"A lot you know. It's perfect timing for you to escort me to church after seeing this project of yours." Beatriz sighed, and her parasol dipped, allowing the sun to shine in Julian's eyes. "Though it won't be the same without Father Telo."

"I apologize again for involving him. It was one in a long string of bad outcomes."

The parasol came back up. "Not at all. Sending the children was the right decision. Most of them made it safely, and I don't believe for one minute those barbarian Northerners would have returned any children if it weren't for the wisdom of Father Telo. No doubt he carried the day and, even now, converts the heathen. He is my preferred priest, you know."

Julian smiled sadly. Did his wife give any of the credit to Telo, or did she consider it all due to her patronage? Likely the bet tipped heavily toward her sponsorship. He drew her arm tighter against his side.

"He's a credit to you. I found him quite . . . enlightening. Since meeting him, I no longer feel the need to attend church. Why, I got all the salvation I needed just looking at the man."

Beatriz bumped him with her hip. "Just like you to be light-minded."

"*Mi amor*, with you I'm positively ridiculous." Beatriz sniffed but laughed right along with him. "In all seriousness," he said, "I pray that Father Telo is safe. That I haven't sent . . ."

Her grip on his arm tightened again, tears shining in her eyes. "The Lord protect and guide us. It shall be as He plans."

"Amen." Julian drew in a deep breath of fresh air as they entered a plaza. The square was nearly empty. All the vendor sheds closed. No crushed ice with fruit juice was for sale. No wine available at shady tables in corners. It might be early, but still, other strollers or shoppers should be out taking advantage of the cooler air. Julian sobered further. Times were too frightening; people kept close to their houses. He couldn't blame them. He, too, fought the urge to hunker down and surround himself with those he loved. Perhaps a walk with his wife was not a waste of precious time.

Several boys had taken advantage of the plaza's emptiness to shed clothes and splash in the large fountain at the heart of the space. Water flew, but they kept their delighted shrieks to whispers, less the first woman to see them drag them out by their ears.

Julian's throat tightened as he remembered his own

small ones, escaping vigilance to participate in just such a lark. From childish joys to grown soldiers. His son's pursuits were no longer carefree—or safe.

Beatriz dropped his arm. Parasol held straight upright, she headed for the fountain. Julian caught her skirt and pulled her back. "Let them play. Let them enjoy their day. Someone should."

Her face went white as she subsided against him. She crossed heart and mind. "Aye. Someone should."

He took them north to a side avenue and away from the gate, and they walked in companionable silence, until at last, the wall loomed overhead. The large stucco buildings became brighter in color as the number of families living inside them increased. Laundry ran from ropes supported from balcony to balcony. Here, as the morning progressed, life and animation returned to the streets, only it was hushed and anxious. People huddled on their steps with morning beverages, talking in whispers. Some children ran errands on silent feet, but the majority were held close to their parents. The smell of sausage and bacon drifted from windows.

Several abandoned houses in this crowded section of Colina Hermosa had been torn down. Their absence left a portion of the wall exposed. Julian headed for the spot. Dirt had been piled carefully against the neighboring house, the piles nearly matching height with second-floor windows. Workmen in sandy boots and dirty clothing hurried with shovels and picks. Twenty feet from the wall foundation, large holes gaped in the earth, big enough to let men walk inside stooped over. Julian nodded in approval at the progress.

"What are we doing here?" Beatriz asked, taking it all in. "What's this about?"

"You'll see."

A marginally less dirty man approached with a bow. "*Alcalde*."

Julian repeated the bow. "Master miner. My wife, Beatriz. You've done well."

"First Wife," the man said. "Progress, but we've struck rock."

"Are you stalled or stopped?" Alarm hit Julian. If they had to start again somewhere else, they might not be ready before the Northerners' ultimatum came due. "The timeline?"

"Still on track, just a little delayed." The man wiped his brow with a yellow handkerchief. "We did expect rock, since the wall had to have been built on a sturdy foundation. But I'm a miner, not a sapper. It's unfamiliar territory for me."

"For all of us," Julian admitted. "There is no one experienced in this field to be found."

"Sapper?" Beatriz asked with a frown.

"A term of war, First Wife," the master miner said, "for tunneling under city fortifications and bringing them down."

"Bringing them down," she gasped. "You're bringing down our wall! I thought you were reinforcing it."

Julian held up his hands. "A few sections only. And not until the right time."

"That's what makes it so difficult," the master miner said. "Controlling the fall."

"You have my entire trust, master miner," Julian said. "And you'll be ready when?"

"With the other sections, tomorrow morning. With this one, tomorrow night—possibly later. If we work around-the-clock shifts."

"You have enough men for that?"

The master miner tucked his handkerchief in a pocket and rocked on his thick boots. "The *concejales* have seen to everything. I have all I need. Do not worry, *Alcalde* Alvarado. Get the people here, and all will go as planned. I must get back to supervising. It's a delicate operation."

As the man hurried off, Julian tucked his wife's arm under his own. He turned for home, waiting for the flood of questions. Her parasol wavered in the air, first riding too high, then too low to deflect the sun.

"The people?" she muttered. "The people. Does that mean what I think?"

"Our people will not burn to death as in Zapata."

Shortly after breakfast, Father Telo sat on the steps of the wagon assigned to him. His new home on wheels was in the inner circle of wagons, close to the strange altar carpet. He rubbed his ankle, where already the manacle and chain bolting him to the wagon were starting to chafe, leaving a red welt on his dark skin.

The length allowed him to go inside or to venture a foot or so from the steps but no farther.

The Lord giveth, and the Lord taketh away.

Better to sit here and study what went on than to brood about his self-imposed captivity inside. *The Lord helps those who help themselves.* And at least it was bigger than the confessional booth. Maybe he could learn something useful or help in some way.

He was reduced to study because no one here spoke his language—or no one who approached him anyway. Neither Santabe nor Ordoño ventured close enough for speech. The way the guards pushed food at him, while ignoring him, made him feel more like a pet bear, a curiosity, than an actually hostage.

His wagon was part of the group where Ordoño lived off to the side of their camp yet with clear trails to everywhere, but few Northerners came and went, except the priests. A fact most interesting in itself. At the moment, there was no one else in sight.

A priestess, in the plain white robe they all wore, came out of a wagon and set a platter of sliced fruit upon the carpet. She was careful not to touch the edge of the rug. A slim slip of a girl, unlike Santabe, her hair was shorn short. One of their white weapons was belted at her hip. She disappeared back inside her wagon and reappeared with a large copper chalice. Telo watched as she sat and washed her feet in the chalice. Only then did she stand and move onto the carpet, retrieving the fruit and taking it to the large table at the center. There were many priests, but only the ones with the large sun-image earring ever ventured onto the altar. It must indicate some type of hierarchy. Telo watched, anxious to learn more.

The girl looked too innocent to be a fanatic like Santabe. Surely that bloodthirsty woman was an aberration and not the normal priestess.

As she vanished behind the screen—to pray, Telo assumed—a voice spoke at his elbow. "Deceptive, at times, how alike you look."

Telo jumped at this echo of his own thoughts, making his chain rattle. "Lord Ordoño. What do you mean?" The man stood at the corner of his wagon, exploring his teeth with a toothpick.

"The priests of Dal. The priests of the *ciudades-estado*. How alike you look with your devotion. Tending your altars. Serene and calm in your prayers."

"But you don't find us alike, my son?"

Ordoño removed the toothpick and leaned against the wagon. "Your sort is all talk. Talk a man into believing. Talk a man into goodness. Talk a man to forgiveness. Trying to talk to a priest of Dal is like holding a conversation with a wall. And about as entertaining. They neither argue, nor do they compromise."

"Intractable?" Telo asked. "Perhaps they take their version of 'The Lord God raised you up. It is to Him you will listen.' too literally. But they cannot be so inflexible. Whose idea was it to give Colina Hermosa seven days to surrender? Not yours, I take it. That does not seem like the act of a completely unkind people."

Ordoño laughed. "It is proof of their obstinacy. True, I would have attacked the moment we had the siege engines. Seven days. 'And Dal did appear before them, and lo, He did give them seven days to decide to worship Him.' Their kindness is an act of superstition, nothing more or less."

Before Telo could answer, a group of soldiers arrived, bearing one of their own between them. They threw the man to the ground in front of the carpet, where he remained prostrate. The priestess reappeared from behind the screen and joined them. She picked up the chalice from the sand and stood on the carpet, holding it.

"What is this about?" Telo asked, waiting for her to offer water to the poor soul.

"A case of blasphemy, Father." Ordoño pointed at the scene with his toothpick. "Watch and learn."

The priestess gave a long speech, then she gestured. One of the standing soldiers said some words in their harsh language, pulling his sword as he spoke. The prisoner kept his head bowed and never tried to escape as his right hand was cut off. Telo climbed to his feet and backed against the wagon, touching his forehead and heart.

The man's scream drowned out the solid thunk as they took off the other appendage. In agony, he reared upright. Quickly, the soldiers stretched the prisoner's arms before him. The priestess knelt with her bowl and caught the bright blood as it spewed forth from his stumps.

Telo wanted to vomit, wanted to look away. The sight of blood had always had that effect on him, worse now that the blood came from a child of God—all men were children of God, no matter their faith. And to see this childlike girl participate in such cruelty somehow made it all the more sickening.

Ordoño's stern, unmoved visage held Telo solid against the wooden wagon as the soldiers struck off the man's head and let the body collapse. Blood sprayed across the spotless robe of the priestess, across the carpet. Telo saw now why they had chosen red cloth.

"A waste of another soldier," Ordoño commented with a sigh. He moved to stand by the steps. "Are you quite well, Father?"

"May the Lord take pity on his soul," Telo said, his voice sounding high. He wondered the man hadn't made an escape for the edge of the quarry and a quick end, instead of suffering such a painful death. "God alone has the right to cast such a judgment. Life is sacred. To do this for a minor sin?"

"For any crime, but blasphemy is the most common. Your compassion is foreign here. Dal must be fed."

Telo shook with suppressed emotion. He hid his hands in his sleeves, hoping to disguise his anger. He wanted to argue that such punishment was not justice, but these people didn't seem to know the meaning of the word. They did not follow the will of any god but a devil. Using execution in this way—against children, too—was an abomination.

He gulped, drawing control around himself like

one of his comfortable and familiar robes. He must mind his tongue, must be careful of every expression. He must not trust any of them if he was to learn about the Northerners and report the information where it could be used. Telo very much feared what this penchant for violence meant for Colina Hermosa's chances—for his future.

"What is considered blasphemy?"

Ordoño twiddled his toothpick. "Quicker to ask what isn't."

The soldiers resheathed their swords and bore the body parts away, leaving a dark stain on the sand. The slim priestess set the chalice of blood on the table. She picked up several of their strange white weapons and laid them in the bowl.

So far Telo had only noticed priests carrying the weapons. What if they intended to arm the soldiers with them, too? Give them a power that could kill with just a touch. How many of these things did they have?

Telo tried to show no reaction. For Ordoño to arrive at just this time made this either a warning or a test to gauge him in some way. Likely it was both. "A strange ceremony. What is the significance of the items they put into . . . the blood?"

"The Diviners?" Ordoño held him with his dark eyes. Did Telo imagine amusement there? "It is how they recharge their weapons in some way."

Telo forced himself to resume his seat on the steps. "I assume these Diviners are no secret as they are worn quite publicly. I cannot get over servants of a higher power carrying weapons, and I've never seen weapons of that kind. They are too smooth for bone. They almost look like gigantic teeth."

"A good guess. They come from the horn of a sea beast. Quite a mundane, lazy animal actually, though rare. As you can see, the priests of Dal are not like the priests of the cities." Ordoño turned from studying the priestess chanting over the chalice. "A strange interest for one such as yourself—to inquire of weapons."

"A strange time for you to arrive to speak with me, my son," Telo said, mimicking the false concern in the man's tone. "Would you rather I inquired on the readiness of the guilty man's soul to meet his God?"

Ordoño shrugged. "What makes you think Dal is interested in what happens to his followers? These people are nothing like your own. Not their values and not their beliefs."

"All the more reason to understand them—to see what we have in common. Through understanding comes reconciliation."

"One doesn't understand them. One survives them—though the numbers who do are few."

Telo met the man's smile with a nod. The scene had been a boast of sorts, along with a test and a warning. Ordoño meant him to appreciate the power he must wield to rise to the top of these Northerners and lead them. "Wouldn't you say the Lord has guided you? You seem to understand them, my son."

"The Children of Dal were directionless before me,

like a child or a flooded river, if you'll allow the clichés, Father."

Telo stared at his strong hands resting on his knees. His host might have given motivation to the Northerners, but whatever hold he had over them could be broken. Would the Northerners fall apart without a leader? Wouldn't the removal of Ordoño be a blessing?

The man stood within his reach, unarmed. Telo was the bigger, the stronger. A grab and a squeeze, and Colina Hermosa would be safe.

Telo shivered and touched heart, mind, liver, and spleen for forgiveness at that sinful idea. He was a humble priest, not an assassin. Where was his faith? The Lord would see them through without delving into sin. "I'll pray for all our souls."

CHAPTER 25

A soft, misting drizzle started to fall. Ramiro held aside a branch to let the witch girl go ahead. She turned her head in his direction as she passed, as if insisting on keeping him in sight. He felt the same on that.

He removed his helmet to wipe sweat from his brow but was stymied by the armor on his hands. Instead, he bent at the waist and propped hands on his knees to catch his breath. Fighting in armor was no picnic. A small burn across the back of his left shoulder told him one of the Northerners had gotten under his plate. The wound would need to be cleaned and soon. "I imagine we put enough distance between us and the Northerners."

The girl stood just out of reach, waiting on him. "I think so, too. The only racket of people crashing through the swamp is you." He caught a flash of a smile at his expense before she swiftly hid it, worry returning. "Where's your friend Teresa?"

"I sent her where she'd be safe with some of the other woman and children to the . . . heart of the swamp." He'd been about to say to where their kin killed each other, but that didn't seem a good reminder at the moment.

"You are going back to the village to find the people you rescued?" She fiddled with her braid, trying to give the impression she didn't care about his answer. He wondered why she did. She'd proved more than adequate at making a fool of him—twice. No doubt she could use her voice to slip away, and he wouldn't even notice. Why stay with him?

"No need." he said. "Someone else is taking care of that for me." Suero had discovered by now that Ramiro wasn't dead but had left a trail of incapacitated enemies behind him. That should put the fear of the Lord into their bargain. Suero wouldn't dare go back on his word unless he wanted to find a sword at his throat. Anger burned. A clean death was too good for that dishonorable snake. He deserved a trial and a—

"Then . . ." The girl pushed her braid over her shoulder, her face solemn. "Do you have any water? Anything to eat?"

He straightened. Her questions were a painful reminder of his thirst and hunger. The girl's lips were chapped and raw-looking. The day would soon be a scorcher. They'd need water. They'd also need a plan, but making any decisions right now was beyond him. Should he go after Teresa? Should he try to persuade the girl to return home with him? By the saints, he feared he didn't have a chance in hell at that.

How many days had it been since leaving home? It was hard to keep track. He couldn't delay if he wanted to get back to Colina Hermosa before the Northern attack. Panic surged but was quickly dulled by exhaustion.

He tucked his helmet under his arm and pretended to turn out nonexistent pockets. "'Fraid I left my supplies in a pile by the village, along with my bow. I was out of food, but I do have water. Just not with me. I guess it's to the village after all."

He looked around to establish a direction, and she turned and pointed. "That way."

"Aye. I was just going to say that."

Her small grin returned, barely affecting her strange blue eyes. She led the way, alternating between keeping her eyes ahead and directed at him. "Can you make less noise? Do you think those soldiers are still there?"

"No and yes. We'll have to be very careful at the village. You ask a lot of questions." He found his gaze drawn with fascination to the way her braid swayed across her back. No adult woman would wear her hair down in that way, and no girl her age would want to be considered still a girl.

The witch girl was silent so long that he decided she was offended again. Teresa would no doubt laugh at him for being an idiot at tact. Saints, but he wished she were here to manage the girl for them. He hadn't the skill for this.

"Thank you," he blurted out, "for saving my life back there."

"We're even." Her eyes latched on him for a

moment, then away. "You put yourself between them and me. Why? For this city of yours?"

"Because I won't let them kill anyone else," he said truthfully though he didn't expect her to believe him. "My turn for a question. Why did you wake me up? From your magic, I mean. Why not slip away?"

"Perhaps I didn't want them to kill anyone else either." She stopped, putting a slender birch tree between them. "That was your brother who died at the lake. What happened there? I don't remember."

"You mean after I choked you?" Ramiro rubbed the back of his neck, the metal of his gauntlet scraping skin painfully. "We saw enemies everywhere. I thought you were one of them."

"And your friends—your brother—turned on each other," she said. "That was my mother's doing."

"I don't know how, but I came out of it. I realized what was happening." Ramiro braced himself for her anger. He'd tell her the truth, even if it caused her to lash out at him. "I brought Salvador back to his senses, and he killed your mother to shut off the magic. Too late, of course. He was dead. Your mother was dead. My friends . . . It wasn't what we wanted to happen."

She wiped at her eyes, leaning against the tree. "I believe it was a mistake, but I can't forgive you."

"Fair enough," he said slowly. The priests would lecture, but forgiveness wasn't in his heart, either. The older witch would have attacked no matter what they had done. He was no longer so certain this girl would have done the same. "Does our truce hold?"

"It holds. For now."

She intended to run as soon as he got her food and water, he guessed. He had until then to change her mind. "If we're going to be civil, can I have your name? What should I call you?"

Instead of answering, she turned back and began walking again. "Stay on the animal trail. I see quicksand. Following the animal trails is the safest way in the swamp." She shot him a glance over her shoulder. "Especially for one as noisy as you."

"Was that a joke?" Ramiro shook rainwater from his eyes and tested the ground before committing his feet. It looked no different here than any other section of swamp, leaf debris covered everything. Could that patch of wet ground be less solid than the rest? "You try hiking around in armor and see how easy it is."

Her head cocked to the side. "Could I?"

He tripped over his feet. "You want to try my armor?"

To his surprise, red crept up her neck. "I . . . um . . . I'm interested in . . . new things."

"Claire."

"What?"

"My name. It's Claire."

"Claire," he repeated, trying out the strange word. "It suits you."

Her neck got two shades redder. Ramiro smiled and swung his helmet by its strap. Maybe he didn't need Teresa after all. Teresa had never pulled a name from the witch girl.

A short time later, she stopped again. "The village."

He stood beside her and could just make out the mud shacks through the foliage. Smoke rose from a few of the homes, but no flames flickered. Either the drizzle had put them out or the fires had been defeated by the mud walls. Except for bodies, there was no one in sight. The village might as well have been a churchyard for all the life it had. He didn't trust it.

"Are they gone?" she whispered.

Ramiro shook his head, unable to say for sure. "Better safe than sorry. We stay as quiet as we can."

She rolled her eyes at him.

"I'll stay as quiet as I can," he amended in a whisper. "I left my supplies on the other side. Where I set the ambush."

They skirted the edge of the village, making their way around. He took her to the bush where he'd left his belongings and drew up short. His bag had been opened, the contents strewn everywhere, slashed and broken. His razor was bent as if purposely bowed over a rock or tree trunk. His bow and quiver was gone as well as anything of value.

The girl rushed to his water bag and held it up with a cry, revealing slits. A few drops leaked onto her palm. "The enemy soldiers? They did this?"

"No," he said, keeping his voice down. The burn of anger returned to his gut. Suero. The razor had been left in plain sight as a taunt—a jab at his youth. It hadn't been enough to turn their back on Ramiro during the ambush. They'd tried to ensure his survival would be difficult. "The Northerners didn't have the time or the manpower."

He set his helmet down, then stooped and seized his blanket roll—it was slashed as if with a large knife, the kind of knife used for hunting and skinning—but underneath waited his second water bag where he'd left it. It looked intact, and its weight meant it had gone unnoticed. He held it out to Claire. "Here."

She stared at him as if expecting a trick.

"It's fine. Do you think it poisoned?"

"No. I just didn't think a man would have any manners toward a guest." She took the bag and drank greedily, head tilted back to ensure no drops escaped.

He held back a curse. Being around her made him feel like he was walking on eggshells. Sharp ones. How was he to convince her to help Colina Hermosa? Was he sure he even wanted her there? "I'll go down to the village and see if I can find anything to eat," he said quietly as he waited. He'd need at least to find a flint. With his own gone, he couldn't boil more water.

The bag came down. "I'll come, too," she said, wiping rainwater from her face.

"No, you won't. I don't know what's down there."

She took another pull at the water bag and handed it back, then she put her hands on her hips. "I'm not eating raw cattail root again. I'm going with you. I can take care of myself. I got away from you, didn't I. Fooled you twice."

He shrugged as he drank deeply. Maybe she could take care of herself—as long as someone watched her to ensure she didn't overreact. Then again, who was he to speak? His record on keeping his head was no better. "Do you still have the knife you stole from me?"

A smug little smile crossed her face. "I do." Claire patted her waist.

"Then keep it there. You don't know what the hell to do with it."

The smile slid from her face, replaced with a frown. He put the water bag back under the blanket, retrieved his helmet, and started toward the village before she could argue some more. She hustled close to his elbow and glared at him. "You enjoyed that, didn't you?"

"Did you enjoy fooling me—twice?"

Red crept up her cheeks. "Maybe." She darted glances all around as they stepped from the cover of the trees. "Will there be soldiers in the village?"

He put on his helmet and checked his sword hilt. "Maybe."

She rolled her eyes. "My mother was right: Men are annoying."

"Then we're even on that, too. Now be quiet."

Nothing moved in the village as they approached. Everything was quiet as the grave, which he supposed it was. The rain lightly pattered down. Perhaps Suero had gathered all his people and evacuated to the swamp. Hopefully he had taken care of any remaining Northerners. But a roll in Ramiro's gut said that wasn't the case.

Everything smelled of smoke and mud and death. The girl turned her face away from the first body—

one of the soldiers he'd hit with an arrow. She already looked green, and they hadn't gotten to the center of the village yet. Ramiro gave the line of dead mules a wide berth, keeping his eyes searching for movement. No sense in getting as sick as the girl. The dead couldn't hurt them; no need to focus on them.

Ramiro passed by the first line of homes to stand in the roadway between the two rows of buildings. The girl breathed heavily at his shoulder, hands clasped under her chin and eyes too large. Before he entered a house, he wanted to be sure no one was here. It would be bad to be caught in one of the huts with no room to maneuver. He sensed . . . something. Almost like a presence waited.

The hairs on the back of his neck rose.

"Anyone here," he called, making the girl jump.

"I guess the place is empty after all—"

A man wearing what looked like a bedsheet made into a robe rushed from one of the huts. An older man with more gray than brown in his hair, he shouted a string of gibberish at them, waving his white stick. Ramiro recognized the Northern man who'd ordered around the soldiers. The madman charged them.

Ramiro relaxed and drew his sword almost casually. The man was not even armed, except for his stick, and that was barely the width of two thumbs. Maybe this one could be captured for Teresa to study. Ramiro stood his ground, waiting on the man—or tried to.

The girl grabbed him by the edge of his backplate and dragged at him. "Don't let him touch you!" she hissed.

"What?" A flutter of panic swelled in Ramiro's breast as if she'd transferred it to him. He seized the girl around the waist with one arm and dodged as the madman went rushing past. The Northerner swung the white stick at their heads, but missed by inches.

The man spun and shouted another string of foreign language at them. Ramiro picked out what sounded like 'dah' several times. "What's going on?" he demanded of the girl, looking from the furious madman to her.

"His stick," she said. "Don't let it touch you."

Ramiro frowned. What was she talking about? The Northerner rushed them again, and this time the madman adjusted as they attempted to evade him. The girl went one way, and Ramiro found himself pressed against a hut, using his sword to keep the man at a distance. He parried a blow from the stick, and a pulse tingled down the length of his sword into his hands, making them sting. His grip on the hilt loosened as his fingers locked in a spasm. What sort of magic was this?

His sword dropped from numb hands.

Angry shouts came from behind the row of huts. "There he is! That's the one! Kill him."

Ramiro took his eye off the madman long enough to see Suero and two of his cronies bearing down on them. They had murder in their eyes, and it wasn't directed at him. Suero held Salvador's sword. The madman paused in the middle of a swipe at Ramiro to turn and confront the new threat.

"Don't!" Claire shouted in warning.

One of Suero's friends lunged at the madman with his knife. The Northerner turned sideways and brought up the rod, touching a bare spot above the villager's shirt. The villager went rigid, every muscle tensed, and he dropped as limp as the inside of a cracked egg, his eyes open and staring. The gentle rain made the only sound.

"*Mierda.*" Ramiro fumbled for the dagger at his belt as his hands regained feeling. Suero and his remaining companion backed away, fear replacing anger on their faces.

A tide of buzzing hornets surrounded Ramiro. He brushed frantically at his face, then shook his head. It wasn't real.

The girl.

Claire stood across the road, head high and shoulders back as she sang. Her damp hair was slicked to her head. Suero and his friend jumped and danced, fighting an invisible threat. Not everyone was affected, though. Ramiro froze. The madman absentmindedly touched the closest man with his stick, sending him to the ground, and walked toward the girl.

Without thinking, Ramiro surged forward. Somehow he crossed the road and got in front of Claire. Before he could bring up his knife to throw, the madman planted his white stick right in the center of Ramiro's wet breastplate. A hum filled his ears. Every nerve ending in his body tried to jump out of his skin. His muscles locked, and pain exploded through his very bones. As quick as it surged through him, though, it vanished, leaving him rubbery and weak as a new-born.

Claire sobbed behind him. He'd lost everyone he cared about; he wasn't about to lose the witch girl, too. He forced his eyes open.

"For Colina Hermosa!" Ramiro brought down his dagger, right into the madman's hand. The man shouted in astonishment, dropping his stick. Ramiro pushed, sending the Northerner to the ground. Suero swarmed forward and thrust Salvador's blade though the madman's back, pinning him to the dirt.

Ramiro forced his legs to support him; now was not the time for weakness. Tense, he held the dagger before him as Suero drew the sword free. The villager had the better weapon, but Suero was unarmored. Ramiro felt weak as a newborn kid, while Suero was uninjured. He hoped it would be a fair match.

"You left me to die, coward," Ramiro said between gritted teeth.

"You harbor a *sirena*, city man," Suero shouted.

"It doesn't change the fact that you *left me to die*."

"We do what we must to survive, city man. I'm not a trained warrior like you." His words grated on Ramiro, and yet he knew Bromisto's father would never be swayed from whatever lies he'd already convinced himself of. As he accepted that disgusting truth, the village leader pointed to the white rod. "What was that? How did he kill my men with that thing?"

Ramiro shook his head. "I don't know, but I'm taking it. Do you intend to stop me?" He wanted that awful weapon to show his father. Having it could turn the tide of the war.

Suero spat. "Take it and welcome. That makes us even. Take it, and don't come back."

"And our bargain."

Suero shook Salvador's sword. "This is mine. I'll keep the bargain. I'll take your city people to safety. Hide them for you. You look for a way to stop these beardless men?"

"Yes."

"Then luck follow you, *ciudad* man. You'll need it." Suero turned and strode for the swamp, leaving his dead without a second glance.

"Saints take you," Ramiro muttered, "and protect the people under your care." God knows Suero wasn't going to risk anything to protect them himself.

The girl stood clutching her braid. "You saved me," she said. "My magic didn't work on him, and you protected me."

Ramiro walked across the road to fetch his sword, trying not to stumble or collapse. Every muscle in his body ached. The smell of burned hair drifted out from his armor; the rain was cool on his face. "Aye," he managed to say. "Thanks to your warning."

"It didn't kill you," she said.

He tapped his breastplate and bent gingerly to pick up his blade. "I think it was the metal. Don't feel too sad. It certainly was plenty painful."

"I didn't . . . you are not what my mother said. She said men were evil."

"Is that a compliment? Thanks?" He turned as slowly as if he'd aged twenty years, and the girl stood right in front of him. Her odd blue eyes were narrowed and ready to split rocks. Had he saved her because it was his mission?

No—it went deeper than that now. He might not want to believe it, but his people's laws weren't just words on paper. They reflected the only way it made sense to live with others . . . even witches.

"Teresa said it. We're *sangre* kin," he said. "Blood kin. Our lives are tied together." He felt it now. A strange connection that made her fate and his joined. She was his responsibility whether she could save his city or not. "And as I said: I'll not let them kill anyone else."

The tension in her face lessened. "I'll go with you to your city. I want to see it for myself. Decide for myself whether my mother was right or wrong."

A smile tugged at the corners of his mouth, and even that hurt. "It's a bargain."

CHAPTER 26

The swamp's trees and brush pressed close to the edge of the road. Drizzle made the thoroughfare into one long mud hole. Ramiro's toes squelched in his socks when he stepped. His boots had succumbed to the inevitable and lost their waterproofing. It irritated him, but his mother had been right about the number of socks he would need. That, and having to leave his armor behind to make better time had him in a fine mood.

He scowled at the cloudy sky. The rainy season had to start now? As if there wasn't enough water.

Without Sancha, the walk would take more than three days—much too long—but it would be even longer if he doubled back for the mare. He only hoped Teresa would forgive him for leaving her behind. It wasn't really an option, no matter the promise he'd made to her. They'd need all the speed they could squeeze from tired legs, backtracking wouldn't help, and three people on one horse would never work. For that matter, a man in armor on foot was hardly swift. He'd kept his breastplate and helmet and discarded the rest in the village—another unintended present for that cheat, Suero, along with both his bows.

I'll come back for all of them, he thought. Teresa *and* my things.

In the meantime, they'd helped themselves to food and water and an oiled tarp that the witch girl currently held over her head. Torn, scraped, and filthy, they looked little better than beggars. By the saints, all they lacked were alms bowls though somehow the girl managed to keep her oddly pale hands and face clean.

She hummed happily to herself as she walked, chewing on a piece of jerky. Ramiro was starting to wonder if her tune was magic directed at causing his black mood. He could have told her to save her breath. She couldn't make him feel any worse.

He had the witch for Colina Hermosa but had lost everything else, and to top it off, they wouldn't arrive in time. Sometimes your best wasn't good enough.

At the ambush, he'd used his head, making a plan instead of reacting. Things had worked out only marginally better than when he'd followed his gut. His bad judgment had sent Sancha away. Maybe Salvador's advice didn't help him because he just wasn't smart enough. Maybe he—

"I saw a bear once," Claire said.

He turned to stare at the girl, suddenly wondering if she was simple-minded.

"You look grumpier." She gave a little skip. "I'd hate to see you when you don't get your way if this is your idea of happy."

"I have much on my mind."

She sniffed. "What's to think about? We go as fast as we can and get there when we get there. No sense in borrowing trouble, my mother would say."

He shook his head. "It is not your city about to be burned or your family put to death by a devastating *army!*" His voice rose until he was shouting by the last word. "We'll never make it in time. And would it matter if we did? I thought the witches could turn the tide, but what you told Teresa before was right: You can only do so much. That mad Northerner in the village wasn't even affected by your magic. And it looks like they have magic of their own. I've been on a fool's errand that cost me my brother, my friends, and now, possibly, my city."

"But we may still help. You don't know anything is over until it's actually over," Claire said. "And even then, there's still hope."

"Hope." Contempt dripped from the word.

"Yes—hope. Like maybe we can turn their magic against them," she said, pointing at his bag.

He looked over at it. The white stick of the madman lay at the bottom of his pack. They had thrown two blankets over the thing before he could bring himself to pick it up. His muscles still ached from whatever it had done to him.

"A frog can only jump so high. A bee can only fly so far. And a fox can only run so fast."

He gaped at her, hands curling into fists, and had to turn away before he shook her. "That . . . what does that mean? I thought I was getting a weapon to stop the Northerners. Instead, I got a silly girl." Mud splattered as he stomped up the road.

She tromped after him. "I'm not a silly girl! And you! My mother told me of your culture. You don't deserve a beard! You should shave it off!" She wrapped the tarp around her head like a shawl. Tears stood in her eyes. "Attacking me because you're lost. You act like a child!"

"Then why are you following me!"

"I don't know!"

To his horror, she burst into sobs. Ramiro put his hands over his eyes and dug for calm. Saints, help him. She'd only been trying to help. "You're right," he said softly. When she didn't respond, he rubbed at his beard and straightened. "You're right," he said louder. "I was acting like a spoiled child and not a man. I apologize. I spoke in wrath."

Her chin trembled, but she no longer cried. The tears left her eyes bright as sapphires. She was small and depended on him, and he'd treated her ill for it. "It made *perfect* sense," she muttered, and he realized she was talking about her silly aphorism. "You're just too dense to get it."

The sad truth was, though, he didn't think she was

wrong: He might just be too dense to understand *any-thing* that was going on. *It was never supposed to be me!* Salvador was supposed to lead him. He would know what to do. Teresa could have talked to the girl like a friend. Alvito could have charmed her. Gomez was the peacemaker. Salvador would have gotten them home in time.

Her saying might make perfect sense, but his world right now made none at all.

To his surprise, she nodded. "I'm lost, too."

He scowled. "I'm not lost. I know exactly where we are."

Claire tossed her braid back and rolled her eyes. "Deny it all you want, but it won't get better until you admit it. Maybe then you can do something about it." She took a firmer grip on the tarp. "I'm a good runner. Probably faster than you. Shall I prove it? We'll make better time."

"There's no sense in exhausting yourself. It's still going to take us over three days. I know what you're trying to do, but it won't help." By his count it had been six days since he had left Colina Hermosa. Even if his father managed to stall and gain extra days, they still wouldn't make it in time on foot.

Claire took off down the road in a sprint before he finished the sentence, the tarp flapping.

He sprang after her in full pursuit regardless of his soggy feet. "I'm not letting you win just because you're a girl."

She turned enough to stick out her tongue and hurried on. Ramiro shook his head, mud flying from his feet. Why had he ever thought the girl reserved or shy? More important:

What had he gotten himself into?

By late afternoon, they were back to walking. The mud and drizzle had dried up, and the sun had appeared to ramp up the heat and swallow the humidity. They'd left the swamp behind and returned to drier grassland. The meadows and wildflowers seemed to fascinate the girl. She'd stared at them for hours, plucking some for a bouquet, which she eventually discarded. Even their weight was troublesome with all the walking still to do. At this time of year, darkness would not arrive for many hours yet.

Ramiro strode along the dry road, grateful for the repeated drills Salvador had put them through. The girl, however, trailed him with drooping shoulders and heavy feet until she caught him looking, then her pace increased.

"We'll stop at nightfall for a few hours' rest," he told her.

Claire shrugged, but already-pale skin was white with exhaustion. "I can go as long as you," she said. He could read the lie in her body, though.

Such dogged determination was admirable—or stupid. She obviously couldn't stand to appear weak before him. He let her catch up, then said, "I'm not lost. I know exactly where we are. And I'm not lost in the way you mean either. I have a mission, a task from the leader of my city. It sustains me."

"If you say so. I can see that you're not worried—and haven't been dwelling on it for half the day. We're just walking until it's dark for the joy of it." She hooked her thumbs in the loops of her filthy skirt that she wore over equally dirty trousers. "My mother told me when times are troubled, the values you hold in here"—she touched her chest—"will see you through. My mother was not one to worry."

Ramiro smiled. "My mother does nothing but worry and fret. It's draining, but my feet will be dry tonight because of it. Extra socks, you know."

She looked at him without understanding, and he laughed. "An inside joke," he explained. His mirth died as he remembered Salvador wasn't here to share it with him.

"A soldier doesn't lose his place, doesn't get lost," he told her. "A soldier has orders to follow. I was forgetting that. I merely have to get you to the *Alcalde* of Colina Hermosa as fast as I may. Protect you from the Northerners like . . ." His eye lit upon a pink coneflower. "A delicate and fragile flower."

Her chin rose. "You have that backward. It is I who protect you and your . . ." She waved her hand. "Fragile and delicate stink."

"You stink just—" He froze. The hair on the back of his neck stood up as it had in the village. Again he felt the sense of someone watching his back. "We're not alone," he whispered. "Off the road. Into the tall grass."

She squeaked as he grabbed her and half dragged her into the giant saw grass lining the road. The tall blades swayed well over his head. It was stifling as the breeze couldn't reach down inside the thick mass, and all was still and silent, except for the girl's panting breath.

"What happened?" she asked in a whisper.

"There's . . ." How did he explain something that only existed as a nagging feeling? And since when did such feelings come to him? For all he knew, it was his imagination and nothing more. "This way."

Ramiro edged through the saw grass; it slid from his shoulders, giving way to him. Below the level of the road, the roots thrived in a wet bog. Already his boots that had begun to dry were soaked again.

The grass concealed, but it also blinded. He could only hope his path ran parallel to the road. Claire stumbled along behind him, sometimes catching his arm for balance, muttering under her breath. He held up his hand to shush her and followed his gut.

A wearisome time later, they paused among the grass, hot and sweating. Ramiro sank to a crouch. The girl copied him. He peered through a gap in the grasses to spy on a squad of Northerners in black and yellow, blockading the road on a wide wooden bridge. Less than a full platoon, they still numbered a good fifty men, and they'd chosen an exemplary spot. A marshy slough covered the other side of the road, allowing a sight line for miles, while a stream passed under the bridge, bisecting their side of the road, dividing the growth of saw grass. They would have to detour a long way to escape the superior vantage point of the Northerners.

The beardless men worked on erecting tents, stacking dry wood, and building cook fires on both ends of the bridge. They were here to stay.

"How did you know?" Claire whispered, puzzled.

"I didn't," he said absently, gripping the medallion of San Martin. Was it a miracle or something else? Maybe the saints interfered to save Colina Hermosa. Or maybe he'd gained a little of his mother's family Sight as he suspected Salvador had. Either way, he didn't want to discuss it with the girl. Her eyes regarded him suspiciously. "I guessed."

None of her doubt vanished. "How did you know they'd be here and not closer to the village?"

"It was just a hunch. They've blockaded all the other roads we use. They discovered we used this one. Now, can we talk about how to get around them?" He rose from his crouch, still keeping low, and led her deeper into the grass. "Can you use your magic to get us through them?"

She shook her head, sweat glistening in the fair strands of her hair. "I can't just march us straight up the road and make them not see us. They're already watching."

"So? You made me not see you."

"No, I didn't. I made you *panicked* so you weren't looking in the right place."

"And that won't work here?"

"I can make them panic, but they'll question why. The magic just doesn't work that way. It can't make people unsee things or forget. In your case, you were already doubting yourself—I just played on that." She rubbed at her chin. "Let me think."

He nodded, trusting her assessment. If she said it couldn't be done that way, then it couldn't. The tops of the saw grass rustled softly as he waited, giving her time. She stood as still as one of the statues of a plaza fountain, hand curled in a fist against her mouth, frowning blindly at it. She looked deceptively soft. He knew now she was anything but. The girl had as much determination as he—and more bravery. Could he set aside everything he knew to put himself in the hands of a stranger?

With a start, he realized he was doing it right this moment.

"The creek is the best choice, don't you think?" she asked. "I mean, the grass grows close to it, so if we cross, we could get right back to cover—and the running water will help. We'd only be in the open as we wade across."

"Yes," he agreed. "But it's wide. Ten yards at least. Can you get them looking the other way?"

"I can." She frowned. "But that would tip them off as much as panicking them or using the hornet song. They'd end up chasing us."

"We're too tired for that," he agreed.

"I can try . . . I mean, I think I can make them see something else, though. Deer. I can try to make them see deer. It could work. Or not."

"Which?" he asked. "Work or not work?"

She shrugged.

That seemed to be all the answer she had. "Why running water?" he asked. "You said that would help?"

Surprisingly, she flushed. "I think it will help. I've . . . I've never used it before. Mother said running water will help carry the sound of the Song. We won't have to get as close." She looked at the sky. "And luckily the rain has stopped. Rain washes out the magic."

He considered her as she gave him a weak little smile. She didn't sound very certain about any of it. Get caught, and they were as good as dead. He'd seen what the Northerners did to spies. His mother would say bypass around. Salvador would likely agree. The risk was too high versus the reward of saving a few miles. In this, however, he must take after his father. If the girl was to prove of any value, she had to be used and tested. Every second shaved off their journey might be important.

She had no confidence. By San Martin, he'd have to have the confidence for both of them. "We try it."

"We do?" She blinked. "I mean, we do. Yes. I can throw them off . . . I think."

What would his father do? Ramiro caught her chin with a finger and lifted her eyes to his. "You can and you will. Let's go." He released her.

"Now?" she said weakly.

"Now." He turned and edged through the grass to get closer to the stream, hearing her follow. No sense in making it harder on the girl. He led them upstream a distance to hopefully make her deception easier and give the Northerners less to see. "Is this spot good?"

Claire nodded, and a wordless hum rose from her throat. It cast no pictures in his mind, made him see no shadows, even when she added words to it. Words that teased at his brain, but which he couldn't understand. Perhaps because he expected the magic, she'd said something about its not working then. Nothing changed about him, but she nodded to indicate she was ready. He stepped from the saw grass and into the stream.

Slow and steady, he lifted his knees high, picking his way across the streambed of stones. Just a deer, unhurried as it crosses shallow water. As the singing girl followed, copying his movements, he froze like a surprised animal and looked directly at the Northerner encampment on the bridge. Ramiro held his breath. What were the odds they had bows, and he might turn out to be a freak surprise instead of a piece of meat for their cook fires?

But the men bustled about, ignoring them. One of the lookouts turned in their direction, lifting his hand in a yawn. Another man joined him and they stared directly toward their spot in the stream.

Ramiro started forward again, trying to keep his pace lazy and unafraid—a wild thing who seldom saw a man.

Shouts came from the bridge. Ramiro's heart leaped.

Discovered.

But when he turned to look, he saw a big gray horse among the soldiers. Sancha! A Northerner shouted in their gruff language, the meaning clear: catch it.

Sancha reared and screamed, fending them off with her waving forelegs. Men with hands held up backed away, frightened of sharp hooves. She flashed between them like mist, a fleeting shadow as she dashed up the road. A last man dived for her trailing reins but missed.

Ramiro darted into the tall grass across the stream, pulling Claire with him. Somehow, she managed to hold her tune. "Hurry," he urged her, running parallel to the road after his horse. Sancha must have broken free from Teresa somehow. The girl clung to his hand. He gave it a squeeze. "You did well, Claire."

If they'd backtracked around the bridge, they'd never have learned Sancha was here. The saints favored them today. And that same hair-raising feeling now told him Sancha would come for his whistle once out of the Northerners' earshot.

Maybe luck did favor them after all.

CHAPTER 27

Amid the buzz of a thousand voices, Julian climbed the steps to the pulpit of the largest cathedral in Colina Hermosa. Behind him, the *concejales* waited at the altar under the center of the high, curved apse dome. The altar statuary embossed in gold and silver and painted in bright colors rose up three stories on the wall, depicting images of the greatest saints. A full-figure representation of Santiago clasping a book was placed front and center, directly above the high altar. San Martin with his cloak, sword, and staff was nearby. To the right, Santa Margarita waited with her girdle and a lamb at her feet. With their shoulders firm and faces serious as the saints above them, the seven elderly men of the *concejales* portrayed a confidence none felt.

People spilled from the nave into the aisles, jam-packed together on the wooden benches, children sitting on parents' laps. Brought from substantial distances, the wood of the long benches was priceless. Private pews reserved for a single wealthy family now contained more life than they'd seen in three generations. Additional people inhabited the second-story choir loft and crowded the ancient doors, where the last rays of the setting sun edged inside, casting long shadows. People spilled all the way down the marble steps to fill the square. A group of priests and the Bishop stood in the north transept, the only ones granted an inch of space in the thick press of bodies. Side chapels overflowed, men shoulder to shoulder with the tombs of long-dead clergy. Even the lower sections of the altar held bystanders, eager for news. It was how the news would be received that Julian couldn't predict.

Beatriz waited for him at the foot of the lectern, touching mind, heart, liver, and spleen as Julian cleared his throat and gestured for quiet. The buzz of voices died to stillness, except for the lone cry of a baby, quickly hushed. He stared out at a sea of expectant faces, light from candles casting an uneven glow over all.

"Our city faces a time like none other," Julian began. "Today is a day to speak only truths, no matter how painful they be. Regardless of the outcome, Colina Hermosa will never be the same. Many of us will perish. But perhaps a core will remain to carry our values forward. The time given us to decide ends tomorrow.

"The Northern terms have been posted in every church for all to see. The *concejales* have been among you to seek your thoughts. The priests have spoken with you also. This unprovoked enemy would have us turn over many of our fellow citizens—men, women, and children—to be killed. They demand we open wide the doors of Colina Hermosa to them. Insist we give up anything *they* consider weapons. Maintain we eliminate our government for theirs. Forsake our very God and the saints who guide us for their bloodthirsty heathen idol!

"They would leave us hanging by a thread. Subject to their power and control. Helpless before any further demands. Powerless to their whims. And they would have this for as long as we live—as long as our children's children live."

Mutters rose and died.

"We can take their terms and live like this. Become like the dead for a chance at a broken life. Their alternative—to be burned along with our city. Already their siege machines have been moved forward in preparation." He dropped his head to tap the contained flame that burned in the core of his heart. "Can we trust the word of an enemy that kills *helpless children!*" he shouted.

From every direction he was met with cries of, "No!"

Julian paused, fighting the lump in his throat. Fear controlled many faces in the crowd, but determination ran through the sacred house in a wave as men climbed to their feet. Pride burned strong in his chest. He knew his people would never accept these terms.

Everywhere he'd gone over the last days, he'd heard the same response.

When the talk died and all who could were seated, he resumed, "So feel the *concejales*. They have voted unanimously to reject the Northern terms." He turned to indicate the councilmen. "But we will not wait for our city to be burned with its folk inside. Our saints did not sit quietly at home when their faith was questioned. They lived their convictions! For us! They sacrificed for us!

"We are men! We are the people of Colina Hermosa! We will make our own destiny! We fight as San Martin did!"

Now they leaped to their feet. A roar spread from wall to wall, traveling out the door and into the square as his words were relayed.

He met Beatriz's worried eyes, and the flame in his heart flickered. His people would stand against the threat. Grievously outnumbered, they would fight. Blood would run. Colina Hermosa would . . . fall. Buildings, businesses, homes—a way of life would perish. Thank the saints his sons were not here. Only in their absence could he keep his head high and force a brave mask for his people's eyes. He willed his knees straight. A core of a core could survive.

"I am an uncomplicated man." The people quieted, taking their seats again. "A merchant. A politician. A father. A husband. It pains me that we are called to leave simplicity and our pleasant lives behind. The Lord forgive me, I want to stay a simple man. I do not

look for violence. But today, there is no other course."
He looked behind him at the *concejales.* "Butchers must
take up blades. Millers must reach for staves. Land-
owners their shovels. Merchants put down their coin
and trust to knives. As a last chance in our final hours.

"Because *we are* honorable, a messenger will go to
the Northerners at dawn to reject their terms." He
very carefully kept his face forward and away from
his wife. "Then our plan will go into action. While
the gate guard and others fight at the west gates, sections of our walls, far from the fighting, will go down.
With our tunnels collapsed, we will destroy our own
wall to get the innocents out. They will be guided and
protected by the members of my *pelotón,* the council's
pelotón, and those of the city and church."

All eyes turned to the back of the building where the
capitanes of each *pelotón* stood like silent beacons with
their shining armor in the vestibule near the doors.
Lieutenant Muño represented Salvador. With crossed
arms or hands on sword hilts, the soldiers nodded.

"The people will take to the hills, go to the swamp,
hide themselves from our enemies," Julian said from
the lectern. "They will try to reach Crueses and find
safety there. Those who go will carry only their children and their elderly and sick. Take nothing but food
that can fit in your pockets or weapons to guard lives.
Take no weight of property because the *pelotón* will not
wait for those who are slow or those who straggle. We
are spread thin; the protection must remain with the
larger group. The priests of every section of the city

can direct you on where to be in the morning." Julian focused on the gilt-embossed wall and frescoes above the great doors as he touched mind, heart, liver, and spleen. "God go with you."

"For the rest with the heart to give their lives so others have time to escape, your district priests can direct you to where you are needed." The core of flame inside Julian burned blue with heat. He would not be there to see any of it. Father Telo had taken his place once—not again. He had a duty above all others.

"Sharpen your swords. Feed your anger. Grease your bowstrings. Hate must be met with hate when the day rises. Fire can burn flesh and topple buildings, but it cannot destroy the spirit. The saints watch over us. The Lord is our guide. Colina Hermosa stands as long as one of us breathes. For love of our families!"

"For love of honor!"

"For love of Colina Hermosa!"

Julian saw it all in his mind's eye: the white buildings coming to life at sunrise, the splash of the fountains where the women met to gossip, the scent and taste of cigars while conversing with friends after a heavy dinner party. All these spelled home.

"For love of Colina Hermosa!" echoed from every throat. Men, women, even tiny children stood to scream their love for their home.

Julian turned and made his way from the lectern, his legs weak. Members of the *Alcalde's pelotón* cordoned him off from the multitude before they could rush to question him. Inside that area of calm, Beatriz waited to clasp him tight. Her lips trembled. "And so we make our last stand, *mi amor*," he whispered. "Now and forever."

A tear spilled over and slid down her cheek. "Last stand. A glorious one, thanks to you. Now and forever."

He shook his head to deny her praise, and a messenger boy in the gate guard uniform of solid gray pushed to his side. "*Alcalde* Alvarado!" the boy hollered in a high voice. "*Alcalde* Alvarado, they ask for you at the gate!"

Concejales Diego and Pedro pushed their way to his side, their own guards trailing. "What does this mean?" Pedro asked. The gray-haired miller clasped his thick hands. "Has something gone wrong? Have the Northerners struck early?"

Julian swung back to question the messenger, but the boy had already wiggled his way into the crowd. "We must go find out."

With the help of a deacon and their guards, they navigated the crowd and squeezed out a back door, across the grounds, and through an arched, wrought-iron gate. The people needed to speak with their priests now anyway and not him. There was no more he could tell them; additional talk might undo the speech he'd just made.

The sunset made a blaze of reds, pinks, and corals across the sky. A few blocks' worth of walking took them to where carriages waited. Pedro got into Diego's as Julian helped Beatriz into their coach. "To the gate," Julian called to his coachman.

"*Mi amor,* shall Carlos take you home after he drops me off? There's no attack, or the bells would be ringing. It's probably some tedious business about who goes where tomorrow." He closed the door and sat beside her on the leather bench.

Beatriz leaned away from the back of her seat, plucking at the lace of her black skirt. "I stay with you. Can't you feel it? Something is wrong. Very wrong. And it has been building for days, getting closer."

"It is the stress of tomorrow, *mi corazón.* We have tonight until the seven days ends. The Northerners will hold to it. I saw it in their eyes. It is their way. In the morning, you will be on your way with the evacuees to find our sons."

"And you? You will be with me."

"I must set an example for the people, mustn't I?" he said evasively. "We will always be together, you and I. The Lord will see it so."

"I hope you are right." Her tone said clearly that he wasn't.

She slipped her hand into his, and he frowned. She was ice-cold, not her usual chilly. A shiver traveled down his spine as the carriage turned a corner onto the main avenue. In minutes, Carlos pulled the horses up, so they could climb down at the entrance to the gate courtyard. As he turned on the coach steps to give Beatriz his help, apprehension grew. Too many men filled the yard. Men who should have been resting off duty.

Soldiers in gray uniforms made way for them, and Julian did not care for the pity on their faces. Beatriz breathed like she'd been running—an activity he hadn't seen from her in forty years, since they were children together, and she wanted to beat him to dessert at her father's table.

"What has happened?" he demanded.

A gate sergeant hurried over to them. "It just appeared outside, *Alcalde* Alvarado. First Wife. We let it in." The man gestured at the gate.

A tall *caballo de guerra* pranced restlessly in front of the great doors, rearing when any of the men crowded around it tried to lay a hand on it. Unsaddled and unbridled, flecks of white foam covered its dappled-gray hide. Its eyes rolled, showing its near panic.

"Oh no," Beatriz gasped in a moan. Julian didn't feel her release his arm.

"It brought . . ." the sergeant began. He stepped back to reveal a man-shaped form covered by blankets, prone on the cobblestones in the center of the courtyard. "I'm sorry, sir."

With a stab of pain, Julian's heart seized and went still in his chest. Another throb of agony, and it resumed beating.

Beatriz had already started forward, a keening wail rising from her. The sound traveled to him as from a thousand miles' distance. The long lace dangling from the combs in her hair shook as if in an earthquake.

"It may not be," Julian said. "Many *pelotón* forces are outside the walls."

Beatriz paused long enough to show him her tear-stained face. "Don't you think a mother recognizes her own child?" She knelt by the blanketed form. "Oh, Salvador." She sobbed.

Julian's feet moved him forward of their own accord, taking him to the dead man. He bent, hand reaching, reaching and shaking too badly to lift the blanket. With a lunge, he managed to pull back a corner to stare at the brown curls of his eldest son, a little messy as if he'd been sleeping. Eyes closed and face solemn and motionless, Salvador did appear asleep. He'd always been a heavy sleeper as a child, able to fall off the bed without waking.

The courtyard spun until only that still face and Beatriz's sobs appeared real. A hand squeezed his shoulder. Pedro.

"Someone fetch my wife and daughters," the old miller instructed. "The First Wife will need women about her now."

"A miracle they got through," the sergeant said to Diego. "The warhorse let us take off the body. It drank, then the creature went crazy when we tried to groom it. None of us can touch it."

Julian lifted dry eyes to regard the horse. Valentía. His son's partner and pride and joy. Valentía spun, kicking his heels dangerously. Gratitude swelled in Julian's breast. The horse had given him final hours with his son before the end.

"Let it out," he said, voice cracking.

"Sir?" the sergeant asked.

"Open the gate," Julian directed. "Let it free to die as it wishes."

Men scrambled to follow his orders. The great bronze gates creaked open just wide enough for the horse. Valentía turned to look at his master, then the stallion disappeared in a flash. Men slammed the gates with the thud of a tomb closing.

Julian could give no thought to how or why it had returned here. He cared not what had happened, grief consumed him. Soldiers began placing candles around the body as if they lay in state in a church. Julian sidled around his son's body to capture Beatriz in his arms. She clung, face pressed into his shoulder, as though nothing could part them. Now and forever. But one thing would—

The first light of morning.

CHAPTER 28

Claire didn't know which made her more uncomfortable: riding for a day with him behind her or when he walked ahead of her like this, leading the horse. Most of the time they rode double, his chin just above her head, and his chest pressed all too close to her back, a patch of burning heat she couldn't escape. Occasionally he demanded they rest the horse he called Sancha and got down on foot, leaving her to ride and giving her a perfect view of his short brown hair above a tanned neck, the width of his shoulders and how they tapered down to a slim waist, and long legs sheathed in knee-high boots. The soldiers back at the village wore such boots, but the sight of them hadn't made her quivery inside like blackberry jam.

Was this the feeling of friendship? Somehow, she didn't think so. It was too tingly and scary at the same time. And it wasn't as if she felt any affinity toward him, any special closeness. She just . . . liked how he *was*. Her mother had never explained this sort of sensation. Perhaps it was due to lack of sleep. Ramiro pushed them, hardly allowing a few hours' rest. Maybe she was simply too tired to feel angry at him.

"It'll be dark soon," he said. "Best we get this over with now before we can't see." He barely finished speaking before dropping the reins and attacking the buckles on his side, loosening one section of his armor protection.

Her eyes widened. What was he doing? "Get what over?"

The armor dropped to the ground, and he pulled his shirt over his head in one smooth motion. A squeak popped from her throat. The parts of him hidden by the sun were almost as brown as the rest of him. He was lean and muscled both at the same time, smooth except for the hair in the middle of his chest that ran down to his navel and into his trousers. She ripped her eyes away, focusing on her hands twisting in her dirty skirt.

"Get down. I'll need your help."

"My help?" she said stupidly. Her mother told her that after meeting her father there was a short courtship, followed by a ceremony in a church. There was no church here in the middle of nowhere. They didn't even follow any road but some long-abandoned trail. Was taking off your clothes courtship?

Just like with the magic, her mother should have given her more details. She had mentioned that some men took what they wanted and didn't bother with ceremonies. Was Ramiro one of those? Would she have to hurt him just when she had started to accept him?

As if he didn't see her sitting there petrified, like a dead stump, he bustled over and rummaged through his saddlebag, handing her a tiny, cunningly made glass jar and one of the waterskins. "Hurry up. Get down," he demanded. "We're losing the light."

The horse twitched an ear like it expected her compliance also.

Ramiro seized her around the waist and slid her down from the horse until she stood crushed between them, his chest in her face. The smell of leather and sweat and male overwhelmed her, masking the smell of horse. She tried to look away, but he caught her chin. "Are you sick?" he asked, turning her face from one side to another. "You don't look well."

"What do you want?" she croaked out.

"Help with this." He released her chin and twisted about to show her his broad back. An old wound and a new one broke the clean surface of his skin. "I can't reach it."

"Oh." Heat mounted into her face until she wondered she didn't burst into flames.

He leaned closer. "What did you think I wanted?"

Why didn't the ground swallow her up?

"N-n-nothing," she stammered. "I just—where I come from, we don't take off our clothes in front of strangers."

"It's only my shirt." A smile crinkled the corners of

his eyes. "And we're hardly strangers now. We're *sangre* kin. A good thing you're not around my *pelotón*. They would give you something to blush about." He backed up a few steps to give her room.

"Well, um . . . there . . ." She cleared her throat, feeling strangely lonely. "There aren't any men where I come from. There aren't really any people where I come from. Just goats."

"So I understand." He went and sat on a rock, turning his back to her. "You know how to clean an injury? Don't use too much water. We'll need it."

"The goats tear themselves on branches sometimes. My mother treated them, but I watched."

"Close enough, I suppose." He turned his neck to look at her. "Well?"

She hurried forward and set down the little glass jar. It must contain some ointment under the cork that sealed it. There was nothing to be done for the old injury; it was well scabbed over, the skin around it clean and healed, though it would leave an interesting scar. The new appeared shallow, like the point of a sword had torn the skin only. Not much worse than one of Dolly's injuries. It had stopped bleeding some time ago.

Lifting the waterskin, she poured just enough water over it to wet it and looked around for something to rub it with. The hem of her dress was dirtier than her hands. She bit her lip, then forced herself to touch him, sluicing away the dried blood. His skin was smooth. The sensation heated her face all over again. Thank the Song, he couldn't see her this time.

She pulled the cork from the bottle and dabbed the honey-smelling mixture across the small cut. Maybe she put more than strictly needed just to avoid having to be done and resume talking to him—and to give her face a chance to cool down—not because she enjoyed touching him.

"We should be near the tunnel leading to my home by first light," he said. "Thanks to Sancha."

The horse had its head down to nose at the sandy ground. Claire gave Ramiro another dab of ointment and looked around for something to use as a bandage. "Good."

"How do you like the desert?"

By the Song. She had hardly noticed, too caught up in looking at him or her own thoughts about her lack of understanding of the magic. Why hadn't Mother told her more? It would have been so useful now on her own. Claire didn't like the feeling of bitterness welling up, so instead she looked around at the landscape, paying attention as she should have done before. The land was dry enough to instantly swallow up all the drops of water she'd spilled and hot enough to quickly evaporate the ones on his skin. The plants were all leafless and spiny.

"I don't see how we can travel in the dark," she said, glad to revert to a practical matter. She corked the bottle and retrieved a clean sock from the saddlebag of the patiently waiting horse, then pressed it to the wound. The thick smear of honey captured and held it. "You're right. These extra socks are handy, but I don't think it will stay."

"Leave it," he said. "It'll be fine. He stood, drawing on his shirt, and she felt a pang of disappointment. "It will be slow and tricky at night. We'll have to really stick to the path, but I think we can manage. I'll have to lead Sancha, but you can ride. Wouldn't want you tripping straight into a barrel cactus."

She frowned at the jibe and gave it up. He probably had a point. The needle spines all around her looked far from pleasant. Besides, she was eager to see his city—any city actually—but maybe more eager to have people around and no longer be alone with him. Despite nervousness about meeting others, these feelings did not belong. They were too different. He was a man, after all. Her mother had warned her over and over that feelings were weak. Not to be depended upon because men couldn't be depended on.

"Why are you going with me?" he asked, shaking her out of her thoughts. "We're an unlikely pair. Not that I mind, I mean. I mean, I'm happy you decided to come . . . home with me. I . . . my city . . . really needs you."

She stared. He was babbling, just as uncertain as she. "I've always longed to see new things. Make a friend. A girl—my age—as a friend," she added, lest he misunderstand and think she meant him.

He shrugged. "Don't get your hopes up. Witches are a story to frighten children where I'm from. They're more likely to run."

"Teresa didn't run."

"Teresa isn't your typical woman." He thought for

a second. "There is one I can introduce you to, though. She's solid and dependable, caring and sweet. Fronilde would be glad to meet you." He went to stand by his horse, waiting to give her a boost to the saddle.

Dummy. Of course he had a girl. Probably several girls. Why was she even bothering with this—by the Song, why did she even care? He had saved her life, but he'd also been part of the reason her mother was dead. Hard-hearted common sense, practical: those were the qualities she needed. She couldn't be a gullible rube who'd never seen or done anything. And yet she couldn't help it . . .

"Your sweetheart?" she said with a smile as if the answer meant nothing. She moved to the horse, stepping into his offered hand to be lifted with one easy swing from his arms.

"My brother's actually. She'll need a friend."

By the time he bent to grab the reins and draw the horse into motion, she'd scolded herself back into sense. Certain men were pleasing to look at, but such thoughts indicated nothing more. "I would be glad to be her friend. Or try. Help if I can with her and the army facing your city."

He smiled, and once more she lost all certainty as to what was happening to her.

Ramiro shook his head. With dawn an hour away, the opening to the west tunnel into Colina Hermosa gaped as a deeper darkness in the side of the hill, hidden behind a screen of tall saguaro. The darkness was to be expected to conceal the location, but not a soul was in sight. His countrymen should have greeted him by now. Something was very wrong though he felt no tingle of warning. "No guards," he whispered to the girl, drawing his sword. "There should be a squad or more." His father had kept a heavy contingent at each of the tunnels. Had the city fallen or something else occurred? "Wait here."

She slid from Sancha and stroked the horse's shoulder. "No. I'm coming, too." Suspicion tagged her voice.

"It's for your protection, not because I plan to deceive you."

"I don't need protection."

"Suit yourself." There wasn't much he could do to get her to stay other than tying her up, and that idea just felt wrong. Besides: He had seen her move, and he had to admit she was even quieter than he—maybe she could even help.

No longer foes, they weren't friends, either. Instead a wary in-between had formed. They had agreed not to kill each other, but building trust was ongoing. He respected her now at least. It might be that newfound respect that made him worry—he now actually *cared* if she might get hurt, especially if she could help the city.

"Sancha, stay here. Wait."

The mare shook herself as if she understood, and he nodded. "See. She listens. Recognizes I know what's best for her."

"She's also covered in fur and has fleas," the girl whispered. "That puts her more like you than me."

Ramiro turned at the entrance of the tunnel to stare at the silhouette of the girl. Sometimes, he respected her more than others. Right now, she was simply a pain in the ass. He *hmmphed* and choked back a smart answer as he remembered Salvador's advice to have patience with those who try you. It was hard, though—Sancha had no fleas.

If anyone did, it was Claire.

Sword in hand, he cautiously walked a few yards into the tunnel. Nothing moved. No one jumped out at them, so he groped blindly for the barrel of torches that had been against the wall.

He touched the barrel with his knee. As his vision adjusted marginally, he set aside his sword long enough to select a torch and pulled out striker and flint. Soon he had a small light established.

Everything looked the same inside the tunnel, except for the lack of guards. The support beams stood solid. The torches were as before. No sign of struggle or violence. Only a fresh scree of loose pebbles and sand covered the floor. No trace the Northerners had ever been here. He led the way as the tunnel sloped down and around in a gradual curve, sword held ready.

"And this will get us into your city without encountering the enemy soldiers?" she asked.

"Right under the Northerners and into the citadel." He frowned, lowering the flickering torch. The scree grew heavier on the floor, piling thick, where before the ground was always swept clean. The scent of dust hung thick in the air. Usually there was a slight breeze in the tunnel with air moving from one end to the other. "It feels—

They rounded a corner and came face-to-face with a wall of boulder, rock, and sand blocking the way forward. A thick, solid mass where digging would take days if not weeks, and the whole ceiling would probably come crashing down.

"—wrong," he finished.

"It collapsed?" Claire asked.

"No. It was done intentionally. A protective measure."

"Why?" she asked.

He shrugged and sheathed his unneeded sword. "I haven't a clue, but the Northerners must have learned of the tunnels." He scrubbed at his tired eyes with his free hand as disappointment rose. So close. Now stymied.

"What do we do?"

"I don't know." He turned and retraced their steps up the tunnel. He'd counted on the tunnels for access to the city. With this one gone, the others must be closed as well. The torch hissed as he plunged it back into the sand filling the bottom of the barrel. The instant darkness pinned him in place to wait for eyes to adjust.

He covered his face and drew in a deep breath, holding it. Without the tunnels, how did they get through the Northern army? It was suicide to attempt to reach the city any other way. Suicide. Even the scouts would have trouble slipping through.

The girl caught his mood and held her distance. "You said the army is before the main gate. We make for a back gate?"

He dropped his hands. "There *is* no back gate. No other gate but the west gate."

"Not a very smart way to build."

"No, probably not." He sighed. "But it always worked to our advantage before. The only other enemies we ever had were smaller *ciudades-estado*. One gate to guard allowed for better distribution of forces. We could assign fewer men to the rest of the wall." Why was he defending his city's strategy to her?

"Well, if these Northerners are all focused on the gate, couldn't we climb over in the back somewhere? With a ladder or something?"

"We have no ladder, and the wall is twenty feet high."

"Oh," she said. "So we give up?"

"No," he said, then louder, "No. Not me anyway. I'm getting closer. Try to see what's going on." Guilt prodded at him. "Perhaps you should go home. As you said, your voice can't carry to an army. You're not going to be much use."

The moonlight allowed him to see her flinch like he had struck her, then her eyes narrowed. "You're trying to protect me again, aren't you?" she huffed, then touched his arm. "I might have misled you on what the Song can do. Honestly, I'm not sure myself of its limits. I'm coming, too."

"You'll get fleas."

"I'll risk it."

CHAPTER 29

All through the long night, the candles burned down into puddles of wax and tallow on the cobblestones. Julian felt that it all happened a million miles away—to another man. It was not himself kneeling next to his dead son with his inconsolable wife.

Women had come and spent much of the vigil with Beatriz, bringing a cushion for her knees, wrapping woolen shawls around her, holding her hand in silence as she cried. A priest had visited with holy water, speaking blessing and absolution over the dead. He could console, but not comfort. And through it all, messengers had come and gone, bringing Julian details of the progress of the preparations for the morning. The morning when the evacuation must go forward whether he cared any longer or not.

Soon, before the hours of daylight, they would come for Salvador and take his son away for burial, without a wake, without a mass. A quick slide into the family tomb without even his parents present, since Beatriz had to evacuate with the others, and he had to face his fate.

People came and went in the busy courtyard around them: for meetings of strategy, preparing weapons for the morning, going to shifts of guard duty. Fronilde had appeared and mingled her sobs with Beatriz's until the heartbroken girl was taken away by her parents. Members of his son's command and other friends and family members had materialized and sat with him for a time. Relatives of Gomez and Alvito had come with questions for which they had no answers, and through it all Julian had knelt by Salvador, numb to everything else.

Gradually, over the long hours of agony, his mind had taken refuge in memories of happier times, back when his sons were young, before he became mayor. When life was simple and good. Before he'd destroyed everything.

"Do you remember," he asked Beatriz, "when Ramiro went missing after mass? How frantic we were." Ramiro had been three and Salvador a sturdy eight-year-old. How silly that day's worry seemed now. How small.

"And it was Salvador who found him, playing in a puddle just up the road," she answered with trembling voice. "I remember. Salvador had the gift from my grandmother. The Sight led him to his brother."

"A fiction," he said gruffly. If his son had the Sight, it had not served him well. "Wishful thinking from

childhood stories, fanciful histories of our people."
He'd heard them, too. Stories of the *ciudades-estado*
people a thousand years before they had cities, back
when they'd been nomadic tribes of the desert, herd-
ing their sheep and goats. Even then they had been
fiercely independent, each group sticking to their own,
traveling to oases, sharing the same beliefs and culture
but not the same leadership, sometimes warring over
water or territory.

"No," Beatriz insisted. "Not just stories. A gift—
from the Lord, before we knew his grace. The Sight has
always been an important part of us, our only means
of warning before we became lazy behind safe walls.
Before the saints performed their miracles and established cities. But that doesn't mean it was lost. Doesn't
mean that stone has blocked it out. It's still there, and
someone from my family has always had it."

"Stuff and nonsense." Julian hardly knew why they
discussed this now. In the days before saints, people
clung to superstition and the belief in small magic.
Those days were over, no longer needed. And to dwell
on it . . .

Even if Salvador *had* had it, it had not served him.
And looking at his son's body, it ended with him, too.

"My grandmother had it." Beatriz sighed. "Of this I
am sure. It skipped me. She told me I did not have the
nature. Always in my life, I would see what is before
me and not what is beyond. She predicted I would lose
myself in home and family, and there my hopes and
worries would lie."

Beatriz shifted as if her knees ached. "I'm old now, old, though not yet at the great age of my grandmother. I remembered the disappointment of that day even now. I could not see beyond, like her." She patted Julian's hand. "But discontent faded with the arrival of husband and children and many happy years."

He stiffened. Many happy years, but not enough. Never enough.

"Now we suffer the setback to so many years of joy as parents and partners," Beatriz continued. "No one escapes this world unscratched. Our time of misery has arrived. As the priests say, there is a time for joy and a time for sorrow. Truly, they comprehended how the Lord works." A tear made its way down her face. "It was the witches who did this."

Julian stirred and drew her into his arms again. How could he argue with her fatalist attitude when his own spirit was crushed? The fault was all his. Him and his risks. He'd destroyed those children with his pride and now his firstborn son. "We cannot know that. We were not there." His voice hitched, but the words would come. "Ramiro, too, could be . . . could be . . ." He choked.

Beatriz pulled away, sitting tall to stare at the wall of the courtyard. Her eyes were glazed and unfocused as if she'd had gone from him. Heartbeats later, she settled against Julian as a whisper, soft as a butterfly wing, her eyes calm. "He lives. He sent Salvador to us."

He stroked her hair, hoping to soothe her addled mind. "We can hope."

"I don't have to hope. I know. I may not have the Sight, but I know in my heart of hearts that my other son lives."

Julian gave her a long stare. She was too calm. He expected her to be out of her mind with grief, for reason to have failed her, but to invent such daydreams? Finding relief in fantasy? It was almost too much to listen to, as if he denied him his own grief with this nonsense.

And yet who was he to take what comfort she could find?

He hated to leave her like this, but time moved forward. It ripped what remained of his heart to go to his death and give her yet more sorrow. One day, she'd understand he did it for her. So she and their people could survive.

He glanced to the lightening sky, where already most of the stars had vanished. "After they take our son away, Carlos will take you home. Your maid and people of the household are waiting to go out of the city with you. I have seen to it, so you won't be alone on the trek. They will support you safely until I get there. My duty is here, to start the battle, then . . . away."

"To leave our son?" She grasped the blanket covering Salvador. "To abandon him with strangers in order to save myself? I cannot."

"You must," he said. "I cannot survive unless I know you are safe. I cannot do what has to be done thinking of you inside the city."

"Then you will meet me at the evacuation route?"

"Certainly," he said, the first time he had to so blatantly lie to her about the plan. It hurt more knowing how easily the words came off his lips. "I will be there soon. Before you can miss me."

She nodded. "That is good. Colina Hermosa cannot survive without your leadership," she said. "You are the *only* thing that keeps us going, my husband."

He took her hand and almost dropped it. "You are warm, *mi amor*." Where before her flesh had been cold as ice, now her hands were warmer than his own. His face remained impassive, but his shoulders twitched in shock. Her words had been perfectly truthful, but he sensed something behind them. "Another could manage just as well . . . if I should fall. Which I will not, as I only direct the start of the battle, then away."

"Away," she repeated hollowly. "Very well. I will see you in the hills." She kissed him tenderly. "After all, any washerwoman could take the rejection of the terms to the Northerners. A washerwoman is needed for nothing else."

He looked at her suspiciously. Did she suspect? She could not. Beatriz would never stay silent about his intended sacrifice. Before he could respond further, a handcart creaked over to them drawn by two elderly men. The priest returned with them. They had come for Salvador. A great rising tide of misery rose in his chest, his throat. He clung to Beatriz as if he could never let her go.

He kissed her face, her eyes. "*Mi amor*, we must

send our son away," he said. "We will return to him in better days. Together now and forever."

"Together," she mumbled. "Let God's will be done. It is our time of sorrow. The test of our belief. You must lead this city." Stiffly, she released Julian so he could go speak to the priest, laying her head on Salvador's chest.

The rough wool of the blanket scratched at Julian's hand as he touched his son's forehead, heart, liver, and spleen. "Be at peace, my son." Soon, he would be with Salvador, then Julian could petition the saints in person to speed his son into heaven. Julian gave the lifeless shell a last caress and touched Beatriz's shoulder, then laboriously climbed to his feet, old bones complaining.

"Father." Julian walked to the priest with hand outstretched, eager to get through this and meet his end. He would arrange the burial, then summon Carlos to take Beatriz to safety. He fought to heed the priest, mind trying to roam once more to happier days. Trying not to think ahead. The man rattled on and on with useless tired expressions that gave no comfort.

At the sound of a door booming shut, Julian spun around. Salvador's body lay alone. Beatriz was gone. A guard straightened from setting the metal bar back in place across the wicket.

"Beatriz!" he wailed in a voice that surely carried beyond the wall to the Northern camp. He ran to the gate. "What has happened?" he demanded of the two guards. "Did the First Wife go out?"

"Yes, sir." the elder said, a grizzled veteran with a

thick and tangled beard. "The First Wife said she was the envoy to the Northerners."

"Envoy? That is insane! Open the door."

The younger guard blanched white, but the older planted his spear in front of the door. "She said you would ask this. You are to stay here and lead the city . . . sir."

"Open it or I will." Julian demanded, trying to brush past them. He reached for the bar, and the guard blocked him, his face set.

"She said to tell you, you must live. That she is the washerwoman today. That she did it for Colina Hermosa, sir. The city needs you."

Julian struggled to get past them. "Beatriz!" Hands grabbed him and pulled him away. He looked up into the concerned faces of *Concejales* Antonio and Pedro and his bodyguards. He continued to thrash uselessly.

The big butcher held him firm. "It is too late, my friend."

"It is done," Pedro agreed. "Your wife has fooled us all. She intends to play the hero and spare you."

Julian dropped to his knees, grappling at his chest. A knife of pain stabbed at his heart. He couldn't breathe. That it should come to this. His love deceiving him, taking matters into her own hands . . . her hands . . . he should have known. The warmth.

He should have seen it sooner. Stopped her. God squeezed at his chest, pain crippling, taking everything. Lances of agony shot down his left arm. It tingled, feeling numb in spots.

"Julian! Julian!" Pedro called, holding him upright.

"The wall," Antonio was saying, head tilted up to look at the parapets. "We can watch what happens from there."

Despite the pain, Julian staggered to his feet. The wall. There he could see what became of Beatriz, just as days before he'd watched Father Telo. The priest had never returned. With Pedro's support, he stumbled to the steps and up, following Antonio's back. Soldiers helped hold him upright, got him a place in the front. A large crowd formed around them, all craning anxiously for a glimpse of the First Wife.

"There, *Alcalde!*" a sergeant called, pointing toward a group of Northerners in the road. "The First Wife!"

Julian shook off the hands holding him and rose to his toes. The tall, black-lace mantilla perched on the back of Beatriz's head stood well above the enemy. As he watched, she settled the heavy wool shawl around her shoulders. The black and yellow of their uniforms circled her.

Only his need to know what happened kept him from throwing himself off the wall to be closer to her. *Mi amor.*

She argued with the Northerners surrounding her. He would recognize that set to his wife's shoulders anywhere. One of the Northerners made a chopping motion across his wrist, then the group was leading her away toward the heart of their camp.

Julian cradled his left arm to his chest as the pain subsided, leaving only a dull ache. He watched until the last bit of Beatriz vanished into the mass of the Northerners. The stars were cold and hard above them, with only a hint of light on the eastern horizon.

"She's done it," Pedro said in his ear. "She's been accepted."

"Then there's no need to wait longer for our attack," Antonio urged. "They have our response. In honor, we can start our resistance now. Perhaps save the First Wife in the process."

Julian stared to hear the wish of his heart repeated. He'd wanted to propose such a thing, but thought it too selfish—to sacrifice the city for his wife. Beatriz would not want that. But Antonio spoke truth. The Northerners had their reply. Why wait? Surely the people were assembled and ready, unwilling to wait until the last moment.

"Yes," Pedro said. "I agree. We should begin the attack now." He shouldered his way through the men to reach a group of messenger boys. "Run to the wall. Tell them to bring it down now. Now. Not at dawn. Get the people out."

Julian spun to find the commanders. "Ready the men. Mass in the courtyard. The gates open for our charge as soon as we have a big enough complement."

"Fetch the *Alcalde* a horse," Antonio shouted. The large butcher flourished his cleaver. "Get him armor. We go to kill Northerners and bring back the First Wife."

Julian took a sword someone put in his hands. Purpose returned, taking the pain away, though his left hand refused to grip strongly. It was a worry for another time. For now he would go to find Beatriz and destroy the Northerners. To give his city a chance to live. Even if all else he loved died.

CHAPTER 30

His ninth day outside Colina Hermosa dawned, bright-
ening the sky and rendering shapes distinct. Ramiro
eyed the last feet of hill before him. His city and the
Northern army should be just on the other side. He'd
followed his best guess, using the darkness and the
land to keep them hidden. Hopefully, his best guess
was correct.

But what would he find over the hill? He feared to
look.

He skirted a group of pincushion cacti growing
in the shade of a tall ocotillo to return to Sancha and
Claire. From atop his mare, the girl dozed, with her
head resting on Sancha's neck. He gave Sancha her
usual morning attention and affection, then lifted the
girl down. Instead of waking, she snuggled against his
shoulder, her eyes closed. The golden glow of the sunlight gave a fragile beauty to the contours of her face,
rendering her radiant. He froze, unsure what to do.

Though close to his age, Claire was unlike any of the other girls with their brazen flirting or their coy, false modesty. Naivety made her in some ways more like a child. Yet her determination and striving to prove herself showed even more strength than some members of the *pelotón* . . . including, he thought ruefully, himself. He frowned. Had his urge to protect her as a possible savior of his city and out of *sangre* kinship become something more? Did he like her for herself, forgiving the loss of Salvador? He wasn't sure he could do that—moving past the loss of his brother—so quickly. And yet . . .

He only knew it would pain him if anything happened to her.

What was he doing? Examining his feelings like a priest? There were more important things to do.

He gave her a gentle shake, setting her feet to the ground. "Claire, wake up. We're there."

Her eyes flew open, and she backed away from his supporting arms as if his touch burned. "We're here?" she asked groggily.

He nodded curtly, scratching at his beard. "I believe so. Follow me quietly and stay low. Sancha, wait for me." They couldn't afford the mare following and appearing above the horizon. Ramiro dropped to his knees and inched over the last few feet of rocky soil to the crest. He held tight to his breastplate and hoped it wouldn't clank too loudly, missing the rest of his armor back in the village. Yawning, the girl copied his movements and soon lay prone beside him.

They had indeed come out on the south flank of the army near the old quarry. In more generous times, when water lay deep, foolish or drunken young men often dared each other to dive from the spot. A dare Ramiro had taken once in his life. Surviving stupidity was a gift from the Lord, but one shouldn't overtax His generosity.

Glancing over the spreading mass of the Northern army between them and the city walls, Ramiro hoped he'd saved enough of the Lord's gift to survive today. He let out a suppressed breath, touching mind and heart. They'd arrived in time. His city was still intact; the enemy camped just as before, only with the siege engines moved into position from rear to front.

A line of house-like wagons were parked just below them and all along the edge of the quarry, then the sprawling camp began, more sparsely inhabited here along the outskirts and thickening as it progressed inward and to the north.

"You want us to go through that?" the girl whispered with awe in her voice. She squinted against the rising sun to see where the citadel of Colina Hermosa rose on its hill, the city tapering down around it to the walls that shared the plain with the army. She inspected the camp full of black-and-yellow uniforms. "I tried to imagine it, but I didn't even come close. It's huge. I've seen termite mounds with fewer inhabitants."

"I was hoping you could disguise us to fit in. Like when you made us appear as deer." He hated to drag her into this. He'd rather she stay behind. But he'd never reach the city without her help. Though the odds were long he'd reach it *with* her help.

Claire shook her head. "All the way through that? I might be able to hold the Song long enough, but what happens when we reach the end? How do I cover us as we run to your city?"

"Get us through, and I'll do the rest."

She rolled onto her side to face him. "That's crazy. We can't take the horse. That, I can't hide. We'll never make it across the distance. We need a better idea. I won't do it unless there's a reasonable chance of succeeding." The mulish expression he had seen often enough when she was his captive overtook her face. "Why doesn't your city just attack and push them over that cliff?"

"I'm sure they'll line up nice and straight and let us push them into the quarry." He slapped down his temper when she flinched. It wasn't the girl's fault he had no better plan. She wasn't the one dying to get home. "I beg your pardon for my hot words." He sighed. "That strategy was considered, but their numbers would outflank our line, even with all our cavalry gathered. Plus, they've obviously prepared for it. Those wagons would give them perfect regrouping spots and act as snags against any attempt. I'm sorry I don't have a better idea—yet."

She resumed her vigil outward, her brow puckered in contemplation rather than anger. "Give it a few minutes. Maybe we can think of something."

With his chin resting on his palm, he dug for inspiration and found none. Bridge the distance between city and army disguised with magic, and they'd be shot full of arrows by his countrymen—not to mention drawing the suspicion of the enemy. Drop the magic and run for it as themselves, and the Northerners would give chase. Perhaps the gate guard would come forth and attempt a rescue when he was recognized, but that was a big if. And he didn't like abandoning Sancha though there seemed no way around that. They could hope they were mistaken for envoys as they approached the city, but how to trigger that when neither one of them knew a word of the enemy language?

He waited for the girl to make excuses, to look for a way of backing away from this situation and him. If their positions were reversed, he wasn't so sure he would stay.

And yet she did.

Claire grabbed his arm. "Look." She pointed toward the outskirts of the camp nearest the gate.

He shaded eyes gritty with exhaustion from the sun with his hand. A figure all in black walked, circled by enemy soldiers.

"It's a woman," Claire said. "I see skirts."

Shivers ran the length of his spine. Ramiro sat up, carelessly exposing himself. "It's my mother."

"What?" Claire seized his arm and tugged, trying to force him down. "You couldn't possibly tell that from here."

His eyesight couldn't distinguish a face or features, but his heart knew. "It's her." He started to turn for his bow and cursed instead. That thief Suero had it. And what good would a bow do among so many or so far?

The butchering bastards have my mother.

He scrambled to his feet only to have the girl throw herself on him, dragging him back to the ground.

"No," she said between clenched teeth. "That will only make it worse."

"It's my mother," he said, preparing to shake her off like a dog with a small cat on its back. The girl clung like a sand burr.

"You think I don't understand," she demanded. "But what is she doing out there? There must be a reason. Wait."

His tense muscles loosened fractionally. He lay still and looked back at the army. His mother neared.

"See," Claire said. "They're coming this way."

"We'll lose her in the crowd," he hissed, as they entered more populated parts of the camp.

"No, we won't. Watch her head covering. It's like a beacon."

Indeed, his mother's stubbornness in clinging to an old-fashioned, tall mantilla proved their blessing. The black lace stood inches above almost every other head.

"What is she doing here?" he asked, not expecting an answer. The small party surrounding his mother progressed deeper into the camp, still headed in their direction. It was his mother. Even with the short glimpse he'd gotten, he wasn't mistaken. His heart and gut agreed. By the saints, why would she be with the army of his enemy? What was his father thinking?

"What if . . ." the girl dropped off whatever she'd been about to say.

"What if what?" he demanded, eyes narrowing.

"What if she's, you know . . . working with them?"

Ramiro choked off a laugh. "My mother? A spy? That's so ludicrous, it's funny. If you'd ever met her, you'd know it was impossible. Besides, if she was working with them, they'd all be decked out in lace by now."

"Just checking," the girl said. "I trust you."

He nodded at the small phrase. But it meant more than three words. She relied on his judgment. She'd made a choice to support him, help him in rescuing or breaking into his city, whichever was necessary. It was a relief to have her support and not to be alone. All his training had always been to be part of a group—part of the *pelotón*. In a way, *she* was his *pelotón* right now.

As the minutes passed, he lay coiled as tight as a clock spring. Claire was right about waiting, but that didn't make it any easier. The girl rested a hand upon his arm, and somehow the contact helped. If anyone understood, she would.

At last, the party with his mother approached a large carpet rolled out on the sand. A table stood on the carpet with some other furniture. One of the house-like wagons blocked his view of Beatriz, but he'd seen enough.

"It's her," he told Claire.

A figure clad in white like the madman they'd encountered in the village came out of a wagon, and the

hackles rose on his neck. She appeared to be following a priest from his city—the bulky, black-skinned
man wore a priest's robe, anyway. They headed for the
carpet and Beatriz. Ramiro struggled to see more, but
again his view was blocked. What happened with his
mother?

Enough!

He brushed off Claire's hand and slid back down
the hill with the intention of grabbing Sancha. Before
he could, a roar came from Colina Hermosa, a sound
unlike anything Ramiro had ever heard. The ground
shook with tiny tremors, causing pebbles to jiggle.

"By the Song!" the girl shouted, jumping to her feet.

Expecting one of their infrequent earthquakes, he
hurried to join her and found that the camp below them
had also turned to look at the city. Another booming,
roar-like outburst shook everything. Pebbles jumped
at his feet. From their vantage on the hill, Ramiro
watched as a back section of the city wall broke into
chunks, collapsing outward in a pile of rubble. First
one . . . then two . . . then another part of the wall
began a slow topple outward.

"Bloody hells!" exploded from his throat. "It's no
earthquake." What had the Northerners done? Whole
back sections of Colina Hermosa's wall slowly disinte-
grated.

The camp below him boiled like a kicked anthill
as people shouted in their foreign tongue, and everyone jumped to their feet or rushed from wagons. He
frowned, thinking for a moment—something wasn't

right. Wouldn't the Northerners be better prepared if they had caused the walls to fall?

"The gate! The gate!" Claire seized him so tightly and unexpectedly, he staggered and nearly took them both down.

The gates of the city yawned wide, and leagues of horsemen boiled out. Not the matching gray of the *pelotón* horses, but brown, and black, plow horses surging beside carriage horses. Swords extended, the whole formation dashed for the confusion of the camp. Bowmen sent flaming arrows at the siege machines. Men on foot—dressed in gate-guard uniforms or no uniform at all—tossed torches at the great wooden machines as they threw themselves onto enemies.

Half the force split away and entered the camp, plunging not through the heart but directly toward their location.

This was his father's doing, Ramiro suddenly realized. If the *ciudad-estado* was going down, it would do so fighting. And another thought came just as quickly:

"Mother."

Horses galloped, using their size to overrun men and penetrate deep into the camp. In minutes, she'd be trampled in the growing madness—caught up in the fighting. Ramiro spun and ran from the conflict, down the hill toward Sancha. A spring took him into the saddle.

Claire still stood on the crest of the hill, her face white and drawn. "Wait for me," she cried. "Don't leave me."

"Catch hold," he ordered.

Claire held out her arm, and he seized it as Sancha took him rushing past. A wrench of his muscles from shoulder to hip and a leap on her part put her up behind him. He touched his medallion and drew his sword, urging Sancha down the far side of the hill.

"For Colina Hermosa!" bellowed from his lungs, joining with hundreds of like cries below.

CHAPTER 31

Father Telo leaned back in the padded chair as Lord Ordoño set out the board and the pieces for a game of *Acorraloar*. The ordinary-looking man who controlled a nation wore shirt and breeches of a plain tan color. His lack of the slightest weapon or any armor made his ordinariness more disturbing. Then again, the other occupant of the wagon was menacing enough for ten people.

Telo didn't exactly find it relaxing to be crammed in this tiny wagon with the enemy of his people and the scowling priestess Santabe, but perhaps having the chain off his ankle made it worthwhile. And it wasn't sinful to find conversation with a living person better than talking to oneself . . . or, if he were to be totally honest, talking to the Lord. Though neither involved chopped-off body parts—usually.

This was the third time Telo had been "invited"

to Ordoño's study for a game. The last two times had involved a middle-of-the-night rousing from sleep and also a most unwelcome third party. Lord Ordoño wanted the priestess to learn the game through observation. Santabe seemed determined to not only cast a glower over everything but also find fault with every word Telo spoke.

Lord forgive him, this round he wanted to play the mute, if only to see if the tall priestess became angrier at silence than calm debate. *Acorraloar* wasn't the only game taking place, and with the blessing, he wouldn't be cornered in either.

Lord Ordoño looked up from arranging the pieces with the light of an *Acorraloar* fanatic in his eyes. The game of avoiding capture while trying to pin down one's opponent had practically been required in seminary, but Telo had never develop an addiction, even after using the game to win free meals. He'd never found conquest a thrill. His host was another story. Here, Telo figured was the real reason for the freedom of the children.

"You may move first," Lord Ordoño said. "After all, it is your home that will surrender in a few hours or be burned."

Telo fought off a shiver, all desire for sleep dissipating. Ordoño said it perfectly flat, without a hint of bragging or even as a dig, as if stating what he planned to have for dinner. *I shall mow down your city, resulting in the deaths of thousands of innocents, and then have a hearty plate of sausage and onions.*

Telo inclined his head and moved the first smooth yellow piece forward one space. The Northerners used balls of colored glass instead of polished stones. Well enough, but the markers had a tendency to roll away at inconvenient moments. Lord Ordoño claimed it made the game more interesting as markers that rolled were forfeit.

"You chose that same opening yesterday," Ordoño said, as if he had scouted some clue.

Telo merely shrugged. Let the man assign more motive to his moves than they deserved.

Santabe sighed. "Must you wake me up for this tediousness?" she said in her heavy accent. She fidgeted with the Diviner rod in her lap, causing Telo to sidle fractionally away from her. One slip with that rod . . . and in her case it might not be a slip at all.

"Dal glories not in games of feints and devious dealings," she continued. "Dal demands direct confrontation."

Her eyes sized him up and found him wanting, dismissing him just as quickly. Still, her honest fanaticism was easier to understand than Lord Ordoño's baffling courtesy.

"Put the Diviner on my desk, Santabe," Ordoño said as if speaking to a child. "I have no intention of becoming one of your sacrifices." The priestess scowled but obeyed. "I would have you learn this game because I believe you capable of more. Humor me." He set forward two black tokens.

Against his will, the white Diviner rod drew Telo's

eyes. Where did their power come from? How did they work? He had a nagging suspicion.

Nothing ventured, nothing gained, sayeth the Lord.

He twisted toward the desk, closed his eyes, and laid a finger on the Diviner. It felt cold like bone, but it didn't kill him. Santabe, on the other hand, seemed intent to do just that. She shouted. A crash and then a crushing weight threw him out of the chair, squashing him down. He opened one eye to find himself very much alive, and the priestess pinning him to the wooden floor of the wagon.

"Blasphemy!" she shouted with burning hate. "He must die!"

The door flew open, and two guards put their heads inside. They relaxed and closed the door again seconds later, as if they saw nothing untoward in their priestess sitting on a man.

Lord Ordoño chuckled, holding the game board high to protect it. "I forbid it. We just started a game. It is the priest's move, and you may kill him when I tire of him. It is my wish."

Her face tightened, but she returned to her chair without another word. Telo picked his bulk up, along with his chair, and returned to it also. What hold did Ordoño have over these people that they obeyed like dogs? She was stronger than some men and not above acting quickly; he'd have bruises. Hands clenched white-knuckled on the arm of her seat, she glared. Her hatred of him as an affront to her Dal had just become personal.

The Diviner rod lay as before on the desk. Not even a burn marred his skin from the odd weapon, which meant this latest brush with death had been worth it. His guess had been correct: anyone could touch it. Only when it made contact with a second person did the lightning or magic in it become deadly.

Ordoño set the board back on its small table without disturbing a single token. "Your move," he said to Telo with elaborate calm. "And if you try that again, I *will* give you to Santabe."

Telo moved the yellow token back to its original spot and set two others forward. Playing the waiting game could be disastrous but had its own rewards. He'd learned much; it remained to be seen if he'd do anything about it.

"I hardly expected a priest to try suicide," Ordoño said. "I don't believe that was your motive. No, a priest learns many things at his mother's breast: deviousness, imparting guilt, false sanctity, pride. Destruction of self is not among them. Nor was murder likely your intent; you haven't got it in you. Yet, interest in weapons hardly seems a priestly direction." The man leaned forward and moved his first marker, then three other black-glass balls.

"Perhaps it is concern for your immortal soul," Telo suggested.

Santabe snorted and let loose a string of foreign words, heat practically radiating from her.

Ordoño showed white teeth and waved her to silence. "I don't credit that either, Priest, despite its fitting nicely with the usual blather."

"Oh, but I've thought about you deeply, my son. I'm very concerned you will be with our Lord soon."

"Long after you." Ordoño crossed one knee atop the other. "If I were you, I'd expend my worry in another direction. I don't need your concern."

Curbing his tongue had never been Telo's talent. Even for penalty of death, he wasn't about to change himself now, and with the recent drama, playing the mute no longer seemed like a worthwhile tactic. "You remind me of the man from the children's tale who bridled and saddled a wild cat. He thought he had control, as the cat went where he commanded. But saddle and bridle don't make anyone civilized. The cat was still wild, and the man had to keep it running, always running. For if the cat stopped, it would turn and rend its rider."

For the first time since Telo had met him, a hint of anger touched Ordoño's eyes. "Fables are for children. Real life is more . . . complicated."

"Is it?" Telo set forth his first stone again and moved the other two back to their old positions, his hand poised over his fourth selection.

"Your children's tales are very boring," Santabe said. "Where is the glory or the gain?"

Telo looked at Ordoño as he moved out two more markers. Ignoring the priestess, Telo said, "It has a nice moral, though: Don't expect the cat to remain stupid." Skin tightened around Ordoño eyes in the only outward sign, but Telo feared he'd pushed too far. The Lord forgive him for not learning wisdom—and not stopping. "Running the cat is the true reason you're attacking our *ciudad-estado*, isn't it, my son?"

Shouting and the bustle of a commotion from outside disturbed the locked silence inside. "FATHER TELO! FATHER TELO! I demand to see my priest! What have you done with my priest? Don't touch me!"

"First Wife?" Telo asked in bewilderment. He shoved back his chair and threw open the door before even Santabe made a move. By the time he made it down the wagon's steps, she was after him, Diviner stick in hand.

A strange scene gathered around the altar carpet. Beatriz pushed and shoved at the soldiers surrounding her. Their efforts to subdue her seemed halfhearted, as if her confidence and bearing deterred them. It reminded Telo of a farce of a fight acted for a holiday play.

Santabe snapped out an angry phrase, and suddenly the farce ended. The soldiers had Beatriz on her knees at the edge of the carpet before a count of three.

"Father Telo," Beatriz said, while Santabe ranted at the soldiers in their language. "Thank the saints you are well. Tell them I'm here as an envoy. I bear a message."

"A message?" Ordoño asked, coming up beside them. "What is this message?" Back in perfect control once more, the beardless man gave a polite bow, motioning for Santabe to be silent. "First Wife."

Beatriz struggled to her feet. "I'm here for my husband. The *ciudad-estado* of Colina Hermosa has rejected your terms."

Telo didn't imagine the flash of delight that crossed Ordoño's face or the dismay in his gut. He touched heart, mind, liver, and spleen. The wild cat would run.

The ground trembled beneath him and a rumbling roar issued from the direction of the *ciudad-estado*.

"Earthquake," Ordoño hissed.

As the first tremors died, a second and third wave arose. Telo frowned as he braced his legs. He'd survived many an earthquake. This did not seem the same.

A cloud of dust marred the blue of the morning sky over the *ciudad-estado*, the wind moving it in their direction. Shouts erupted from the army camp. People, who had stood still as the earth shook, dashed into motion, hurrying with purpose, grabbing weapons. Dozens of white-clad priests emerged from wagons, holding their Diviner sticks.

Ordoño shouted what were obviously orders and strode away. A servant ran to him with a shining coat of mail and another offered a belted sword and long dagger.

The shouting grew in volume and mixed with clashes of metal. Fighting. The whole time, Beatriz held on to Telo's arm, and now they watched as Ordoño vanished into the chaos, a crowd of high-ranking soldiers surrounding him.

"What do we do now, Father?" Beatriz asked.

"Pray," he said. Surely, *Alcalde* Julian had a plan. Why would he send his wife here without one?

The priests of Dal converged on Santabe much as

the soldiers had on Ordoño. White-clad figures appeared like wraiths out of the dust cloud from the city. Telo shrank back to put as much space between him and them as possible, but they crowded too close for comfort. Santabe answered them in her language, her large sun earring swaying with the quickness of her response. Many drew their Diviners as they dashed off. Only two remained behind with her.

Telo had the sinking feeling that these priests wouldn't sit quietly on the sidelines praying, offering water, or helping with the injured. He wished he'd had time to learn more of their language. He'd barely caught a single word. The chaos around them slowed and grew more organized even as the dust cloud dissipated. Though caught unaware, the Northerners regrouped all too soon.

He must do what he could to keep the high priestess off-balance. "Not what you expected from us. Did you think kindness made us meek?"

"Where is your protector now?" Santabe looked around, as if seeking something. "You are not important, false priest. And no one will miss you. Ordoño will forget you ever existed and find another for his silly game."

She advanced on him, the white rod held in front. Yet before she could take more than a few steps, the immediate world around them exploded. Beatriz clutched Telo's arm in a tight grip as a group of horsemen broke through a line of wagons and into the clearing around them, and Santabe whirled to see what was happening.

Swords swung. Northerners died before they could turn. Horses collapsed in a slow scream of agony. More horses appeared, using their speed and size to bully their way forward.

Small metal boxes flew at wagons, glowing coals spilling out of them onto canvas roofs or wooden walls. Tinderboxes. First one wagon caught on fire, then another. Ordoño's study smoked.

Telo smiled. The two scouts *had* gotten word to the *Alcalde*. Santabe gripped her Diviner rod in both hands and twisted it like she was clutching someone's neck.

A group of five horsemen broke loose and headed in their direction, led by the hefty miller and *concejal*. "First Wife—!" *Concejal* Pedro shouted, as they plunged closer toward the small group gathered by the empty carpet on the sand.

The two priests who had remained with Santabe strode forward. Casually, one touched Pedro's horse with her Diviner. The mare tumbled headfirst, dead before she could make a sound. As she plummeted past, the priest brought the rod up and made contact with Pedro. The other priest worked his Diviner against horse and human flesh with equal efficiency. In seconds, two horses veered away at a gallop, one riderless, and four men and three horses lay dead.

"Your god makes you weak," Santabe gloated.

Visible overhead, the tall siege machines rumbled

forward. One burned, but the others released their giant arms to fling fiery debris over the roofs of Colina Hermosa. All around him, the horsemen of his city dropped, wildly outnumbered.

Telo's gut clenched, but he shook his head. "He shows us the way and will not desert us. These men will dine in paradise tonight with the saints. Can your people expect as much?"

Santabe hissed what sounded like an oath and said something to the handful of soldiers surrounding them. Then she turned to Telo. The hate in her eyes had given way to satisfaction. Very deliberately she stepped onto the altar carpet. "I tell them to kill you first. Meet your paradise!"

Despite his struggles and Beatriz's shrieks for help, they drove him to his knees and stretched his arm out. A sword rose, blade glinting in the morning sun. Telo shut his eyes.

CHAPTER 32

Ramiro screamed a war cry as he urged Sancha down the hill. The rising sun blinded him. So bright and just at eye level, it reduced his visibility to a few feet, making it impossible to sight enemies. And yet he plunged on—for the mission, for the city, for his family.

The weight of Claire against his back lessened as Sancha leveled out, entering the army camp. He squinted against tearing eyes and just got his sword up in time to deflect the first Northerner soldier. He sensed others homing in—one man alone, easy pickings.

Then Claire opened her mouth and sent out her hornet song. The Northerners lost focus, swatting at the air. This time her song created barely an itch along Ramiro's skin. As she mentioned, it didn't work when one expected it.

Ramiro sliced through the first and stabbed another as Sancha took them on past. He almost felt guilty; this wouldn't have counted toward earning a beard. With a bow, he could have slain dozens. Yet, they were at war. Feeling sick to his stomach, he settled for incapacitating only those within reach.

The girl clutched his shirttail where it emerged from under his back plate. Salvador would argue he should get Claire to the safety of Colina Hermosa. That she was too valuable to risk. Salvador would remind him always to see first to their city, even at the expense of his mother. He should be taking Claire to the city so his father could find a way to use her. He should, he should, he should . . .

He was done with precepts.

Today, family came first. He was done with whether he should stop and consider or follow his gut. He was done wondering if he was good enough. Done with worrying what his brother would do and trying to be Salvador. Today, in this new day, he would just be Ramiro.

He applied pressure with his right leg to guide Sancha left, hopefully in the direction he'd last seen his mother. The sun shifted out of his eyes, allowing his first clear look around. The influence of the girl's song appeared to extend fifty, maybe even a hundred, yards around them, affecting friend and foe alike. A small girl, with a small voice, yet despite that or the shrieks and clashes of metal, Claire's power was effective for a greater distance than Ramiro believed possible—all within that span fled or showed other signs of broken concentration. Beyond that, the Northerners fought as usual, paying scant attention to them.

Ramiro battled his impatience to hold a slow, steady pace so Claire's voice could maintain a bubble of safety around them. Ahead a group of enemy servants with empty buckets watched a wagon house burn; unaware in the desert, sand was the best weapon against fire. As they threatened no one, he gave them a wide berth.

A crawling along his spine twisted Ramiro in the saddle. A large Northerner rushed him from behind, axe upraised, bursting into their safe space. Ramiro braced himself, but the man drew up short, face grimacing in pain. He toppled to the ground to reveal an arrow shaft in his back. A peasant on a big draft horse raised his bow in salute and an instant later was pulled from the saddle to disappear under Northerner swords before Ramiro could utter a word of thanks.

Ramiro shook his head at a death he couldn't prevent and stepped up his vigilance. Arrows wouldn't be stopped by the magic, nor those enemies driven by determination. In fact, it probably made them a larger target. All around him gate guards and untrained civilians died, outnumbered and outskilled. And he could do nothing for them.

Where were his *pelotón* brothers?

Glances around confirmed his suspicions: men from the *ciudad-estado* fought from horseback or afoot, but no *pelotón* members were among them. Perhaps they engaged the siege machines. Even from the rear of the camp, the tall structures of the scaling towers were visible, trundling forward toward the walls of Colina Hermosa. Tiny forms of archers stood atop them, waiting to rain fire. Behind them, Ramiro caught the flash of trebuchet arms already throwing flaming debris. Smoke rose from the city. The *pelotón* would not have failed so drastically. Once again he asked himself, *Where were they?*

Heat from the burning wagon warmed his face as he took them around it. The girl clung to him, her voice starting to weaken as she tired. The reach of the magic grew smaller. How long before she could do no more and they were left to the scant protection of his sword? He directed a quick prayer to the saints that he found his mother first.

The battle calmed on the other side of the wagon. Here seemed to be only the dead. Piles of horses and men lay, all the men bearded. Then a man and woman in white robes stepped from behind a heap of bodies. Ramiro went cold. They each held one of those deadly rods.

The few Northern soldiers who had approached Ramiro suddenly turned around and found somewhere else to go. The woman was no older than himself, a slim figure, but she set her rod athwart crossed arms with no less determination then the steely muscled man next to her. They stood shoulder to shoulder, unmoving. The song had no effect on them. Ramiro recognized soldiers at guard when he saw them, even if these soldiers wore strange uniforms.

Sancha pranced under him as he hesitated. They could probably just avoid the deadly pair. Then behind the pair, he detected a small group of soldiers, another white-robed figure, a man dressed in priestly clothing and . . . his mother.

Claire's song cut off as she recognized the black-lace mantilla, too.

"Keep this for me." Ramiro handed her his bloody sword. The last time he'd used a sword against one of these white-dressed strangers, it resulted in a numb and useless hand. Sweat ran from his neck and back. Then his full armor had diffused whatever magic the rod wielded, leaving him only exhausted and aching. He had no such protection today, only his breastplate.

"This isn't a good idea," Claire said, grabbing his hand and holding on.

"Probably not. When I die, get yourself back to your swamp and don't look back." She looked at him with eyes too large in a white face, and he leaned down and kissed her cheek.

Her hand went slack on his with surprise. He took advantage of her relaxed grip to dismount. "Sancha, wait." The number of dead horses professed the magic weapon worked equally well on animal flesh. Sancha needed to stay well clear.

The white-robed man tapped his deadly stick against his opposite palm in anticipation. A smile stretched his face, while the girl waited impassively, cool and fresh as if already assured of victory.

Ramiro felt for the San Martin medallion at this

throat. He feared it might come to this. One touch would be the end of him.

Face tight, he took a step forward. He'd not give them the opportunity to get close.

In a flash, he threw his dagger at the man. His boot knife—retrieved from Claire—followed before the dagger even struck true in the man's chest. Neither one had time for more than a shout as the boot knife protruded from the girl's throat. She raised her hands to her neck before she dropped beside her lifeless partner.

Ramiro firmed his knees. It had been a gamble. He hadn't practiced in a while. Thank the saints for Alvito's prowess with knife throwing and his insistence on lessons.

A glint of metal caught his eye. In the group surrounding his mother, a sword came down. The priest he'd seen from above screamed in agony. His mother shrieked.

He was halfway across the distance before he realized he had no weapon left but his empty hands. "Hold, damn you!" he yelled. Five soldiers and another of those white-robed maniacs turned at his call, allowing his mother to drop to her knees beside the priest, using her skirts to try and stem the flow of blood from the holy man's severed wrist.

Ramiro quickened his pace and put his hand in a pocket, pretending he knew what the hell he was doing. The woman in white wore a gloating smile that couldn't spoil her attractiveness as if she prepared to make a conquest at a dance. She had the height of a man and enough muscle to back it up. The hot light in her eyes would make a sane man step back. Fear tightened his belly, but his mother knelt by the woman's feet. The white rod was dangerously close to Beatriz's hunched back.

His eyes narrowed, and he came on. A force plowed into him from behind and his sword was thrust into his hands.

"You won't get rid of me that easily." Claire sang, and for a second, even he saw clouds of angry insects. *Crazy girl*, he thought fondly, then had time for nothing more.

With the soldiers hopping at the manipulation of their minds, the tall woman pushed back her braid and picked her opponent.

She came at him.

He threw the rolled ball of socks from his pocket at her. She flinched, giving him enough time to gauge a feel of the ground around him: level but rocky.

Recovering, she swung at him. He spun, desperate to get behind her. His sword would be worse than useless. He'd have to rely on his feet. She proved too quick. The white rod swiped at him. He leaped away, feeling the wind of its passing. She kept him jumping as if they were dance partners, and he feared she would prove the swifter.

How long could Claire keep the soldiers off him? Once they swarmed forward, he was done for. He had to think of something before then. Even overpowering the madwoman would only give her opportunity to reach out and touch him.

The madwoman feinted left and swung right. He stumbled over a melon-sized rock and had to bring his sword up to block her. A vibrating burn ran down the metal into his hand as he lost his balance, falling. Fingers going numb, he heaved the blade at her. She batted it aside with her rod like it was nothing.

Gravel and sand cut up his palms as he scrambled back across the ground. Retreating.

Her eyes burned hot. "So dies another heretic," she said in a thick accent. She stretched forth her rod.

A gray blur shot between them. The madwoman wheeled her arms in shock as Sancha's teeth snapped an inch from her face.

Ramiro screamed in horror. Veins corded in his neck. *Not Sancha.* He stopped breathing.

Terror gave him wings. His tingling hand landed on the melon-sized rock as he got his feet under him. He sprang upright with it, but Sancha was a barrier between them. *No time.* The madwoman brought her weapon toward Sancha, and Ramiro leaped onto his horse's back. He drove the rock down with all the force he could manage, crashing it into the madwoman's skull.

The woman collapsed, and air rushed backing into Ramiro's lungs. He slumped, winding his arms around Sancha's neck. She twitched an ear and swished her tail as if to ask what he'd been worked up about. The hammering of his heart left a painful ache in his chest wall.

"That's two females who saved me today," he whispered to the mare.

But there was one he had to rescue.

Mother.

He slid from Sancha onto wobbly legs. Claire and his mother had dragged the priest away from the soldiers and onto a carpet spread out on the sand. The dark-skinned priest lay propped against a table, his mother at his side. Claire stood between them and the soldiers, back straight and chin high as she sang. Worry turned to relief as he caught her eye.

The five soldiers caught in Claire's magic were soon incapacitated with blows to the head, then Ramiro searched the sand for his sword, only to find fresh prickles ran down his spine.

They had an audience: A half dozen Northerner soldiers watched from a short distance away, their eyes hard as they mumbled to each other

The sight unnerved him. There seemed no reason why the group didn't rush them. But he thanked the saints for the respite as he clutched his sword and hurried to lead Sancha over to the carpet, then going back and hefting the madwoman's limp body by her robe and depositing her on the rug. He wanted her under his eyes. An oozing spot of blood matted her hair over an ear, but she breathed, if shallowly. Instinct and common sense said not to leave her at his back or near her weapon.

A quick nod to Claire, and he dropped down next to his mother at the priest's side. "You were right about the socks, Mother."

She didn't bat an eye but seized his arm with her free hand. "My *niño*." She reached up to touch his beard and burst into tears, while still keeping the pressure intact on the priest's wound. "My *niño* with a beard."

"Nostalgia later," he said, winding the leather strap taken from the equipment on Sancha around the priest's arm. The poor man wore a sheen of sweat, tossing fitfully against the table leg and muttering to himself.

"Off. Off."

Ramiro examined the wound at the priest's wrist. It was a neat job done with a very sharp blade. "It's cleanly off, Father. Once cauterized, it will heal. You'll survive." Or he would if the rest of them did.

The priest opened his eyes. "No. Off. Altar."

"Alter what, Father? You need to rest." Ramiro glanced over his shoulder. Their crowd of watchers had grown in number and looked. . . . well, upset was too mild a word. He had a very bad feeling.

He finished tying off a knot in the improvised tourniquet, and his mother clipped him on the ear. "Father Telo is trying to tell you something," she said. "You listen."

Ramiro glared. *Mothers.* "This is not the time—"

"Altar. Holy Spot," the priest muttered. "Off."

"Yes, Father Telo," Beatriz said. "We'll light many candles at holy spots for your recovery, just as soon—"

"No, wait," Ramiro interrupted. The prickles down his spine turned to panic. He took in the gold piled atop the table—Sancha nosed at them as he watched, knocking a few statues to the rug—the eerie growing crowd full of discontent. "We're on their altar. Their holy spot."

The priest managed to nod, face set in pain. "*Gotteslästerung,*" he said, repeating one of the frequent angry shouts from their watchers, "means blasphemy."

"Mother, who is that?" Ramiro asked, pointing to the crumpled madwoman, lying in a heap.

"One of their false priests."

Ramiro groaned. "*Mierda.*" So their priests were vicious killers, ordering the massacre of innocent villagers. What did that make the rest of the people like?

Saints.

Get off the altar and the waiting group of fanatics would tear them apart. Stay on, and they'd eventually work up the courage to cross the carpet. Either way, he and his companions were dead. The Northern soldiers had grown to over twenty and started to edge closer.

"Claire," he called, waving her over.

"I heard," Claire said, her face pale with strain. "The Hornet Song won't help, will it?"

He shook his head.

"You've brought a witch, Ramiro?" Beatriz asked, her face puckered.

"She's . . ." Witch seemed a nasty word. One that didn't begin to describe Claire. "She's my friend, Mother, and she's here to help." He turned to Claire. "Have you another song? Something stronger. What about the one your mother used?"

The girl held her hands clasped together, twisting

them. "I don't know what she sang. She never taught me that." Her eyes pleaded for reassurance. "We're going to die, aren't we?"

Words stuck in his throat. Anything he said would be a lie, better to say nothing. He stood. Flames came from the hill of Colina Hermosa. His city burned. Everything seemed to fall apart. Even his rescue had been but a temporary reunion.

He tightened his grip on his sword. "The three of you get under the table."

The priest plucked feebly at his trouser leg. "Dal. They fear. Their god."

Ramiro knelt again. "What, Father?"

"Dal. They are. Terrified of their god." The priest pointed toward the low-rising sun with his whole hand. "Dal." He gripped Ramiro again and indicated the crowd, which now surrounded the carpet. "The witch. Can she . . . ?"

"Use it," Ramiro finished. A painful hope grew in his chest, and he turned to Claire.

"Can you make them fear their god?"

"How?"

He racked his brain. What did one fear about God? Correction. What did one fear if your god had cruel and evil priests? If your god collected gold tribute? If your god called trespass on his altar blasphemy? If your god was also cruel and evil?

The crowd had grown to over fifty and gathered a yard from the carpet. They shifted their feet, mutters rising to yells. A stone struck Ramiro's shoulder. Another came at Claire but missed. Time was up.

Beatriz began dragging the priest under the table.

What did you fear? You feared his presence. You feared his attention on you.

"Claire." Galvanized, Ramiro tripped over the priest's legs in his hurry to get to the girl and whispered, "Can you make them feel their god is here, come for them?" He pointed at the sun and more stones flew. Beatriz cried out as she was struck. "Dal. Tell them this Dal is here, and angry at them."

"I'd have to make it very simple," she said. "One wrong word, and it would all fall apart. They have to be willing to see it. I'm not sure I can."

"If you can't, no one can. Just try." Rocks flew faster. One dinged against his breastplate. "I don't want to pressure you, but soon." He placed himself in front of her to block the rocks.

A glance back showed Claire stood with the sun shining on her golden hair. Instead of being able to make out words, all Ramiro heard was a humming that rose in intensity. From low and hesitant, it became a great force. The light seemed to dim. A great well of darkness rolled over him. Even knowing something was coming, his knees buckled. His mother whimpered. A blast of hate and evil surrounded him.

Northerners looked over their shoulders at the red-orange ball of the sun. A sun that boiled with fury. Their faces went slack with terror. Weapons and rocks dropped to the ground. One, then another broke and ran. They babbled and shouted as they fled, startling more and more into flight.

"Dal! Dal!"

For once, he could understand their words.

Ramiro threw his arms over his head and sensed his mother weeping, huddled against the priest. A foul force bore down upon him like a thumb on an ant. It was only Claire's magic or so he tried to tell himself. But the angry pressure cried out for his blood—for the blood of all humans. It craved death and destruction. The removal of everything kind and good.

Shaking, he fought the sweep of fear. This was not his god or any god. The terror lessened a trifle. It was only Claire's magic. An illusion. There was nothing to dread. With effort, he raised his head to check their surroundings.

Many of the soldiers dodged between the wagons and launched themselves off the edge of the quarry, crying with what sounded like joy as they fell. Others ran directionless, and still more escaped toward the bulk of the Northern army, shouting as they ran. One man remained near the carpet, pitched on his face in an apparent faint or fit.

To Ramiro's astonishment, men far beyond the reach of Claire's voice threw down their weapons and joined the retreat. By the dozens, then by the hundreds, they fled, leaving the fight and everything behind. Wherever Northerner priests tried to stop them, those impediments were soon trampled by the mindless mob.

Even as those fled, though, many came directly toward them. Ramiro climbed unsteadily to his feet, fumbling for a weapon, even as the force continued to bear down, but he need not have worried. They avoided the carpet and threw themselves off the edge of the quarry. Ramiro blinked and rubbed at his eyes but the scene remained the same. Claire stood beside him, no longer singing, her mouth round with astonishment.

The entire Northern army ran as if pursued by demons.

They fled into the dark embrace of their god.

CHAPTER 33

As the crushing weight of blackness lifted, gone as quickly as it had come, Ramiro spun in a circle. He held his sword loosely but saw only more of the same. The battlefield had emptied except for corpses, wounded, and his fellow countrymen. They were as frozen with bewilderment as Ramiro. He touched mind then heart to settle himself . . . and before the latter organ burst from relief at their salvation. Silently, he sent a swift prayer to Santiago for their deliverance.

"How did you do that?" he asked Claire as he moved to stand next to her. Her mouth hung open. "How did you make that wall of foulness?" he asked. "It felt . . . it felt like a god truly was angry at us." Only now, with it gone, did the air feel breathable again or his lungs strong enough to do their work.

"I didn't. I just sang, 'Dal is here for you. He is the sun.' Simple, like I said. I didn't put anything into it."

She tugged at her braid. "It shouldn't have affected anyone beyond the reach of my voice. They must have spread it themselves."

"But that evil?" he persisted. "That malevolence? Did you feel it, too?"

She nodded, brow furrowed. "That wasn't me. It came when I said . . . that name. I . . . it . . . it was dangerous. It could have turned on us." She swallowed. "Do you think it was real?"

He didn't want to consider that possibility. If that was the real Dal, he was viler than the darkest sin.

"You saved us," he said instead, reaching out to take her hand and show his gratitude with a salute. He hesitated when she stiffened. Instead of the formal gesture, he dragged her to his arms, holding her tight against his chest. Her head fit neatly under his chin, her body trembling. His own guts felt like water. As he tightened his hold, she stood rigid, then gradually relaxed with a sigh.

"I don't ever want to do that again," she begged in a whisper.

"It's done," he soothed. "Over. I promise. Never again."

Claire nodded against his throat. A loud *hmmph* sounded behind him. He swung around to find his mother, hands on broad hips and eyebrows raised.

Ramiro gave Claire one more squeeze and stepped back. His arms felt strangely empty with only his sword in hand. He barely set himself before his mother barreled into his arms.

"My son. My son," Beatriz said tearfully, then she drew herself upright. "This may be a battlefield, but there are still standards of behavior. Or am I mistaken? A *caballero* minds his manners, whether or not his mother is present."

The unspoken word "witch" hung heavy in the air. Ramiro wondered exactly how long it would take his mother to create a whole new list of etiquette pertaining to what one could and couldn't do around a witch.

Awkwardly, he used some time sheathing his sword to evade his mother's clutching arms, then patted her back. "Mother, meet Claire," he said. "Claire, my mother, Beatriz."

"Yes, well." Beatriz cleared her throat, looking oddly at a loss. "First names. We'll discuss that." Her face wiped clean of severity, to return to tears. "Tell me what happened to your brother. I want every detail."

He cast about for a way to deflect her. He didn't want to talk about it. There hadn't been time to invent a suitable story that wouldn't involve his family's hating Claire forever. If they had a chance to get to know her first, then possibly he could tell them the truth. Until that time, he'd go with blunt and rude. "Claire saved all our lives and risked her own. We owe her. I think we're passed formality."

His mother stared at him in shock.

"Your city," Claire said in the awkward silence that followed. "I'm sorry. It's burning."

Ramiro turned to follow her gaze. The siege towers and machines had stopped in their tracks, abandoned, but they had done their work. Colina Hermosa was engulfed in a fiery rain. Timbers crashed down, taking whole roofs. With no men in the city to counter it, even the thick stucco walls couldn't rebuff the flames racing up the hill toward the citadel, infecting everything in their path—including churches—and casting a ruby glow over the white walls in the early sunlight. The astronomy tower of the university fell straight downward with an audible crash though miles away.

His heart dropped.

Lost. They were too slow. Too late. Everything he'd worked to save. What Salvador had died for. Gone. For naught.

He reached up to wipe away a tear before someone saw it. "The people?" his voice sounded hoarse. Inside, he felt stripped and hollow. His refuge from the bustle of the day was gone. His place to put cares aside—gone. No retreating to the rooftop with a book or to the kitchens to steal a snack. The jewel of a city would soon be no more. Only char and cinder.

"Your father arranged to bring down the wall." Beatriz said. "They got out." She came to lean against him, her tears flowing freely.

Now he knew where the *pelotóns* went. His father would have put the best soldiers to guard the people. He put an arm around Beatriz, holding them both up. How much worse this must be for her who had lived her whole life there. To lose home *and* child.

He'd made his choice: mother over city. He stood by it.

"Rest in peace," the priest said from his spot against the table, crossing himself with his uninjured arm. "As the blessed Santiago said, it is only a stone and wood and labor. It can be replaced."

Ramiro thought of the splashing ripple of fountains and the lazy scent of jasmine on the breeze and wasn't so sure. His heart ached. Some things could never be the same again. Claire came over to stand beside him, her face full of sympathy.

The four of them watched as more and more of Colina Hermosa was consumed. At least the people had escaped.

Finding nothing of interest, Sancha had wandered to the edge of the carpet. Her ears pricked forward at the arrival of a troop of horses. *Alcalde* Julian and some *concejales* rode at the fore. *Concejal* Lugo's face looked as sour as the hard candy he sold in his stores.

"Take any useful supplies and burn all the rest," his father said even as he pulled his mount to a stop and hurried from the saddle. "Ho, Father Telo!" The priest raised his good hand in a salute, which the *Alcalde* returned.

"Santabe," Julian said, pointing to the unconscious woman. "You caught her. And their leader, Lord Ordoño? Did he get away?"

"Gone," Father Telo gritted out, his dark face tight with pain.

Ramiro shrugged as a troop of gate guard took the priestess into their custody. The rest rode off to see to their orders, and a few healers scurried to help the priest.

"*Mi amor,*" Julian said as he ran forward to embrace his wife, pulling up short when he took in Ramiro. "Son! You're alive. Both of you." He sobbed into their shoulders.

Ramiro clung to his sadly reduced family and let their misery wash over him. The fragile peace he'd reached with his brother's death threatened to topple.

"The disruption of the Northern army was your doing?" *Concejal* Lugo said, interrupting the reunion.

"Indeed it was," Father Telo affirmed. "The Lord provided."

Glad for the excuse, Ramiro pulled away and gave a quick report of losing Salvador, Alvito, and Gomez, finding Claire in the swamp, leaving Teresa behind, their trek here, and what occurred after. "Basically, the magic fooled them," he concluded.

"Then we have the weapon to hold back the Northerners when they regroup," Julian said.

Eyes swung to stare at Claire, filled with fear and suspicion, or downright hostility. *Witch* they all said. Her shoulders hunched under their scrutiny as she stood alone. The prickles returned to Ramiro's back, whether it was the promise given to Claire or something else. He recalled Salvador's words from a lifetime ago when they'd bluffed the unit of Northerners on the road to Aveston:

"The Northerners are not fools. They will not give us the opportunity to trick them again. Don't count on your enemy to be stupid."

Ramiro put on a brave face, willing Claire to know

he had her back. He had brought her here, and he would see her safe. "The same deception will not work a second time," he said. He met her eyes and saw the same resolve. She might not be of their blood, but she had made their cause her own. "No—not again. But we'll find a way. As the father said, the Lord will provide." And He would have to. His people were homeless. Many were dead. But the Northerners would be stopped if they returned, just as they had this day.

His mother had returned to Father Telo, to fuss and boss the healers. His father was deep in discussion with *Concejal* Lugo and his other advisors. "Ramiro, come here," Julian called. "We need to discuss rounding up the evacuees and finding safe shelter. I'll need my son's help."

Ramiro walked toward them, drawing small puffs of dust from the dry ground. "You sent them to the swamp?"

Julian spared him a glance from the sharp debate of the advisors. "Some of them."

"Teresa is there," Ramiro said. "I told her to take charge. She'll see to the people when they arrive. Get them settled until the rest of us get there."

His father barely gave him a nod before *Concejal* Lugo and others interrupted, all with their own version of what they should do now. He heard calls for scouts to investigate the Northern army to be sure they weren't regrouping. For men to secure the treasure on the barbarian altar to pay for their survival. For everything to be dropped and an attempt made to save the city. His father looked harried under the barrage of opinion. The advisors closed ranks in a circle, and his father's form disappeared.

Ramiro shook himself and turned to leave them to it. Let the politicos sort it out. There would be a time for remembering the dead, time for going back and finding Teresa, time for gathering survivors, but right now, he couldn't think about it. It was a day of miracles. His people had survived. They lived. He had earned his beard and come through the other side. It was time to set worry apart, even if it was just for an hour. They'd won, and if only for a little while, he wanted to forget that it seemed as if everything was falling apart.

Claire had wandered off to stand by the edge of the quarry. The soldiers picking through Northern belongings and loading supplies onto their back or into piles gave her a wide berth. They worked in silence, watching the girl with half an eye as if she would unleash her magic upon them for moving too fast or making too much noise.

He was the only one who would see the girl as human after this. To everyone else, she would be the witch who destroyed the Northern army single-handed.

Ramiro caught up Sancha's reins and the mare followed with a toss of her head. A scuff of his boot sent a pebble flying over the edge of the quarry to fall and fall, then bounce off stone with an echo in the stillness. Northern bodies lay sprawled at the bottom. Their shapes twisted and broken. Claire turned to look at him.

"Maybe my mother was right, and the Song *is* terrible. I did this." Her eyes were limpid with unshed tears.

He took Claire's hand, ignoring the shocked surprise of the nearest people. They had gotten past acceptance of each other; he hoped they headed toward friendship. The saints knew he needed friends, and he could tell she needed one, too.

"I felt much the same . . . when I earned my beard." He struggled to find words that would console her. "There are times we have to do what we must . . . to save our lives . . . to save the lives of innocents." He drew them away from the edge. "It gets easier. You only have to be strong enough to bear it. Don't let doubt break you."

The flames dancing over Colina Hermosa caught his eye. He had found that strength, the courage to let defeat and death fall onto his shoulders and yet still manage to carry the load. Could she do the same? They all had to find peace in their own way. He gave her hand a squeeze. She looked so fragile with her pale skin, her head barely coming to his shoulder, but the smile she gave him was strong.

Sancha butted him in the back, making him stumble, letting him know in no uncertain terms she'd had enough of standing around doing nothing. Claire laughed, the sound a bright throb in the solemn battlefield of death.

Ramiro touched his breastplate for luck. "I'm a man of the *pelotón*. I'm going after the refugees to protect them as best I can." As soon as he said the words, tension rushed from his body. Planning and organizing was his father's job. He would defend Colina Hermosa and its people. Soldier. It was what he was and where he belonged. Salvador would approve.

He vaulted to the saddle, holding out a hand for the girl. "Will you come with me?"

She worried at her lip. "The Song . . . it scares me. Mother didn't want me using it, didn't tell me enough about it. But . . . I *need* to know." She studied him. "It would be easier . . . I'd feel braver with a person at my side as I explored it."

"I could be that person," Ramiro said gravely, keeping his hand out.

"And if that person *needs* to go . . . well, I could go with him."

To his relief, Claire seized him and swung up behind, an arm secured around his waist. He put stirrups to Sancha and turned the mare west toward the swamp. He had his place, and for now, the girl was content to make it hers.

Let the saints take care of the rest.

ACKNOWLEDGMENTS

Recently, I heard that people who follow their child-hood dreams of employment to adulthood are the happiest. As a child, I never wanted to be a writer, didn't put pencil to paper in some school notebook and fill it with stories. My every-girl-must-have teenage diary boasted mostly empty pages. According to my parents, I wanted to be Underdog or possibly Mighty Mouse. I never learned how to fly like them, but I had an imagination that didn't stop. My first characters were stuffed animals. That moved on to joining my cousins and little sister in acting the parts of Tom Sawyer or Robin Hood. Somehow, many years later, imagination returned, and this time I put those worlds on paper for others to, hopefully, enjoy.

Thank you to readers everywhere for wanting to live in someone else's imagination.

Also, I want to thank some of those people who

nurtured and made this book possible. The Speculative Fiction group at Agent Query Connect taught me the ropes of writing and provided guidance. My critique partners Carla Rehse, Angie Sandro, and Joyce Alton deserve so much thanks for reading the early drafts and pointing out where it went off the tracks. I couldn't have managed without their shoulders to hold me up.

My terrific agent, Sarah Negovetich, for her support and always knowing when I needed to cut a character point of view or add more. And, more important, like the knights of old, I want to thank Sarah for having my back.

I thank all the team at HarperVoyager. To my editor, David, thanks for deciding you needed more epic fantasy and making *Grudging* one of them. I appreciate Rebecca for answering my unending line of questions. Sara, thanks for smoothing out my typos, and Zea for leading me through the scary world of promotion.

Huge hugs to my parents for encouraging me to always have a book in hand—even if it was sometimes at the dinner table. To my sister, Tracy, for being my first fan. My teenagers, now young adults, who brought me down to earth in a way only your children can. But most of all thanks to my husband, who was the first to think I should be an author and who also reminds me there is a world that isn't in my laptop.

The battle is over . . . but the threat to Ramiro and Claire's peoples has only just begun.

Read an exclusive excerpt from Book Two in the Birth of Saints series

FAITHFUL

On-sale Fall 2016

CHAPTER 1

Ramiro held the reins loosely in his left hand and combed through Sancha's mane with his right. There hadn't been time to give his horse a proper grooming in the two days since the walls fell at Colina Hermosa, and guilt for neglecting the mare added to the burdens on his shoulders. Sancha would forgive him.

He was not so sure others would.

A patrol through the desert, looking for lost evacuees in the middle of the afternoon, was pure duty. No one would do so for fun. Yet, the missing people had to be found, and his brother Salvador had beat the precepts into his head: *Always see first to Colina Hermosa and its citizens, then fellow pelotón members, other military brothers, and last self.* So Ramiro tried to live to honor his brother.

Hot sunshine beat down on the back of his breastplate, making sweat run freely, and turning the metal into an oven. Heat waves shimmered off the packed sand of the hill ahead, and the air smelled of salty sweat, summer, and distant smoke. As he rode, his naked sword lay ready across his lap. Not all the Northerners had thrown down their weapons or leaped to their death on the orders of an illusion of their god. It paid to be vigilant.

But no matter how hot or unpleasant, he'd much rather be on patrol, broiling in full armor and saving lives, than lugging corpses from the bottom of the quarry to the burn pile. And it was a thousand times better than sitting around with too much time to think.

It's way too hot to think. . .

Sancha's ears twitched, and Ramiro darted sharp glances to the men riding spread out on either side. A search-and-rescue party worked better with distance between them to cover more ground, but that meant most of his patrol was out of eyesight. He relied more on Sancha's sharp senses than his own. Yet, even the nearest men rode on without a word, as they had for hours.

A pang of what could only be termed homesickness washed over Ramiro and a knot formed in his throat. He hadn't expected riding a patrol without his friends Alvito and Gomez would create such a hole in his gut. Or that orders given to him from a captain other than his brother would sting quite so much.

It had been over a week, but he felt their loss more keenly in the silence out here, only broken by the desert wind and calls of cactus wrens.

He unclenched his fist from Sancha's mane and forced himself to resume freeing an embedded sandbur. The new captain of the *pelotón*, Muño, was a good man. Ramiro had known him forever, and he'd been a loyal and capable lieutenant for years. The sergeant from the gate guards they'd brought in to replace Gomez seemed competent. But nothing was the same. Not the fact that he could never see his brother Salvador again, or that he could never return home to a city burnt by the Northern army.

He didn't even have Claire for company, having left the witch girl behind with his mother as he attended to duty. His mother might not be a warrior—or approve of Claire—but she would do the best she could for his sake to guard the girl from harassment and catcalls. He just wished he felt right about leaving Claire with *anyone*, once more thinking how strange it was he thought of her at all, considering he hadn't always worried for her safety.

"Hi-ya!" came distantly from his left.

Ramiro dropped the burr and scrambled to don his helmet and pick up his sword. To his relief the men closest to him did the same, proving just as unready. That call could mean anything from a party of aggressive Northerners to a group of lost refugees to simply a break to eat. Sancha picked up her feet and pranced as Ramiro used his knees to guide her toward the call.

"Steady, girl, steady," he told her as her urged her in the direction of the call. No matter what it was, there was enough time to assess the situation. He was no longer the naïve *bisoño*, striving to earn his beard and be considered a man. Those days of eagerly throwing himself forward were also gone.

A bit of bright yellow peeked above an outcropping of rock. His mind dismissed it as a prickly pear flower before his eyes jerked him back. The yellow was too large and too flat to be a flower. Ramiro edged Sancha in that direction and saw a piece of bright shirt. Cornering around the rock revealed a plump woman clutching two children to her breast, all three crouched small against the stone. They had the same brown hair and brown skin as himself, proclaiming they could not be the pale Northerners.

Eyes clenched shut, one boy had his hands clamped over his ears. The other boy had burrowed his face into the woman, as if her presence could save him. They trembled and shook in the grip of great terror, though all around them was calm.

A shiver ran up Ramiro's back. He hastily glanced around but saw only sunshine, rocks, and cacti. What had happened here to instill so much fear?

"San Andrés protect us," the woman was chanting in a dry whisper. "Santiago shield us. San Andrés protect us. Santiago shield us." When she looked up, he was shocked—he knew her.

"Hi-ya!" Ramiro called out before sheathing his sword and swinging down from Sancha. "Over here! Survivors!" He stepped forward and grasped the woman's shoulder. "Lupaa, you're safe now." Even without the woman's apron, he recognized the motherly face of the citadel's head cook, the woman always ready to sneak him bread slathered in her special honey. What were the odds that of all the people of Colina Hermosa he should rescue someone he knew?

"What happened here?" he asked. "Lupaa!" He shook her.

Only then did her eyes open slowly, as if doing so pained her after clenching them too tight. But instead of greeting him, her gaze darted in all directions, passing over him.

One of the boys moaned and actually folded himself smaller, pressing into the rock. The new sergeant, Jorge, and a second soldier arrived and dismounted from their *caballos de guerra*. The horses had the same dapple-gray coloring as Sancha, and every *pelotón* member had their own bond with one of these intelligent animals.

"Report," Sergeant Jorge said. Everything about the sergeant spoke of precision and exactness to detail, from the crease in his uniform to the careful placement of his equipment on his saddle. His beard, simple and cut close, reminded Ramiro painfully of his brother's.

No time for that now. Ramiro drew himself up. "Refugees, sir. This one is Lupaa from the citadel kitchen. One of my mother's cooks."

"It's not every *bisoño* who has his own chef," the other soldier teased. Gray tinted Arias's hair and spread liberally through his thick beard. The man had been a member of the *pelotón* for longer than Ramiro had been alive, but he remained lean and fit.

Ramiro bristled and grit back a sharp retort lest he look childish in front of Sergeant Jorge. "I'm a rookie no longer."

Arias held out his hands. "Old habits. No offense meant."

Sergeant Jorge cleared his throat. "The matter at hand, *caballeros*."

Ramiro bent over Lupaa and met the woman's brown eyes but found no recognition in them. "Lupaa. Lupaa." He snapped his fingers close to her face.

"Santiago shield us. San Andrés . . ." She started and recognition flooded back. "Ramiro? Thank the saints! Is it over? Tell me it's over!"

"Over? What happened here? Why . . . this?" He waved a hand at her and the boys. "How did you get here?"

"I . . . we assembled at the Santa Teresa section of the city. Ran with the other evacuees when Colina Hermosa's wall fell to let us out. I couldn't keep up." She gave the boys a squeeze, and one lifted his head. "My grandsons stayed with me. We ended up with a smaller group, going in what we hoped was the right direction."

"You are south of the swamp," Ramiro said. The evacuees from the city had meant to head west for the swamp of the witches to hide, or to Crueses, the closest safe city. It was his father, the *Alcalde's*, plan to save the people of the city from the Northern army, and it had worked well . . . for the most part. But many of the people were too slow to stay with the soldiers guarding them, too old or weak, and had been left behind. "Off course. And then? Why this hiding?"

"Northerners found us. We took what shelter we could and prayed."

"Then the screaming started," the boy added.

Ramiro looked around again. There was no sign of Northerners or of other evacuees from his city. He turned to Sergeant Jorge and shrugged. Perhaps fear had caused Lupaa to imagine things. Maybe she mistook normal sounds of the desert for the enemy.

"I told my grandsons not to look, never to look, and we prayed," Lupaa said. She struggled to get her legs under her, and Ramiro took her arms, levering her to her feet. "We prayed so hard." The taller boy, probably twelve winters old, stood under his own power. The smaller child still clung to his grandmother.

Sergeant Jorge waved Arias to go ahead toward where the first call had originated. "You're safe now, ma'am. In our custody. Soldier, bring her and catch up with us." The sergeant followed after Arias, pulling his *caballo de guerra* after him.

"Hi-ya," Ramiro acknowledge, though the man had already forgotten about him. It shouldn't sting that the sergeant didn't remember his name. The man had barely time to learn all the officers, let alone every ordinary soldier under his command—though maybe he pretended not to remember in order to avoid showing favoritism toward the *Alcalde's* son.

Sancha sidled up against him, and Ramiro plucked a water skin from his saddle, offering it to Lupaa.

"Drink." By the time they had all taken a turn, color came back to their faces and the younger child had his eyes open.

"You hid from the Northerners," Ramiro said. "How many were there?"

"Many," Lupaa said. "I could not count them all. It was dark, and we were few. Unarmed. I ducked against the rock with my boys and prayed for the evil to stop. Thank you. Thank you a thousand times for saving us. My kitchen is always open to you. We owe you our lives."

"You are most welcome, but the danger was long gone." Ramiro glanced at the sun. If her story was true, they'd been against the outcropping for at least six hours. No wonder they looked to be in shock. But he couldn't quite figure out something: *Why had they stayed like that once the Northerners passed them by?* "You said screaming."

The youngest put his hands back over his ears, eyes wide. "Horrible," the older said. "For hours." He shook, and Lupaa drew them close again.

Something didn't add up. The Northerners would have done their killing and moved on. Unless they'd spent time on some elaborate torture. That sounded like the enemy's way, but again, he was missing something, because Claire had routed them. Her magic had sent them running like devils were in pursuit. Most believed the Northerners would not stop until they reached their distant homeland. Indeed, none of the patrols over the last two days had met with sizable resistance, if any at all.

That *had* been two days ago, though. What if the Northerners managed to regroup? His own people were far from recovered. Still in smaller groups and spread over distances, they reeled from the loss of their city and from the death around them. The people of Colina Hermosa were not up to fighting an organized enemy.

The feeling of unease along his spine grew, urging him forward to investigate. His mother's stories of the Sight in his family came to mind again, but this felt more like a suggestion than an outright warning of danger. "Which direction did the screaming come from?"

The boy pointed after the sergeant, and Ramiro gripped Lupaa's hand. He fixed a relaxed smile on his face to reassure her. "Wait here for me. Then I'll take you to the camps. Sancha, stay," he ordered. The warhorse would keep them safe for the few minutes it would take to scout around and discover what had happened here.

He pushed through a cluster of tall ocotillo, its thorny branches spreading out six feet in all directions. He could see that most of the fifteen members of his small patrol gathered in a spot ahead. The needles of a barrel cactus scraped against the steel of the greave below his knee. Too many flies filled the air. A rust-colored stain spotted the flat leaf of a prickly pear. He bent closer. *Blood*. Dried by the sun.

He soon spotted another splotch on a rock, and then larger discolorations in the dirt. Puddles he would have walked right past if not for the tingling along his spine.

The first clump of what could only be flesh showed a few steps later, a torn and unidentifiable bit the size of his thumb. It could be from an animal.

Ahead, one of the soldiers vomited into the sand. Ramiro stopped, heart racing.

Saints.

An arm hung from the crook of a tall saguaro cactus, the skin intact and too pale to be from one of his countrymen. It ended near the elbow in a jagged tear. The hand was missing.

Ramiro's stomach rolled, the hair at the back of his neck standing up. As Santiago had taught centuries ago, he touched mind, heart, liver, and spleen in quick succession to clear his body centers of negative emotion.

It almost helped.

That wasn't done with a sword or ax, he thought. *Nothing sharp.* None of the vegetation nearby looked hacked or disturbed as if a battle had taken place. He quickly spotted more body parts and pieces of flesh. Here a torso missing its head and wearing the bright colors of an evacuee. There, under a pincushion cactus, an ear. A scrap of fabric in the black and yellow of a Northern uniform. An eyeball under a buzz of flies. Blood covered everything, as if thrown from buckets. Too much blood even from the number of bodies he could see. The smell, sharp and metallic, filled the air. Some of it in the shade still looked wet.

He'd seen death many times in the last few days, but this wasn't death. These people had been torn apart.

This is savagery.

He scrubbed his hands on his breastplate and forced himself to join his fellow soldiers.

"A wildcat?" Arias was saying. "The Northerners didn't do all of this. There are more of them dead than civilians."

Sergeant Jorge shook his head. "Bears perhaps." It was clear, though, he didn't believe that either. Bears would kill for food. This wasn't hunting. This was a massacre.

Ramiro remembered the white-robed priests of the Northerners and the rod they carried that could kill a man with one touch. His fellow soldiers hadn't seen the fanatical light in their eyes or witnessed their depraved cruelty. They killed from more than necessity. They *enjoyed* it. This must be a new devilry of the Northern priests. He could picture the fanatics killing their own soldiers for running from Claire's magic.

Claire.

Ramiro's heart leaped, and his hand darted to his sword hilt. If the Northern priests sought revenge, she would be their prime target. Claire was alone, except for his mother. The girl might have magic, but she was immature in so many ways. He had to return to the camp. "Sergeant, I'll escort the civilians we found back to safety."

Sergeant Jorge gave him an absent nod, waving off the flies. "Arias, go with him. The rest of you spread out and look for more survivors. Try and get a count on the dead. See if anyone can find any signs of what happened here. Animal prints. Anything. Otherwise all we've got is a group of Northerners killed some refugees, then turned on each other. Insane devils."

The sergeant's voice fell behind as Ramiro returned to Sancha, only to be brought up short. He'd rode double on Sancha before with Claire, but the girl was small and he'd been without most of his armor when it was left behind and stolen by that blackguard Suero. Now he wore borrowed armor from fellow soldiers . . . and Lupaa was no slip of a girl.

Arias arrived, and they traded glances, both aware of the difficulty. "I'll take the boys and you the woman," Arias said. "It's going to be a long walk back."

Ramiro turned to help Lupaa mount. The prickle along his spine demanded he hurry. Ramiro closed his eyes for calm as he realized his volunteering had actually harmed his cause. Camp was only a few hours away, but leading Sancha while the civilians rode meant they'd be lucky to be back by nightfall. The rest of the patrol would beat them there.

He just hoped his mistake didn't cost Claire.

ABOUT THE AUTHOR

MICHELLE HAUCK lives in the bustling metropolis of northern Indiana with her hubby and two teenagers. Two papillons help balance out the teenage drama. Besides working with special needs children by day, she writes all sorts of fantasy, giving her imagination free range. A bookworm, she passes up the darker vices in favor of chocolate and looks for any excuse to reward herself. She is the author of the YA epic fantasy *Kindar's Cure*, as well as the short story "Frost and Fog," which is included in the anthology *Summer's Double Edge*.

Find her on twitter under @Michelle4Laughs or her blog Michelle4Laughs: It's in the details.

www.michelle4laughs.blogspot.com

Discover great authors, exclusive offers, and more at hc.com.